STEPHEN BOOTH

Stephen Booth was born in the Lancashire mill town of Burnley, and has remained rooted to the Pennines during his career as a newspaper journalist. He lives with his wife Lesley in a former Georgian dower house in Nottinghamshire and his interests include folklore, the internet and walking in the hills of the Peak District. *Scared to Live* is the seventh in the series featuring Derbyshire detectives Ben Cooper and Diane Fry. The second, *Dancing with the Virgins*, was nominated for the coveted Gold Dagger Award.

For automatic updates on Stephen Booth visit HarperCollins.co.uk/stephenbooth and register for AuthorTracker

www.stephen-booth.com

STEPHEN BOOTH

Scared to Live

HARPER

Harper
An imprint of HarperCollins*Publishers*
77–85 Fulham Palace Road,
Hammersmith, London W6 8JB

www.harpercollins.co.uk

This paperback edition 2007
1

First published in Great Britain by
HarperCollins*Publishers* 2006

A catalogue record for this book is
available from the British Library

ISBN 9780007808403

Set in Meridien by Palimpsest Book Production Limited
Grangemouth, Stirlingshire

Printed and bound in Great Britain by
Clays Ltd, St Ives plc

This book is dedicated to
my parents, James and Edna Booth

1

Sunday, 23 October

Even on the night she died, Rose Shepherd couldn't sleep. By the early hours of the morning, her bed was like a battleground – hot, violent, chaotic. Beneath her, the sheet was twisted into painful knots, the pillow hard and unyielding. Lack of sleep made her head ache, and her body had grown stiff with discomfort.

But sleeplessness was familiar to Miss Shepherd. She'd started to think of it as an old friend, because it was always with her. She often spent the hours of darkness waiting for the first bird to sing, watching for the greyness of dawn, when she knew there'd be people moving about in the village. There might be the sound of a van in the street as someone headed off for an early shift at the quarry, or the rumble of a farmer's tractor in the field behind the house. She didn't feel so completely alone then, as she did in the night.

For Rose Shepherd, this was the world. A distant noise, a half-heard voice, a snatched moment of indirect contact. Her life had become so confined that she seemed to be living in a small, dark box. The tiniest crack of light was like a glimpse of God.

By two o'clock, Rose had been out of bed twice already, moving aimlessly around the room to reassure herself that she was still alive and capable of movement. The third time, she got up to fetch herself a glass of water. She stood in the middle of the bedroom while she drank it, allowing her toes to curl deep into the sheepskin rug, clutching at the comfort of its softness, an undemanding gentleness that almost made her weep.

As always, her mind had been running over the events of the day. There was no way she could stop it. It was as if she had a video player in her head, but it was stuck in a loop, showing the same scenes over and over again. If they weren't from the day just past, then they were snapshots from previous days – some of them years before, in a different part of her life. The scenes played themselves out, and paused to allow her to fret whether she could have done things differently. Then they began over again, taunting her with the fact that past events were unalterable. What was done, was done.

It was one of the reasons she couldn't sleep, of course. Her brain was too active, her memories too vivid. Nothing seemed to slow down the thoughts that stalked backwards and forwards in her consciousness, like feral animals roaming the edge of the forest, restless and apprehensive.

But Rose was glad that she'd been out the previous day. She'd been doubtful about it beforehand. No journey was without its risks, even if it was only three miles over the hill and down into the village of Matlock Bath. Despite a diversion to the shopping village, she'd arrived in the village too early, and had time to kill once she'd parked the Volvo.

Standing in her bedroom, Rose smiled at the recollection of her own weakness. Matlock Bath had been busy, as she ought to have known it would be. At first, she'd been disturbed by the number of people on North Parade, and nervous of the motorcyclists in their leathers, clustered by their bikes eating fish and chips out of paper wrappings. When she passed too close to them, the smell had been so overpowering that she thought she would faint. And that would never do.

She turned slowly on the rug, fighting the muzziness and disorientation of being awake when her body wanted to sleep. There were only two points of light in her bedroom – the face of her alarm clock, showing two thirty-three, and the echo of its green luminescence in the mirror on the opposite wall. She found it difficult to focus on the light, because she couldn't judge its distance from the reflection.

She could smell those fish and chips, even now. The odour was so powerful that for a moment she had no idea where she was. Time and place began to blur, a street in a Derbyshire tourist village merging into an image of a deserted roadside with the smell of gunfire in the air, then whirling back to her bedroom, with those two green points of light rushing towards her out of the darkness. Feeling giddy, Rose steadied herself with a hand on the wall and sat down in a chair by the window.

No, no, she was wrong. It was a bad mistake she'd made yesterday. The sort of mistake she'd taught herself to avoid, that she had made such careful plans against. But she hadn't been able to avoid it. There was no other way out.

Rose breathed deeply, trying to control the dizziness. For a moment, it had been just as if those motorcyclists had entered her bedroom. She could hear the creak of their black leathers, the thud of their heavy boots against the doorframe. There was the rustle of their paper wrappings, the acrid tang of the vinegar. Somewhere, perhaps, the rumble of an engine, coming closer.

The bikers had been irrelevant, though. Waiting in Matlock Bath, Rose's first impressions had been the steepness of the hills above her, the denseness of the trees, the roofs of houses perched among them in apparently impossible places. Soon a sense of her vulnerability had become too strong, and she had to get off the street, to find somewhere she could feel safer.

So Rose had paid her money to enter the aquarium, and for a while she'd watched children feeding carp in the thermal pool. Even now she could remember feeling the shape of the item she carried in its plastic bag, and knowing she was making a fool of herself in the most dangerous way. But perhaps no one had noticed her nervousness, because people were too wrapped up in their own interests.

She thought about taking some more of her herbal tablets. But that would mean walking as far as the bathroom for another glass of water, and it wouldn't make any difference anyway. Not now.

Her doctor knew about her anxiety and insomnia problems. She'd gone to him out of desperation, breaking her own rules and knowing it was a mistake. But he hadn't been able to help her. For a start, he'd never understood why she wouldn't continue taking the sleeping pills he gave her. Rose had felt quite sorry for him when she saw his perplexed frown, his fingers hovering over the keyboard to tap out an automatic prescription for Nitrazepam. In the end, she'd told him the pills gave her heartburn, and he'd accepted that as a reason.

Of course, he was a rural GP, and he hadn't met anyone like Rose Shepherd before. He didn't understand that she wasn't just another neurotic, middle-aged woman. He couldn't possibly have known that she was even more frightened of never waking up than of not being able to sleep.

Rose had always known she'd be killed. Well, it felt like always. She could barely remember a time before she'd known. She expected to meet her death because of the way she'd led her life. It was a question of when it would happen, and how. All she could hope for was that it would be sudden, and painless.

Two forty-five. The house was very quiet, wasn't it? Even her bedside clock had a tick so faint that she had to listen hard to be sure it was working. There was an Edwardian longcase in the sitting room downstairs, but it would be another fifteen minutes before it was due to strike. Its chimes had counted away many of her nights.

In some ways, knowing her fate only made things worse. It meant that she lived every day in fear of a phone call, a knock on the door, the smashing of glass in the middle of the night. Every time she went out of the house, she expected not to return. Whenever she looked through the window, she was surprised not to see dark figures in the garden, watching her house. For a long time now, she'd considered it more difficult to live than to die.

She tried to imagine what the neighbours would say about her when they were asked. No doubt they'd all agree that Rose Shepherd was a very private person, who never called round to say 'hello' and didn't mix much in the village. They knew she'd lived alone for the past ten months at Bain House in Foxlow, deep among the Derbyshire Dales. Some would put her age at nearly seventy; others would frown and say she could only be in her fifties, surely? But they hadn't really got a close look at her. The postman might recall she had an accent that wasn't local, but she'd never spoken more than a few words to him.

And that was pretty much all anyone would know of her. The details of her life were shrouded by trees and protected by electronic gates. And that was the way it had to be. It was what had kept her alive until now.

Rose smoothed out her sheets, turned over her pillows and went back to bed. Ten minutes later, she was hovering fearfully on the edge of consciousness when a black Mitsubishi Shogun with tinted windows drove into Foxlow and stopped outside her gate.

Leaving through the back door of a cottage on the corner of Pinfold Lane, Darren Turnbull saw the black car as it drew away from Bain House. He stepped back into the shadows, wishing that Stella wouldn't insist on having that security light. He had to walk right through its glare to reach the lane by the church, and it didn't do much for his anonymity. In this place, he felt sure that some nosy neighbour would see him and find out all about him before he got his car keys out of his pocket. Stella sometimes talked about him leaving her house like a thief in the night. With that bloody security light, he was more like an actor stepping out on to a stage. He prayed there was no audience tonight.

Darren watched the vehicle coming back towards him from the corner. He was slightly puzzled by its speed. There was no other traffic anywhere on the road at this time, and most drivers would whizz through a place like Foxlow in seconds. But maybe this was some old fogey who thought you had to obey speed limits, even when there was no one around.

He wasn't as good at recognizing makes of car as some of his mates were, but Darren could see this was some kind of four-wheel-drive job. A big one, probably Japanese. He liked black cars – there were too many grey and silver models around these days, and they all looked the same. Tinted windows, too. That was cool. He could barely distinguish the outline of a driver as the car passed under a streetlamp near the phone box.

Finally, the car had gone, and Darren began to move again, keeping close to the wall of the cottage to avoid the light as he made his way to the back gate. His blue Astra was parked under the trees on Church Walk. No streetlamps here, not even any houses where he could be overlooked. There was just the old church somewhere in the darkness. If he looked up, and through the trees, he could see the top of its square tower against the sky, with its little stone ramparts like broken teeth.

Darren shuddered when he thought about the church and its graveyard. He'd been scared silly of these places when he was a kid, and even now he preferred to stay away from them. They made him think of bats and vampires, and dead people coming up out of their graves. He'd rather not even go to funerals, if he could avoid it. All those folks dressed in black with their long faces gave him the creeps. He always tried to make an excuse that he was too busy working, and then he'd go along for the sausage rolls afterwards, if he could get away with it.

Why Stella had decided to move here when she got divorced, he had no idea. It wouldn't suit him at all – it was too far out in the sticks, miles from anywhere and full of old nosies who wanted to know every detail of your life. The city was a lot better. You could move around there without anyone knowing who you were or where you'd been. But at least he didn't have to live in Foxlow himself.

He grinned to himself as he got into his Astra and reversed it in front of the lych gate. A visit to Stella was always worthwhile, he had to admit. As long as no one found out, of course – especially Fiona. That would be a disaster. She'd murder him for sure.

Darren shivered again as he drove out on to the street. But this time it was nothing to do with his superstitions. The village of Foxlow suddenly felt very cold.

A few minutes later, the Shogun had turned at the top of High Street and was being driven too fast down Butcher's Hill. Its headlights were on full beam, sweeping across the hedgerows, reflecting off gateposts. Anyone coming in the opposite direction would be momentarily blinded, too dazzled to see the vehicle's model or colour, let alone its driver. In a burst of sodium light, it would be gone as soon as it appeared.

When it reached the bottom of the hill, the Shogun slowed to a halt. It idled for a moment in the road, with its front windows half-open and its engine ticking over. Then the driver swung the wheel to the right. He rammed his foot on the accelerator, and the car surged off the road through an open gateway. Its headlights dipped and swayed as it bumped along the field boundary and followed an uncultivated strip of land close to the hedge. With its four-wheel drive engaged, the vehicle growled towards the top corner of the field, where it turned and coasted along the back gardens of the houses in Pinfold Lane.

Finally, the headlights died and the Shogun rolled the last few yards in darkness. After it stopped, there was silence for a moment, then the whirr of a window lowering, the creak of seat leather as a body shifted position, and the slow, careful scrape of metal. With a final click and a grunt, the movement stopped. From a position near the driver's seat came a green glow and a faint electronic beeping.

A hundred yards away, in Rose Shepherd's house, the clock was softly chiming three as the bedside phone began to ring.

2

Detective Sergeant Diane Fry pushed at the half-open door and stepped carefully past the tape. In the hallway, she had to squeeze past a child's bike propped against the wall, one wheel off and a spanner on the saddle. She almost tripped over two bulging bin liners full of clothes, ready to go to the charity shop, or maybe the launderette. The smell in the house was overpowering, despite a cold draught blowing through the rooms from the broken windows.

'Home, sweet home,' said a voice behind her.

DC Gavin Murfin leaned on the front door, forcing it back against the bin liners with an ominous creak of hinges and a popping of plastic.

'I hope you remembered to wipe your feet, Diane,' he said. 'We wouldn't want to ruin the décor.'

Fry felt her shoulders stiffen inside her jacket.

11

From the moment she'd entered the house, the fabric of her clothes had begun to feel prickly and uncomfortable, as if the sensitivity of her skin was suddenly heightened, her nerve endings screaming in sympathy with the dead.

'Shut up for a bit, Gavin, will you?'

Murfin sniffed, and rattled the empty sweet wrappers in his pocket. Fry did her best to ignore him. Everyone dealt with these things in their own way, of course. Gavin's instinct was to retreat behind a flippant façade. For Fry, the urge was to focus on small details, the trivialities that could so easily be missed if you saw only the big picture.

The first thing she needed to know was how much evidence had been preserved from the original scene, and what had been interfered with. Here, in this house in Darwin Street, she could see at a glance there had been far too much interference. For a start, someone had disturbed the opened post that lay on the hall table, where it lay in a pool of dirty water. She poked at the envelopes with a finger. One of them seemed to be a packet of photographs back from the printers, and another was a BT phone bill. On the bottom were a couple of polling cards for next month's county council by-election. Some local politician had just lost a voter.

Surrounded by the remains of a family's day-to-day existence, Fry paused for a moment, listening to the slow drip of water from a ceiling, the crack of a splintered window frame. Her eyes drifted across the muddy carpet to the walls, scratched and gouged by passing equipment – hose reels, breathing apparatus, stretchers. Her attention settled on the incongruous chrome gleam of the spanner, still waiting for someone to pick it up and replace the wheel of the bike.

'Ugh. The *Marie Celeste*, with extra charcoal.'

Fry lacked the energy to answer Gavin this time, let alone to shut him up. It was too early in the morning, and she was too depressed at having been on call when something like this came in. Derbyshire's E Division didn't catch an incident like this more than once every ten years or so. Of course, Edendale had house fires like anywhere else, but it was bad luck when someone died in one. Today was unlucky all round.

At least the structure of the building was intact. From the street, it had been hard to tell that anything serious had happened, except for the broken windows and the scorch marks where flames had licked the walls. It might just have been a rowdy party that had got out of hand. Inside, it was a different story. Whether the story was anything to do with her, Fry had yet to find out.

Fry tried to tune down her senses as she followed the approach path towards the tape that marked the inner cordon. She realized that the hallway smelled a bit like her kitchen – charred bacon and evaporated steam. When it was her turn to kick the bucket, this was the way she imagined it would be. She'd be a kitchen accident statistic, one more victim of a faulty toaster, killed by an exploding microwave. Death in the throes of breakfast.

At the foot of the stairs, she turned right into the sitting room, keeping carefully to the stepping plates. Judging by what the neighbours reported, the occupants of 32 Darwin Street had been taken by surprise. Six weeks ago, Lindsay Mullen had ordered a new carpet for her lounge. It had a deep, thick pile, and it was a shade of cream Lindsay had always wanted, but her husband insisted wasn't practical. It would show up the dirt, he'd said. It was a shameful waste of money.

Royal Wilton in chamomile, that was it. According to the uniforms who'd taken initial statements, the lady in the house to the left had heard the entire argument as Brian Mullen left for work one morning.

Fry looked around the wrecked lounge. Mr Mullen had been right. The carpet was black now, and trampled with charred debris. Dozens of boot prints had sunk into two inches of filthy sludge.

The problem was, the bottom edge of the door into the kitchen had sealed so tightly against the new Wilton that there was no gap for air to get through. When the sofa ignited, thick smoke would have filled this room in minutes, choking fumes that seared the lungs and stung the eyes. If only a few wisps of it had seeped under the door into the kitchen, they might have reached the smoke

14

alarm, and the outcome could have been different. Unlike so many others, the Mullens' alarm had been working, the batteries recently replaced. It just hadn't detected any smoke until it was too late. Far too late.

'They never stood a bloody chance, did they?' said Murfin.

Fry glanced at him. His flippancy was gone, and he was sweating a little despite the draught stirring the curtains behind him. Of course, Gavin was a family man, with children of his own. There were some things that got to you, no matter how hard you tried to keep up the exterior.

'They say it's better to die of smoke inhalation than burn to death, anyway,' she said, though she didn't expect it to help. Her own flesh still crawled at the thought of the flames.

She looked away from Murfin before he could distract her concentration. This room had been packed with plastics, too – TV, video recorder, racks of CDs and DVDs, boxes full of children's toys under a shelf in the corner. Most of the toys were just a molten mess now, multi-coloured pools of lava that had run on to the carpet and congealed in the spray from the firemen's hoses. There were recognizable shapes here and there – the twisted controls of a PlayStation console, the burned edge of a Monopoly game. The head and one arm of a Barbie doll waved from a skin-toned puddle, like someone drowning in a sea of their own flesh. Something scorched and wooden gazed accusingly at her from blackened eyes.

Then a tiny flash of colour caught her attention. A glint of bright yellow, like a drop of sunlight in the blackness. She crouched towards the floor and gently blew away the ash. A broken section of Monopoly board lay at her feet: Piccadilly and the Water Works.

Of course, the untreated polyurethane foam in the furniture had been the real problem. Brian Mullen had definitely had a point. Lindsay could have spent her money more wisely if she'd replaced the cheap sofa instead of the carpet. The outcome really could have been different. For a start, her children might still be alive.

When she walked through into the kitchen, Fry found it almost pristine and untouched, apart from a few muddy footprints on the vinyl flooring. From the condition of the teak-effect units and the white painted walls, she would never have guessed there had been a fire at all. She felt as though she'd stepped out of one film set and into another, where an entirely different story was taking place. This one suggested a harmless domestic comedy – a family eating breakfast together in their spotless kitchen, Mum and Dad and the kids, all chattering and laughing, hurrying to get ready for work or school. Behind her, the other room might have been the scene of a cheap horror film, except the credits had already rolled and the crew had packed up and gone home.

'Diane, do you want to have a look upstairs?' called Murfin, without enthusiasm.

'Yes, in a minute.'

Fry took a last look at the kitchen, with its silent smoke alarm. She noticed that the cooker was new, too. A Smeg dual-fuel with air-cooling system. A thousand pounds or so, she guessed. Money wasn't all that short in the Mullen household, after all.

She went back through the sitting room and joined Gavin at the foot of the stairs. She wasn't sure that she needed to visit the bedrooms. They might have been where the victims died, but they weren't where the fire had started. If there had been a crime committed, it was here on the ground floor that the evidence would be found, surely?

As she was debating with herself, Murfin settled the question by hauling himself slowly up the stairs, sighing at every step. Fry had no choice but to follow him.

And, in a way, the bedrooms weren't quite so bad. It was clear that the flames hadn't reached here. The furniture was almost untouched, though covered by a layer of soot. The covers of the beds had been pulled back, revealing clean, unmarked sheets. The first room she saw might simply have been waiting for Lindsay Mullen to come home and clean up the mess. Apart from the markers where her body had lain when she collapsed from smoke inhalation, of course.

'Have you got the photos there, Gavin?'

Murfin grunted and passed her the file. Fry had seen the photographs before she came out, and remembered the condition of Lindsay's body, the cotton pyjamas she'd been wearing, with the left leg rucked up to expose a thin, white calf. Her face was only visible in the close-ups, turned to the right, her left cheek pressed tightly to the floor.

It wasn't Lindsay Mullen's face that Fry was interested in, but the position of her body, the angle of her limbs. She turned one of the photos to align it with the room, and checked the direction of the door. Lindsay had almost certainly been going the wrong way. It wasn't too difficult to picture her, blinded and disorientated by darkness and dense smoke, feeling her way frantically round the walls in an effort to find the door, while her children screamed in the next room. It wasn't difficult at all. In fact, it was too easy for comfort.

'Next room, Gavin,' she said.

'That's the kids' bedroom.'

'I know that.'

Jack and Liam Mullen had died without leaving their beds, according to the incident reports. They woke up choking, and died from the effects of smoke inhalation. Died calling for their mum, probably.

The house must have been so full of smoke by then that the boys would never have made it to the stairs, let alone through the flames in the hall. Still, their bedroom wasn't a pleasant place to be. Gavin wouldn't even come inside the door. He knew the bodies had lain here for some time, since the boys had obviously been dead and beyond rescue. Coroners' rules required the bodies to be left *in situ* until forensic evidence had been gathered to establish the cause of death.

Of course, the vast majority of house fires were tragic accidents. Faulty wiring, a fag down the back of the sofa, clothes left too near an electric heater. If sudden deaths didn't go automatically to CID, she wouldn't even be here. Fire service codes on this incident were ambiguous – but then, the firefighters on the scene would have had other priorities than looking for a cause.

Fry heard a rustle and a cough, and turned to find a uniformed PC standing at the bottom of the stairs. He was wearing a yellow reflective jacket, and he held his helmet in one hand as he wiped the sweat from his forehead with the other.

'DS Fry?' he said, looking up at her. 'They said you'd be here. I thought you ought to know straightaway –'

'What is it?'

'Well, we've been talking to the neighbours again. We ought to have found out earlier, I suppose, but we never thought to ask. You know what it's like, everyone is in shock when a thing like this happens, and with the husband being taken off to hospital –'

'Out with it, for heaven's sake.'

He coughed again and turned the brim of his helmet in his fingers. 'I've been speaking to the

19

lady next door. She says it's only just occurred to her to mention it . . . Well, it seems there were three children living at this address. Mrs Mullen had a daughter, as well as the two boys.'

Fry stared at the charred wreckage and thought about the bedrooms. There was a closed door at the end of the landing, a third room she hadn't entered. But the firefighters must have been through the whole house, surely? They wouldn't have left a bedroom unchecked for victims, would they?

'The daughter could be away from home,' she said. 'Staying over with friends for the night or something. What age is she?'

The officer swallowed. 'According to the neighbour, the third child is about eighteen months old.'

Fry bit her lip. She hated incidents that involved children. Someone else ought to have taken this job. She ought to have sent one of her DCs. Not Gavin Murfin, though – well, not on his own. But Ben Cooper would have been a good choice. Cooper understood children. He knew all about families. Fry thought he'd probably read far more into the circumstances of this house than she could herself. But Cooper hadn't been on early call this morning. You couldn't always get the right officer for a job.

Her eyes were drawn past the PC and back to the two bin liners standing near the front door. It was only then that she realized the bags weren't bulging because of the amount of clothes stuffed inside them, but because the plastic had melted and sagged into obscene lumps and swellings. One of the bags had split completely when Gavin pushed the door against it, and the skirt of a blue Baby Gap denim dress protruded from the rip.

'Where's the husband now?' she asked.

'Edendale General,' said the PC. 'He suffered minor burns and smoke inhalation trying to get into the house.'

'Did you say "trying to get in"?'

'Yes. He wasn't at home when the fire started. I thought they would have told you.'

'There seem to be a lot of things that no one's telling me,' said Fry. 'Has everyone around here taken a vow of silence, or what?'

Postman Bernie Wilding was already late with his deliveries in Foxlow that morning, when he remembered the package for Rose Shepherd. That was unusual in itself – Miss Shepherd rarely got more than bank statements and junk mail. Most days, there was nothing in his van for her at all.

Bernie did a three-point turn at the end of Pinfold Lane and drew up to the wrought-iron gates of Bain House. He was listening to Ken Bruce on Radio Two, and he turned the volume down a bit before he lowered the window. He reached out to press the button on the intercom, but got no answering voice. That was a bit odd, too. Folk in the village said Miss Shepherd never went anywhere. She was supposed to be a bit of a hermit, shut up alone here in this big house. And sure enough, she'd never been out before when he'd called with a package.

But he supposed even a hermit must do her shopping some time. A visit to the doctor, the dentist, the optician. Well, it was nothing to do with him, anyway.

Bernie scribbled a message on one of his cards, and was about to push it into the letter box mounted on one of the gates. But when he opened the flap, he saw that a furniture store leaflet was still in there, along with a free newspaper that was delivered by local kids over the weekend. And that definitely wasn't like Miss Shepherd. Even if he didn't see her for weeks on end, he knew she was around, because she emptied the letter box. It was a sensible thing to do, otherwise it gave the impression there was no one at home. There were criminals who drove around these villages every night, looking for signs of empty properties.

Uncertain what to do now, Bernie peered through the gates at the house standing among the trees. The curtains were drawn at the front, even on the ground floor. He didn't know the internal layout of the house, but that must be a lounge or something. You wouldn't leave the curtains drawn during the day, unless you were sick.

Bernie liked to think of himself as an old-fashioned rural postman, who knew his patch and the people he delivered to. He'd heard so many stories about a postman being the first to raise the alarm when someone was ill or dead and even the neighbours hadn't noticed. It had never happened to him yet, not in fifteen years with the Royal Mail. But he was always on the lookout for elderly people on his round, the ones who lived alone and didn't get many visitors. Not that Rose Shepherd was all that elderly – but you never knew, did you?

Ken Bruce was announcing the ten o'clock news bulletin. Was it so late already? Bernie knew he ought to get on – he'd already lost enough time this morning, with having so many special deliveries to make and getting stuck behind the tractor that overtook him every time he stopped. Miss Shepherd was probably out doing her shopping in Matlock, wasn't she? Monday morning was a good time to go to the supermarket. Nice and quiet. She'd just forgotten to empty the post from her box for once. She'd do it when she got back from the shops.

Bernie pushed his card through the flap, put the package back behind the van seat, then reversed into the road and drove on. He'd missed the news headlines, but Bruce was playing a song he remembered from the sixties – the New Seekers, 'Now the Carnival is Over'. Bernie was singing quietly to himself as he headed back through Foxlow.

3

Detective Constable Ben Cooper opened his fridge door, then closed it again quickly when he caught the smell. Another thirty seconds of breathing that in, and he'd lose his appetite for breakfast. He had a brief after-image of something nasty wrapped in plastic, caught by the interior light like an exhibit at a crime scene, sordid and decomposing, its DNA degrading beyond use.

'Well, do you want me to call in and see the solicitor again tomorrow morning?' he said into his mobile phone. 'I can manage that, if you like, Matt. But I'm not sure it'll do any good.'

'He wants a kick up the pants, that's what'll do him some good. Maybe I ought to go in and see him myself. What do you reckon? I'll go straight into his office when I've finished the muck spreading tomorrow.'

Cooper smiled at the thought of his brother bursting into the offices of Ballard and Price, his overalls covered in slurry. Matt could be a bit

24

intimidating at the best of times, especially in an enclosed space. In his present mood, the solicitors' receptionist would probably call the police to have him removed.

'It wouldn't help, you know.'

Matt sighed in frustration. 'Bloody pen pushers and bureaucrats. They seem to spend their time making life difficult for everyone else.'

'I suppose Mr Ballard has a job to do, like the rest of us.'

'Oh, yeah. He takes a lot longer about it, that's all.'

Cooper ran a finger round the fridge door, checking the rubber seal for gaps. It hadn't occurred to him things could get as bad as that so quickly, just because he hadn't bothered checking inside for a few days. It wasn't as if the weather was particularly warm or anything. It was nearly the end of October, and summer was over in the Peak District. But the fridge had come with the flat, so he wasn't sure how old it might be.

'I don't know what else I can do,' he said. 'You're the executor, Matt.'

'I hadn't forgotten.'

Of course, he knew what was bothering his brother and making him so impatient. Probate on their mother's will was taking so long that he was starting to get worried about the future of Bridge End Farm. If money had to be found from the estate, the only way it could happen would be if assets were sold off.

'I thought you'd know a bit more about the law than I do,' said Matt.

'Well, not this part of the law.'

He didn't bother to tell Matt that his knowledge of criminal law was also a bit sketchy. There were eight thousand criminal offences on the statute books – and more than a thousand of them had been invented since Cooper became a police officer. Without the manuals, he'd be lost, like everyone else.

Cooper left the fridge alone and crossed the kitchen, dodging the cat that was sitting looking at him expectantly, having heard a rumour there might be food. On the days he was at home, meal times seemed to come round every hour.

'Besides,' he said, 'don't forget how much Mr Ballard charges for his time.'

'You're right, Ben. Just a phone call then, I suppose.'

'At least it'll keep the subject fresh in his mind.'

There was silence for a few moments. The Cooper brothers had always been comfortable with silence. They'd grown up together on the farm hardly needing to speak, because each understood what the other was thinking. But that was when they were physically together. You could read a person's thoughts in their face, in the way they moved or breathed, or what they did with their hands. It was different on the phone, though. Silence felt awkward and wrong. Not to mention a waste of money. With his mobile pressed to his ear, Ben started to wonder whether he could get a reduced tariff from Vodaphone for the amount of non-talk time he used.

But in this case, he sensed that there was more to his brother's silence than awkwardness.

'Is there something else, Matt?'

'Yeah . . .'

Ben felt his stomach tighten. For a second, he thought he was going to be sick, and he looked to see if the fridge door had fallen open again and released the nauseous smell into the room. After the death of their mother, there surely couldn't be more bad news already. But he could read a lot into one word from his brother.

'What is it? Something wrong with one of the girls?'

'No, they're fine,' said Matt. 'Well, I think so.'

'You're not making much sense, Matt.'

'Look, Ben, I've made an appointment to go into the surgery on Friday. I want to talk to Dr Joyce. And if necessary, I'll ask to see the specialist who treated Mum.'

'Why? We know what happened to her – it was a series of strokes. It happens all the time in people of her age.'

'I don't mean the strokes. I mean the other problem.'

The family had rarely referred to Isabel Cooper's condition by name. For a long time, it had been 'Mum's problem'. Towards the end, before she died in Edendale District General from a brain haemorrhage, it had become 'the other problem'. Now, it seemed to Ben there was no point in trying to avoid spelling it out. Mum wasn't around any more to be upset if it inadvertently slipped out in her presence.

'Oh, the schizophrenia.'

'Yes.'

'I don't understand, Matt. What do you want to find out that we don't already know?'

'I can't talk to you about it on the phone – it's too complicated. Can you come over some time? I've got a lot of stuff to show you.'

'Well, I'm going to be a bit busy this week –'

'So what's new?'

'All right, what if I call at the farm tonight when I come off duty?'

'That'll do.'

'See you, then.'

Cooper put out a bowl of cat food and placed it on the floor in the conservatory, near the central-heating boiler. Randy was an animal with a fixed routine and firm ideas about his territory.

Then he went back to the fridge, took a deep breath and eased open the door. He scooped out some rotten tomatoes, half a carton of sour milk, and a wedge of Stilton with its blue veins blossoming into a furry carpet. They all went into a plastic bin liner. He wasn't sure any of the items accounted for the smell, though. Poking in the salad tray at the bottom of the main compartment, he found a liquefied lettuce, which probably did.

When he'd got rid of the worst, he tied up the bin liner and put it to one side. Now he ought to remove everything else from the fridge and give it a good clean. Probably it could do with defrosting, too.

But then Cooper hesitated. It would do later on, wouldn't it? Tomorrow, even. He closed the fridge, put the bag near the back door, and returned to the sitting room. He put on his shoes and jacket, and checked how much money he had in his wallet. Then he made sure his phone was fully charged. Allowing your phone battery to go flat was as bad as letting your car run out of petrol. Both things happened now and then, but it was better if they happened to someone else.

Finally, he left the flat. For once, even the smell of the morning traffic was like a breath of fresh air.

He was unsettled by his conversation with Matt. He hoped his brother wasn't having to cope with too many worries at once. There were certainly some decisions to be made about the future of Bridge End, though. The new farming support payments favoured the more productive farms in the valleys, and an upland farmer's income could be halved, unless he changed his ways. The suckler herd might have to go, for a start – no matter how environmentally friendly and picturesque they were, grazing cattle were becoming as economically unviable as sheep.

Matt could intensify the dairy herd, or leave

part of the land unfarmed, in return for environmental grants. On the other hand, he could abandon the idea of running a profitable farm altogether and get himself a job stacking shelves in a supermarket.

On his way through the market square, Cooper pulled out his mobile and chose a number from his phone book. His call was answered almost straightaway.

'Hi, it's me. How are you this morning?'

She sounded pleased to hear from him, and the sound of her voice alone made him feel better. He didn't know how she did it; perhaps it came of being a civilian.

'Oh, I'm fine, too,' he said. 'No, really. There's nothing wrong at all. I just wanted to find out how you were.'

He listened to her talk for a while, neither of them saying much, but enough to put a smile on his face as he crossed Hollowgate towards the Raj Mahal and the pedestrianized area.

He had to end the call when a couple of acquaintances stopped to say hello. Cooper couldn't place their names at first. But he knew so many people around Edendale that it wasn't surprising. Faces from his childhood haunted him constantly. He'd see an old schoolfriend passing in the street, then immediately another and another. It was like the way a phrase he'd heard for the first time suddenly seemed to be repeated everywhere, as if someone was trying to send him a message. What sort of message could these familiar faces be trying to convey? *This is where you belong*, perhaps.

Later that morning, Cooper found himself watching a man in a grey sports jacket approaching a cash machine outside Somerfield's supermarket. Running his finger along the edge of the card slot, the man glanced over his shoulder with an apologetic smile. He wasn't sure whether he liked being watched or not.

There were two ATMs at Somerfield's, both set into the outside wall near the trolley park, about fifteen yards from the main entrance. A small queue of shoppers had formed at the other machine, fidgeting with their carrier bags and purses.

'If you feel an obstruction of any kind, don't use it. That's the best advice. Usually there are a couple of tiny prongs. Here, see?'

With a flick of the finger, the man pulled out a thin, clear sleeve of rigid plastic. He held it up to reveal a loop at the back.

'This is the old Lebanese Loop trick. The loop retains a card when it's inserted. Since the machine can't read the magnetic strip, it keeps asking you to re-enter your PIN. Someone standing behind you watches you tap your number in. When you walk away, the suspect removes the card and empties your account. Bingo.'

'Surely that type of device is easy to detect?' said someone in the watching group. 'We just saw you do it.'

'But I know what to look for.'

PC Steve Judson had greying hair, a little longer than favoured by most police officers. He worked with the Plastic Crime Unit, a team struggling to deal with a mounting wave of cash and credit card fraud. According to the latest figures, it was big business – worth at least forty million pounds a year across the country.

Judson looked at the queue for the adjacent cash machine. 'This is a typical location. The ATMs would be more secure inside, but the store isn't open twenty-four hours. Some customers want to use them late at night, when this car park is probably deserted.'

'Is that when the biggest risk is, rather than when the cash machines are busy?' asked a female DC, one of two who'd driven over the hills from B Division for the plastic crime session.

'The risk is different. If you look at the people in the queue there – they're close enough to each other to make shoulder surfing easy. But at night, when the place is empty, you'd be pretty damn suspicious of somebody who came and peered over your shoulder, wouldn't you?'

There were other officers present in the car park who'd come from Nottinghamshire and even from Leicestershire. Strangers, but probably future colleagues. No one was talking about their future this morning, but it must have been in everyone's minds when they greeted each other.

'It isn't so long ago that the NCIS bulletins were warning of cash machine gangs spreading out of London down the M4 to the West Country. Did they get it wrong?'

'No, not at all. Those gangs did good business in the West Country, so they decided to go nationwide. Now they operate in any place they can recruit enough illegals.'

'Illegals?'

Cooper could hear a few sets of antennae going up, alert for derogatory remarks. It was always a tough call, knowing when to report a colleague for political incorrectness. If you tolerated it, your own career could be on the line.

But PC Judson seemed not to have noticed the reactions from the group.

'Some illegals are being trained for cash machine work within twenty-four hours of coming off the boat. That way, they can pay back the traffickers. It's better than slogging your guts out in a carrot field in East Anglia for two quid an hour, I suppose.'

Nobody laughed, or even dared to nod in agreement. A Nottinghamshire detective next to Cooper shuffled his feet in the shredded tree bark around the roots of an ornamental birch.

Somebody at the front asked a question about identity theft, which set Judson off on a new tangent. The Nottinghamshire officer leaned towards Cooper.

'Are you Derbyshire?' he said quietly.

'Yes, I'm based right here in Edendale. DC Cooper.'

'Ross Matthews. Hi. What's it like working here?'

'It's OK,' said Cooper defensively.

Matthews nodded. 'I'm at St Ann's, and it's a nightmare. I might put in for a transfer when we go global.'

He didn't need to explain what he was talking about. Everyone knew that the number of regional police forces would soon be reduced dramatically. A government commission had concluded that any force with fewer than four thousand officers was too small to deal with serious crime. So Derbyshire was certain to disappear. Even its bigger neighbour, Nottinghamshire, had suffered highly publicized problems that had led its chief constable to admit his detectives couldn't cope. Within a few months, all the officers here this morning might be working for one huge East Midlands Constabulary.

'Why not?' said Cooper. 'We can always do with some help here.'

He realized that Judson had finished speaking and was looking at him over the heads of the group, waiting for his attention.

It was then that Cooper's mobile rang. Probably he should have switched it off. He bet everybody else had put theirs on to silent vibrate, but he'd forgotten this morning.

He looked at the number on the display, and

saw it was Diane Fry. His DS shouldn't be calling him, not when she knew he was on the plastic crime exercise. Cooper looked at Judson and shrugged apologetically, then walked a few paces away from the group.

'Yes, Diane?'

'Where are you right now, Ben?'

'Somerfield's supermarket.'

'I suppose that makes sense, does it?'

'They have ATMs,' said Cooper. 'You know – cash machines.'

'Yes, I know what an ATM is. Wait – you're on the plastic crime initiative.'

'Did you forget?'

'No, I've been a bit busy this morning, that's all.'

'Something on?'

He heard Fry hesitate. 'Don't get excited. Just something I'd like you to take a look at when you're finished. Get away as soon as you can, will you?'

'Are you going to tell me what it's all about?'

'A house fire last night. Multiple fatalities.'

'Where?'

'One of the Edendale estates. The Shrubs, I think they call it.'

'I know where you mean.'

For all the time she'd served in E Division, Fry still didn't seem to know the area all that well. Perhaps she didn't think it was worth the effort because she wasn't intending to stay long enough.

Yes, that was the impression she gave. A visitor caught in a depressing stop-over while she waited for a connection to somewhere better.

Cooper remembered a few of the initial reactions to Fry when she'd first transferred from West Midlands. 'A bit of a hard-faced cow'; 'Could be a looker, but she doesn't bother'; 'Too tall, too skinny, no make-up'; 'Stroppy bitch'. None of them had been fair, of course. But Fry hadn't done much to make herself popular with her colleagues. In fact she seemed to relish her image.

In the background, he could hear Judson answering a question. 'A blank piece of plastic, embossed and encoded with a stolen account number. Some of these plastic crime merchants practically steal your identity.'

'Can you hear me, Ben?'

'Yes, you mentioned a fire on the Shrubs.'

'Great. Well, three deaths. A mother and two children.'

'Evidence of suspicious circumstances?'

'Not yet. But . . .'

'You're expecting some?'

'We haven't had the forensics yet. But I want to know if you'll be around.'

'OK,' said Cooper, trying not to sound surprised. 'I'll see you back at the office after the session with Steve Judson. Is that OK?'

'Yes, that's absolutely fine.'

When he ended the call, Cooper frowned. Somehow, Fry hadn't sounded her usual self.

Judson caught his eye across the group and raised an eyebrow. 'They get your PIN by focusing a camera on the keypad,' he was saying. 'At the end of the day, they retrieve discarded receipts. They match up the time of your withdrawal with the tape from the camera, and they've got both your PIN *and* your account number. They can produce a duplicate card and make fraudulent withdrawals as easily as if they'd stolen the genuine card. And you won't even know anything's happened until you see your next bank statement. That's more than bingo – it's the jackpot.'

Edendale District General was on the northern edge of town, occupying a greenfield site where new wards could be added as funding became available. Fry had never seen the old hospital on Fargate. It had closed years ago, its Victorian buildings so primitive and crumbling that nobody had bothered saving them from demolition. But its location must have been very handy. Even at this time of the morning, it would take her fifteen minutes to get across town to the new site, once she got away from Darwin Street.

'Tell me again, who made the emergency call?' she asked Murfin when he came off the radio to the control room.

'One of the neighbours dialled 999 when he saw the smoke. Bloke by the name of Wade. A bit of a know-it-all, by the sound of him. FOAs took a statement earlier.'

37

'You know, we should have made sure we had complete information before we came out.'

Murfin looked aggrieved. 'You said you wanted to get the job out of the way as soon as possible. In and out, and turn it over to the coroner, that's what *you* said.'

'OK, Gavin, thanks.' Fry didn't like her words being quoted back to her, especially when she'd been wrong. 'It's a bit irritating, that's all.'

'Is that why you made me look in that last bedroom?'

She sighed. 'It had to be done, Gavin. You aren't here just to wreck the place and make stupid jokes. There was nothing in the bedroom, anyway.'

'You didn't know that at the time.'

'Right. How come the hospital staff have more information than we do, eh? So the youngest child wasn't even at home, but with the grandparents? It shouldn't have needed a call to the ward sister to find that out.'

Murfin was silent as he watched her get into her car. 'You know I've got kids of my own, don't you?' he said quietly, before she closed the door.

Fry bit her lip, caught out by a moment of tricky human emotion when she hadn't expected it. 'Sorry, Gavin.'

But he didn't seem to have heard her as he walked away. And by the time she caught up with him later, he was back to his old self, so she didn't mention it again.

*   *   *

Brian Mullen was in a side room off one of the newer wards, with a PC on duty outside the door. Mullen was in his early thirties, sandy-haired, with a faintly pink complexion, as if his skin had been freshly scrubbed. His hands were bandaged, but otherwise he looked quite fit and healthy.

He was also sedated and deeply asleep, as motionless as the dead. There was no point in asking questions of a comatose body.

'Naturally, he was in a very distressed condition when he was admitted,' said the ward sister. 'Apart from his physical injuries.'

'But otherwise he'll be well enough to be interviewed later?' asked Fry.

'You'll have to get permission from the doctor.'

Fry didn't like hospital doctors much. They seemed inseparable from a smell of disinfectant and a tendency to interfere. White coats and professional obstinacy; both unwelcome obstacles when she was intent on finding the truth.

'Were you on duty when Mr Mullen's parents-in-law came in this morning, Sister?'

'Mr and Mrs Lowther? Yes, I spoke to them myself. It was helpful they came, because we'll be able to reassure Mr Mullen his daughter is safe, at least. She was with them last night, apparently. Oh, but you'll know that – someone called earlier.'

'Yes, thank you,' said Fry. 'So when will Mr Mullen come out of sedation?'

'Some time this afternoon.'

'I need to know as soon as he's awake and fit to answer questions, Sister.'

'I'll inform the officer over there, shall I? I presume he's going to carry on hanging around here making a nuisance of himself?'

'I'm afraid so.'

'Well, I hope we have less trouble with the patient when he wakes up. He almost injured one of my nurses when we had to sedate him earlier.'

Fry had been about to leave the ward, but she stopped halfway through the swing doors. 'What do you mean, you *had* to sedate him?'

'He was completely wild, shouting that he couldn't stay here, he had to get out. You know, we see some troubled cases in this hospital, but Mr Mullen was in a dreadful state.'

'He must have wanted to go back to his house. He knew his family were trapped in the fire.'

'Probably you're right . . .' The sister hesitated, sounding doubtful. 'I suppose it's not my place to say this, but that wasn't the way it seemed. If you'd asked me at the time, I would have said he was frightened.'

'Frightened?' Fry glanced back at Brian Mullen, lying motionless in his bed. 'Well, whatever it was, I expect he'll have forgotten it when he wakes up, won't he?'

'Not necessarily. It's his brain and body that are sedated. Deep-rooted fears are in the subconscious. And the subconscious never sleeps.'

* * *

After a wasted trip across town and back, Fry was feeling even more irritable. When she pulled up near the Mullens' house, she found just one miserable-looking uniformed officer standing outside the gate. He had his hands folded behind his back, and he was bouncing slightly on his toes, as if auditioning for a part in *The Pirates of Penzance*. At any moment, he might burst into 'A policeman's lot is not a happy one . . .'

'Where's the fire officer?' she asked, when Murfin emerged from the house.

'He's nipped off to get a bit of something for a late breakfast, lucky bugger. He said to tell you he wouldn't be long.'

'SOCOs here yet?'

'There's someone on the way, I'm told.'

Fry looked around at her available resources. One Gilbert and Sullivan extra, and Gavin Murfin. There was nothing like trying to do things on your own, was there?

Coming up behind the same tractor one more time, Bernie Wilding had to slow down on the road between Foxlow and Bonsall. But the tractor driver pulled over into a lay-by to let him pass, and the postman saw that it was Neville Cross, who owned Yew Tree Farm. His land ran right up to the garden of Rose Shepherd's property.

Bernie slowed to a halt alongside the tractor and tapped his horn to get the farmer's attention.

'Morning,' said Cross.

'Just thought I'd mention – I couldn't get any answer at Bain House earlier on. You know, Miss Shepherd's place? I wondered if you've seen her about at all?'

'Can't say I have. We don't see her in the village much.'

'No, I know. I thought it was a bit funny, though. Her post was still in the box from yesterday, too.'

The farmer nodded almost imperceptibly. 'I'll keep an eye out.'

'Thanks a lot.'

Bernie waved and drove off, watching the tractor pull into the road again as soon as he'd passed. He'd probably get behind it again when he reached Bonsall. Sometimes he thought these farmers drove around the lanes all day just for the sake of it. They loved being a bloody nuisance with their tractors, and their trailers full of slurry. Now and then, Bernie wished he could put a bomb under one of them.

4

Lindsay Mullen's parents lived on the hillside above Darley Dale, a couple of miles north of Matlock. Following the directions she'd been given, Fry watched out for the Shalimar Restaurant, then turned left into Northwood Lane and climbed the hill. The Lowthers' address was near the top, a large bungalow with its rear windows looking down on the A6 from Bakewell.

She and Murfin had to walk a long way up a garden path to reach the front door. This was a garden that seemed to be mostly gravel and stone flags, apart from the obligatory water feature, and dozens of terracotta pots that didn't contain very much.

'I like this sort of garden. No plants.'

And Gavin was right. There was a birdbath, a sundial, a statue of an angel in ornamental stone. And so much furniture, too – a patio set on the terrace under a green parasol, a wooden bench in the shade of an arbour, and a garden barbecue on

43

timber decking at a lower level. In the last few yards, they found themselves walking on cast-iron stepping stones in the shape of flattened tortoises, between solar lights like Edwardian gas lamps. Near the door stood a cast-iron chiminea with a mesh door, its surface just starting to rust.

A few minutes later, they were sitting with Henry Lowther in a conservatory, on either side of an oak coffee table that matched the flooring.

'Sorry to bring you in here,' he said, 'but Luanne is asleep, and we don't want to disturb her. It's going to be stressful enough for the child in the next few weeks, poor thing.'

'Luanne is your youngest grandchild, sir?'

'Yes.'

'How did she come to be here with you last night?'

'We've been looking after her for a few days. Luanne hasn't been sleeping through the night, you see. Poor Lindsay wasn't getting much rest, so we offered to give her a break for a bit.'

'I see. And are you coping all right yourselves? Talk to your family liaison officer if you need any help, won't you?'

'No, we're fine,' said Lowther. 'Luanne needs us, and it's best to have something to concentrate on. You know what I mean . . .'

Lindsay Mullen's parents seemed to be quiet people – no sign of hysterics, or outbursts of anger. But Fry hardly caught a glimpse of Mrs Lowther before she disappeared, clearly on the verge of

44

tears, her eyes already red from previous bouts of weeping.

'My wife isn't up to talking about it yet,' said her husband. 'I hope you understand.'

'Yes, of course. I'm sorry to have to bother you with questions, sir.'

'It's something you have to do.'

It was much too warm for Fry in the conservatory. Looking around, she saw that the central heating radiator had an individual thermostat control. She wondered whether Mr Lowther would notice if she surreptitiously turned it down. But he was watching her too expectantly, the way people did sometimes after a sudden death, as if they thought she might be able to bring their loved ones magically back to life.

'Could you tell me when you first heard about the fire, sir?'

'Yes. Brian phoned to tell us. That's our son-in-law.'

'Brian did? What time was that?'

'Good heavens, I'm not sure. It was in the early hours of the morning. I was too shocked to check the time. Well, I might have looked at the clock, but I didn't take it in. Brian said he was phoning from the hospital – I remember that. At first, I thought it was him that had been in an accident, and I didn't understand what he was trying to tell me. I suppose I was still half asleep.'

The conservatory was probably so warm because it was full of plants – fuchsia, tree ferns, bougainvillea. In the kitchen, Fry had noticed cacti and tradescantia, and a wooden herb wheel on the window sill. She might be ignorant of what grew in the countryside, but she was familiar with house plants. During a spell with a foster family who'd run a small-scale plant nursery in Halesowen, her job had been to write out the labels for the pots – and God help her if she got one wrong through not recognizing a species.

There would be spiders and small insects crawling among these plants, too. She'd tried to sit in the middle of the two-seater cane settee to keep away from the jungle, forcing Murfin to take one of the chairs.

'How did Brian describe what had happened?'

'Describe it? Well, he said he'd arrived home and found the house on fire. I gather he'd been out for the evening. Brian was very distressed, you know – understandably. And he'd suffered some injuries trying to get into the house. In the circumstances I'm surprised he had the presence of mind to call us at all. But I'm glad he did. I don't know how we'd have heard about the fire otherwise.'

'Well, we'd have found your details somehow, and a police officer would have called on you.'

'That would have been worse, I think,' said Lowther. 'If anything could be worse than this.'

Mr Lowther was officially described in the forms as a managing director. In Fry's experience, most managing directors looked as though they'd eaten too many corporate lunches and Rotary Club dinners. But Lowther didn't. He was a big man, but had kept his leanness. Regular squash, or business not so good?

For a moment, Mr Lowther was distracted by the fronds of a tree fern that hung near his chair. He reached out to tear a bit off the plant, with the air of someone who had no idea what he was doing. When he leaned over, Fry noticed that Mr Lowther's shirt buttons weren't fastened properly. One hole was empty, and its button had been fastened too low, so that part of his shirt hung untidily over his waistband.

'That was all Brian could tell me, really. He said that the house was on fire. And that he thought Lindsay and the children were still in there.'

'What did you do?'

'We went up there, of course – to Darwin Street. But the fire was all over by the time we arrived. They wouldn't let us go into the house. So then we went to the hospital, but Brian was sedated. We sat around for hours before someone came and told us that Lindsay and the boys hadn't survived. It was horrible. It seemed as though we were almost the last to know.'

'It can feel like that sometimes. But people have their jobs to do.'

'Yes, I know. But it doesn't really make it any better. Can I ask *you* something now?'

'Go ahead, sir.'

'Do you have any idea how the fire started?'

'Not yet. We think the seat of the fire was

47

downstairs in the sitting room, but we need to examine the house more closely before we can be sure about anything.'

Mr Lowther's gaze drifted away again, and Fry's attention was caught by the traffic on the A6. It had slowed suddenly as an unexpected type of vehicle mingled with the cars and vans, displaying an entirely different pattern of movement. Even through the double glazing, Fry thought she could hear the creak and rattle. For a moment, she wondered if *Pride and Prejudice* was being filmed again somewhere nearby.

'A stagecoach has just gone past on the road down there,' she said. 'It was being pulled by four big grey horses.'

'Yes, they're Dutch Gelderlanders.'

Fry turned, surprised to see Mrs Lowther standing in the doorway, her eyes dried, her voice almost steady, as if she'd made a great effort to bring herself under control.

'Beautiful, aren't they?' she said.

'Right. You've seen them before, then?'

'Sometimes there are two of them drawing a landau.'

Henry Lowther glanced at the window, but didn't seem interested. 'The fire must have been caused by faulty wiring or something, I suppose. They'll find out what went wrong, won't they?'

'We don't know yet whether it was an accident,' said Fry.

But Lowther shook his head. 'No, no. It can't have

48

been started deliberately. I might just about imagine one of the boys playing with matches. But not arson.'

'We should know soon enough, Mr Lowther.'

'You don't understand. There's no one who could have had any reason to start that fire deliberately,' he said. 'It just isn't possible. Lindsay would never upset anybody. And as for Jack and Liam –'

He stopped, as if finding himself unable to express the impossibility in the case of his grand-sons. His anguished expression suggested that the idea of harming them was physically beyond comprehension. His wife caught a surge of his emotion and began to cry all over again.

'What about Brian?'

'He wasn't even at home,' said Lowther.

Fry watched him, trying to detect an accusatory note in his voice. But perhaps it hadn't occurred to the Lowthers yet that their son-in-law ought to have been at home with his family, should have been there to protect them, even if it meant he'd have died in the fire too. It would come later, that anger, the readiness to find someone to blame, if only for not being there.

'Nevertheless, do you think there might be anybody he could have got on the wrong side of? Someone who might want to take revenge on him?'

'You've met him, haven't you?' said Mrs Lowther, between sniffs. 'You can see he's harm-less. What could he have done to anybody to make them commit an evil act like that, just to get back at him? It doesn't make sense.'

Her husband nodded. 'Besides, Brian doesn't mix with people who'd do that sort of thing. He's a despatch manager in a distribution centre.'

On the corner table was a set of photographs in silver frames. Smiling faces, boyish grins, a baby balanced on someone's knee – the Lowthers' grand-children. Fry could see that Jack and Liam were fair-haired, with the pale look of their father. But the baby, Luanne, was much darker. The biggest frame contained an entire family group – Brian and Lindsay with all three children, their youngest child held proudly out front, taking centre stage as if it was her birthday or something.

Fry felt an urge to pick the photos up and look at them more closely, but she was afraid it would distract the Lowthers' attention. Pictures of the fire victims had already been obtained for the case files and the media. She could look at them back at the office, more safely.

Instead, she looked down at her notebook. 'Could we talk about the house for a few minutes? I mean, your daughter's address in Darwin Street. I presume you know it quite well?'

'Yes, of course,' said Mrs Lowther. 'We go there often. We were with them when they moved in. I helped Lindsay choose some of the furniture.'

Hearing that, Fry knew she'd have to pick her words carefully when she asked the next few ques-tions, or she was likely to lose Moira Lowther al-together. The untreated polyurethane foam wasn't her fault, but guilt knew no logic.

'First of all, the smoke alarm. They had one installed in the kitchen.'

'Yes, it was installed as soon as they moved into the house. Brian insisted on it.'

'Who advised him where to put it?'

'Advised him? I don't think anyone did. The kitchen was the obvious place. It's where accidents are most likely to happen.'

'I see.'

Of course, in one way the kitchen *was* the obvious place for a smoke alarm. Every day, the fire service could be guaranteed a tea-time call-out to an overheated chip pan somewhere. But if Brian Mullen had bothered to read the manufacturer's instructions he would have seen a different recommendation. If he'd taken any notice of it, he might have kept his family alive. But there were too many 'ifs' in that equation.

Nevertheless, Fry filed away the impression of Brian Mullen as the sort of man who'd toss the instructions disdainfully aside as he whipped out a screwdriver and relied on his masculine instincts to get the job done.

'Lindsay was proud of her kitchen,' said Mrs Lowther. 'It's not six months since she had new units put in, and a canopy cooker hood with a double extractor. It was immaculate.'

'Yes, I've seen it,' said Fry. 'I wonder, during the past few weeks, did Lindsay or Brian mention anyone hanging around near their house, or someone suspicious coming to the door?'

'No, not at all.'

Before much longer, Fry had exhausted her questions. To be honest, she was glad to get out of the conservatory and away from the plants.

'What sort of business do you run, sir?' she asked.

'I own a very successful export company. We deal mostly in machine tools, which we sell all around the world. We've been planning a shift towards computer technology, but that's not our core business right now.'

Not a wholesale florist's, then. She'd just wondered. As they went back through the house, she saw begonias and chrysanthemums in the living room. And there were foliage plants everywhere: monstera, yucca, palms. It was like the hothouse at Kew in here.

'Oh, you have a visitor,' she said when they reached the door.

A man was coming up the path towards the Lowthers' door. He was taking his time, pausing to smile sadly at the stone angel, stepping carefully on the flattened tortoises. He looked to be in his mid-twenties, smooth faced and wearing an overcoat of a kind that you didn't see very often these days. Fry wondered if he was a journalist.

'Oh, it's John,' said Mr Lowther. 'Our son.'

'Does he live here?'

'No, he has his own apartment, in Matlock. Poor John, he's very upset – he and Lindsay were so close.'

'Is he older than your daughter?'

'No, two years younger.'

John Lowther looked at Fry and Murfin curiously as they met on the porch step.

'These people are the police, John,' said his father. 'They're here about Lindsay and the boys.'

'We were close. Did they tell you?'

'Your parents? Yes, they did.'

'I'm shut up completely.'

'I'm sorry?'

But Lowther was looking at Gavin Murfin. 'I like your tie.'

Murfin looked aghast at getting a compliment. 'Er, thanks.'

'Are you all right, Mr Lowther? I know it must be a very difficult time for you.'

His eyes travelled back towards her, but failed to focus. 'Pardon? What did you say?'

'Have you thought of seeing your doctor?'

Lowther laughed. 'I don't see my doctor, because he's not here.'

He went into the house, where his mother greeted him with a sob and a hug. Fry and Murfin walked back to the car. For a few moments, neither of them spoke. Then Fry started the engine and drove slowly back down the road.

'A bit of a teacake,' said Murfin.

'What?' said Fry, thinking he was talking about food, as usual.

'That Lowther bloke. He's a bit of a teacake.'

'You mean John? Come on, Gavin, you just didn't like him because you thought he was gay.'

'What if he was?' protested Murfin. 'I don't

judge people like that. Well, not any more. I've done the course.'

'Yeah, right. You've learned not to say out loud what you're thinking, that's all.'

Murfin sniffed, but didn't deny it.

'Besides,' he said, 'you don't have to be gay to admire my tie.'

'No, just colour blind.'

'Well, did *you* like him?' asked Murfin.

'He was a bit odd, I suppose.'

'Two sandwiches short of a picnic, more like.'

Fry sighed. 'Is it getting near lunchtime by any chance?'

'Well, now you mention it –'

'All right, all right.'

Fry knew when to give in to necessity. She couldn't understand the way Gavin lived to eat, instead of the other way round.

Sometimes she thought that most of the people around her had life upside down, or back to front. Take the Lowthers, for instance – they had a garden full of furniture, and a house full of plants. Something wrong there, surely?

In Foxlow, a police patrol arrived outside the gates of Bain House at about a quarter past one that afternoon. Thirteen sixteen hours, according to the incident log. PC Andy Myers pressed the intercom button on the gatepost a few times, but got no response.

'Maybe it's not working,' said his partner.

'I can hear it buzzing.'

'Well, Control can't give us a phone number for her.'

'She must be ex-directory.'

'So what do we do, then?'

Myers looked at the wrought-iron gates and the stone pillars on either side. 'One of us has to get his arse over these gates. There should be a release on the other side. Mind the spikes when you get on top, Phil. They look lethal.'

'Oh, thanks a lot. Don't strain yourself, will you?'

'I'm the driver. I have to stay with the car.'

Myers watched his partner struggle over the gates, grumbling all the way as he tried to avoid ripping his uniform or impaling his hand on a spike. Finally, his boots crunched down on to gravel at the other side and he found the release button to open the gates.

'The bloke who phoned in was a farmer name of Cross,' said Myers from the window of the car. 'He says there's a bedroom window open round the back somewhere, and a light on.'

'Why didn't *he* climb over the bloody gate, then?'

'Him? He'll be long gone, ploughing his sheep or something.'

'You don't get out into the country much, do you, Andy?'

The two officers went up to the front door and knocked. They still got no reply. Myers began to walk round the side of the house.

'Yes, I can see the open window,' he called. 'I'm trying the back door.'

'Anything?'

'No.'

'Nor here, either. Think we ought to go in?'

'I don't like this open window,' said Myers. 'There's a burglar alarm – you can see the box up there on the wall. And security lights, too. She's not some careless householder who'd leave her property insecure.'

'I'll call in and let Control know what we're doing.'

'OK, Phil. Then you'll have to find a window to get through on the ground floor. I wouldn't give much for your chances of reaching that open one.'

'Hey, wait a minute –'

When Fry and Murfin arrived in Darwin Street, a man was standing in the garden of number 34. He seemed to have appointed himself some kind of supervisor, checking that everyone attending the fire scene did their job properly. He was holding a small digital camera and squinting through the viewfinder at a SOCO in a scene suit carrying two bulging plastic bags towards a van.

'Hoping to sell some photos to the press, sir?' asked Fry.

He glowered at her. 'No such luck. They've all been here and done their own pictures, TV cameras and all. These are for my records.'

'Records?'

'I'm in Neighbourhood Watch. This'll come up

at the next meeting, you can bet. I was right here from the start, you know. In fact, it was me that rang 999.'

'Would you be Mr Wade?'

'That's me: Keith Wade.'

He was either overweight or so bundled up in sweaters that it was impossible to judge his shape. He was sweating a little, but whether that was from excitement or exertion, she couldn't tell. Keith Wade looked like a man who'd spent all his life in the driver's seat of a lorry, eating egg and chips at truck stops and gradually turning pear-shaped.

'Did you happen to take any photographs during the fire, sir?' she asked.

''Course I did. Look –'

He turned the camera round and held it up as he fingered the controls. A picture appeared on the LED screen. It was very dark – almost black, but for a dull, reddish glow. Only the faint outline of a roof and chimney stack could be made out at the top of the picture.

'Are they all like that?'

'I followed the progress of the fire, and recorded how quickly the emergency services arrived. I took some with the flash when the firemen were here, but all I got was a lot of glare off the reflective strips on their jackets.'

'We'd like copies of any shots you took during the fire.'

Wade looked pleased, then his face fell. 'I haven't got a colour printer.'

'That's all right. Have you got internet access? You can email them to us.'

'Yes, I can do that.'

Fry gave him her card, and he fingered it happily.

'Detective, are you?'

'That's right.'

'Is that usual?'

'What?' said Fry, ready to react to some sexist remark.

'Sending a detective to a fire.'

'When there are fatalities, yes.'

'Fatalities, right. The two kids were killed, weren't they? Never stood a chance, they reckon.'

'And their mother, of course.'

He nodded. 'Tragic. I knew Lindsay and Brian pretty well. We've been neighbours for six years.'

Wade's house was so close to the Mullens' that the smoke had stained his walls, too. Pools of water lay in his garden, and someone had trampled a flower bed on their way to the fire.

'Mr Wade, has anyone been around in the last few weeks asking questions about the Mullens?'

'Asking questions? Other than you lot, you mean?'

'It's a serious enquiry, sir.'

'Sorry. No, there hasn't been anyone.'

'Think carefully, please. It might have been someone who appeared perfectly innocent at the time. A market researcher calling at the door, then dropping in a casual question about your next-door neighbours?'

'No, I'd remember that.'

'What about your wife? She might remember someone being around while you were out.' Seeing Wade hesitate, she probed further. 'I'm sorry. Are you married, sir?'

'I'm divorced,' he said.

'OK. Tell me again what made you first notice the fire.'

'Well, I think I smelled the smoke. I suppose the smell of it must have been strong enough to wake me up. At first, I reckoned it must be someone's bonfire that had been set alight. Kids do that around here, you know – they think it's fun to see the fire engines arrive. But when I got out of bed, I saw a funny light on the bedroom curtains. It was sort of flickering, like someone was watching a huge TV screen outside. Do you know what I mean?'

'So what did you do?'

'I put some clothes on, went outside to have a look, then made the emergency call.'

Yes, and that sweater was probably the first thing he'd put on. It looked as though he'd been wearing it for months. The thing was brown and shaggy, with little threads of wool springing out everywhere.

'Did you see anyone outside at that time, Mr Wade?'

'No, not a soul. But I wasn't looking up and down the street, just at the fire. It had broken the sitting-room window by then, and there were flames going up the wall. Come to think of it, I suppose it might have been the sound of the window breaking that woke me up, not the smell of the smoke.'

'Why do you think that, sir?'

'Well, like I said, I'm in Neighbourhood Watch. I've sort of trained myself to hear the sound of breaking glass at night. We've had some burglaries round here, as I suppose you know. So I have to be on the alert.'

'I see. But you don't actually *remember* hearing glass breaking last night?'

Wade looked disappointed. 'No, not really.'

He was so transparent. Fry imagined he was a bit of a nuisance at Neighbourhood Watch meetings, always claiming to have seen something that he hadn't, to make himself more interesting. She wondered whether Wade was a member of other organizations, too. The Police Liaison Committee, the Keep Edendale Tidy Group – anything that would let him stick his nose into other people's lives.

'What about traffic, Mr Wade? Were there any cars going by when you first saw the fire?'

'Not that I noticed,' he said. 'Just a minute.'

He raised his camera to his face and focused on something past Fry. She turned to see a liveried police car pull up outside number 32, and the driver spoke to a uniformed officer on duty outside.

'Would it be all right if I took your photograph as well?' asked Wade. 'I don't think I've got a detective.'

'No, it wouldn't be all right.'

He sighed. 'Fair enough.'

'Mr Wade, did you make any attempt to get into your neighbour's house when you saw the fire? Or were you too busy taking photographs?'

He looked hurt. 'Of course I tried to get in. After I'd made the call, I ran back out and went over the fence to their house. But there were already flames coming out of the windows, and I couldn't see a thing for the smoke.'

'You must have seen Brian Mullen arrive home later.'

He shoved the camera away in a pocket and wiped the palms of his hands on his sweater.

'Yes, poor bugger. He was going out of his mind. Is Brian all right, do you know?'

'His injuries are only minor.'

'That's something, anyway.'

Even out here, the smell of smoke and charring was very strong. Mr Wade himself seemed to reek of burning, like a smoked kipper. If he'd stood in his garden wearing that same sweater while the fire was burning, it was probably impregnated with the smell: smouldering wood and singed flesh.

'Are you normally at home during the day, Mr Wade?'

'Sometimes I work late shifts,' he said. 'I make deliveries for the supermarkets.'

'I see.'

'I ought to be in bed now. But I couldn't sleep with all this excitement going on.'

Fry looked across the fence at number 32. The SOCOs had erected a crime-scene tent over the doorway, so it was impossible to see inside the house now, except for a vague shape moving past a blackened window now and then. The bodies of the victims had long since been removed, and the firefighters had finished damping down, leaving nothing but a few streams of muddy water running into the gutter.

'Yes. Riveting, isn't it?'

By the time she got back to E Division headquarters in West Street, Fry had a headache. She looked in her desk for some Paracetamol, but found only an empty box, not even a broken foil strip. She glared angrily around the CID room. Light-fingered bastards. She never let herself run out of Paracetamol, so someone in the office had been nicking them from her drawer without asking. In this place, they'd steal your fillings if you left your mouth open too long.

She took a few deep breaths instead and drank a cup of water. She had to be fit and on the ball. This wasn't a time to screw up; it was the perfect opportunity to demonstrate her ability. Had she done everything that needed to be done right now?

She'd left Gavin Murfin at Darwin Street to liaise with the fire investigator and chase up the SOCOs. She'd also asked for a search team to examine the vicinity of the house. What she needed was some indication of malicious intent, so she could go to the DI with a view on the case. That would show she could deal with a challenge.

The pain tightened across her forehead. She ought to have asked Cooper to bring her a new supply of Paracetamol from the supermarket. The day was about to begin in earnest, and there were bound to be more problems coming her way before long. It was going to be one of those weeks, all right.

The dead body lay at an awkward angle, half on a rug by the bed. It had been a nice sheepskin rug once, soft and white – until it soaked up most of Rose Shepherd's blood. Now it was stained dark red and caked into stiff clumps. When Miss Shepherd died, she'd been wearing her nightdress, a cotton one designed for comfort rather than style, with enough folds to conceal the source of the blood.

PC Myers raised a hand to the light switch, but remembered the light was already on. His partner stood in the doorway, tugging at his radio.

'What do you think she's done to herself?'

'Can't tell,' said Myers. 'She's dead, though.'

'Back off, then. Don't touch her.'

But Myers was crouching closer to the body, and he could see the circular hole punched neatly through the cotton near Rose Shepherd's heart.

'Bloody hell, Phil,' he said. 'The old bird's been shot.'

5

Ben Cooper drove out of the Somerfield's car park before the plastic crime session was over. He wasn't sorry to be leaving. He didn't think Steve Judson would be sorry to lose him, either. Two calls on his mobile were two too many.

As he accelerated his Toyota into Fargate and crossed the junction towards Chesterfield Road, Cooper considered phoning Diane Fry to let her know where he was heading. But if she hadn't heard about the Foxlow incident already, she'd find out soon enough.

But, wait . . . a triple death, she'd said, in a house fire. If that turned out to be malicious intent, E Division would have its work cut out. Caseloads were always a headache when a major enquiry cropped up. There were only eighteen DCs on the division, most of them scattered across the sections. Every officer in Derbyshire Constabulary had an average of three crimes on his desk at any one time – well, except in Glossop section, where they claimed to have five. But then, Glossop always had been a world of its own.

Oh well, it looked as though his social life might be put on hold again. And just when it was getting more interesting.

He crossed the bridge over the River Eden and hit the A623 into Calver. To the west, beyond Abney Moor, was his old home, Bridge End Farm. The town of Bakewell was a little further on, and then it was a straight run down the A6 to Matlock.

This was one of his favourite parts of the Peak District, because it seemed to have the best of both worlds. The high gritstone edges rose to the east – Curbar Edge and Baslow Edge. Dark, bare and ancient. But down here in the valleys, the dense woodland gave the landscape an entirely different character. At this time of year, he could start to think of it as his own world again, almost free of tourists, settling under its blanket of fallen leaves.

And beneath the trees, among the fields and the drystone walls, were the small farms. Each one, like Bridge End, trying to face up to its future.

Finally, he reached Foxlow. It was one of those villages that looked as though nothing ever happened, but where the worst things often did. Not much traffic during the day, and no one out on the street. The residents were all at work, or in their gardens, or shut away in their front rooms, wondering what all the activity was outside.

The scene at Bain House was already swarming

with personnel and vehicles. When Cooper reported to the RV point, he was amazed to see officers from the Firearms Support Unit patrolling the outer cordon with their automatic weapons cradled across their bullet-proof vests. That could only mean one thing.

His DI, Paul Hitchens, was coming across the garden with the crime-scene manager, Wayne Abbott. Hitchens was dressed in a dark suit and tie, keeping up his image as one of the smartest detectives in E Division. Abbott was wearing his pale blue crime-scene coverall, and neither the colour nor the shapeless outfit suited his muscular build and stubbled jaw.

Waiting patiently for them at the incident control unit was the divisional head of CID, Detective Chief Inspector Oliver Kessen. Until potential forensic evidence had been preserved and recorded, the scene was Wayne Abbott's domain, and crime-scene managers were jealous gods. Everyone had to wait for his permission to enter.

It was somehow reassuring to see Kessen at a crime scene, though it indicated the seriousness of the incident. Although he wasn't a big man, the DCI had the ability to become a focal point for activity wherever he happened to be. He was the still centre at the heart of events that might otherwise descend into chaos. Today he looked as calm as ever, using his mobile phone to deal with some administrative problem at the office as he waited for Hitchens and Abbott to reach him.

Cooper admired that. Better to be calm and unhurried than to rush around doing all the wrong things in the early stages. It was the way he'd like to be himself, if he ever made it to a senior level. But he wasn't sure he had the right temperament. Maybe that was why he was still a DC.

He joined the fringes of the group, hoping for more information. The details he had so far were scanty. A woman found dead in her home, possible signs of an intruder.

The DCI took his time ending his call. 'Definitely a shooting?' he said finally, turning his gaze on Abbott.

Abbott pulled the hood and collar of his scene suit away from his neck and peeled off his gloves. 'Absolutely. At least three shots were fired, I'd say.'

'Why would you say that, Wayne?'

'You can see for yourself. We've got the video, of course. But I can let you do a walkthrough on this one, if you like.'

The DI was signalling. Cooper fell in step alongside him as they headed towards the house.

'The victim's name is Rose Ann Shepherd. Unmarried, so far as we can tell. It appears she lived completely alone – no other family members, and no staff. She's been resident in the village for about ten months.'

'Who found her?' asked Cooper, pulling out his notebook.

'Well, a neighbouring farmer raised the alarm, but it was actually the postman who first noticed something wrong – his name's Bernie Wilding. Mr Wilding could see that the victim hadn't emptied her letter box.'

'So she's been dead since yesterday?'

'At least.'

They followed the path marked out for them to climb the stairs and reach the master bedroom. The victim's body still lay where PC Myers had found it, half on and half off the rug, twisted at an unnatural angle. She looked as though she'd been turning towards the door, one arm outstretched, but bent awkwardly by the fall. The red stains on the sheepskin ran on to the carpet and soaked the victim's nightdress. Cooper noticed that the nightdress was blue, only a shade or two darker than Abbott's crime-scene suit.

The bedroom was noticeably cooler than the rest of the house. And there was an obvious reason for that – the casement window stood open. A cool breeze blew through the back garden of Bain House, and a few dead leaves had drifted on to the window ledge.

'So,' said Kessen. 'Three shots, you said?'

Abbott stood over the body. 'Well, two shots hit the victim. The medical examiner says either one of them might have been enough to kill her. Certainly enough to put her on the floor.'

'So where did the third shot go?'

'That was a miss. The bullet embedded itself in the bedroom wall there, high up near the ceiling. See it?'

'Yes.'

'We'll be able to give you an idea of the weapon once the bullets have been recovered.'

'Time of death?' said Kessen, without much sign of optimism.

'Between thirty and forty hours ago, according to the ME. Rigor mortis was almost gone when he examined the victim, but for a bit of residual stiffness in the abdomen.'

'My God, forty hours?'

'At the maximum.'

Hitchens looked at his watch. 'That would put the earliest time of the incident at nine p.m. Saturday. And the latest at seven a.m. Sunday.'

Kessen shook his head. 'For heaven's sake, how does a woman get herself shot and then lie dead for nearly two days without anyone noticing? Why didn't someone somewhere miss her? Why didn't they get worried when she wasn't out and about doing all the things she usually did?'

'The time is just a temperature-based estimate, of course,' said Abbott. 'You'll need some other evidence to pin it down more closely.'

'Yes, thank you.'

'Well, temperature-based methods of calculating time of death are the most prone to error, you know. Newton's Law of Cooling isn't the most modern approach.'

Ah, Newton's Law of Cooling. It was a familiar phrase, one that had stuck in Cooper's mind from his training. When he first heard of it, he'd pictured some seventeenth-century eccentric sitting under a tree with an apple bouncing off his head. He didn't know the mathematics behind Isaac Newton's theory, but he knew it was almost always inaccurate – hence the medical examiners hedging their bets and stretching out time scales like Play-Doh.

Like everyone else, he'd been taught that rigor mortis in a dead body was complete by twelve hours and gone by thirty-six. But later he'd discovered that there were as many differences of opinion as there were experts, and too many factors involved. Time of death should be based on witness reports, not physical evidence. But he hadn't heard a hint of any witnesses yet.

'Surely we can send FSU home?' said Hitchens. 'Whoever did the shooting will be long gone.'

'Not until we've completed a sweep of the area and done door-to-door in the village,' said Kessen. 'For all we know, he might be holed up somewhere nearby.'

'Yes, understood. It just seems to be making the residents a bit jittery, seeing armed police officers on the street. They're not used to it around here.'

Kessen shrugged. 'Point of entry, Wayne?' he said. 'On the face of it, this open window looks like the way the assailant came into the house.'

'Perhaps. But it wasn't forced – there are no tool marks on the frame. We lifted several latents, though. I should get results on those within the hour.'

'The first officers to arrive came in through a

side window,' said Hitchens. 'But they had to smash it themselves, which set off the intruder alarms – Control got a call from a monitoring room somewhere, but we were already on the scene by then. The alarms were still going like crazy when I got here.'

'Our officers set off the alarms? They weren't activated by the assailant?'

'No, sir.'

Kessen walked out on to the landing and looked down the stairs. A SOCO was crouched over something in the hallway.

'What have you got there?'

'A video intercom system. It must be connected to the unit on the front gate.'

Hitchens came over to look. 'I don't even have a gate at my house, let alone an intercom. I live on one of those open-plan estates. Any bugger can run across my front lawn, or up my drive.'

'They call that community living,' said Abbott.

'I know what I'd call it. So how does that thing work?'

The SOCO picked up the handset. 'When someone presses the button at the gate, there's a tiny camera in the unit on the gatepost that shows their image on the screen here.'

'So the householder can see the postman in the flesh, and know he's not an impostor.'

'That's it.'

Cooper looked down at the body again as the exchange went backwards and forwards around

71

him. Voices echoed strangely in the house, as if it wasn't fully furnished. Actually, the furniture *was* fairly sparse. Nothing unnecessary or frivolous cluttered the rooms that he'd seen. It made him think of his flat in Welbeck Street when he'd first viewed it. Furnished, but empty. Empty because no one lived there.

He felt uncomfortable for the victim, lying there on the floor. He knew nothing about Rose Shepherd, but he was sure she'd have hated anyone to see her like this. Her grey hair was dishevelled and fell in loose strands across her face. Her mouth had fallen open, and a trail of saliva had dried on her lips. Crime-scene photographs would show up a small rip in the victim's nightdress and the white, crinkled flesh on the back of her thighs. The flash would cruelly expose the crow's feet around her eyes, the loose skin at her neck, the beginning of liver spots on the back of her hand where it clutched the rug. Death did nothing for the appearance. But this was the way Miss Shepherd would be immortalized.

Kessen walked back to the bedroom and looked out on to the garden. 'Correct me if I'm wrong,' he said, 'but there's quite a bit of money tied up here, isn't there?'

Abbott nodded. 'A few hundred pounds for that intercom unit alone, I'd say. Probably double that for the installation of the gates.'

'So it looks as though the victim really needed to know who was calling on her, doesn't it?'

'We've got house-to-house under way. But so far, everyone we've talked to is in agreement on one thing: Miss Shepherd never got any visitors. Apart from the postman – and even he didn't get past the gates.'

'No visitors at all?'

'So they say.'

'No. We just haven't talked to the right people, yet,' said Kessen.

'Why?'

'Well, that can't be true, can it, Paul? You're a property owner. What about all those folk who come to your address? The refuse men to collect your wheelie bin, the tanker driver to deliver your central heating fuel, the man who reads your electricity meter? No one can build a moat around their property and keep everyone out. It isn't possible these days. Life has a way of intruding in all sorts of ways.'

'Rose Shepherd does seem to have been a very solitary person, though. She lived on her own, and she didn't mix with the neighbours, by all accounts. No one in Pinfold Lane knows who Miss Shepherd's next of kin could be, or whether she had a family at all. We found an address book near the phone downstairs, but we can't see any obvious relatives listed. In fact, the entries seem to be all routine stuff – doctor, dentist, a local garage.'

'There must be something in the house to give us names. A diary, letters . . .?'

'Well, we're still looking. But it seems odd.

There ought to be somewhere obvious for her to keep information like that. Why make us hunt for it?'

'Try a phone bill. See what numbers she called most often, who was on her Family and Friends list.'

'Yes, sir.'

'How long had she lived here? Do we know that?'

'The neighbours say about a year. Miss Shepherd moved in on her own, with no sign of a husband or anything. No secret lover sneaking in through the back door either.'

'If the lover was secret, no one would know about him, surely?'

'This is a village,' said Hitchens, as if that explained everything.

'You know, this is a large house for one woman living on her own.'

'She doesn't seem to have employed anyone, not even a gardener or cleaner. The lady at the next property down the lane says Miss Shepherd did some gardening herself now and then. She used to see her from her bedroom window, pottering about on the other side of the hedge.' He looked up at Kessen. 'See what I mean about a village? Who needs surveillance?'

'But the house?' Kessen brushed at a cobweb. 'It looks as though it could have done with the attention of a cleaner now and then, to be honest.'

'Presumably Miss Shepherd was less keen on housework than gardening.'

Kessen turned back to Abbott. 'What about security? We know she had an intruder alarm.'

'A top-of-the-range monitored system, too. She wanted to be sure that there would be a police response if she had an intruder. Motion sensors – so possibly an audio connection or a CCTV camera somewhere. We can check with the monitoring centre whether she ever had any alerts. This is more than a DIY job, or a bells-only system.'

'Doors and windows?'

'Five-lever mortice deadlocks, and hinge bolts.' Abbott tapped the fanlight. 'Laminated glass – almost impossible to break in the normal way. Oh, and there's a restrictor on the inside of the letter box to stop anyone reaching through to release locks and bolts. She didn't use the letter box on the door, though. There's one on the gates.'

'Probably the gates came later.'

Abbott moved around the room. 'We've got double glazing, key-operated window locks. Venetian blinds, so she could stop people looking in without blocking the light. Outside, I noticed there were bulkhead lights as well as the floodlights fitted with motion detectors.'

'She seems to have had good advice on security.'

'There's even a shredder next to the desk here. She wasn't taking any chances.'

'She knew about bin raiding, then. Not everyone has that sort of nous. I wonder where she learned about the risk of identity theft.'

'What about that Notts exercise a while ago? Wasn't that in the local papers?'

'Could have been.'

Cooper remembered that, too. Nottinghamshire Police had decided to take the contents of hundreds of household bins and analyse them to see what people were throwing away. A messy job, but interesting results. They found nearly ninety per cent of domestic rubbish contained information that would be helpful to fraudsters. Most of the bins had the full name and address of someone in the household, and many had details of bank account numbers and sort codes. Some had the full set. Helpful? That was more like making someone a Christmas present of your bank account. PC Judson would be horrified.

'The one thing we've found is her passport,' said Hitchens.

'A UK passport?'

'Yes. Rose Ann Shepherd, British citizen, born 1944 in London . . .' He flicked through the pages. 'No stamps.'

'What about an address?'

'Your address doesn't appear in your passport.'

'No, but most people give a next of kin. A friend or relative, anyway – maybe two.'

'You're right.' Hitchens turned to the back page again. 'Nope, not in Miss Shepherd's case.'

'No one she wanted informed in the event of an accident?'

'I guess not. You know, this passport looks

almost unused to me. Mine has got a bit creased at the spine and started to turn up at one corner.'

'Well, that would explain why there are no stamps.'

'Not necessarily. It just means she hasn't been outside Europe with it. Or rather, outside the Schengen area. You don't get stamped moving between Schengen countries.'

In her passport photograph, Miss Shepherd was smartly turned out. Her hair was a darker shade of grey, swept back in a business-like manner to match a white blouse, discreet ear studs and a hint of make-up. She had sharp blue eyes and a direct gaze, with the faintest of smiles at the camera.

Hitchens took a call on his mobile. 'OK, that's great. Thanks.' He turned to Kessen. 'There was a Vauxhall Astra seen in the village in the early hours of Sunday morning. It doesn't belong to any of the residents, so far as we can tell. One witness is almost sure she's seen it in the village before – and the previous occasion was late at night, too.'

'Any details?'

'Blue.'

'Dark blue? Could have been black in the dark?'

'Nope. Light blue, seen under the streetlight near the phone box. No reg, but it probably started with an X, so it wasn't a new model.'

'You know, we need the media to come on board early in this one, Paul. There are no obvious leads from the house. We've got to get appeals out to locate the driver of that Astra, and anyone who had contact with Rose Shepherd in the last forty-eight hours. No – the last two weeks. God, I don't know – any contact with her, full stop.'

Cooper looked up, surprised to hear the DCI getting even a little bit rattled in public.

But he could see what was bothering Kessen. The first twenty-four hours were the vital period after any murder. If you didn't have a strong lead within that time, you were destined for a long drawn-out enquiry – and the odds were against bringing the case to a successful conclusion. This murder might be forty hours old already, according to the ME, and there wasn't a single lead in sight.

But why didn't someone miss Rose Shepherd? That was the question the DCI had asked earlier. And it was a good question.

'You know, there's absolutely no sign of an intruder being in the house,' said Kessen. 'Apart from this open window, which shows no traces of having been forced. No tool marks, no damage. Right, Wayne?'

Abbott had his phone to his ear. 'And no fingerprints either,' he said. 'I just got an update. The only prints we found on the window are a match for the victim's – and they were on the inside.'

'And every other window in the house is locked down tight. Why wouldn't this one be locked, too? Can anyone suggest an answer to that?'

'Yes,' said Hitchens, looking anxious. 'Because someone used this window to get *out* of the house. I don't know how he got in – I can only guess the victim let him in through the front door. But he must have gone out this way.'

'We're on the first floor. Did he clamber down the drainpipe?'

'Probably.' Hitchens looked out of the window. 'Actually, there isn't a drainpipe. Not within reach.'

'A nice dense ivy, then? Russian vine?'

'Nothing. It's a blank wall . . .' Hitchens hesitated. 'He must have jumped.'

'From this height?'

'Er, yeah.'

'In that case, Paul, I expect you'll find the intruder's prints on the window frame, perhaps some fibres from his clothes on the stone ledge. There'll be some pretty deep footwear impressions in the ground down below, where he landed. Oh, and you'll be looking for a suspect who ran away with two broken legs and a cracked spine.'

Hitchens sighed. 'So what's the alternative?'

Kessen joined him at the window. 'There's only one other possibility. That there never was an intruder in this house. The victim was shot from outside.'

Hitchens stared. 'From the garden?'

'No, look – the angle is completely wrong. The shots must have come from the field.'

'But the window – why was it open?'

'Wayne said there were no prints on the outside. What about the inside?'

'Just the victim's.'

'So that's pretty clear, isn't it?' said Kessen. 'The

victim opened the bedroom window herself. And someone waiting in the field shot her.'

'Jesus,' said Hitchens.

Kessen turned back and addressed the room in general. 'Close off that road up there, seal the gateway, and get the SOCOs and the search teams into the field. That's where our gunman was.'

Before the action moved outside, Cooper took a chance to study the interior of the house. One of the first things that had struck him was the amount of dust. Of course, there had been no cleaner. And Miss Shepherd had only done the minimum amount of housework herself, by the looks of it. A bit of attention to the sitting room, the kitchen, the bathroom, and her bedroom.

But there were other rooms that seemed to have lain untouched. Opening the door into a guest bedroom set balls of dust rolling across the carpet, spiders scurrying away from the movement. The curtains were closed in here, so Cooper switched on the light. Fine particles of dust hung in the air, swirling in the draught from the landing.

Most people had no idea where the dust in their homes came from. As far as the average householder was concerned, it might as well come from the Moon, floating down from the sky every night and settling on available surfaces like drifting snow. An inconvenience, perhaps, but something natural and inert that was just part of the atmosphere, like oxygen.

But Cooper knew different. It was one of those

facts that he'd learned as a teenager and never forgot. He knew that all human beings in the world shed thousands of dead skin cells every hour, an entire layer of skin over three days. That was what hung in the air and danced in a shaft of sunlight from the window. That was what lay on the shelves and gathered in restless clumps under the bed, or shrouded the junk in the attic. Ninety per cent of the dust in any house consisted of dead human skin.

Also, the décor in the sitting room struck him as odd. Off-white and charcoal grey, almost no colour. It seemed a bit modern for a house of this age, let alone for the sort of woman that Rose Shepherd seemed to have been. As far as anyone could tell, anyway.

Hitchens stuck his head round the door. 'Ben, we've brought the postman back to the scene. Go and get a statement from him, will you? He's fretting about getting back on his rounds.'

'Right, sir.'

Cooper took a last look at the charcoal grey wallpaper around the fireplace. It showed up the dust badly, and it was undisturbed by finger marks. And then he remembered another fact he'd learned about house dust. Each speck of it carried tens of thousands of dust mites. Right at this moment, they were busy feeding on those dead skin cells.

6

'Years ago, I used to work on a delivery round out Leek way,' said Bernie Wilding when Cooper found him sitting in his red mail van. 'I saw those wallabies out there about as often as I saw Miss Shepherd in Foxlow.'

'The wallabies?'

Cooper laughed. Most rumours of exotic animals surviving in unlikely parts of the country were rubbish. But sometimes the creatures turned out to be real, like the scorpions on the London Underground – or the wallabies of the Roaches.

'Did you really see the wallabies?' he asked.

'Only as an odd shape in the distance once or twice. I was never quite sure whether I was looking at a wallaby or a hare, really. But I always told everybody I'd seen the wallabies. Well, you do, don't you?'

'Yes, I would too.'

It was one of Cooper's genuine regrets that he'd never seen a wallaby, despite his thirty years in the Peak District. No one who lived or worked on the western fringes of the national park doubted they existed. Plenty of drivers had seen them, and a few had run one over at night on some remote road. The original animals had escaped from a private zoo during the Second World War, and bred on the moors. According to the stories, a yak escaped at the same time. But the last yak sighting was back in the fifties. Pity, really.

'Too late now, I reckon,' said Wilding.

'So they say. Too many people and dogs invading their habitat.'

'Oh, aye. And too much traffic. People have killed them off, when the bad winters couldn't.'

Cooper thought he'd probably passed the test. Some of his colleagues would have had no idea what Bernie was talking about. But he'd proved his credentials as a local.

'What about Miss Shepherd? You saw her often enough and at close enough range to recognize her, didn't you?'

Wilding screwed his face up thoughtfully. 'You know, the few times I did catch a glimpse of her, she always seemed to be wearing a headscarf, or something that hid her face. I could never be entirely sure it was her. Not so that I could absolutely swear to it, you understand?'

'So you don't think you'd be able to identify her, Mr Wilding?'

'Not for certain. Sorry.'

'You spoke to her, though, didn't you? What did she sound like?'

'Well, I reckon she had a bit of an accent,' said Wilding. 'But I couldn't really place it. I didn't speak to her that often, and even then it wasn't to hold a conversation. Most often, it was through that intercom thing on the gate. And, to be honest, I wouldn't recognize my own mother speaking through one of those.'

'Did you ever see anyone else coming or going from Bain House?'

'No, never.'

'Any cars parked there?'

'Just Miss Shepherd's. It's a Volvo, I think.'

'And these gates were always closed, as far as you know?'

'Always. She kept everyone out, including me.'

'One last thing,' said Cooper. 'What was it you brought for her this morning?'

'Oh, there was a package. It was a bit too big to get in the letter box. Can I give it to you?'

'Yes, please. I'll let you have a receipt.'

Wilding handed him a small parcel about nine inches long. 'Miss Shepherd never got much mail. I hope it was nothing to do with what happened to her.'

'Well, it was the reason she was found today, instead of in a week's time.'

By the time Diane Fry arrived in Foxlow, there was no room for anyone to park anywhere near

Bain House. She had to leave her Peugeot on the roadside close to a stone wall and walk to the RV point. Cooper met her near the gates as he was clearing the way for Bernie Wilding to get his van out.

'Can you bring me up to speed, Ben?' she asked.

'Sure. I've made notes.'

'I thought you would have.'

Cooper ran through the details. Fry listened carefully, finding nothing to fault him on. He thought he'd done pretty well, considering he hadn't been at the scene much longer than she had herself.

'She sounds like a bit of a recluse,' said Fry when he'd finished.

He wondered if Fry felt the same slight shiver of recognition that he did at some of the details. There were times in many people's lives when they went to great lengths to avoid contact with anyone else. It wasn't so unusual. Just a bit extreme, perhaps, in Rose Shepherd's case.

'Actually, I used to know a lady who was a real recluse,' he said. 'Old Annie, we called her. When I was a child, she lived in an old cottage near the farm. She must have been there for donkey's years, because the place was getting very run down. But she didn't seem to have any relatives – or if she did, they never bothered to visit her. Annie stayed in her house watching TV and listening to the radio, much like Miss Shepherd must have done.'

They began to walk towards the house. The

front door stood open, officers still coming and going with bagged items for examination.

'No one visited Annie at all?' asked Fry.

'Well, Mum used to call on her occasionally to see if she was all right. A few times a year, she was invited to our house. Boxing Day, that was a time when we always had to have her round. As kids, we used to dread her coming.'

'Why?'

'Annie was one of those lonely people who didn't speak to anyone for weeks on end, then couldn't help talking far too much when she finally got into company. It was as if she had to prove to herself that she could still hold a conversation, that somebody would listen to her when she was speaking. I suppose she needed to be sure that she still existed in other people's eyes.'

'Were you psychoanalysing people even then?' said Fry. 'Yes, I bet you were. I can just see you as an eight-year-old Sigmund Freud.'

But Cooper took no notice. He knew her well enough by now. She made those remarks out of a sort of defensive instinct sometimes. In fact, whenever he talked about vulnerable and lonely people, it seemed.

'Of course, the result was that everyone tried to steer clear of Old Annie,' he said. 'It was probably why her relatives never visited her, and why even the postman kept his van door open and the engine running. Mum always said she had trouble getting away from the cottage once she was inside.'

'No one likes being trapped by an old bore.'

'Yes, I suppose Annie was a terrible old bore, but it was more than that. When I was a small child I found her quite frightening. She had that slightly hysterical tone to her voice that always makes people nervous. So people went out of their way to avoid her.'

'God help me, but I hope I die before I get like that.'

They found Hitchens and Kessen at the edge of the field backing on to the garden of Bain House. The DCI seemed to be sniffing the air, trying to detect the scent of his suspect, like a dog. Wayne Abbott was walking across the field towards them, his boots crunching through the ridges of ploughed soil.

'I was always taught to go around the edge of a field so as not to damage the crop,' he said. 'But I'm making an exception today, because the edge of the field is exactly where your tyre marks are.'

'The tyre marks of what?'

'A black car possibly, but a dark colour certainly.'

Kessen looked surprised, and perhaps a bit irritated. 'Why do you say that?'

'Well, I'm betting if they drove openly across this field they were hoping that residents living nearby would think they were out lamping.'

'Lamping?'

'That's when people go out into the country-side to shoot animals at night. Lampers use a bright light to dazzle their quarry.'

87

'Yes, I know about that – rabbits and such like.'

'Well, not just rabbits. Badgers, deer, sheep – you name it. Anything that'll stand up and be shot at.' Abbott's eyes flickered around the group. 'DC Cooper will tell you about it. I'm sure he must have done a bit of lamping himself.'

'Well . . .' began Cooper. But no one was listening to him.

'But the thing is,' said Abbott, 'if local people thought somebody was out lamping that night, they probably wouldn't have bothered to dial 999, even when they heard shots.'

'You're kidding.'

'It's different in the country – you get used to hearing gunshots. In the city, someone might call the police, but out here you wonder how many brace they've potted.'

'I understand that. But the colour of the vehicle . . . ?'

'Well, you wouldn't go lamping in a white car, would you? You want your target to focus on the light, not on the paintwork of your bonnet.'

'Nothing else, apart from the tyre marks?'

'Nope. I was hoping for some shell casings. A brass casing could give us some prints, or there might be marks left by the weapon's extractor or firing pin. But there's nothing here that we can see.'

'All right. Thanks.'

'So it looks as though the suspect didn't bother going into the house. Clever.'

'Clever?'

'Well, it makes it more difficult for us. We always have a better chance of coming up with something from a closed scene. Like the bedroom, for instance. But a ploughed field? And two days after the incident? Better start praying for a miracle.'

Kessen stared at the house. 'All right, it was clever. But I wonder what the shooter did to get Rose Shepherd's attention.'

'What do you mean?' asked Hitchens.

'Well, if he made the hit from the field, he must have found some way to get his victim to the window. I can't believe he was prepared to sit out here all night on the off-chance that she'd decide to get out of bed and take a look at the stars.'

'A phone call, I reckon,' said Hitchens. 'It'd be easy enough to phone her on a mobile from the car.'

'Yes.'

'It's starting to look like a professional job, isn't it?'

'I'm afraid so.' Kessen nodded. 'Yes, he could easily have phoned Miss Shepherd and woken her up. But what did he say to get her to come to the window? What *could* he have said that would make her walk straight into his sights?'

While Abbott organized a detailed search of the field, Cooper took the chance to report what the postman Bernie Wilding had told him about never seeing Miss Shepherd's face clearly.

'I could understand it if she was physically disfigured,' said Hitchens. 'If she was a burns victim, or something. That would explain why she never went out, and didn't want people to see her.'

'But she wasn't disfigured, either in real life or in her passport photo. How old is that passport? When was it issued?'

'Issued May 2000. Expires 2010.'

'What about motive?' asked Fry. 'Do you think someone in the village might have had a grudge against her?'

'If she didn't have contact with anyone in the village, how could someone have a grudge against her?'

'Well, I don't know. Maybe that's *why* she didn't have contact with anyone. We don't know anything about her history, so we can't guess. Where do we start?'

'There's one place we can start,' said Kessen. 'We need a list of individuals in the locality with firearms certificates. What about this farmer, what's his name?'

'Neville Cross?'

'He's a neighbour, isn't he?'

'He owns the land at the back of Bain House. But I think his farmhouse is way down there, two fields away.'

'He'll have a firearms certificate. Most farmers do – for a shotgun, at least. But maybe he has a serious rabbit problem and needs a rifle.'

'Yes, and maybe he's a retired SAS sniper,' said Hitchens sceptically.

Kessen spun sharply on his heel. 'Well, maybe he is. We don't know that he isn't, do we, Paul? This is a man who had the opportunity – the shots were fired from his property. No one would question Mr Cross driving over his own land, even at night. Perhaps no one would question him taking his rifle with him either.'

'We don't know that he has a rifle,' persisted the DI.

'He's also the man who reported the open window at the back of the house,' said Kessen, as if Hitchens hadn't spoken. 'Thereby ensuring that he was involved in the investigation as a witness. You know the typical behaviour, Paul.'

'He was alerted by the postman that something might be wrong. That's why he took a look.'

'That doesn't mean he wouldn't have done it anyway, sooner or later. We don't know, do we?'

'We don't know anything,' said Hitchens.

'That's why we have to start by eliminating whoever we can get hold of locally. And we'll see what that leads us to.'

'What if he doesn't admit to having a gun? We don't have any justification for a search.'

'We could ask him to co-operate with a gunshot residue test. At least we'd know if he'd fired a gun recently.'

Listening to the discussion between the detectives, Wayne Abbott shook his head. 'Sorry, it's too long since the shots were fired. A GSR test has to be done within the first few hours to get meaningful results. After forty-eight hours, any suspect will have washed and wiped his hands enough to have removed all detectable traces.'

'A trace metal test to determine whether he's held a firearm?'

'Has to be within twenty-four hours.'

Kessen cursed quietly. 'Twenty-four hours is useless to us. Useless.'

The DI pointed at his two detectives. 'We've done the initial house-to-house, but the immediate neighbours will have to be interviewed properly. They must know something about Rose Shepherd. Take one of them each, will you? Someone will give you the names.'

'Right, sir.'

'A woman with no family and no friends,' said Hitchens bitterly. 'How can we reconstruct the life of someone like that?'

'She must have had at least one enemy,' said Fry. 'That's a start.'

'It's some kind of relationship, anyway.'

'Of course it is,' said Kessen. 'It means she had a close enough relationship with someone for that person to hate her. To hate her enough to kill her. That's not some casual passer-by that she once said hello to in the street. There's a history between them.'

'But as far as this house is concerned, the victim

seems to be a woman without a history. Without a life almost.'

'Look, if there's no evidence of Rose Shepherd's past in this house, it means only one thing – that she had a past she was trying very hard to hide.'

Fry touched Cooper's arm.

'Ben, have you got your car here?'

'Sure.'

'Give me a lift down the road, then. I had to leave mine miles away.'

'No problem.'

Fry brushed some cobwebs off her jacket. 'This house is dirty, isn't it?'

'Yes, I noticed that. Have you seen the décor in the sitting room, though?'

'That charcoal grey? Yes, very minimalist.'

Cooper stopped in the doorway to take a last look at Bain House before he left. Was the house dusty because Miss Shepherd couldn't be bothered with housework, or because she'd never been used to doing her own cleaning? Or might there be another reason?

On an impulse, he crouched towards the floor and looked into the sunlight flooding the pine boards. A layer of dust showed up clearly, glittering in the light from the windows. It would be possible to tell immediately if anyone had walked across this patch of floor. Their footprints would be visible in the dust. Perhaps that was why it had been left undisturbed.

Abbott's lamping theory was an interesting one.

When a rabbit was caught in the lamper's beam, it was mesmerized by the light and seemed to forget to run away. Yes, Cooper had seen it happen. He could picture the unnatural stillness of the animal, its eyes reflecting light like two glass beads, stunned by the sudden glare when it thought it was safe in the darkness.

Fry was waiting outside for him, no doubt getting impatient. But for a moment, Cooper thought about Rose Shepherd, shot down at her bedroom window as she stood in her nightdress and slippers. She must have been an easy target in a sniper's sights, silhouetted against the light. It was impossible not to picture her frozen to the spot, waiting for the bullet to strike.

7

'Nice barn conversion,' said Cooper. 'Somebody's done a good job of it. Probably worth a bit of money, wouldn't you say?'

'More than I'll ever see.'

Fry got out of the car and walked across the gravel as Cooper drove away. Actually, it was more than a barn conversion. She could see an entire range of farm buildings here. They formed three and a half sides of a square, facing on to a central courtyard. A two-storey stone barn, cleaned up and fitted with patio doors and casement windows. A tractor shed converted into twin garages and workshops. The door of one garage stood open, and the nose of a blue BMW was visible.

According to information from the control room, the neighbours on this side were called Ridgeway, Martin and April. Fry took a small detour before crossing the courtyard to their house, and looked in through the windows of one of the outbuildings. Games room. A gym. And a sauna. Very nice.

The Ridgeways themselves could have stepped straight out of *Derbyshire Life*. They had perfected the country look: corduroys and cashmere, tweed and waxed cotton. Fry wasn't at all surprised when she heard their accents and discovered they both came from Luton.

'We noticed all the activity, of course,' said Martin Ridgeway, who wore the corduroy and waxed cotton over an Antartex shirt. 'And a young constable called about an hour ago to ask us if we noticed anything suspicious in the early hours of Sunday morning.'

'And did you notice anything, sir?'

'No.'

He invited Fry into the house, which she thought was probably further than the young constable had got. She was taken into a dining room, with six spindle chairs around a polished table. A spiral staircase with cast-iron balustrades led to a first-floor gallery, what must have been a hayloft or something at one time.

'We're members of Neighbourhood Watch, you know,' said Ridgeway. 'But our co-ordinator says the police won't give him any information. Has there been another robbery?'

'Another?'

His eyes widened in astonishment. 'You don't even know about them?'

'No, I'm sorry. Right now, we're conducting enquiries into a suspicious death.'

'Good heavens! We didn't know that. But I suppose we ought to have guessed it was something more high profile, to justify all this activity. Who is it that's died?'

'Miss Rose Shepherd, at Bain House.'

'Oh,' said Ridgeway.

He sounded distinctly non-committal, as if he didn't want to appear either too upset or too pleased at the news.

Fry thought of Keith Wade, the Mullens' neighbour back at Darwin Street. It was odd that both Ridgeway and Wade were members of their respective Neighbourhood Watch schemes, one in a well-off rural community and the other on an Edendale housing estate. There were no superficial similarities between them, but theoretically Martin Ridgeway ought to be equally well informed about his neighbours.

'What do you know about Rose Shepherd, sir?' she asked.

Ridgeway turned his head. Fry could see a room through a doorway that appeared to be a home office, a desk loaded with computer equipment.

'Was she foreign?' he said vaguely. 'We heard a rumour in the village that she was foreign.'

'Not so far as we're aware. Did you never speak to her yourself, Mr Ridgeway?'

'No. Why would I?'

'Well, she lived right next door.'

He shook his head. 'It's not as if these are semi-detached properties. I don't know anything about her.'

Fry found herself staring at a mahogany barometer on the dining-room wall. She'd never understood those things. If the mercury was up or down, what did it mean? She preferred those weather houses, or whatever the things were called, with two little Jack and Jill figures. At least it was always clear what they were telling you. Sun or rain, and no ambiguity.

'Didn't you say you were in Neighbourhood Watch?'

'We keep an eye on the security of property, we don't spy on our neighbours.'

Fry could see a woman doing something in the garden. 'Is that your wife? Could I ask her?'

'If you like.'

Sliding doors stood open to the garden, because it was still warm enough for that, even in late October. At least it was preferable to the Lowthers' overheated conservatory.

April Ridgeway was wearing the cashmere, with a waxed body warmer and gardening gloves. When asked, she gave a similar story to her husband's. She had never spoken to the occupant of Bain House. There might have been some talk about Miss Shepherd in the village, but she made a point of not listening to gossip.

'Have long have you lived in Foxlow?'

'Nine months.'

'So Miss Shepherd was already living at Bain House when you moved in.'

'I suppose so.'

'You're interested in wildlife, Mrs Ridgeway?' asked Fry, watching her tighten some wire netting on a bird table.

'Very much so. We both are, aren't we, Martin?'

'It's one of the reasons we came to live here, in the national park,' agreed her husband. He stood back from the bird table and inspected his wife's handiwork.

'That netting is to stop the grey squirrels,' he said.

Fry frowned, struggling to understand why wildlife enthusiasts would put food out in their garden and then try to stop wild animals eating it. But during her time in Derbyshire, she'd learned that there were things about the country she would never understand.

'Our only regret was that we couldn't go somewhere that still has red squirrels. We're members of a conservation society that supports work to protect them. Reds have been wiped out in Derbyshire, you know. In fact, the whole of the Midlands.'

Fry didn't know, and didn't really care. Perhaps she should have sent Ben Cooper here and taken the neighbours on the other side of Bain House instead.

'You know, it was once possible for a red squirrel to cross from one side of Britain to the other without touching the ground,' said Ridgeway, taking advantage of her silence. 'That was when we had the true wild wood, the ancient pine forests that had grown here since the Ice Age. But those trees died, or were cut down. And then the grey squirrels came.'

'If you have an interest in wildlife, I wonder if you've been aware of anybody lamping in this area?' asked Fry.

'Lamping?'

'You know what that is, sir?'

'Oh, we know what that is, all right. If we knew about anything like that going on around here, we'd report it straightaway. But what has that got to do with this suspicious death you're investigating? Was the lady killed by poachers?'

'I'm afraid we just don't know.'

He took her ignorance as confirmation of his own fears. 'That's another problem our native wildlife is facing, you know. Animals are the first victims when society starts to fall apart. Look at all those stories of illegal immigrants stealing swans and butchering sheep in the fields.'

'You read the *Daily Mail*, then?' said Fry impatiently.

'You're not from this area yourself, by the sound of your accent.'

'No, I'm not.'

'A city person? Birmingham, at a guess?'

'Very close.'

'Ah, I can understand why you came here,

then. Seeking to get back to the real England, like we did.'

'No, not at all.'

'I know it's not politically correct to say it, but many of your colleagues agree with our views.'

'Not me.'

Ridgeway smiled and gestured at the bird table. 'We sometimes think of grey squirrels as the immigrants of the animal world. They're nothing but vermin, after all – rats with furry tails.'

Fry felt the anger rising, but she'd promised herself she was going to be more tolerant of people she had to deal with. Even those who infuriated her as much as Martin Ridgeway.

She consulted her notebook, partly to cover her irritation, and partly to remind herself of the questions she would otherwise fail to ask.

'Have either of you noticed a blue Vauxhall Astra in the village recently? No? A vehicle of any kind acting suspiciously?'

'No.'

'Any vehicles at all visiting Bain House?'

'We can't see the entrance to Bain House from here, so we wouldn't know.'

'And did you hear anything unusual on Saturday night, or in the early hours of Sunday morning?'

'Our double glazing is very good. We don't hear much noise at night.'

'One final question, sir – do you possess a firearm of any description?'

101

Ridgeway hesitated. 'I do have an air rifle.'

'Oh? What power?'

'No more than twelve foot pounds, so I don't need a licence for it. I'm a law-abiding citizen, you see.'

'What do you use an air rifle for? No, don't tell me – let me guess. You use it for shooting squirrels.'

'Also crows, rooks and magpies, which steal the eggs of song birds. They're all classed as pests, so it's lawful to shoot them on private property.'

'I can understand that. But what's the problem with squirrels?'

'The invasion of grey squirrels has driven our native reds into remote sanctuaries, protected forests in Wales or Scotland. Now all they can do is cling on in dwindling numbers, powerless against an alien species.' Ridgeway took a step towards her and lowered his voice. 'Our kind of people are just like those red squirrels. We're being driven out by the vermin.'

'I think I'm finished here,' said Fry.

As she was shown out, she wondered why the Ridgeways had bothered joining Neighbourhood Watch if they knew nothing about their neighbours and couldn't even see the adjoining properties. But she supposed there was only one reason, from their point of view – they thought it would provide protection for themselves.

In the dining room, Martin Ridgeway tapped the barometer, as if out of habit. It appeared to be some kind of ritual before he opened the door of his barn conversion.

Fry looked over his shoulder. One hand pointed at 'Stormy' and the other at 'Change'.

'Is that good or bad?' she said.

Ridgeway scowled. 'The same as bloody usual.'

Rose Shepherd's other neighbours were called Birtland. Cooper found their address to be a bungalow, with a long curving drive leading off Pinfold Lane. The property was only a few decades old, but built after the introduction of national park planning regulations. There were no red brick terraces and plaster porticos here, no incongruities like those allowed in some of the forties and fifties developments. This place was stone clad and mullioned, designed to blend in with its surroundings.

Even so, Cooper thought he would never get used to some of these new properties. They gave the impression that someone had sliced off a piece of landscape with a bulldozer and flattened an area big enough to plonk down a bungalow. There seemed to be no regard for the natural contours of the land.

'Mrs Birtland?'

'Yes?' The grey-haired woman who answered his knock peered cautiously past a security chain.

He showed his ID. 'DC Cooper, Edendale CID.'

'Is it about the murder?'

'Oh, I see someone's been talking. Was it the officer who called earlier?'

'No, but word gets around.'

Cooper smiled. He was pleased to hear that, for once. 'May I come in? You can check my ID, if you want.'

'No, that's all right.'

She took the chain off and let him into the bungalow.

'Edward and Frances, is that right?'

'I'm Frances, Edward is my husband.'

'And is Mr Birtland in?'

'Yes, Ted's in the back. Would you like a cup of tea, Mr Cooper?'

'No, thank you, Mrs Birtland. I won't be keeping you long.'

Being called 'Mr Cooper' made him smile even more. That really was a rarity in this job.

'Ted,' called Mrs Birtland, 'we've got a visitor.'

Edward Birtland didn't get up when Cooper entered. He was seated in a well-used armchair by a random stone fireplace, a fragile man of about seventy. He held out a hand politely, and Cooper couldn't do anything else but shake it. The grip of Mr Birtland's fingers hardly registered.

'So,' he said, 'how did you hear someone had been killed?'

'The murder?'

'Well . . .'

Frances Birtland chuckled. 'It was Bernie. Our postman knows everybody.'

'Of course he does.'

'You brought him back to Foxlow when he'd nearly finished his round. He stopped and told a few people about it on the way home.'

'I understand how Bernie Wilding knows everybody. The question I've come to ask you is how well you knew Rose Shepherd.'

'We didn't know her at all. She hadn't been in the village long.'

'About ten months,' said Cooper. But it wasn't the first time he'd heard that sort of period dismissed as if it was yesterday. Your family had to have lived in some of these villages for generations before you belonged.

'Are you Foxlow people yourselves?'

'Of course,' said Mrs Birtland. 'We've lived here all our lives. We had a house on the High Street when we were married. We bought this little bit of land when Ted retired, and had the bungalow built. It took all the money we'd ever have – though we didn't know it at the time.'

Cooper glanced at Mr Birtland, who smiled sadly and patted his wife's hand.

'I thought I had a good pension put away,' he said, 'with the company I worked for. But it didn't turn out the way we planned. Once we'd paid for the bungalow, suddenly there was nothing left. So we just have our old age pensions to live on.'

'The only way we could live any better is by selling the bungalow,' said his wife.

'And moving away from Foxlow, I suppose?'

She nodded. 'And we could never do that.'

'Can you think of anyone in the village who would have known Miss Shepherd better?'

Mrs Birtland shook her head. 'No, not really.'

'Have you tried the Ridgeways on the other side?' said her husband. 'They live in the barn conversion. Well, I say barn conversion – that was Church Farm until a few years ago. My grandfather was a cowman there. He worked for the Beeley family all his life. It's gone now, and so have the Beeleys.'

'One of my colleagues is talking to Mr and Mrs Ridgeway. Do you think they might have known Miss Shepherd well, then?'

'We couldn't say.'

'Don't you talk to the Ridgeways either?'

The Birtlands glanced at each other, exchanging some thought that they decided not to share with their visitor.

'They moved into the village about the same time as Miss Shepherd,' said Birtland finally. 'So I suppose we tended to associate them together in our own minds. We didn't know where any of them came from. Being located where we are, at this end of Pinfold Lane, we've started to feel as though we've been cut off from the rest of the village by incomers.'

'I see.'

Birtland looked at him expectantly. 'You haven't asked us yet whether we heard anything,' he said.

'It was the next question, sir.'

'Ah, good. Well, we've been thinking about it since we heard that Miss Shepherd had been killed. Was she shot?'

Cooper leaned forward. 'Did you hear shots on Saturday night?'

'Well, that answers my question,' said Birtland with a chuckle. 'We think maybe we did.'

'What time would that have been?'

Birtland reached out to pat his wife's hand again. 'We disagree on that, I'm afraid.'

'Ted thinks it was about two o'clock in the morning, but I think it was more like three,' she said. 'I don't sleep too well sometimes, and I'm often starting to come awake by then.'

'But you didn't look at the clock to make sure?'

'No, we didn't. We didn't take much notice, you see. We often hear people shooting around here. We always have, all our lives. As long as the shooting isn't too near our house, we don't bother. I don't think Ted even woke up. If he did hear the shooting, he must have gone straight back to sleep, that's all I can say.'

Birtland laughed. 'I don't suppose that's much use to you.'

'Could you say how many shots you heard?' asked Cooper, afraid to go back to the DCI with anything so vague.

'Two or three,' said Mrs Birtland.

'Or four,' said her husband.

Cooper sighed. 'Thank you.'

'We would have come forward anyway when

107

we heard somebody had been killed, you know. But we were told you'd be calling today.'

'That's all right.'

Mrs Birtland accompanied Cooper to his car. 'I'm sorry if we don't appear very hospitable,' she said.

'Don't worry. But if you do happen to remember anything more about Miss Shepherd, or about any visitors she had –'

'Yes, of course, we'll let you know.'

'Thank you.'

Frances Birtland looked up the street towards the village. 'You know, we always thought we'd be comfortably off when we got old,' she said. 'But look at us now. There are young kids around here who get more pocket money to spend than we get in pension. The world's gone crazy, don't you think? And it was just our luck to be at the wrong end of our lives when it happened.'

Cooper knew what Fry would have said if she'd been at the Birtlands' with him. *So much for neighbourliness. What happened to that famous community spirit you're always telling me about, Ben?*

When he picked her up, Fry was about a hundred yards further down the road from the Ridgeways' barn conversion, on the corner of the High Street. She seemed to be looking at the square tower of the church rising above yew trees in the graveyard, and at a cottage next to it, with honeysuckle hanging from the roof of the porch.

'Any luck?' he said when she got into the car.

'They didn't hear anything. Their double glazing is too good. You?'

'The Birtlands might have noticed the shots. But they've been here all their lives, and they're used to hearing people shooting rabbits.'

They pulled in through the gates of Bain House and parked behind a dog handler's van.

'By the way, the Ridgeways think Rose Shepherd was a foreigner,' said Fry.

'That's funny. The Birtlands think the Ridgeways are foreigners.'

Fry snorted. 'They're from Luton.'

'Exactly.'

'Oh, I see. So the Ridgeways are the awful incomers. What happened to that famous –'

'I know, I know.'

'Also, Mr Ridgeway kept banging on about grey squirrels. He seems to have a bit of an obsession with them.'

'They're a big problem,' said Cooper. 'The government ought to do something to eradicate them.'

Fry just groaned. And Cooper wondered what he'd said wrong this time.

8

Moira Lowther gave her son another hug. 'Take care, John. Give us a call if you need to talk. You know we're here, don't you?'

'Yes, that's all right.'

She looked suddenly anxious and tried to hold him back. 'And you're taking – You're doing everything you should, dear?'

'It's fine. Everything's under control.'

He walked back down the path, no longer seeming to care whether he stepped on the tortoises, or whether the angel was close enough to speak to. His green Hyundai stood at the kerb, just out of sight below the wall.

Moira watched him until he vanished from view, and listened for his car driving away. Then she turned back to her husband. 'Who was that on the phone?'

'Just Tony.'

'Who?'

'You know, he used to work for the company.

He went off a few months ago to set up on his own account.'

'Oh, yes, I remember. He was the one I didn't like.'

Lowther laughed. 'You and your likes and dislikes. Tony was always loyal to the company. Unlike some of these others, deserting a sinking ship.'

'Is it that bad, Henry?'

'Oh, we'll survive.'

'I don't want to have to think about it right now.'

'None of us do.'

She gazed down the road, though the Hyundai was long since gone.

'Do you think John will be all right?' she said.

'We'd better keep an eye on him. He's very upset.' Lowther put an arm round his wife. 'And how are you coping?'

The question seemed to start her tears all over again, and tears turned to deep, racking sobs. It was a few moments before she could get her breath back.

'How did it happen?' she said. 'How on earth did it happen?'

'Hell, I don't know.'

Mrs Lowther pulled out a tissue to dry her eyes. They both stood in their garden in silence for a while, listening to the trickle of water, the chatter of a blackbird. No one watching them could have told what they were thinking, or whether the Lowthers were even thinking the same thoughts.

'Well, we have to make sure we look after the living now, don't we?' said Moira. 'That's the most important thing.'

Henry Lowther patted her shoulder. 'That's all I've ever wanted,' he said.

'Between two and four a.m.?' said Hitchens when Cooper and Fry returned to Bain House. 'Is that the best they could do?'

'Sorry.'

'Well, it falls bang in the middle of our time scale, anyway. So it helps a bit, I suppose.'

'We're no closer to filling in details of Miss Shepherd's background, though,' said Fry.

Hitchens shook his head. 'Not much nearer. Although the owners of the village shop think Rose Shepherd's accent might have been Irish.'

'Do they? But her passport says she was British. Born in London.' Fry laughed. 'It's possible, though. Irish is foreign enough for folk round here.'

'Why don't we put it to Bernie Wilding?' suggested Cooper.

But Hitchens shook his head. 'It would be leading him too much. At the moment, he can't identify Miss Shepherd's accent, but if we suggest a particular nationality, he might try to make all his recollections fit in with the suggestion. I bet we could get him to agree that Rose Shepherd was an Iraqi or an Australian – anything we like the sound of.'

'The name Shepherd sounds more Australian than Iraqi,' pointed out Cooper.

'I meant those as examples,' said Hitchens. 'Wake up, Ben.'

'I was joking.'

'Right. Well, it hasn't been a laugh a minute round here, I can tell you – not with Mr Kessen in the mood he's in. We have found a laptop, though. It was in the bottom drawer of the victim's wardrobe.'

'Well, that's good news,' said Fry. 'Has it been checked out yet?'

'We haven't had time to go through the files, but Miss Shepherd definitely had internet access. It looks as though she used an ordinary modem dial-up connection, so she could have used the laptop right there in the bedroom, plugged into the socket for the bedside phone.'

'Any interesting email correspondence?'

'Nothing obvious, apart from some junk mail. God knows why she kept that. But it looks as though she might have joined some online groups, because there were different aliases and screen names. It seems Rose Shepherd did have a social life, of a kind. But it was all online.'

'By the way, I've got the package that the postman was trying to deliver,' said Cooper. 'It isn't all that big, but it's heavy for its size.'

'Open it up. But be careful.'

When the cardboard packaging came off, they were looking at three books from an internet book-seller. Maeve Binchy, Danielle Steele, Josephine Cox.

'Does that give us any clues?' asked Hitchens.

'I don't think so,' said Cooper. 'I once saw a Muslim woman in full chador buying a Danielle Steele novel in a supermarket, so I don't think we can make any assumptions.'

'The only surprise to me is that she ordered three books at once, since it meant they wouldn't go into her letter box,' said Fry.

'Maybe they were on special offer,' said the DI, moving away to answer his phone.

Fry waited for a quiet moment, then approached him between calls.

'Sir, I'm going to need to review the house fire enquiry. You know, the triple death?'

'Not now, Diane.'

'But –'

'Well, not unless you have firm evidence of malicious intent. Do you?'

'No, sir. Not yet.'

'Come back to me when you do, then.'

Fry bit her lip. She obviously wasn't going to get a look-in on the Rose Shepherd enquiry. She was too junior in this company. But she had an enquiry of her own that she could make a mark with – if she could find the time to work it properly. The Darwin Street fire was low priority until malicious intent was proved. But there were ways around that problem.

She went outside and found Gavin Murfin. Ben Cooper would have been more useful, but his absence was likely to be noticed, so Murfin would have to do.

'Ah, Gavin, you're not doing very much,' she said, taking hold of his arm and steering him towards her car.

'Well, actually –'

'Good. You're with me.'

Somehow, Murfin had obtained a pork pie, which he was eating out of a paper bag. He'd got into the habit of bringing food with him if he thought he was going to be away from civilization for a few hours.

'But if you drop bits of that pie in my car, Gavin, you know what'll happen. And it won't be pretty.'

Fry had to negotiate the lines of vehicles in Pinfold Lane to find somewhere to turn round. The only space was the entrance to the Birtlands' driveway.

As she reversed to do her three-point turn, she saw Ben Cooper standing in the gateway of Bain House. He'd stopped to speak to one of the SOCOs, Liz Petty. It wasn't clear whether she was working the scene, because she was still wearing her navy blue sweater with the Derbyshire Constabulary logo rather than a protective scene suit. Fry watched them for a moment as she changed gear. She saw Petty push back her dark hair and confine it in a clip behind her head. Her cheeks looked slightly pink as she laughed at something Cooper was saying.

'They make a grand couple, don't they?' said Murfin, picking crumbs off the seat. 'Ben and Liz, I mean,' he added, as if it needed explaining.

'Are they sleeping together?' asked Fry, as casually as she could manage.

Murfin stopped hunting for crumbs. She could feel his eyes on her, wary and suspicious.

'I dunno,' he said.

'You're his friend, aren't you, Gavin?'

'Me and Ben? We go back years.'

'You must know, then.'

Murfin shook his head. 'It would only be gossip.'

He lowered his head between his knees, as if searching the floor for more debris.

'I just wondered,' said Fry.

In reply, all she got was a mumble from somewhere under the seat.

'What did you say, Gavin?'

'I said I can't hear you.'

Fry let out the clutch suddenly. As the car jerked forward, Murfin's head shot up from the footwell. His face was beetroot red from the blood rushing into it.

'Bloody hell,' he said. 'You really *are* trying to kill me.'

Cooper went into the back garden of Bain House to look at the field where the SOCOs were still working under a white tent. Liz Petty had confirmed what he'd already guessed – the Foxlow shooting had put a lot of extra pressure on Scientific Support.

116

One of the complications was obvious. In effect, there were four separate crime scenes to be examined. For a start, there was Rose Shepherd's bedroom, and the other rooms of her house. Officers conducting the search might hope to learn something about the victim's life that would lead to her killers, or at least suggest a motive for her murder. But if, as they suspected, the attacker hadn't entered the victim's home, or even made direct contact with her, there would be no traces of him in the house. No DNA or fingerprints; no fibres or evidence of any kind.

Then there was the field. That at least had yielded some tyre marks. How clear they were would depend on how soft the ground had been, whether it had rained before the incident, and what the weather had been like since. Cooper looked at his watch, and pictured DCI Kessen doing the same thing, cursing the delay in the body being found. There wouldn't be much else in the field, of course. If there were no shell casings or footwear impressions, then there wouldn't be any dropped matches or cigarette ends either. But the suspect's car had been driven close to the edge of the field. A tiny flake of paintwork left on a branch of the hawthorn hedge, maybe? A bumper scraped on the corner of a stone wall? But in a fifty-acre field? From dark paintwork? Needles and haystacks came to mind.

The most useful scene might be the third one: the suspect's vehicle. If they ever found it, of course. There should be fibres on the seats, finger-prints on the door handles, sweat stains on the gear stick.

Cooper turned at a sound in the garden. A squirrel ran across the lawn and scuffled among the dead leaves on the flower beds. It was burying nuts before hibernation time came. Across the garden, another squirrel chattered with that strange cry they had, somewhere between the call of a bird and the mew of a cat.

From what Diane Fry had said, Mr and Mrs Ridgeway would hate this, if they saw it. If they were breeding here, there'd be a continuous supply of them to raid her neighbours' gardens.

Cooper was approaching the end of his shift. His DI seemed to have forgotten him, Fry had already left Foxlow, and no one had mentioned overtime. Tomorrow would be hectic, though. By then some lines of enquiry would have emerged. Suddenly, there would be an insatiable demand for resources, and everyone would be rushed off their feet. He might as well take advantage of the lull.

He walked back into the house. Downstairs, the rooms were full of people. He could hear them opening drawers, taking photographs, rustling papers, talking and laughing among themselves. There were probably more people inside Bain House at this moment than had been over the doorstep in the whole of the last year. If Rose Shepherd walked in now, she wouldn't recognize the place.

She'd be like a shocked parent who'd come home unexpectedly to find the teenage children had moved the furniture, rolled up the carpets, and thrown a party that got out of hand.

The image of her bewildered reaction brought Cooper to a halt as he remembered the fourth crime scene. At this moment it was lying in the mortuary, waiting to be examined for whatever information it could yield. It was Rose Shepherd's body.

After Fry had dropped Gavin Murfin off at West Street with his instructions, she drove straight back to Darwin Street. Things were happening here, at least. All the appropriate people were gathering, including the fire service's divisional officer and his investigation team. Their brief was to work with the appointed investigating police officer – which was her, for now.

Her next job would be to decide whether the attendance of a forensic scientist was needed. Of course, she'd be mad to try to manage without an expert when three deaths were involved. It would be too late to change her mind once the scene had been compromised. But there was a procedure to be followed before she could commit resources.

Right now, the fire service had taken possession of the scene. They'd brought in their own dog team from Alfreton, and a chocolate brown Labrador bitch wearing blue protective boots and a reflective harness was being deployed by her handler in the ground-floor rooms of the Mullen house. A firefighter told her the dog was called Fudge, though her official title was 'post-fire search tool'.

Never mind the fancy names. The important fact was that the dog could search the scene faster than any conventional equipment. It had been trained to locate the presence of flammable liquids that could have been used to start the fire, and then give a passive alert to the handler, so that evidence wasn't disturbed.

To the dog, it was all a game. There'd be a reward when it found what it was looking for. More than Fry would get, probably. No one would be waiting to pat *her* on the head and give her a chicken-flavoured Schmacko.

Well, she didn't like animals much, but she had to admit the Labrador's expertise was a good example of focus, considering all the other smells that must have bombarded the dog when it entered the house. Lucky animal, not to have to worry about what these humans had been up to inside 32 Darwin Street.

Fry's mobile rang. It was Murfin, his voice sounding slightly muffled as usual. If he wasn't actually eating, he was salivating at the thought of his next snack.

'Hi, Gavin.'

'I called the hospital, like you told me. They say Brian Mullen is awake. He'll be fit to be interviewed in the morning.'

'Great.'

'I suppose you'll want to do that after the morning briefing?'

'Yes, I want to get to him as soon as I can.'

'Want me to come along?'

'Er . . . no thanks, Gavin. There'll be plenty for you to do on the Shepherd enquiry.'

'OK. I don't like hospitals anyway.'

As she ended the call, Fry saw the fire service dog padding across the debris in its blue boots. The animal was wagging its tail, happy to have done its bit. Was it Schmacko time already?

'So what's the result? Did the dog find anything?'

'Yes. She identified accelerant in two locations in the sitting room,' said the handler. 'I've marked the locations for further investigation by the DO – or the forensic scientists, if you're calling them in.'

'Great job. Thanks.'

Fry was already reaching for her phone again. Traces of accelerant were evidence of malicious intent. A chocolate Lab called Fudge had just upped the stakes in this enquiry.

9

Below the hill, most of the fields at Bridge End Farm were still good grazing land. But much use that was to anybody now.

According to Matt, he would soon be a glorified park keeper instead of a farmer. Without headage payments, there was no way he could raise sheep, for a start. In future, British lamb would cease to exist, and everything the consumer bought would be flown in from New Zealand. It would happen the same way it did with Brazilian beef and Danish pig meat, he said. Countryside Stewardship schemes were all very well. Maintaining the landscape and conserving biodiversity? Fair enough. But Matt was baffled that the country didn't see any value in an ability to feed itself.

Ben drew his car into the yard in front of the farmhouse, trying to imagine the place empty and deserted, cleared of its animals. Not just a silent spring, but silent all year round.

Bridge End had been one of those traditional mixed farms that had once characterized British agriculture. Animals were fed with crops grown on the farm, and in turn they fertilized the fields with manure for the next crop. For Ben and Matt, growing up on the farm, it had seemed such a logical and natural cycle that they assumed it would go on for ever. But even by the 1990s mixed farms had already become a quaint eccentricity.

Perhaps his father wouldn't have cared too much. Joe Cooper had never really been interested in the farm. True, he had occasionally rolled up his sleeves to help. With his shirt open at the neck, he would reveal a rare, vulnerable flash of white skin and a proud smile at working alongside his two sons. It was one of the abiding images that Ben still carried – though, at the time, he hadn't thought of his father as remotely vulnerable. Like the farm, it had seemed that Sergeant Joe Cooper would go on for ever.

He'd been trying to train himself to remember those happier images, instead of the one that had tormented him for years: the bloodied body on the paving stones that he'd never actually seen. Some of the youths responsible for Joe Cooper's death were already back out in the world at the end of their sentences. Two years for manslaughter, that was all. First-time offenders, of course. Ben knew he was bound to run into one of them some day soon. It was probably futile to hope that he wouldn't recognize them.

'Bad do about that family in Edendale,' said Matt when he greeted his brother in front of the house. 'The fire, I mean.'

'Yes, really bad.'

'Are you working on that?'

'We don't know if it was malicious or not yet.'

'It's not good when kids are involved, whatever it was.'

Matt removed his boots and stripped off his overalls in the porch. A tabby cat immediately jumped up and inspected the overalls to see if they'd make a decent bed.

'Actually, I was down at Foxlow earlier,' said Ben. 'We had a shooting.'

'Oh, I heard,' said Matt.

'Did you?'

'It was Neville Cross who found the body, wasn't it?'

'Well, not quite. But he made the call.'

'Neville's the NFU rep, you know.'

'So the farmers' grapevine has been busy, has it?'

'Something like that.'

Matt stroked the cat absent-mindedly. His hand was huge, so it covered the animal's head completely. Only its ears protruded, trembling with the vibration of a deep purr.

'Come into the office, Ben. There's something I want to show you.'

'Is there room for two people?'

'As long as you don't mind sharing your breathing space with a smelly old dog.'

The farm office was cramped and untidy. It was the aspect of the farm that Matt paid least attention to, because it meant being indoors. Occasionally, Kate came in to help out with the paperwork and sort the mess into some kind of order, so they muddled through year by year, driving their accountants up the wall. 'I'm a stockman, not a filing clerk,' Matt would say. But deep down, he probably knew that this failing was the reason he was doomed. These days, farmers had to be business managers and entrepreneurs above anything else, if they wanted to survive.

Matt eased himself on to the office chair in front of the computer. He was filling out so much as he got older that he looked too big for the desk, like an adult sitting in an infants classroom.

'I've been looking at the internet,' he said.

'Blimey, we're going to have to watch you. At this rate you'll be catching up with the twenty-first century.'

Matt scowled. 'Most of it is a load of crap.'

'Yes, I suppose so.'

'In fact, I've never seen such crap.'

'You have to learn how to filter out the rubbish to find the useful stuff.'

'I'm a livestock farmer, so I know what crap is.'

'Yes, Matt.'

Ben perched on the arm of a deep armchair. The chair itself was already occupied by an aged Border collie called Meg, who didn't even bother opening an eye. She was there by right, and wasn't moving for anybody. Ben wouldn't have dreamed of booting her off.

Matt booted up and frowned at the screen as he waited to enter his password. 'I've got something I want to show you.'

'Don't tell me you've been looking at ideas for diversification again? What is it this time – rock festivals? You've got the fields, and the mud.'

'That'll be the day, when I let thousands of hippies camp on my land.'

'It worked for Lord Montagu of Beaulieu.'

'No, it didn't. He had riots between gangs of rival jazz fans.'

Ben laughed. 'What is it, then?'

'It isn't about the farm at all,' said Matt gloomily, still staring at the screen.

Realizing that he wasn't even denting his brother's morose mood, Ben leaned forward to see what he was looking at. He'd brought up a website that must have been bookmarked in his favourites, because he hadn't used the keyboard to type out a URL. Ben was surprised that Matt even knew how to do that.

'It's an article I found about schizophrenia,' said Matt. 'Well, to be more exact, about its inheritability.'

For a moment, Ben was thrown by the word 'inheritability'. It was an expression he was accustomed to hearing from Matt, but strictly in relation to livestock breeding. Was a high-yielding cow likely to produce offspring that were also good milk producers? What percentage of lambs sired by a Texel ram would have the same muscle ratio? That was inheritability. Genetics played a big part in breeding animals for desirable characteristics. But schizophrenia? It didn't make sense.

'What on earth are you trying to tell me, Matt?'

'It was something I heard one of the nursing home staff say, before Mum died. It hadn't occurred to me before, and nobody ever mentioned the possibility. Not to me, anyway. I don't know if they mentioned it to you, but you never said anything.'

'Matt, I don't know what you're talking about.'

'It occurred to me that it might be like other conditions. Do you remember that family of Jerseys that were prone to laminitis? It was passed on from one generation to the next, and we never could breed it out. We had to get rid of them all in the end.'

'Yes, I remember.'

'Well, according to this, schizophrenia is heredi-tary, too.'

'What?'

'Ben, it's for the sake of the girls as much as anything. I need to know what the odds are – the chances of schizophrenia being hereditary. Will you read it?'

Almost against his will, Ben ran his eyes over the text on the screen. *It has been verified that schizo-phrenia runs in a family. People with a close relative suffering from schizophrenia have an increased chance of developing the disease. Parents with schizophrenia also increase the chances of passing the disease to their child.*

He straightened up again. 'I don't want to know this, Matt.'

'There's more. Read the rest of it.'

'No. This is ridiculous.'

'I'll print it out for you. You can read it later.'

'I don't want to read it later, thanks. I can't understand why you're doing this, Matt. What's the point?'

'*What's the point?* It says that members of families vulnerable to schizophrenia can carry the genes for it, while not being schizophrenic themselves. They're called "Presumed Obligate Carriers".'

'Matt, you don't know anything about this stuff.'

'I'm trying to find out. Look, there's a bit of research here that talks about anticipation.'

'What?'

'The progress of an illness across several generations. They studied families affected by schizophrenia and found that, in each generation, more family members were hospitalized with the condition at an earlier age, and with increasing severity.'

'And your conclusion, Doctor . . . ?'

Matt pressed a couple of keys, and the laser printer whirred into life. He turned to face his brother.

'My conclusion is, I reckon my kids could be eight times more likely than average to have schizophrenia.'

Ben shook his head. 'It's still a small chance, Matt. We were told that one in every hundred people suffers from schizophrenia. So even taking heredity into account, that's only a maximum risk of, what . . . eight per cent?'

'It's a bit less than our risk, admittedly.'

'Ours?'

'Yours and mine, little brother. The children or siblings of schizophrenics can have as high as a thirteen per cent chance of developing the disease.'

Matt took a couple of sheets off the printer, stapled them together and held them out to his brother. Ben didn't take them.

'You actually believe all this stuff?'

'Look at it, won't you?'

But Ben shook his head and sat back down on the arm of the chair. Meg groaned and looked up at him accusingly with one tired eye. She was a dog who liked peace. Raising your voice in her sleeping area just wasn't on.

Matt held up the pages again. 'They think some families might lack a genetic code that counter-acts the disease. You know, I'm wondering now if Grandma had schizophrenic tendencies. She had some strange habits – do you remember? But everyone in the family used to talk about her as if she was only a bit eccentric.'

'I do remember her being rather odd, but that

doesn't mean a thing. It certainly doesn't mean you'll pass something on to the girls.'

'You know, I'm trying to picture it,' said Matt. 'I can see myself, forever on the lookout for early-warning signs in Amy and Josie. It would be sensible, in a way – early intervention and treatment would result in the best prognosis. But what kind of effect would it have on the girls if we were watching all the time for tell-tale signs?'

Ben wasn't sure who his brother was talking to now. He might as well be alone in the office with the dog.

'Sometimes, I'm stopped cold by the thought that one of the girls could grow up to be like Mum. I might end up being afraid of my own child. At other times, I imagine what a relief it would be if my children turned out to have any other problem at all but schizophrenia. I feel as though I might be able to make some kind of deal with God.'

'You don't believe in God,' said Ben.

'No, I don't. But it doesn't stop me. It's the idea of a bargain, playing with the percentages. I go over and over the figures in my head. Chances are, I say to myself, both the girls will be fine. And genes aren't the only factor. Schizophrenia is only about seventy per cent inherited – which means thirty per cent is due to environmental factors, right?'

'Yes.'

'So if we knew what other factors could influence people . . . If we knew, we might be able to create a different environment, so the genetic switch wouldn't be flipped.'

'Matt, you're making far too much of this. You said yourself most of what you find on the internet is rubbish.'

' "Crap", I said. A steaming pile of cow flop, if you like. But not this. You know this isn't rubbish, Ben.'

'You're worrying about nothing. Your children are perfectly OK.'

Ben's attention was caught by a movement outside. The window looked out on to the narrow front garden and the farmyard beyond. His youngest niece, Josie, was sitting on the dividing wall.

'That's what I'm worrying about,' said Matt.

Ben tapped on the window so that Josie looked up, and he waved. She giggled, waved back, then blew him a kiss.

'There is absolutely nothing wrong with Josie,' he said. 'Or Amy, for that matter.'

'Do you remember before she started school, Josie had an imaginary friend? She used to say her friend was with her, and talked to her all the time.'

'For God's sake, every child has an imaginary friend at that age, Matt.'

'I didn't.'

'That's because you had no imagination.'

'Thanks.'

131

Turning back to the window, Ben saw Josie poke her tongue out at him, perhaps because she'd lost his attention for a moment.

'Does she still have that imaginary friend?' he asked.

'I don't know,' said Matt. 'Josie doesn't mention her any more, not since she started school. But that might be because she realized other people found it odd, so she stopped talking about it.'

'Or it might be because she has real friends now and doesn't need the imaginary one.'

'Do you think so, Ben?'

'With the best will in the world, it was a bit lonely up here for Josie when Amy was already at school and she wasn't.'

'Time will tell, I suppose,' said Matt. 'But I have to find out the facts. It was me who made the decision to have children. Well, me and Kate.'

'Have you talked to Kate about it?'

Matt ran a hand across his face. 'I need to know what to tell her first.'

'When you were looking up all this information on the internet, did you come across any advice? What do they say you should do?'

'Talk to a psychiatrist.'

'And that's what you're going to do, right?'

Matt sighed. 'According to some of these websites, the genetics of mental illness will be much better understood in twenty years' time. But there isn't much chance of research having practical applications within five years – when it would be useful to me. Or useful to you, Ben.'

'I'm not planning on having kids any time soon.'

'You're past thirty. You won't want to wait that much longer. Men have a body clock, too.'

'If you say so.'

'What about that girlfriend of yours?'

'Liz? We're just . . . Well, we're just going out together, that's all.'

Matt raised his eyebrows and gave him a sceptical glance.

'What?' said Ben.

'Nothing. I just think you've been different since you got together with her.'

'No, I haven't.'

His brother snorted. 'Be that as it may. In the end, Ben, you'll have to face the fact that no one can tell you whether a child of yours will be healthy, or vulnerable to schizophrenia.'

'That's one thing I'm *not* going to worry about,' said Ben firmly.

A few minutes later, he left his brother in the office and went out into the passage that ran through the centre of the house. When he was a child, the passage and stairs had been gloomy places. He remembered dark brown varnish, and floorboards painted black alongside narrow strips of carpet that had lost its colour under layers of dirt.

Things were very different now. There were deep-pile fitted carpets on the floor, and the walls were painted white. Or maybe it was some shade of off-white. Kate would know the exact name from the catalogue. The wood had been stripped back to its original golden pine and there were mirrors and pictures to catch the light.

Reluctantly, Ben turned and looked up the stairs. At the top, he could see the first door on the landing, the one that had been his mother's bedroom. After the death of his father, she had gradually deteriorated until the family could no longer hide from each other the fact that she was mentally ill.

Isabel Cooper had been diagnosed with chronic schizophrenia, and finally the distressing incidents had become untenable, especially with the children in the house. Ben shuddered at the memory. He never wanted to witness anything like that, ever again.

On a Monday night in October, Matlock Bath's Derwent Gardens were deserted. There was no one to be seen on the paths between the flower beds and the fountain, no one near the bandstand or the tufa grotto. The sycamores along the riverside were turning golden yellow. Their leaves drifted across the paths, undisturbed by passing feet.

At the far end of the gardens, past a row of stalls under striped awnings, was a temporary fairground. An old-fashioned waltzer and a ferris wheel, a train ride, a set of dodgem cars, all silent and still.

A figure approached from the direction of the Pavilion, a man in an overcoat, walking along the river bank, past the jetty where boats were tied up ready to take part in Saturday's parade. He wandered apparently aimlessly, kicking at tree roots, making the fresh, dry leaves crackle under his feet.

He passed the waltzer and ferris wheel and found himself near a small hut that served as a ticket booth for the rides.

By the door of the hut, he stopped. There was no one visible in the darkness inside. But still he kept his eyes turned away, gazing up at the tower on the Heights of Abraham, high above the village. That was the place he'd rather be, surrounded by rushing air, with the wind loud in his ears. But the hilltop amusement parks had closed for the day.

'It's done, then? All over with.'

He froze. The whisper might have come from the hut, or from the river bank behind him. Or it might have been inside his head.

'Yes, all over,' he said.

Beyond the hut, he could see the dodgems lurking in the gloom of their wooden circuit, like a cluster of coloured beetles. There was a Rams windscreen sticker on a Leyland truck, backed up on the other side of the circuit. One of the operators of the fairground must be a Derby County fan. He wondered if the truck contained the generator that ran the cars, bringing life to the beetles, making them crackle and spark.

'You're evil, aren't you?'

'Am I?' he said.

'Really evil.'

He was distracted by the sound of the fountain splashing. A spray of water caught by the breeze spattered on to the rose bushes. Tip-tap, like tiny footsteps.

'I'm not listening any more.'

Laughter swirled in his mind, making him shiver. 'Too late.'

John Lowther pulled his overcoat closer around his shoulders as he walked away, scuffing his feet in the leaves. He didn't know what he was supposed to do next. And he wasn't at all sure about the voice, that awful disembodied whisper. It had sounded like the voice of a child.

10

An incident room had been opened up in Edendale for the Rose Shepherd enquiry. A fatal shooting was still rare enough in Derbyshire to make Miss Shepherd's murder a high-profile case, even if she hadn't been a respectable middle-class woman gunned down in her own home.

Watching the staff arriving at E Division head-quarters, Cooper deduced that the HOLMES system was being activated. He recognized an allo-cator he'd worked with on a previous enquiry. The others would be data inputters, a receiver, an analyst.

With no obvious lines of enquiry that might lead to a quick conclusion, the HOLMES computer indexes would be vital in sniffing out correlations as information came in. One tiny detail could send the investigation in a new direction.

Before the morning briefing started, Cooper

joined a small crowd examining the display of crime-scene photographs from Bain House and the field behind it. Some of the interior shots showed the victim from different angles before her body was removed to the mortuary. On the lower part of her torso, where it was in contact with the floor, there was a large, bruise-like discoloration that he hadn't noticed before. That was dependent lividity – the effect of gravity on blood that was no longer being pumped through the veins. At least it showed that no one had moved the victim after she was killed.

'The victim was killed with a semi-automatic weapon, at least three shots fired in rapid succession,' said DI Hitchens, opening the briefing. 'We know it wasn't a bolt-action rifle. Since even one of the shots would have put her down on the floor, the second shot has to have followed rapidly to strike the victim before she fell. Otherwise, she'd have been out of sight below the window sill, with no chance of a second shot hitting its target.'

Officers around the room began to call out questions, their voices difficult to distinguish.

'What about the third shot?' asked someone.

'If we follow a rough trajectory from the impact to a point in the field where the suspect's vehicle was positioned, we see that the third shot passed through the window at about the same height and the same angle as the others. Exactly where the victim had been standing, in other words. So the third shot was probably fired after she'd already started to fall. That's why it missed.'

'Could that have been the first shot, rather than the third? I mean a miss, followed by two hits when the shooter got the range?'

'Possibly. But the other two shots were very accurate. A head shot, and one near the heart. Besides, if you heard a shot and felt a high-velocity bullet whizz past your head, your first instinct would be to dive for cover.'

They all looked at the photographs of Rose Shepherd with a dark hole in her chest and another near her left eye. Her right eye remained open, staring in amazement at the ceiling.

'This lady did none of those things, so far as we can judge,' said Hitchens. 'It appears the bullets struck her before she could react. But we'll get the opinion of the pathologist, of course.'

The DI paused, but there were no questions, so he continued: 'We've got preliminary reports from the teams on house-to-house. We're looking for a blue Vauxhall Astra that was seen in Foxlow in the early hours of Sunday morning, about the time of the shooting.'

'Just one sighting?'

'No, two. The Astra was seen driving into the village about eleven thirty, and leaving at about three a.m. It's possible some of the neighbours heard shots between two a.m. and four, but we can't narrow down the time of the shooting any further than that right now. So I've asked for input from the intel unit. We need a list of possibles who fit the MO.'

'What about prison releases?'

'Yes. Any suggestions?'

'You know our intelligence feed from HQ is never up to date, sir.'

'We'll have to use the informal mechanisms, then,' said Hitchens.

'You mean "phone a friend"?'

'That's right.'

There were a few ironic laughs around the room. Yes, sometimes the old ways *were* still the best, they seemed to say.

Another hand went up. 'What about the gun, sir?'

'Well, we don't have the weapon yet,' said Hitchens. 'But we do have some bullets. Unfortunately, the heat generated by firing a gun destroys any DNA on the bullets. It's sometimes worth having a look at the casings, though.'

'But there aren't any casings.'

'Yes, there are. We just don't know where.'

At one time, Cooper would have tried to stay at the back of the room during these briefings. If you sat at the front, you might be expected to contribute, and he'd never really had the confidence to do it in front of a crowd of people, most of them more experienced than he was. When he did have ideas, he usually preferred to share them discreetly with his DS or the DI, in case he was scoffed at.

But today, he found himself near the front, propped against the wall where Hitchens could see him. Cooper suspected the DI would pick him out at some point. He'd been a member of the force's competition shooting team for several years, and he knew a bit about guns. Just as he did about lamping – though he'd only ever taken part in the legal kind. Well, probably. Even better, he knew a few people who were obsessed with guns, including some Territorial Army members, the weekend soldiers who trained in their spare time for reserve duty in Bosnia or Iraq.

Hitchens cocked an eye towards him. 'Anything you want to contribute at this stage, DC Cooper?'

He straightened up, trying not to notice all the eyes suddenly turned towards him.

'If we're looking at the possibility of a professional hit, I can tell you that snipers are trained to pick up their brass,' he said. 'That would explain why there are no casings. They're also told not to leave other clues to their identity or their shooting location. A trained person reconnoitres the site and selects a place that gives him cover and an escape route. Then he takes his shot. But normally only one – the sniper's motto is "one shot, one kill".'

'But this suspect took three shots.'

'To me, that doesn't sound like a real professional.'

'There was no sign of any casings in the field, so we presume our suspect stayed long enough to pick them up.'

141

'Well . . .' began Cooper.

'Yes?'

'At night, in a ploughed field, that would be quite tricky. You'd be lucky to find one, let alone all three.'

'True,' agreed Hitchens, looking at him with interest.

Cooper leaned back for a moment and pictured the scene. He imagined himself sitting at the wheel of a car at night, in a ploughed field, with the driver's window open and three bullet casings lying on the ground somewhere outside the vehicle.

'Not just tricky,' he said. 'It would mean the suspect getting out of the car and leaving his footprints in the soil. He would pick up earth on his shoes and trail it back into the vehicle. That's three possibilities for trace evidence. But the scenario doesn't fit, does it? It's not consistent with the planning before and after the hit.'

'And there were no footprints in the area where the shots were fired from, just tyre marks,' pointed out Hitchens. 'Maybe the casings fell close enough to the car that the gunman was able to lean out of the door and pick them up without leaving the vehicle.'

'No, that won't work. It was a high-powered rifle. The casings would have been ejected at speed.'

'What, then?'

'The only possibility I can see is that the casings must have been ejected *inside* the car.'

'Is that possible? If he was firing a rifle from the driver's seat?'

'The car was facing northwards, up the field, wasn't it? With the back fence of Bain House on the driver's side?'

'Yes.'

'Then, no,' said Cooper. 'I don't think it is possible. Whoever fired the rifle would have had to be in the passenger seat.'

There was a sudden buzz of interest. Cooper felt himself flushing – not with embarrassment, but excitement. He was sure he'd got this right. He could see it so clearly.

'We'll have to get this checked out properly,' said Hitchens.

But Cooper mimed holding and pointing a rifle. 'Imagine it. With the window wound down, you'd want to rest the barrel of your weapon on the door for stability while you were aiming. It wasn't too distant a shot – a hundred yards is nothing. But even so, you'd want to be sure. That means the stock and the chamber would be well inside the vehicle, so your casings would eject against the back of the seat.'

'He was shooting from the passenger seat?'

'No, it would have to be from the back seat,' said Cooper.

'Wait a minute. This would suggest two suspects, right?'

'One to drive and one to shoot. It's the only way.'

'Two suspects . . . It makes sense,' said DCI Kessen, speaking for the first time. 'They went into the field, did the job and drove straight out again. No one would want to hang around climbing over seats or packing a weapon away. From their point of view, they were already taking a bigger risk than they might have cared for. Having a separate driver would cut down tremendously on the time they were exposed. Unfortunately, our witnesses say there was only one person in the Astra.'

'OK. That was useful, Ben. Thanks.' Hitchens looked at his file, indicating that he wanted to move on. A discussion could last all morning if they got stuck on one subject.

Cooper glanced across at Fry, who was watching him closely. She nodded and almost smiled. That was high praise indeed, coming from her.

'The good news is that we've got some calls coming in from the public in response to photos of Rose Shepherd in the media this morning,' said Hitchens. 'So her passport photograph wasn't too out of date. Most interestingly, we've got a couple of potential sightings in Matlock Bath on Saturday afternoon. That would be between six and sixteen hours before she was killed – in fact, around twelve hours, if we put any reliance in the evidence of her neighbours.'

The DI brought up a map of the area for everyone to see. 'Matlock Bath is no more than three miles from Foxlow – on the A6, just south of Matlock itself. It's a popular tourist spot, even at this time of year, so it would have been busy on Saturday afternoon. Maybe that's why she chose it – anonymity in crowds. But if these are positive sightings, it didn't work out that way. She must have stood out somehow for members of the public to remember her.'

'There's no CCTV in Matlock Bath, is there?'

'No. This isn't Glossop we're talking about. They don't expect major crime on the street. There will be some limited CCTV systems on commercial premises, but nothing on the street.'

'There's a webcam,' said Cooper.

'A what?'

'A webcam. You can go on the internet and see a view of Matlock Bath promenade. I think they have it running pretty much every day.'

'Who operates this thing, Cooper?' asked Kessen, leaning forward in his chair.

'I think it's a photographic museum.'

'Time lapse, I suppose?'

'Yes, sir. But no worse than most CCTV systems.'

'It would be too good to be true if it caught Rose Shepherd. But let's check it out anyway.'

Hitchens waited to see if the DCI had finished. 'Next thing,' he said. 'We've had the victim's phone records checked, and we now know that a call was made to Miss Shepherd's home number at three o'clock on Sunday morning. The call lasted only twelve seconds. As you might have guessed, the caller used an unregistered pay-as-you-go mobile. No account, no address. If our suspects knew what they were doing, they'd have bought a phone specifically for this one call, then dumped it. And it looks as though they knew exactly what they were doing.'

'Pay-as-you-go phones,' said someone gloomily. 'The biggest gift that was ever made to drug dealers.'

'And paedophiles. And terrorists. We need some legislation on this one, don't you think, sir?'

'That's way above our heads, I'm afraid.'

'Right. We're just the poor buggers who have to pick up the pieces.'

Hitchens sighed, and departed from his notes. 'Actually, true anonymity is hard to achieve these days. We might not be able to identify the purchaser of a prepaid mobile, but if the call credits are paid for by card or cheque, the payments can be traced back. Also, we can track the phone's physical location, provided it's switched on. But, in this case, assuming our suspects do still have the phone, it's been switched off since the call to Miss Shepherd.'

'Dumped it, like you said, sir.'

'Exactly. Now for the victim's background. You're probably aware that this is proving a real headache. Whatever her reasons, Rose Shepherd went to extraordinary lengths to protect her privacy. She left almost nothing of a personal nature to give us an angle on her life. However, we've had time since yesterday to go through her cheque books and bank statements.'

'Anything interesting?'

'To be honest, I've never seen such a boring credit card statement as hers. I was hoping for something a bit revealing – I don't know, a purchase of expensive wine, or a subscription to a porn website. But nothing out of the ordinary. Not a thing. Her bank statements show her Council Tax, electricity bill and water rates going out on direct debit. Her BT phone bill was paid online by credit card. There's nothing here that tells us anything about her. All the evidence we have points to Miss Shepherd being a model citizen, paying her bills on time, being no trouble to anyone.'

'Much too perfect to be true.'

'Absolutely. I think we can all agree on that.'

'Perfect citizens vote, don't they? Is she on the electoral register?'

'No. And she's not in the phone directory either,' said Hitchens. 'All we've got is her passport, plus her bank statements and utility bills. The other strange thing is that there are no obvious personal contacts. There *is* an odd entry on a blank page in her address book, though. It's just three digits: 359.'

'A dialling code, perhaps,' offered Kessen.

'Well, we checked it out. The Highbury area of London comes closest – 0207 359.'

'Inner London?'

'Yes, London N1.'

'What about the 0359 code? Where's that?'

'Nowhere. It's a BT code all right, but it's allocated for future network expansion.'

'Could it be a country code?' said Cooper. 'Is there a directory somewhere?'

'On the shelf.'

He picked up the directory and leafed through the pages towards the back. 'They don't list international codes by number, but by country, in alphabetical order. Hold on . . . well, that didn't take long. It says here 359 is the code for Bulgaria.'

'Oh, great. There's a job for someone to follow up. Any volunteers?'

There was a ripple of laughter round the room as the atmosphere eased and officers recognized the end of the briefing approaching.

'I know it's going to be a pain in the neck for Scientific Support, but we should get someone to go over the whole house for fingerprints,' said Kessen. 'The fact that the victim didn't spend too much time dusting should work in our favour.'

'Meanwhile, the IT team are giving the laptop a going-over,' said Hitchens. 'If Rose Shepherd had information stored somewhere, it might be online. There are plenty of sites offering free web storage space.'

'Protected by a password, of course. So we just have to hope we strike lucky.'

'Basically, the victim's story seems to be this: she kept herself hidden away in Bain House for the best part of a year, then for some reason decided to go for an afternoon out in Matlock

Bath. That same night she was murdered by person or persons unknown.'

'It's as if she was hiding from someone. Do you think she was frightened of being recognized if she went out?'

'Yes, she thought she was in danger. And it looks as though she exposed herself to that danger on Saturday. But we don't know why. We're working on the theory that the victim was seen in Matlock Bath by someone who followed her home to find out where she lived. Somehow, they also obtained her ex-directory phone number. Then they wasted no time in eliminating her.'

'She must really have upset someone in the past.'

'Absolutely. If we can establish why Rose Shepherd was in hiding, it should give us a lead on her killer. At the moment, she's still something of an enigma. But that was all her own doing. In making it difficult for anyone to find her, Miss Shepherd also made it harder for us to identify her murderer.'

After the meeting, Cooper collected the actions he'd been allocated on the enquiry, then went straight to his computer. He Googled the Matlock Bath webcam and soon found the site. Life in a Lens, that was the name of the photography museum. The camera seemed to be mounted on the roof.

According to the caption, the webcam picture was updated every sixty seconds on weekdays, but it seemed to be more like thirty seconds when it began to reload. The picture was pretty grainy, of course. They'd have a hard time identifying anyone, unless there was detailed information available about what they were wearing at the time.

Matlock Bath was a bit like a seaside resort, but without the sea. Beyond the railings to the right there was just the shallow water of the River Derwent. The camera covered only a section of the road and the river beyond it. This was North Parade, looking northwards to Jubilee Bridge. But the picture showed almost nothing of the shops and cafés on the promenade, except for a glimpse of some buildings in the background.

It was a grey, damp day in Matlock Bath. The river was brown and choppy, and Cooper could see mist hanging on the slopes of the narrow valley. Cars and people were reflected in the wet tarmac of North Parade.

Fry stopped to look over his shoulder. 'Is that Matlock Bath?'

'Yes.'

'It looks pretty miserable.'

'It's one of those places that changes completely at weekends, or in the summer. On a busy bank holiday, you wouldn't recognize it.'

'I'll take your word for it.'

Cooper looked up at her. 'Diane, do *you* think the internet is how Rose Shepherd created a social life for herself?'

'It's beginning to look that way, isn't it? Why?'

'I always find that a bit sad. I don't think the internet was ever intended to replace social contact, only to make communication easier for people who were isolated from each other.'

'As far as we can tell, Miss Shepherd *was* isolated,' said Fry. 'It's just that she'd cut herself off deliberately.'

'I can't even begin to imagine living like that,' said Cooper. 'I'd get desperate very quickly.'

Fry reached for her phone as it rang. 'It looks as though Miss Shepherd must have been a pretty strong-willed, self-sufficient woman, don't you think?'

Cooper couldn't answer her, because she began to talk into the phone. He thought about it for a moment, though. No matter how strong-willed and self-sufficient Rose Shepherd had been, she'd still got desperate in the end. So desperate that she'd made a bad mistake.

Then he noticed the webcam picture reloading on his screen. Within the space of thirty seconds, the stretch of promenade he was looking at had become deserted. The people had run for cover, the cars had moved on. Now there was no one at all to be seen in his grey, misty glimpse of Matlock Bath.

In response to a summons, Fry had joined Hitchens in the DCI's office. Kessen didn't look happy, despite his attempt to strike a positive note for the enquiry team when he wound up the briefing.

'Sir, Rose Shepherd wasn't on someone's witness protection programme, was she?' asked Hitchens.

Kessen shook his head. 'I've already asked the question, Paul. But where's her panic button? Where's her minder? There's no sign of anyone ever being in the house with her.'

'It's still possible, though.'

'If she was an individual our intelligence is aware of, we'll hear back soon enough. If not, one of the phone numbers in her book ought to turn something up. And if that still doesn't bring anyone running, let's hope the media coverage does.'

'It's like you said yesterday, there must be someone somewhere who's going to miss her. But there doesn't seem to be any family, no one to give us the background on her relationships.'

A family liaison officer had been assigned to Brian Mullen and the Lowthers. But in Rose Shepherd's case, there was no grieving family, no one for an officer to be assigned to.

'I wonder if I could borrow DC Cooper some time?' asked Fry. 'I could use a bit of help on the triple-death fire for a while.'

'You can have him – once he's completed his actions on the Shepherd enquiry. He and DC Murfin are going to check the sightings in Matlock Bath.'

'Perhaps first thing tomorrow morning?'

'I suppose so, Diane. All being well.'

*   *   *

When Cooper put his jacket on, he noticed some sheets of paper sticking out of his pocket. He pulled them out and unfolded them.

'Damn you, Matt.'

They were the pages his brother had printed out the previous evening. He must have slipped them into Ben's pocket when he wasn't looking.

Cooper threw them down on his desk, intending to put them in the bin later. He walked to the door and opened it. Then he turned, went back to his desk, and picked up the papers. He felt tugged by some sense of obligation, but he wasn't sure who to. His brother? His mother? Or perhaps to himself, or some unborn generation.

Researchers are studying genes that may be involved in schizophrenia and looking for ways to direct treatment according to genetic make-up. Brain imaging has identified differences in the brain for people at risk. Many studies have found evidence of abnormal brain structure and function in unaffected siblings.

The advice is to talk with a psychiatrist face-to-face about what you're experiencing, even if it is only occasional forgetfulness or a feeling that you're 'losing it'. What you're experiencing may be related to stress, and not to schizophrenia.

Cooper shuddered. Everyone thought they might be losing it at some time in their lives, didn't they? It didn't necessarily indicate a deeper problem.

But occasionally, such ideas did rise from the depths of his mind to settle on the surface, like a scum of decomposing leaves. It was best not to disturb them. They were black and slimy with putrescence. Leave them alone, and they'd sink to the bottom again, vanish in a bubble of gas. That was the best way. He wished Matt would understand it.

11

Flowers had started to arrive at Darwin Street. Floral tributes to Lindsay Mullen and the two children. They came from relatives, friends and neighbours, and even from people who'd never known them. Communal grief had become fashionable, even in Edendale.

Next door, Keith Wade was complaining to a uniformed constable that he'd had to park his car at the end of the road because of the outer cordon. Fry saw that he was still wearing the same sweater. It must smell like a badger by now. No wonder Mr Wade lived alone.

And, of course, the fire investigator from the Forensic Science Service had arrived at Darwin Street when Fry wasn't looking. As a result, he'd already assessed the scene and was setting out his equipment in the Mullens' sitting room when she found him.

'Glad you could make it,' she said. 'DS Fry.'

He was a small, middle-aged man whose white

paper suit emphasized his pear-shaped body. And when he spoke, he revealed a Scottish accent.

'Quinton Downie,' he said, taking off a glove to shake hands.

'Do you have all the background information you need?'

'All that you can give me, apparently.'

'You know the time of the call to the fire service, and the apparent seat of the blaze, based on the firefighters' observations. We can't tell you anything about the contents of this room.'

'Yes, yes. So what is my objective? The cause of the fire? Mode of spread? Want me to comment on the accuracy of witness statements?'

'The cause of the fire will do for now, thank you.'

'Just so we're clear. It would be very useful to examine photographs of the scene during the fire.'

'Oh?'

Downie looked up at her. 'Try asking around the neighbours – someone may have taken photos or videos of the fire. It's amazing how often the offender stays on to watch the fun.'

'It's already been done. Right now, I just need you to concentrate on your own job.'

'OK. So . . . Locate seat of fire. Consider possible ignition sources. Excavate seat?' Downie tilted his head to one side and looked at the charred remains around him. 'Yes, I think so. Then take samples, formulate hypotheses. And report conclusion.'

'I'll look forward to it,' said Fry.

Downie was unpacking what looked like a series of pre-prepared forms. 'You'll get a location plan, as well as photographs as I excavate the seat of the fire. Samples will go straight to the lab.'

'Fine.'

'By the way, I examined the outside of the building before I came in. Do you know that you have unsooted broken glass in the vicinity of a side window?'

Fry had been about to leave the room, but turned back. 'What?'

'A broken side window. I wondered if your people had noticed it already. There don't seem to be any markers round there.'

'A lot of these windows are broken,' said Fry. 'That's the result of heat from the fire, surely?'

Downie looked up and smiled. 'If that were the case, the glass would be sooted on the interior surface. It isn't, which implies it must have been broken either in the early stages of the fire – or before it started.'

'You mean a point of entry?'

'Could be. I took samples anyway. But you might want to get that window examined for fingerprints or tool marks before the evidence is compromised any further.'

'You don't have to tell me my job.'

Downie just sniffed, as if she wasn't even worth a reply.

Fry glared at the back of his head as he continued to lay out his equipment. Looking around for someone to give instructions to, she caught sight of the fire officer standing in the doorway, grinning.

At that moment, her phone rang. It was the sergeant in charge of the search team.

'I thought you'd want to know straightaway, we've found an empty lighter fluid can. It's butane, but quite an unusual brand, I believe. It looks like someone found a use for a hundred millilitres of Swan Extra Refined recently.'

'Where did you find it? How near the house?'

'It had been chucked in a wheelie bin a hundred yards down the street, near the corner of Lilac Avenue. The householder says no one at this address smokes, and she has no idea how the can got in her bin. She insists it wasn't there on Sunday when she last put some rubbish out.'

'You've got it bagged properly?'

'You bet.'

'Thanks.'

Fry ended the call and turned back to Downie. 'Show me this side window,' she said.

He sighed and stood up. Together, they made their way out of the house and into a side passage near the garage. Brian Mullen's car still stood on the drive. It was a red Citroën, almost the same colour as the fire appliances that had surrounded it on Sunday night.

'OK,' sighed Downie. 'Look, you have plumes of soot deposited on the exterior wall by smoke emitted from the window. But the broken glass on the ground beneath the window is unsooted. So, we can conclude that the fire didn't touch this glass.'

'Yes, I see.'

'Even from here, I can see tool marks on the window frame,' said Downie. 'You might care to check whether the firefighters obtained entry this way.'

'They didn't. They came in through the doors.'

'Right.' Downie turned to look at her. 'Pity about the shoe impressions, though.'

'What shoe impressions?'

'Precisely.'

Fry looked at the ground where they were standing. It was a muddy mess, covered in crushed vegetation and trampled by size ten boots.

'Shit.'

Downie shrugged. 'Think yourself lucky to get this much. The site of any fire is a challenge to the principles of crime-scene management.'

'If the lab finds butane in your samples, it won't be up to me any longer anyway, lucky or otherwise,' said Fry. 'It becomes a murder enquiry.'

'I know, I know.'

Fry felt herself getting angry. 'Three people died in this fire. The evidence mustn't be compromised.'

'I can assure you, Sergeant Fry, everything will be done by the book.'

Fry looked at the rest of the houses in the street. A few neighbours were clustered outside the cordon. By the book, eh? That was all she needed, some civilian lecturing her about procedure. She knew what 'by the book' meant.

She also knew the principles Downie was referring to: protect, record and recover. Crime-scene examiners said that contamination only really occurred after the scene had been preserved. Anything before that was normal procedure.

But in this case, procedures had involved smashing down the doors and flooding the place with water, then sending in firefighters in big boots to trample the sodden evidence. Well, the principles still applied. As long as compromises were recorded and reasons given.

'By the way,' called Downie, passing the RV point on the way to his vehicle, 'the usual advice is not to fit a smoke alarm in the kitchen. Steam and cooking fumes can set it off too easily. For a two-storey house like this, the bottom of the staircase is the best location, with a second one on the landing as an extra precaution.'

'I'll be sure to let Mr Mullen know,' said Fry.

'Who?'

'The householder. The husband of the dead woman, the father of the two dead children. He's in hospital right now, but I'm sure he'll be pleased to know that he installed the smoke alarm in the wrong place. I bet it's the information he's been waiting to hear.'

Downie scowled, and seemed about to lose his temper. 'I'm just doing my job,' he snapped.

'So you said.'

She watched him stamp off in his scene suit, like an angry paper bag.

It wasn't much of a moral victory, though. Fry knew how much she relied on people like Downie following procedures to the letter. If she didn't have a watertight chain of custody when evidence was presented in court, it could undermine the whole case.

Now the scene was filling up with personnel. Scientific Support had allocated a couple of SOCOs, who'd waited for Downie to arrive from the lab at Chorley. And the two civilians she could see approaching the outer cordon looked as though they might be the insurance assessors. Great.

Fry tried to look on the bright side. This would make a good impression on her next personal development review. It was real team work.

Brian Mullen's hands were still bandaged, and he fumbled a bit taking off the radio headphones when he saw his visitor coming. From the look on his face, Fry thought he was going to leap out of bed and make a run for it. The ward sister had said yesterday that he'd been so frightened he'd fought against being kept in hospital. But what was he frightened of? Not her, surely.

'How are you getting on, Mr Mullen?' she asked, pulling a chair up to the side of his bed.

'Oh, not too bad,' he said warily. 'You're the police, are you?'

'Yes, sir.'

'Everyone's been very good to me. A vicar came round. And there was a counsellor, to see if I needed help.'

Now the pinkness in his cheeks had subsided, Mullen looked very pale. He had the sort of narrow, angular face and waxy skin that she'd only ever seen in Englishmen and some Scandinavians. His voice sounded hoarse from the effects of smoke inhalation, and he reached for a glass of water standing on the bedside cabinet. He had to hold the glass carefully between the tips of his fingers because the bandages got in the way.

'I hope the hospital have managed to keep the press away, sir,' said Fry.

'The press? I never even thought about them.' Mullen looked suddenly panicked. 'You've got to talk to the doctors. Tell them they have to let me go home. I need to get out of here.'

'You're much better here for now, sir. You'll be able to leave when you're fit. Meanwhile, we need to talk to you about what happened at your house.'

'I've already given a statement, you know.'

'An initial statement, yes. But that was only the start of our enquiries. There are a lot more questions to be asked.'

Mullen lay back on his pillows and sighed. 'Oh God, I suppose it's necessary.'

'If we're going to find out what happened, it is.'

'Tell me something, though – is Luanne all right?'

'Your daughter, sir?'

'Yes. Is she safe?'

'She's with your in-laws. There's no need to worry about her. Why shouldn't she be safe?'

'I don't know. She's only eighteen months old.'

'A family liaison officer has been assigned. There'll be support from Social Services, too, if it's needed.'

'Right.'

Fry watched his bandaged hands twitching, his eyes roving anxiously around the room. She was puzzled by his reactions. But Brian Mullen was a victim right now, a bereaved relative. Protocol called for politeness and consideration. Perhaps she ought to have brought him some grapes.

'Your daughter wasn't in the house at the time of the fire, was she?'

'No. Henry and Moira had been looking after her for a few days, to give us a bit of respite. Luanne wasn't sleeping, you see. She was having us out of bed every couple of hours.'

'I don't have children myself, but isn't eighteen months quite old to be still having that problem?'

'It varies.'

'Did your wife take anything to help her sleep, Mr Mullen?'

'Well, she couldn't when Luanne was in the house, obviously.'

'But on Sunday?'

'Yes, I think she might have done. A couple of pills, maybe.'

'Any idea what she took?'

He shook his head, and Fry decided to leave it for a while. She could easily get the information from Lindsay's GP – or even from her bedside drawer.

'As for you, I believe you'd been out for the evening?'

'I won't ever be able to forgive myself for that. I should have been there with my family. I could have saved them, couldn't I?'

'Probably not, Mr Mullen. You could have ended up a fatality yourself.'

'I've been lying here thinking it would have been better if I had died with them. To have survived seems . . . well, it seems like a punishment somehow.'

Fry nodded cautiously. Statements like this always sounded false to her. She couldn't help thinking that Brian Mullen had been rehearsing the phrases in his head for maximum effect. But her instinct was sometimes wrong – there *were* people who had difficulty expressing the most genuine emotions in a convincing way. On the other hand, Mullen had also tried to divert her from her line of questioning.

'Who were you out with that night, sir?'

'Just some mates.'

'Anyone in particular?'

'Oh, my mate from work, Jed – Jed Skinner.'

'And you arrived home at about one thirty a.m. Is that right?'

'Yes, I got the taxi driver to drop me off at the corner of Darwin Street. I'd already paid him off before I noticed anything wrong, and I didn't realize what was happening at first. I saw the flashing lights from the fire engines. There weren't really any flames then, you know. Just a lot of smoke. An awful lot of smoke.'

'When did you realize it was your own house on fire?'

'Not until I was almost there. Things looked so different with the lights and the smoke, and the hoses running across the road. It felt as though there ought to be a film crew somewhere. And all the neighbours were standing outside in their nightclothes. I was thinking, "Some poor bugger's got a real problem there," and wondering who it was. It didn't seem possible that it was *my* house they were all looking at.'

'I suppose you weren't thinking too clearly at the time, either.'

'What do you mean?'

'Well, I expect you'd had a few drinks, hadn't you, Mr Mullen?'

The look on his face changed then. His colour went a deeper pink, his mouth twisted into a less relaxed shape. Fry tried her hardest to read his expression as guilt, but it looked more like petulance.

'Yeah, a few.'

'Which club had you been in, by the way?'

'The Broken Wheel. There are only two places

that stay open late in Edendale, and the other one is full of kids on drugs.'

'All right. So when you finally realized it was your house on fire . . . ?'

'I looked around for Lindsay and the boys, obviously. There was a crowd of people gawping, and a copper trying to sort out the traffic. I couldn't see my family anywhere.'

'So you ran into the house?'

'Yes . . .' He hesitated. 'No, not straightaway. I saw my neighbour, Keith Wade. I asked him where Lindsay was. He said he hadn't seen her, or the boys either. Well, I knew from the way he said it, and the look on his face . . .'

'Knew what?'

'That they were still in there.'

Even Fry could detect a frisson of genuine emotion in Brian Mullen as he reached the next part of his story. A physical reaction was evident in the tightening of his mouth, the half-closed eyes, the sheen of sweat that appeared on his brow. Fear, yes – and a memory of pain, too.

But, of course, he had been burned by the fire, as proved by his bandaged hands and the notes on his chart at the end of the bed. His breathing had been affected by smoke inhalation, but that was only evident in the hoarseness of his voice, and perhaps in a peculiar inability to vary the pitch of his speech. That might be why his words sounded almost mechanical and insincere. Just might be.

'The firemen took no notice of me at first,' he said. 'They were too busy. But I could see some of them getting kitted out in masks and oxygen tanks – all that gear, you know.'

'Breathing apparatus.'

'That's it. But they seemed to be doing everything so slowly. My house was burning, and my kids were in there, but these blokes were fiddling about with tubes and helmets. So I went in.' Mullen stared at her defensively. 'I knew my way about the house a lot better than anyone else. I knew exactly where Lindsay and the boys would be. So it made sense.'

'Perhaps at the time it did,' conceded Fry.

He bridled at her tone. 'I couldn't stand there and do nothing.'

'So how far did you get?'

'Only to the stairs.'

'Tell me about it, please.'

Mullen subsided, wincing at the memory. 'The stairs are straight off the hallway. I could find them easily, even in the dark. I ran in and got maybe half a dozen steps up. But then the smoke was so thick that I suddenly didn't know which way I was going. It was in my eyes and in my throat, and I was trying to hold my breath, but I couldn't. I started to feel dizzy. I went down on my knees. I wanted to carry on, I really did. But I only managed one more step.'

'And then the firefighters caught up with you and pulled you back out of the house?'

'Yes, that's right.'

Fry pointed at his hands. 'What did you burn yourself on, Mr Mullen?'

He looked at the bandages and frowned. 'I'm not sure. I think it must have been the banister rail. That would have been the only thing I touched, wouldn't it?'

'With both hands?'

He shrugged. 'I suppose so.'

She let him think about that for a moment. 'You didn't go into any of the rooms downstairs? The sitting room, for example?'

'No. Why would I? I knew my family would be upstairs, in the bedrooms.'

'How could you be so sure of that, Mr Mullen?'

'For heaven's sake, it was almost twenty to two in the morning. Where else would they be, except in bed?'

'Your wife might have been waiting up for you to come home.'

'No, she never did that.'

'You see, the sitting room is where the fire is believed to have started. It must have been obvious when you entered the house that the smoke was coming from there.'

'So?'

'Well, we agree that you weren't thinking straight at the time, so perhaps your instinct might have been to go to the seat of the blaze and try to put it out. Or you might have feared that your

168

wife was in the sitting room, and had started a fire in there accidentally.'

'None of those things went through my mind,' said Mullen. 'I assumed they were upstairs. I had this picture in my head –'

'Yes, I see. So you're quite sure you didn't go into the sitting room, or touch the door maybe?'

'I'm sure. Look, I can't understand why you're asking me these questions.'

'It's for purposes of elimination, Mr Mullen. It will help us to establish the cause of the fire.'

'What? Are you saying it was started deliberately?'

'It's one of the possibilities we have to leave open. We can't rule anything out until it's been confirmed one way or another. That's why it's important to establish your movements, Mr Mullen. If the fire investigators find evidence of someone entering that room during the night of the fire, we'll know it wasn't you, won't we?'

Fry smiled at him, but he didn't look reassured. She often found that reaction. Perhaps she ought to work on the smile.

'Yes, that's right. But –'

'Don't worry about it now. You have a lot of things to think about. Let us know if we can be of any assistance. They've offered you counselling . . .?'

'Yes, all of that stuff,' said Mullen impatiently.

'And you do have some family in the area to support you?'

'There's Lindsay's parents. My dad is in Ireland. I don't know when he'll be coming over. He hasn't been well himself, so he might not make it.'

'Is there no one else locally?'

Mullen shook his head. 'There's only John.'

'John?'

'John Lowther. My brother-in-law. But Henry and Moira say he's devastated about Lindsay.'

Fry stood up. 'Well, take care, sir. We'll keep you informed.'

Mullen looked up at her, anxious now that she was leaving. 'I tested that smoke alarm regularly, you know. It was working all right.'

'Yes, well don't worry about that now.'

Mullen sank back on to his pillow, as if he'd put a lot of effort into that last statement and was now exhausted. Fry began to move quietly away, but his voice stopped her.

'We promised Luanne we'd take her to see the illuminations in Matlock Bath,' he said, his voice whispering with hoarseness. 'You know, with the parade of boats on the river, and the fireworks? We were going to take all the kids there, for a treat. The illuminations started a couple of weeks ago, but we were going to wait until half-term. The boys always liked the boats, but it would have been Luanne's first time. We won't be taking them now, will we?'

Fry hesitated in the doorway.

'No, sir. I'm sorry.'

She walked out of the ward and past the nurses'

station, trying to make sense of Brian Mullen. At times, the emotions underlying his responses had been too complicated to pin down. But one thing she was sure of. Despite what Mr Mullen had pretended, the idea that the fire might have been set deliberately had come as no surprise to him at all.

12

Upriver from Matlock Bath, the town of Matlock was going through another of its transformations. In the eighteenth century it had been John Smedley's 'mild water cure' that had changed the place for ever. Nearly thirty hydros had opened to exploit the thermal springs, with vast numbers of infirm visitors pouring in to immerse themselves in warm baths and try out the treatments on offer. On the hillside, Cooper could still see Smedley's Hydro, the biggest of them all. The vast building was now full of local government workers, soaking the public on behalf of Derbyshire County Council.

'It's right at the roundabout and over the bridge,' said Murfin.

'I know the way, Gavin.'

'And watch out for pedestrians on the bridge. Some of them are suicidal.'

'Gavin, I'm not your wife. I don't need you to tell me how to drive.'

He followed the A6 out of the town towards

Matlock Bath, and drove into the gorge where the River Derwent snaked beneath the face of High Tor. He slowed briefly at the point where the 'box brownie' sign came into view, warning of speed cameras ahead. The roundel gave the speed limit as fifty miles an hour. Despite the sign, there were no permanent cameras installed here. The safety team's van might be parked by the side of the road occasionally, that was all. And the van hadn't been in this area on Saturday. He'd already checked.

Although it seemed to form one continuous promenade along the west bank of the river, Matlock Bath's main street was split into two halves: North Parade and South Parade. In the middle were a couple of three-storey stone villas that had somehow escaped being converted into amusement arcades or fish restaurants.

Like so many resorts, this place was biker heaven. Even today, motorbikes were parked against the kerb on South Parade. Kawasakis, Suzukis and Ducatis, all polished and gleaming. Most of the bikers on the pavement seemed to be well past their youth, though. Their leathers bulged in the wrong places, and when they took off their helmets, their hair was grey and straggly, or missing altogether. There didn't seem to be one aged under fifty.

'Hell's Granddads,' said Murfin. 'They don't bother doing the ton any more, they just park up for a cup of tea and a fairy cake.'

'And to show off their bikes to each other, by the looks of it.'

'That's it, Ben. Nothing too strenuous at their age.'

But the statistics told a different story, and it wasn't funny. Despite the road being lined with *Think Bike* signs, a motorcycle rider forming each 'i', a map behind the Pavilion car park kept a record of the rising toll. New markers were added frequently to show where bikers had died in Derbyshire. Last year, two had lost their lives in one day in the Matlock area. That had been in October, too, but on a Sunday. One of the victims had been in his forties, the other in his fifties.

In fact, this stretch of the A6 was one of the designated 'hot routes' – the most popular roads among bikers, especially on bank holiday weekends. There was another section between Buxton and Taddington, but it was the Cat and Fiddle road into Staffordshire that had received most attention, ever since a bikers' magazine described it as more exciting to ride than the Manx TT. The latest figures showed motorcyclists accounting for a quarter of all fatalities and injuries on the roads in the county. No surprise, perhaps, when they seemed to be drawn to the most dangerous places.

Despite their appearance, some of these bikers would be riding circuits around the valley later in the day. And if it was a good day, no one would actually die.

'So where are these people who think they saw the shooting victim on Saturday?' said Murfin, yawning extravagantly.

'Rose Shepherd was seen at the Riber Tea Rooms

on South Parade, and the Aquarium on North Parade. Oh, and the Masson Mill shopping village. That's a bit further down the road from here.'

'We'll have to split up, I suppose.'

'It'll be a lot quicker, Gavin.'

'Hey, we're not going in all these shops, are we?'

'We ought to go into any that are close to where Miss Shepherd was seen. We've got to be thorough, while we're here. The DCI wants a picture of what the victim was doing here, and who she met in the hours before she died.'

'Shopkeepers, eh? I just hope they're friendly.'

'You'll survive.'

Murfin wasn't the only officer Cooper had heard expressing reluctance to enter shops on duty. Talking to shopkeepers had been part of the routine in his father's time. But that was before they started measuring police performance against key indicators – which didn't include retail crime. So shoplifting had become low priority. The larger businesses hired their own security guards and adjusted their budgets to account for 'slippage'. Small businesses couldn't do that. And an unsuspecting police officer made a handy target for a shopkeeper's frustration.

He managed to park the Toyota on the roadside between Hodgkinson's Hotel and a shop called The Biker's Gearbox. Then he and Murfin took a parade each.

'Tell the missus I died a hero's death,' said Murfin as he got reluctantly out of the car.

Cooper had drawn North Parade, and had to walk

back the way he'd come. There must be a dozen cafés and fish restaurants in this length of road alone: Taste of the Waves, Frankie and Joe's, the Promenade Fish Bar . . . And then there were all the pubs and restaurants, and the big hotels on the hillside.

Between them, they accounted for the most distinctive feature of Matlock Bath, a characteristic that Cooper remembered so well from previous visits and which was still present now, undiminished by the years. It was the smell of fish and chips, hot and vinegary, hanging permanently over the promenade like a haze.

Many of the shops, amusement arcades and restaurants were closed. Of course, it was a weekday and out of season, with the children back at school for the new term. But some had opened to cater for the bikers and a few other visitors.

He passed the photograph museum, Life in a Lens, and noticed that a Victorian tea room had been opened on the ground floor. He'd have to call and ask about the webcam later.

The aquarium had a window display of a deep-sea diver and a treasure chest, but the ground floor was taken up by an amusement arcade. He asked at the pay booth for the member of staff he wanted and was directed past the slot machines and up the stairs into the aquarium.

'He'll be with you in a minute.'

'Thanks.'

At the top of the stairs, he waited by the original petrifying well. This was what the first visitors to Matlock Bath had come to see – ordinary items apparently turning to stone. Thermal water still ran down a channel through the building, pumped up into sprays and gurgling ominously somewhere beneath his feet. The objects he could make out under their layer of calcium included teapots, a bird's cage, a telephone and a deer's skull, complete with antlers. As usual, visitors had thrown coins into the water, forever hoping for a bit of good fortune. This was one belief that seemed to survive, no matter what – an enduring faith in the magical properties of water.

Cooper wondered if Rose Shepherd had tossed a coin in here on Saturday. She sounded like a woman who'd desperately needed a bit of good luck.

Suddenly, a man was standing beside him.

'Is it me you've come to see?'

'Yes, if you called the police in response to our appeals.'

Cooper fumbled for his ID, but the man didn't even look at it.

'I'm a bit busy, so you'll have to keep up with me while I'm working. I have to check all the safety precautions and signs while it's quiet.'

'All right.'

'Through this way, then.'

'Before we go any further, is this the woman you remember seeing here on Saturday?'

The man glanced at the photograph. 'Yes, that's her. It's the same photo that was in the papers, isn't it?'

'Yes, I'm just making sure. The reproduction is sometimes a bit poor.'

In the aquarium itself, red-eared terrapins basked on a concrete beach under halogen spot lamps. There were vegetarian piranhas and South American snakeheads that swam with their long bodies hanging in graceful curves, ready to travel across land to find more water if their habitat dried up. One glass tank contained only the hands of an unseen man scraping the silt off the bottom.

'She came in on Saturday afternoon, about two fifteen. Didn't stop here for long. She had a quick walk round, then spent a few minutes by the thermal pool.'

'What made you notice her?'

'Well, it's not often we have people coming in on their own. A woman of sixty or so? She seemed harmless, but you never know.'

'So you kept an eye on her?'

'Discreetly. On my own initiative.'

'What did she do?'

'Pretty much what you did – stopped at the petrifying well, then came through here and looked at the fish. She liked the terrapins, as I recall.'

He opened a door, and they walked out of the heat of the aquarium on to a cool, tiled walkway beside an outdoor pool.

'This was the original baths, you know. The Victorians thought the water cured rheumatism. The pool is still fed by the thermal spring. It's a constant twenty degrees centigrade.'

Cooper looked over the side of the pool. It was full of colourful Japanese fish and fat mirror carp.

'Twenty degrees centigrade? Lucky fish.'

'The lady stood out here for a bit. There were some children feeding the fish. See? You can buy a carton of food from the machine for twenty pence.'

'Did she speak to anyone?'

'No, she was just watching.'

Despite the temperature of the water, it was much cooler out here, because the pool was open to the sky, with only a few rusty girders remaining of the roof. Looking up, Cooper noticed a camera mounted on the wall, focused on the feeding station.

'Are you sure? No one standing near her? Or someone that she took a particular interest in?'

'Only the children.'

Cooper waited on the red and black tiles while the man walked off to check a side door. There was a plop as one of the larger fish surfaced at the other end of the pool. And then he saw that people had thrown coins in here, too. Instead of buying food for the fish, visitors had tossed their twenty pence pieces into the water, so they lay glinting on the bottom.

'We go out this way. Through the hologram gallery.'

A moment later, Cooper was back in darkness, standing in front of a pocket watch that seemed to float in mid-air. When he moved his head, the time on the watch face changed. The hands flicked from eight minutes before ten o'clock to six minutes past, and then to a quarter past. Disturbingly, the Roman numerals were in the wrong place, too. He wondered if it was symbolic. *Look, it's later than you think.*

'Before you ask, there wasn't anyone else in here. Did you think the lady might have come in the aquarium to meet someone?'

'It was a possibility. Was she carrying anything when she came in?'

'Come to think of it, yes. A carrier bag of some kind.'

'And did she still have the bag when she went out?'

'I can't recall.'

In another hologram, Cooper watched an elephant turn into a pig, then a hippopotamus. Further along the wall, a man metamorphosed into a werewolf, and Dr Jekyll became Mr Hyde. Piped music played in the background, something soothing and a bit New Agey. But it was interrupted by noises from the amusement arcade downstairs: the rattle of coins, the blaring music of the video games. Real life intruded, even into a room full of illusions.

'And that was it?'

'Yes, that was it. Then she left.'

'Back down the stairs?'

'You have to exit through the amusements, but she didn't stop in there. She was in a hurry to get out by then.'

'When she got out on to the street, which way did she go?'

'I couldn't tell you.'

'All right. Did you notice anything unusual about her manner?'

'No. I got the impression she was killing time. In fact, I'd have said she came in to get out of the rain – except it wasn't raining that day.'

'How was she dressed?'

'Oh, I dunno. A jacket of some kind. Not a coat . . . Like I said, it wasn't raining, or even particularly cold.'

'Colour?'

'Black, I think. And slacks – trousers, you know, not jeans. She wasn't scruffy.'

'Oh? Did you get the impression she'd dressed up a bit to come out?'

'Well, she'd made an effort, definitely.'

'But not to come here? She was just killing time, right?'

'She wasn't looking for anyone in here, I don't think. She hardly seemed to notice other people, except the children. She looked like a self-contained sort of person. Do you know what I mean?'

'Yes, I know what you mean. Thank you for your time.'

As he left, Cooper noticed that a view from the camera in the thermal bath was projected on to a screen over the entrance. On a busier day, you could watch from the street as children fed the fish or threw their coins into the water, hoping for good luck.

In fact, if he'd been standing here at the right time on Saturday afternoon, he would probably have seen Rose Shepherd. Cooper imagined a ghostly likeness of her now, superimposed on the tiles. For a second, Miss Shepherd really seemed to be standing at the edge of the pool in her black jacket, clutching her carrier bag. But the moment he moved his head, she disappeared again, vanishing like an image in one of those holograms. And she'd given him no sign – no clue at all why she'd come here on Saturday, all dressed up for an afternoon out in Matlock Bath.

There wasn't much chance to talk at a Home Office post-mortem. There were always too many people present – the SIO, crime-scene examiner, photographer, pathologist and her assistant. And without the distraction of conversation, Fry found it difficult not to think about the smell.

She had no problem with the sights, or with being passed unidentifiable, bloody items for packaging now and then. She wasn't even bothered by the pathologist eating a snack during the proceedings, as some of them did. But the smell was something else.

Some old hands suggested putting Vicks VapoRub up your nose before attending a PM. Others pointed out that Vicks was designed for clearing the nose, so it actually heightened your sense of smell, instead of masking odours. Two extra strong mints might help, though, they said. Fry hadn't found anything that worked.

'In the absence of any other priorities, I've scheduled them in the order they came in,' said the pathologist, Juliana van Doon. 'So it's fire victims first. But since there are three of them, I've requested a colleague to come in and assist me. So we shouldn't be too long getting to your shooting.'

'That one isn't mine. I'm on the house fire.'

'Oh, I thought you'd been promoted.'

Everyone in the autopsy suite was fully suited and booted to avoid infection. The suits were also supposed to prevent your clothes from trapping the smell, so that members of the public and their dogs didn't shy away from you and throw up when you went out on to the street.

It was Lindsay Mullen who lay on the dissection table. The mark of the incision where the pathologist had opened her up glared a startling red against her waxy skin. Fry was glad she hadn't witnessed the removal of the skull for examination of the brain. The noise of the saw and the smell of singed bone were the worst part of a postmortem for her. Well, there was one other stage that was as bad – the moment when the loosened scalp was folded forward over the corpse's face with the skin inside out, like a towel thrown over the beer pumps at closing time.

'A well-nourished Caucasian female, physical condition consistent with a stated age of twenty-nine. Sixty-one kilos, one hundred and seventy-three centimetres.' The pathologist looked up. 'That's about nine stone nine pounds, five feet seven inches.'

'Thank you.'

'Physical injuries are all superficial. No signs of external trauma.'

'Any signs of recent sexual activity?' asked Fry, to take her mind off the smells.

Mrs van Doon pursed her lips and flicked back her sleeves. 'You have all the best ideas, don't you?'

'I need any indication I can get of whether there was another person in the house that night.'

'Yes, I understand where you're heading. I can see why they employ you on these cases. I imagine you don't leave any bit of dirt unexamined.'

'We have a lot in common, then,' said Fry coolly, surprised by the sharpness of her tone. But she supposed even pathologists were human sometimes.

'No, no signs of sexual intercourse. This is the only item that's of real interest –'

The pathologist held up a body part that had been cut free and sliced open with a scalpel. Fry didn't recognize it, which was probably what Mrs van Doon expected.

'This is the oesophagus. The black stains you can see on the inside are soot. They suggest that your victim was alive when the fire started, because she breathed in smoke. There's enough in the oesophagus to have resulted in asphyxiation.'

'So that's the cause of death?'

'Possibly . . . There's a sort of triple whammy in these cases. Inhalation of soot particles damages the airways, because the particles are super-heated and contain toxic agents. Hot air burns the upper passages, too, and can cause vagal inhibition. But there's a third factor. Carbon monoxide is normally associated with soot inhalation, and I can deduce some CO poisoning from the cherry pink discoloration on the torso. We'll get blood samples analysed for carboxyhaemoglobin levels. But anything above fifty per cent is fatal.'

'I presume there'll be a report soon.'

'When I get time.' The pathologist began to strip off her gloves. 'The other two fire fatalities are children, I see.'

'Yes.'

'You know, the children look almost undamaged, but for the carbon monoxide discoloration and some smoke staining.'

Fry searched for something to say. 'That makes it worse, I suppose. They don't look as though they should be dead, do they?'

'On an emotional level, that's true.'

She watched the pathologist drop her gloves into a bin, wondering if she'd just been the object of a subtle insult, or a slur on her professionalism. *On an emotional level?* But perhaps it had been a moment of personal confession. It was difficult to tell with Juliana van Doon.

13

In Matlock Bath, houses seemed to climb on top of each other in their haste to escape the valley floor. Above them were the two Victorian pleasure grounds on Masson Hill – the Heights of Jacob, the Heights of Abraham. Their biblical slopes were occupied by modern leisure parks now, the fairy-tale shapes of castles and towers poking up among the trees.

For the past twenty years, there had been no need for anyone to slog up the winding paths to reach the hilltop park at the north end of the village. Strings of white cable cars now rode high over the valley from a base station near the railway line, carrying visitors up to enjoy the play areas, the Treetops gift shop, the Hi Café and the Summit Bar. A grey stone tower was visible on the summit, a flag fluttering in the breeze.

The weather had been warm right through into October, which felt wrong in the Peak District. After another dry summer, the trees had burst into an explosion of yellows and golds. Where the turrets and battlements of Lilliput Land Castle had lurked among dense foliage all summer, now they were emerging slowly from a sea of reds and golds. Some of the other features of Gulliver's Kingdom were being revealed, too, like the chairlift and the campanile on Fantasy Terrace.

Cooper could see the new indoor facility standing out prominently on the hillside. It was designed to stay open during the winter, and it housed everything from Wild West shoot-outs to an ice palace. Or so his nieces told him. He supposed he'd have to take them there one day, when he got some time off.

Turning left out of the aquarium, he called at the neighbouring properties, which happened to be the two villas housing B&Bs. There was a chance that Rose Shepherd had come into Matlock Bath to meet someone who was staying here, although there didn't seem to be any reason why she should have killed time next door in that case.

Drawing a blank, he walked a bit further up North Parade, where he found another amusement centre and a shop selling hand-made chocolates, both of which were closed.

Across the road was the Jubilee Bridge – wooden planks and iron girders, with an old gas lamp on a central arch. It led across the river to a bandstand and the remains of a switchback. There were more wooded slopes lying above Lovers' Walk. Their steepness called for erosion controls: log revetments, brush and board hurdles, a dead hedge. Here and there, sycamores and beeches had been felled, no doubt condemned because they weren't native to Derbyshire.

An artist had set his easel up on the bridge, trying to capture the scene downriver towards the Pavilion, with trees reflected in the moving water. Cooper often came across painters, though usually in the summer. He had to admire the effort they put in, if only to carry their equipment from the car. But they were setting themselves a hopeless challenge. This landscape was constantly changing. No set of watercolours was going to preserve it on a canvas.

He noticed that Life in a Lens stood on the other side of the aquarium, with a Victorian tea room on the ground floor. This was his chance to call in and ask about the webcam.

When he came out a few minutes later, a school party was queuing to enter the mining museum further down the road. There were two cameras on the outside wall nearby, but they were focused on the entrance to Brody's nightclub. When he was a teenager, Brody's had been known to the local kids as 'The Pav', because it was located on the upper floor of the Pavilion, above the mining museum and the tourist information centre.

But where the heck was Gavin Murfin? Cooper stood by his Toyota for a while, looking up and down the street. Then he walked a few yards along South Parade, past the ice-cream parlour and the antiques centre to the corner, where he found that a science-fiction bookshop he remembered had closed down. He supposed it had been a mistake to let Gavin take the interview with the waitress at the tea rooms. The smell of fish and chips on the promenade was so inescapable that he must be giddy with hunger by now.

Finally, Cooper pulled out his phone and called Gavin's number. Strangely, the ringing tone seemed to be echoed by a tune playing somewhere nearby. He turned and looked into the windows of the building behind him. There was Gavin, eating a choc ice. And waving.

'OK, I did the waitress at the Riber Tea Rooms,' said Murfin when Cooper got him away from his choc ice. 'Nice lass, name of Tina. Get this – reckons she saw Rose Shepherd talking to two other people at a table in the café on Saturday afternoon.'

'Wow, you got more than I did,' said Cooper.

'That's why I thought I deserved a reward.'

'What time was this, Gavin?'

'Around two thirty, she thinks.'

'That must have been after Miss Shepherd came out of the aquarium.'

Murfin used the tip of one finger to wipe a bit of chocolate from his front teeth. 'I chatted Tina up a bit, and I got her to do her best with descriptions. But the tea rooms were full that afternoon. She did say the woman she recognized from the paper was wearing a dark jacket.'

'That fits. What about the other two?'

189

'Ah, there she was struggling a bit, poor lass. She says they'd come in earlier, a man and a woman. But she had no reason to take particular notice of them. The Shepherd woman came in about a quarter of an hour later, and she was on her own, which is more unusual. She ordered a coffee, paid for it, then took her time looking round, and went and sat at the couple's table.'

'Did she seem to know them?'

'That's what Tina's not really sure about. There were no empty tables, so Miss Shepherd would have had to sit with someone, and she chose those two.'

'Right. We don't know why, though?'

'Maybe because they looked the most harmless. All Tina can say is that when she took the coffee to the table, the three of them weren't talking and the atmosphere seemed cool. But they did chat a bit later on. The couple left the café first, and Miss Shepherd went out right after them. The money for the couple's bill was left on the table.'

Cooper unlocked the car. Standing at the kerb behind it was an entire family of bikers – mum, dad and two small children, all dressed in matching leathers and gathered round a pair of purple Suzukis.

'Well, it's something at least, Gavin,' he said. 'She must have come down into Matlock Bath for a reason.'

'Oh, and I did a couple of shops,' said Murfin.

'Yes, the ice-cream parlour. I saw that.'

Murfin groaned theatrically. 'You know, Ben, you're getting as bad as Miss.'

'Get in the car, Gavin. We've got to call at Masson Mill.'

Masson had been the world's oldest working textile mill until production stopped fifteen years ago. Here, in the middle part of the Derwent Valley, was where industrial history had changed. It had all started for Sir Richard Arkwright at Cromford Mill, just downstream. But Masson was his great flagship.

Cooper couldn't remember details of the innovations that led to Arkwright's success, the industrial secrets German manufacturers had gone to great lengths to get hold of. But he could see how Arkwright's status had risen purely by looking at the building. This mill hadn't been built, but designed. Instead of a dark, cavernous shed, it was an edifice intended to impress. The three central bays were built out towards the road and decorated with half-moons of glass between Venetian-style windows. Above the windows stood a shuttered cupola, and Sir Richard's name spelled out on the brickwork in proud capital letters.

One of the later extensions to the mill had been converted into a car park. Cooper drove up a ramp and parked on the roof near a side entrance to the shopping village. Over the wall, he could see the convex weir built to take advantage of an outcrop of rock on the opposite bank of the river. From there, the water ran into a goyt, the fast-flowing channel that had driven the mill's waterwheels.

'What are we looking for here, Ben?'

'Eva Hooper. She runs a retail unit on the road level.'

Murfin opened the door into the shops. 'Mmm, cakes.'

There were four open-plan retail levels, accessed from a central staircase like an old-fashioned department store. Each floor was divided into areas selling discount designer clothes, furniture, food, golf equipment. The mill clock was still on the wall at road level, but for some reason it had stopped at twelve noon. On the lowest level was a restaurant, lined with windows overlooking the river. A patch of brown scum had formed on the water, as if a few gallons of coffee had been spilled there.

'Gavin, why don't you find the offices and ask about CCTV footage? There's a camera over the main entrance.'

'All right.'

Cooper had seen signs on this floor for the working textile museum. Could it have been part of Miss Shepherd's afternoon out, before her visit to the aquarium? Perhaps Arkwright's legacy had some significance for her. Come to think of it, she was old enough to have worked here at the mill. Had she been revisiting old haunts, re-living memories one last time?

Cooper shook himself. He'd begun to imagine the victim having some kind of premonition that she was about to die. But no one knew the time of their death in advance, unless they had some terminal illness. Or they were intending to commit suicide. That was the only way to be *really* sure.

The museum was reached by leaving the shopping area and passing through an echoey room over uneven wooden floors that creaked and shifted underfoot, worn by decades of use by Arkwright's millworkers. Bobbins and shuttles were on sale here, along with other mementoes of the textile industry that had once employed so many.

He found a man taking money on a flight of stairs that led down into the spinning and weaving sheds.

'Do you issue admission tickets here?' he asked.

'No. You get a leaflet with a map of the route through the rooms of the museum – see?'

'Were you working on Saturday?'

'In the afternoon.'

'Do you remember this woman coming in?'

The man looked at Cooper's photograph.

'No, sorry.'

In the rooms below, two enormous machines rattled away unattended, and stacks of shuttles sat in alcoves along the walls. There were wicker baskets and wooden trolleys, shelves full of old tools and equipment. An ancient typewriter, dusty cardboard boxes. Cooper could smell lubricating oil and hear the chug of the looms, leather belts spinning over wheels in the glass-roofed sheds. A tiny cubicle looked to be an overseer's office, dusty ledgers still open on the desk, wire-framed glasses poking out of an ancient spectacle case. Visitors' direction signs pointed towards a distant doorway – the bobbin room.

Cooper turned back. 'Thanks for your time,' he said.

In a distant corner of the shopping village, he found Eva Hooper. Her unit sold prints of Peak District landscapes, ethnic gifts, pottery, leather-work, gemstones. And, of course, a range of post-cards, calendars and greeting cards – anything that tourists might be interested in.

'Yes, I think she was here,' she said. 'It was Saturday, so we were quite busy.'

'Yes, I understand.'

'If it had been during the week, I might have remembered her better.'

'Did she buy anything?'

'I'm not sure. If she paid by cash, there won't be any record of her name.'

'OK.'

'You could ask my assistant, but she's not here today. She works for me part-time when I'm busy.'

'What's her name?'

'Frances – we call her Fran.'

Cooper paused with his pen poised over his notebook. He'd spoken to a Frances very recently. It wasn't a common name, but coincidences did happen . . .

'Frances what?'

'Birtland. She lives a couple of miles away, in Foxlow.'

'Yes,' said Cooper. 'I know.'

Fry was satisfied that she'd done everything she could to prevent any further loss of evidence from the house at Darwin Street. She'd taken all the actions necessary to preserve the scene and create a log. The examination had been thorough. True, in an ideal world, it could have happened a bit sooner. But since when had this world been ideal? At least it had been done before any cleaning up or salvage operations started.

Now she was anxious to get Brian Mullen back at the scene as soon as she could, in case any more items came to light that needed to be recovered. Once that had been done, she could relax and let the clean-up get under way.

The good news from the fire officer was that significant evidence often remained, even after the most destructive of fires. She recognized some of the terms he used, but mostly his optimistic tone. The experts had even agreed on where the fire started, though apparently Quinton Downie had insisted on defining a radius of error about a metre around the likely source.

One of the SOCOs assigned to Darwin Street was Liz Petty. Some people turned up everywhere. Inside the hallway of the house, Petty was unpacking another holdall full of stepping plates.

'Watch where you're walking,' she said, without looking round.

'Yes, all right.'

She looked up then. 'Oh. Hi, Diane. How are you doing?'

'Fine.'

'Making progress on the enquiry?'

'Yes, thanks.'

'There'll be some publicity on this one, I suppose. There was a TV news van outside earlier. I don't know what they were filming.'

'They can film what they like. There's nothing for them to see.'

She was aware of Petty watching her as she moved around the room. But after a moment, Fry became focused again. She was noticing all the changes that were taking place in the house – the plastic sheeting, the evidence containers, the yellow markers and flags that decorated the carpet, creating a bizarre new pattern on what had once been Lindsay Mullen's cream Wilton.

'Actually, I heard you weren't getting on well with Quinton Downie,' said Petty.

Fry turned. 'Where did you hear that?'

'People talk. Even firefighters have ears, you know. Otherwise, their helmets would fall off.'

'Very funny.'

Petty looked up at her from her position crouched over a stepping plate. 'Downie is very well respected in his field. He lectures regularly at Centrex.'

But Fry wasn't impressed by the mention of the police training centre. 'That doesn't mean he has any right to lecture me.'

Downie was in the sitting room packing his equipment away. He looked satisfied with his efforts, reminding Fry of the fire service dog, the chocolate Labrador. He wasn't quite wagging his tail, but it was a close-run thing.

'Liquid accelerants are volatile, so it's good that we collected debris samples early,' he said when Fry entered. 'Arsonists tend to use petrol products, because they're easy to obtain and have a low flashpoint. But petrol has rather a narrow flammability range – it stops burning when the oxygen level is reduced. Hydrogen and acetylene are far more dangerous.'

'The accelerant in this case could have been a butane-based lighter fluid.'

'Butane? Well, the flashpoint is about the same as petrol, well below ambient temperature.' Downie looked around the sitting room. 'In fact, you're lucky we're not looking at radiation-induced flashover.'

'What?'

'In a closed room like this, there normally isn't sufficient ventilation for unlimited burning. In fact, if it had been a bit more airtight, the fire might have gone out. But there was just a little bit of ventilation, and that made it worse. The room was pretty cluttered, items of furniture pushed close together, flammable materials on the floor. In conditions like this, flashover can happen very quickly. If you're there to see it happen, it's quite dramatic.'

'OK, I believe you.'

Downie smiled, a man who enjoyed the small details of his job. 'Old houses are the worst. A lot of them are like bonfires waiting for the first match. Wooden floors, wooden beams and window frames. With a bit of breeze blowing through, you can get a fire going that's hot enough to melt the fillings in your teeth. Of course, it isn't actually the wood that burns but the gases released from it by heat. The solid material disintegrates, and you're left with a pile of ashes.'

'But the victims died upstairs,' said Fry. 'Smoke inhalation.'

'Oh, yes. Absolutely lethal. If you get a lungful of smoke from a house fire, you're in trouble.'

'I can't understand why the victims never even made it to the stairs.'

'Look, it goes like this . . .' Downie demonstrated by closing his eyes and clutching his throat. 'You've taken a breath and you can't open your eyes because as soon as you do they water. You take another breath and the irritants hit the back of your throat. You retch and take an even deeper breath – it's a natural, involuntary reaction. It fills your lungs with toxic fumes. That disorientates you, makes you dizzy, and puts you down on the floor. While you're incapacitated, the toxicity takes over.'

To Fry's amazement, he lay down on the floor and demonstrated what it was like to be dead. She'd never seen anybody look less dead in her life. But if there had been a weapon handy, she might have felt tempted to help him achieve authenticity.

Then he opened his eyes and looked up. 'We used to say you had seven minutes to get out of a burning building. Now, with all the materials we've put inside them, it's more like three minutes.'

'And that's why we advise people to install smoke alarms.'

'Ah, yes. The smoke alarm. Pity about that.'

'It was functioning, wasn't it?'

'After a fashion.'

'Mr Mullen says he tested it regularly.'

'No doubt he did. But, like most people, all he was doing was pressing the button. That proves the sound works, and the batteries aren't dead. It doesn't tell you whether the detector is functioning.'

'What are you saying?'

'I took a look at the smoke alarm earlier. And I'd say your Mr Mullen never bothered reading the manufacturer's instructions. He should have vacuumed around the detector regularly to prevent the build-up of dust. Apart from battery failure, there's nothing worse than accumulated debris for interfering with an alarm. This one hadn't been cleaned for a long time. There was even a thin layer of cement and plaster particles, so I'm guessing the family had building work done in the kitchen at some time.'

'Yes, they had new units put in about six months ago, and an extractor fan installed.'

'There you go, then. Cement and plaster, with a couple of layers of dust. It was almost as if they'd built a wall inside the detector. I'm sorry for the chap, and all that. But facts are facts.'

'What about where the fire started?'

'Now, that's interesting,' said Downie. 'The point of origin would normally be near the area of greatest damage. But there are three items of furniture in this room with differing upholstery. The nature of the upholstery makes a big difference.'

'Do you mean polyurethane foam?'

'Well, all three items contain polyurethane foam padding. It's the covering that matters. Anyway, it appears to me that the initial fire was started by applying flame to a quantity of papers adjacent to this chair here, right among these toys.'

'But the other chair seems to have suffered most damage. That, and the settee.'

'It's rather deceptive at first glance, isn't it? You see, the chair this side of the room is upholstered with a thick cotton weave. It was probably a nice piece of furniture.' Downie moved across the room. 'The settee, on the other hand, was padded with polyurethane foam *and* covered in a partly synthetic fabric mixture, probably poly-cotton. Now the third item of furniture. This, I'm afraid, is a cheaply upholstered armchair, with a wholly thermoplastic cover over polyurethane foam, without any inter-lining.'

'So the quality of the furniture varied. Perhaps the Mullens should have gone to Ikea and bought a complete suite. But they probably couldn't afford it.'

Downie didn't seem to hear her. 'You see, despite the fire having been lit directly adjacent to it, the cotton-weave chair sustained less damage than the other two items. The natural fibre cover charred and pyrolized, but the weave didn't fall away, so it provided some retardation of heat release. However, the cheaply constructed armchair was completely consumed, and the synthetically upholstered settee was also severely damaged. Both would have been ignited by radiated heat. The thermoplastic material melts and falls away to expose the underlying foam to the fire. Not so good.'

'I think I see,' said Fry, surprised to realize that she actually did.

'Excellent,' said Downie. 'Well, that's my theory for now. I'll examine remaining fabric from the three items and test their burning characteristics. But the carpet is probably going to be most helpful to us. Carpet absorbs accelerant well, and retains residue longer.'

Petty had moved into the sitting room and was concentrating her attention on a heavily damaged area of carpet.

201

'Is this where the accelerant was used?'

'We think so. It's one of the sites identified by the dog.'

Petty was photographing the burn pattern before she began to cut into the carpet. She rolled up a sample with the foam backing on the inside and eased it vertically into a container.

Fry left the house to look outside. Someone was bound to have left their fingerprints somewhere in the house, in an area undamaged by the fire. The trouble was, it might well be a firefighter or a police officer. Not to mention members of the household and their various friends and relations. The footwear impressions were going to be useless, too. The layer of mud wasn't deep enough, and the lab would never get a match, or identify a pattern.

She watched Downie carefully placing his evidence samples and control samples separately in his van. And she saw that he'd completed the most important items of all – the chain of custody forms.

Then she spotted Wayne Abbott standing in the road near one of the Scientific Support vehicles and walked across to him.

'Is there any particular reason we got Liz Petty?' she asked him.

Abbott turned in surprise, and she saw that he had a mobile phone pressed to his ear. 'Hang on a minute,' he said, and held the phone away to free both ears. 'What was that?'

'I wondered how we came to get Liz Petty,' said Fry.

He stared at her, reflecting her hostility like a mirror. 'Liz attended an inter-service fire investigation course at Ripley not so long ago. She was the obvious choice for this job. Why?'

'Oh, no reason.'

'She was up to her neck in volume crime, dealing with burglaries on the Southwoods Estate,' said Abbott. 'But we gave this priority for you. What's the problem?'

'Nothing.'

Abbott turned his back and resumed his phone call. 'Sorry . . . no, it was just someone wasting my time.'

14

Hitchens was waiting for Cooper and Murfin in the garden of Bain House. 'The chiefs are talking about bringing in the NCOF,' he said.

Murfin looked puzzled.

'The National Crime and Operations Faculty,' Cooper told him quietly.

'That must be at Bramshill – Acronym City.'

'Yes.'

'If Mr Kessen puts in a request, their regional officer will provide us with assistance. In fact, the NCOF can turn out a full team. Their own SIO, psychologist, forensic scientist, pathologist –'

'With respect, sir, we don't need all that.'

Hitchens looked at Cooper and smiled. 'That's what I think, too. But let's prove that we don't need it, shall we?'

'I don't think it will be much use to us, sir,' said Cooper as he followed the DI into the house, 'but I've asked for footage from the Matlock Bath webcam for Saturday afternoon. They were very helpful. They're sending me a QuickTime movie file.'

'OK, Ben. Well done. We have to try everything.'

DCI Kessen was sitting in an armchair in the sitting room of Bain House, looking thoughtfully at the white and grey walls.

'How do you think the victim would have spent her time, all alone in this house?'

'Well, there are two TVs,' said Hitchens. 'One in the sitting room, another in the kitchen. Also a couple of radios, including a digital on the bedside table. When we turned it on, it was pre-tuned to BBC 7.'

'Sorry, I haven't gone digital yet. You'll have to enlighten me.'

'Re-runs of old BBC comedy shows and dramas. You know, *Hancock's Half Hour* and *Round the Horne.*'

'OK.'

'There's a decent stereo system, too. Nothing special – but women don't care much about the technical details, do they? She obviously used it, because it was plugged in and switched on, just left on standby. And there was a CD in the slot – an Abba compilation.'

'Why am I getting the impression of someone living on nostalgia?'

'She certainly seems to have surrounded herself with sound. Or noise, at any rate.'

'I think I'd be the same if I lived on my own.

I'd need to drown out the silence somehow,' said Murfin.

'There's quite a collection of CDs in the racks. She had some DVDs, too. *Sleepless in Seattle*. I still haven't seen that.'

'She must have bought those things from somewhere.'

'Mail order, probably. They're small enough items to go into the letter box. Unlike the package of books that Bernie Wilding tried to deliver.'

'You know, there's something strange about this house,' said Cooper tentatively.

'What do you mean?'

'It doesn't feel lived in.'

'Rose Shepherd lived here.'

'Hardly. She just seems to have existed.'

Kessen nodded at him, 'What's your impression, Cooper?'

'Well, you can still detect traces of the family who lived here before her. On the other hand, Miss Shepherd has hardly left her imprint on the house at all. It's almost as if she'd never been here.'

He looked out of the window at the garden. At least the armed officers deployed on Monday had been withdrawn, and the scene looked more peaceful again. Then he saw a tortoiseshell cat sitting under a tree, watching the house. When a SOCO walked across the lawn, the cat crouched cautiously, but didn't move away.

'Who searched the kitchen?' said Cooper. 'Did they find any cat food in the cupboards?'

Hitchens laughed. 'I don't think so. There was some fish in the fridge, though. Fresh salmon.'

'That makes sense.'

'Why, Ben?'

'I think I've spotted Rose Shepherd's means of not being alone.'

WITNESS APPEAL AFTER
FOXLOW SHOOTING

Detectives are appealing for witnesses after the murder of a woman in Foxlow on Sunday.

Miss Rose Shepherd, sixty-one, was killed by two shots from a high-powered rifle, fired from a field behind her house in Pinfold Lane during the early hours of the morning. Miss Shepherd had lived in the village for the past ten months, and police have yet to establish a motive for her killing.

Meanwhile, officers are keen to talk to witnesses who might have seen anyone suspicious in the area during the last few days. They would particularly like to trace the owner of a blue Vauxhall Astra saloon which was seen in Foxlow around the time of the murder.

The driver of the car is described as a white male, aged around thirty-five years old, about five feet ten inches tall and of medium build. He was wearing a black Parker style coat with the hood up.

Anyone with information is asked to contact Edendale CID, or call the Crimestoppers line in confidence.

'A Parker style coat?' said Murfin when he saw the press release. 'Will that be from the same people who make pens?'

'Oh God,' said Cooper. 'That's embarrassing.'

'They mean "parka", don't they? Even I know that.'

Murfin folded the press release up and tried to create wings so that he could throw it across the CID room.

'It's not reading enough that does it, you know,' said Cooper. 'People hear "Parker" and "parka" on the TV and they sound like the same word.'

'Now, we'll have a load of old biddies going round looking for coats that say Parker on the label. I don't think "parka" is even a brand name, is it?'

'No, it's an Inuit word. It means a coat made from a fur pelt.'

'Well, I can see you read books all right, Ben. No one else I know would have that sort of information at their fingertips.'

'I might even find a use for it one day.'

'Our local pub has a quiz on Tuesday nights. Fancy going in for it some time? You can win a keg of beer.'

'I don't think so, Gavin. Thanks.'

'Oh, I forgot. You've got better things to do in

208

the evenings these days. Not allowed in the pub with your mates any more?'

'You've got it all wrong.'

To change the subject, Cooper asked Murfin if he'd heard about the fire service dog and its identification of accelerant at the house in Darwin Street.

'Now, me – I'm not a big fan of dogs,' said Murfin. 'Cats need less work to look after. And they don't crap on your lawn just because you haven't mowed it for a few weeks, like.'

'Working dogs are different,' said Cooper. 'I've seen that fire service dog in action at previous incidents. She has a great time when she's working. Absolutely loves it.'

'Well, I have to admit, the bitch did a good job at Darwin Street.'

Cooper caught a movement from the corner of his eye, and saw Diane Fry frozen in the doorway. She was staring at Murfin, and Cooper suddenly realized that she'd heard only the very last part of their conversation.

'Hi, Diane,' he said. 'We were just talking about the accelerant detection dog.'

Fry unfroze slowly. 'Oh, yes. That bitch.'

She moved forward into the room, waving a copy of the press release. 'Have you seen this?' she said. 'It's ridiculous.'

'Yes, we know,' said Murfin. 'We spotted it straightaway.'

'Somebody should speak to Media Relations.

This sort of thing makes us look stupid. I mean, what use is an appeal for information when they leave our phone number off?'

Murfin looked at the press release again. 'Oh,' he said. 'So they did.'

'The DI says we have a meeting tomorrow to review progress.'

'Another review? We never seem to do anything else.'

'It's better than wasting time and effort rushing off in the wrong direction,' said Fry. 'Regular reviews ensure the most effective use of resources.'

Cooper glanced at her. She was sounding more like a manager every day.

'Progress? What progress?' said Murfin.

Fry flushed. 'All right. That's enough.'

'Diane, before you go,' said Cooper. 'How obsessed would you say the Ridgeways were with exterminating squirrels?'

'Oh, very.'

'Obsessed enough to drive around the village at night shooting them out of the trees in other people's gardens?'

'Like Rose Shepherd's garden, for example?'

'Well, she has grey squirrels. If Mr and Mrs Ridgeway had taken a peek over her garden fence, they might have seen she was encouraging them and even feeding them, so decided to do something about it.'

'Without speaking to her about it?'

'Does that seem to fit their character?'

'Oh, yes. I can believe they'd opt for direct action. In fact, I think Mr Ridgeway probably blasts everything in sight that doesn't fit his criteria for being allowed to survive. You're thinking Rose Shepherd went to her bedroom window at the wrong moment and got hit by a stray shot?'

'Something like that.'

'In fact, there'd have to be three stray shots, wouldn't there?'

'True.'

'And – I'm sorry, Ben – but Mr Ridgeway only has an air rifle.'

'So he says.'

Fry gave it some thought. 'I didn't like either of the Ridgeways – as you probably gathered.'

'You don't always make a secret of your opinion.'

'And it's true that they sounded as though they were already offering some kind of justification. When they talked about alien invasions, they didn't just mean squirrels.'

'Can I hear a "but" coming?'

'Well, I think they're probably all mouth. The really dangerous ones act on their beliefs – they don't talk about them to any police officer who happens to come calling.'

'I see.'

'And, unfortunately, we don't have any evidence to justify searching their house for an automatic weapon.'

'Ah, that *is* true. We could ask them to let us do it voluntarily, though.'

'Tell you what, why don't you suggest your idea to the DI yourself, Ben? I'm only a supernumerary on the Shepherd enquiry. I've got other fish to catch.'

Before he switched off his computer, Cooper checked the Matlock Bath webcam to see if it was still running, as the site claimed.

When the picture came up, he saw it was already dark in Matlock Bath. He looked at his watch. Six o'clock. He hadn't realized it had got so late.

When he looked back at the screen, the webcam picture was reloading. Now the headlights of two cars were approaching the camera. But the only other colour in the image came from strings of lights hung along both banks of the river, and across the road. Some of the illuminations came close to the camera, mounted on the roof of Life in a Lens. Coloured lights also framed the iron girders of the Jubilee Bridge. The bridge was reflected on the surface water as a black, shapeless mass that disappeared into the trees on the other side of the river.

Across the river and into the trees. Where did that phrase come from? It must be a song, or possibly a book title. It made him think about the gunman who'd shot down a harmless middle-aged woman. If he was a professional, then there was something that no one was admitting out loud. He would be long gone from the area by now.

Never mind across the river and into the trees – their suspect could have been on the other side of the world before the clock even began to tick on the Shepherd enquiry.

Later that evening, Liz Petty sat in the upstairs room of Aitch's Wine Bar in Bakewell and accepted a glass of Merlot.

'Thanks, Ben.'

'Cheers.'

Cooper sat down next to her with his bottle of beer. The remains of their dinner had been cleared away, and he was starting to wonder whether chocolate truffle cake would go all right with the plum-and-chilli sauce that had been on the char-grilled chicken.

'Anyway, Quinton Downie was right,' said Petty. 'Fire can be one of the most difficult things to investigate. So many factors influence its behaviour that a scene can be very misleading.'

She took a drink of wine and gazed out of the window at Buxton Road. Liz lived just off Fly Hill, a couple of minutes' walk from the wine bar, in a three-storey terraced cottage she rented from her uncle. The third-floor bedroom had a terrific view beyond Bakewell towards the golf club.

'I remember something we were told on the course I did,' said Petty. 'It was a real incident, with photographs. A young child who'd died in a fire. It made me think of that case when I heard there were two children involved at Darwin Street. I know these two weren't burned to death, but still . . .'

Cooper waited, recognizing that she needed to sort her feelings out before she put them into words. Whatever it was that she wanted to tell him, it might be the first time she'd talked about it to anyone. He'd learned when to listen and not interrupt.

'You know that under the effects of intense heat, your brain expands?' Petty said at last.

'Yes, I think so.' Cooper put down his glass. He had a feeling it was going to be worse than he'd imagined. Chocolate truffle cake was suddenly less appealing.

'Well, a child's skull is a lot weaker than an adult's. The bones are very soft at first, you know. They showed us some photographs from this scene, where the young boy had died. The fire was so rapid and the temperature so high that when the child's brain expanded, it burst the skull. The captions said *skull failure and brain protrusion in a two-year-old fire victim*. And I was thinking, if you came on a scene like that, your assumption would probably be that the child had died from a serious head injury before the fire.'

'And that a fire had been started to conceal the evidence,' said Cooper. 'It happens.'

'Right. But it would be a wrong assumption. Chances are, it might just have been the fire.' Her voice dropped lower. 'It might only have been skull failure and brain protrusion. Only that.'

Cooper heard the break in her voice, and let the silence settle. It was as if a bubble had formed around their table, insulating them from the rest of the wine bar. He felt he could almost reach out and touch that rare thing, the ability of two people to think the same thoughts and share the same emotions without having to speak them out loud.

Then Liz reached out for his hand. 'You didn't want dessert, did you, Ben?'

'No, not really.'

'Let's pay the bill, then.'

Stella Searle looked away from the TV set in her bedroom towards the shower, where she could hear water running. Darren had bought her the TV himself. He'd do almost anything to keep her happy, except the one thing she really wanted.

'Daz!' she called. But she only heard him humming some tune to himself, like a cocky child, and she had to call him again. 'Darren!'

'What's up?'

'Come out here.'

'I'm having a shower, darling.'

'Come out here. There's something on the telly you've got to see.'

'It'll wait. I won't be a minute.'

'No – now,' she said, using the tone of voice she knew he'd recognize.

'Oh, bloody hell.'

The water stopped, and after a moment he padded out into the bedroom with a towel wrapped round his middle, his hair wet and feet making damp marks on the floor.

'What is it, Stell?'

She looked back at the screen, but the newsreader had moved on to another item, something about petrol prices.

'It's gone off now.'

'Fuck's sake, darling. If I don't get finished in the shower, I'll be late home. Fiona will throw a bloody fit.'

Stella took no notice of his mood, or his swearing. Darren was all mouth. She knew she had total control over him.

'They were doing a bit about the woman who got shot in the village the other night.'

'Oh, that. Yeah, I heard about it.'

He turned and began to head back towards the shower, clutching at the towel to keep it in place. His backside was too big, excess fat padding out his hips. Darren thought he was fit, but he spent too much time driving, or sitting around with his mates drinking beer.

'It said the police are looking for a car. And a man that someone saw in the village that night.'

Darren hesitated with his hand on the door of the shower cubicle. 'Good. They'll get the bugger that did it, then. We can't have blokes walking about shooting old women dead like that.'

'She wasn't all that old,' said Stella. 'Sixty-odd, they said. It's nothing these days.'

'If you say so.'

Darren slipped off the towel and went back into the shower. The water had started to trickle from the shower head, but she knew he heard her when she spoke again.

'I reckon it was your car that someone saw,' she said. 'Daz, I think it's you they're looking for.'

'Give over.'

'I think you should go to the police,' she said.

'You must have got it wrong. It wasn't anything to do with me.'

'I'm only telling you what it said.'

'Well, what did it say *exactly*?' he snapped.

'I can't remember *exactly*. It was something about a blue Vauxhall Astra. That's your car, isn't it?'

'Well, it might be,' said Darren. 'What else did it say?'

'A man in a parka – that was it. Aged about thirty-five.'

'I'm not thirty-five.'

'You look it, though.'

He gave her an incredulous stare. 'Thanks a lot.'

'It was you, Darren,' she said stubbornly. 'Well, it sounded like you. Your car, and a man in a parka, seen in the village about the time of the incident. That's exactly what it said. I think.'

'And they reckon this man in the parka did the shooting? That's ridiculous, Stell. That's stupid.'

217

'No, that wasn't quite it.'

'Oh, for God's sake. Why can't you remember anything properly? You're so bloody thick, Stella. I don't know why I bother with you.'

'Piss off, Darren.'

He stamped off sulkily, but came straight back again. 'I need to know exactly what they said, Stella. This is important.'

'Witnesses, that was it. They said the police were looking for witnesses. And they particularly wanted to speak to the bloke in the parka, with the blue Astra.'

Darren didn't reply. She glanced at him, and saw that he'd gone pale. He still wasn't fully dressed, and the water was drying in patches on his arms. He shivered, like somebody had walked over his grave. She remembered him saying how much he hated being next to a graveyard, and all those dead bodies and stuff.

'A witness, that's what they reckon you are. Maybe the police think you might have seen something important. Did you see anything, Darren?'

Darren was silent for longer than she thought was natural. For him, anyway. He wasn't the sort of bloke to be stuck for a word, even if it was to tell her to 'eff off'. He was staring at the TV screen, though the news had long since finished, and there was some football match on.

'Did you, Darren?'

'No,' he said finally. But he didn't sound too sure.

Stella touched his chest, then flinched away at the coldness of it.

'No,' he said again. 'I didn't see anything.'

'Was there anybody about in the village when you left that night?'

'I just told you, I didn't see anything.'

'You might be able to help the police find who did it.'

He grabbed her arm then, and for the first time Stella felt a chill of fear. He was stronger than she thought, and he had that possibility of violence in him, after all.

'Get it into your head right now,' he said. 'I didn't see anything that night. Got it, Stell? I didn't see a bloody thing.'

Cooper always woke automatically to the sound of sirens, even when he was in unfamiliar surroundings. He listened for a few moments, until he recognized the distinctive rasping bullhorn of a fire tender approaching a road junction somewhere to the north. So it was nothing to do with him – not for a while, at least. At this time of year, the call-out was probably to a bonfire that had been prematurely set alight. It happened every year; some people just couldn't wait for the fifth of November. Soon there'd be fireworks, too. Night after night of explosions over the town. Complaints to the police about youths pushing bangers through pensioners' letter boxes.

The sirens receded gradually into the distance.

219

Cooper remembered where he was, sighed, and turned over again. He felt the comfort of a warm body beside him in the bed, the reassurance of steady breathing that meant he wasn't alone in the middle of the night.

It made a big difference, not to be alone. And for once, it wasn't the cat.

15

It was Jimi Hendrix. When Cooper saw the can of Swan lighter fluid next morning, he knew immediately where he'd seen one before. It featured in one of those classic rock posters. Hendrix setting fire to his white Stratocaster at the Monterey Pop Festival.

Could it have been 1967? Somewhere around that time. The legend said that Hendrix felt upstaged by The Who, because the British group had ended their set by smashing their equipment. During his own last number, the guitarist had grinned at the audience, squirted lighter fuel on his guitar and struck a match, playing the final notes through the flames. It was one of the seminal moments in the history of rock music. Mad, and dangerous.

'You can buy the hundred millilitre can for about three pounds, but it isn't stocked everywhere,' said Fry, when he'd examined the can.

'That gives us a chance of tracing the shop it was bought from, then.'

'Yes, it would do, if we had the manpower.'

In the poster Cooper remembered seeing on a friend's bedroom wall, the can had been clearly visible in the guitarist's hands. It was just like this one – square-sided and yellow, the same colour as Hendrix's frilly shirt.

'Anyway, we've got an initial report faxed through from Downie's people at the FSS lab this morning.' The neutral tone of Fry's voice didn't give away whether it was good news or bad news.

'What does it say?'

'I'll read it for you: "The laboratory received two evidence containers of debris taken from the suspected seat of a fire. A head space sample from each container was subjected to gas chromatograph analysis. The chromatogram shows characteristic peak patterns of a common hydrocarbon fuel, n-Butane."'

'Lighter fluid, then.'

'Right. Specifically, butane lighter fluid. The positive samples were taken from a section of carpet in the Mullens' sitting room, and from the toy box in the corner near the video. Not much accelerant used – but then, it wouldn't have needed a lot.'

'It could have been an accidental spillage, couldn't it?' suggested Cooper.

'Have you tried accidentally spilling lighter fluid, Ben?'

'I don't even smoke. I never have.'

'Well, it comes in an aerosol can like this one, with a pressure valve that fits into the lighter.'

'OK, I've seen it.'

'The most you can do accidentally is create a bit of mist that makes your fingers feel cold. To spill it, you have to prise the top off the can.'

'Even so, Diane, one of the Mullens' kids could have done that.'

'Maybe. So which of the Mullens was a smoker – Brian or Lindsay?'

'I don't know.'

'The answer is, neither. And why didn't the SOCOs find a lighter fluid can in the house? They're metal, so it wouldn't have been destroyed in the fire.'

'I don't know that either.'

'Because there wasn't one, Ben. The only can that's turned up is this one, which was found in a wheelie bin down the road. And if this is the right one, then it wasn't put there by accident.'

Fry had called a meeting of what was left of her team. They were waiting for Murfin, but he was finishing a phone call, typing one more paragraph of a vital report, trying to make the point that he had too much work to do already.

'Right, there are things to be done in the Darwin Street arson enquiry,' she said.

'Such as?' asked Murfin.

'We need to chase up forensics from the fire scene – particularly that sitting room. Brian Mullen swears that he never went in there that night. If we find any evidence of his presence in the room after the fire started, then we can demonstrate that he's lying.'

'Right.'

'Obviously, somebody will have to interview this Jed Skinner. That should happen as soon as possible, before it occurs to Mullen to contact Skinner and they get their story straight.'

'I'll do that, if you like,' said Cooper.

'No, let Gavin go.'

'OK. What, then?'

'You can come with me to the hospital. I want your opinion on Mr Brian Mullen.'

'Really?'

'Don't look so surprised – it isn't the first time I've asked for your opinion, Ben.'

'Well . . .'

'Also, Mullen's story is that he arrived home from the Broken Wheel in a taxi, which dropped him off at the end of the street. I've already spoken once to the next-door neighbour, Keith Wade, but I want to know about a conversation they supposedly had. Wade must have witnessed Mullen going into the house on his abortive rescue mission. It would be useful if he happened to see his neighbour arriving in the street, too.'

'From the taxi?'

'That's another thing –'

'You want us to find the taxi driver.'

'Exactly. Confirm the time and place he picked

Mullen up, and where he dropped him off. And then I'd like to know what happened to Skinner. Did the driver see him outside the club? Did he and Mullen share a taxi, even?'

'I wonder if Mr Wade is aware of any problems between Mullen and his wife?' said Cooper. 'If he lives in an adjoining semi, he might have been close enough to hear any arguments.'

'We should ask all the neighbours that,' said Fry. 'Discreetly, of course.'

Cooper looked at the map to check the relative locations of the fire and the wheelie bin where the lighter fluid can had been found.

'By the way, this isn't the Shrubs,' he said, pointing at the map. 'The area's called that because of the names of the streets.'

'I know that.'

'Well, since when has Darwin been a shrub?'

'It's close.'

'Close? In an evolutionary sense, or what?'

'Geographically. Look, Lilac Avenue is just over there, no more than three hundred yards away. Myrtle Drive is next to it. It's nothing to make a fuss about.'

'No one on Darwin Street would consider themselves to be living in the Shrubs,' said Cooper. 'These things are important to people.'

Before they left, Cooper saw that two bin liners full of clothes had also been brought back from the Mullens' house by the SOCOs for examination, though no one seemed to have any idea what

225

they were expecting to find. Sometimes they took protect and preserve a bit too far.

'Oh, you're back,' said Brian Mullen when they entered his room at the hospital. His voice sounded a bit better now, but for a slight tendency to squeak on the last syllable of a sentence.

'Sorry to bother you again, sir,' said Fry. 'This is my colleague, DC Cooper.'

'Do you have some information?'

'Sorry?'

'You said you'd keep me informed.'

'Oh, yes. Well, I'm afraid it's still early days yet. But I do have a few more questions.'

'Questions again?'

'I'm trying to get things straight in my mind. To clarify what happened the night your family died. Is that all right, sir?'

He lay back wearily. 'I suppose so. As long as I can get out of here.'

Fry opened her notebook. 'According to what you told me previously, you arrived home at about one thirty after your taxi dropped you off at the corner of Darwin Street. You saw the fire, but didn't realize it was your own house until you were closer.'

'That's right.'

'Who did you say you were out with, by the way?'

He was distracted by the question, which was what she wanted.

226

'One of my mates, Jed Skinner. I work with him at the distribution centre.'

'Oh, you're a despatch manager, aren't you?'

'That's right. Jed's in the transport department.'

'Just one mate, was it?'

'Eh?'

'Just you and Jed out for the night?'

'Yes, like I said.'

Fry looked at her notebook. 'You told me you were "out with mates". That's "mates", plural.'

'Well, I might have said that.'

'Why?'

'Look, we were in the pub first off – the Forester's Arms. I know a lot of people in there, I'm a regular. So I *was* with lots of mates then.'

'But only Jed at the Broken Wheel?'

'Like I said.'

'You went there alone, the two of you? And you left together, just the two of you again?'

'Yes.'

'And that was just after one. So the next person you spoke to must have been the taxi driver. And then there was your neighbour, Mr Wade. Shortly after that, you ran into the house, then the fire-fighters pulled you back out.'

'I've told you all this. For God's sake –'

Mullen controlled his burst of anger, then raised his still bandaged hands, as if presenting the evidence.

'And you can't remember what you burned yourself on, Mr Mullen?'

'I told you, it was the banister rail. It must have been that, because it was the only thing I touched.'

'Ah, yes. And it's made of wood, so it would have been burning, or at least smouldering. But the banister rail is only on one side of the stairs – the other side is a blank wall. Would you have touched the banisters with both hands?'

'I must have done.'

Mullen held up his hands again, as if he thought she couldn't see them. The facts were indisputable, he seemed to say.

Fry wished she could have taken swabs from his hands to test for traces of accelerant on his skin, but she had no evidence to push it so far. And it was too late now anyway.

'Look, maybe I panicked and touched it with the other hand on the way down,' said Mullen.

'It's possible.'

'Of course it is.'

'And you didn't go into any of the rooms downstairs?' asked Fry. 'The sitting room, for example?'

'No. Why would I do that? Like I told you yesterday, I knew my family would be in bed at that hour.'

'We believe the fire started in the sitting room. It must have been obvious when you entered the house that the smoke was coming from there. Are you quite sure you didn't go into the sitting room, or even touch the sitting-room door?'

'Yes, I'm sure.'

Mullen was starting to look sulky and irritable.

Fry gave Cooper a look that told him to take over for a while.

'Do you smoke, sir?' asked Cooper.

'No.'

'What about your wife? I'm sorry to ask –'

'No, Lindsay didn't smoke either. I can see what you're driving at, but we both agreed not to smoke a long time ago, for the sake of the kids. Passive smoking is very damaging to young children. Their air passages are so small they breathe in far more smoke than an adult would.'

'I see. What about other members of your family?'

'There's only John who's ever smoked. But he knows not to when he's in our house . . .'

'. . . for the sake of the kids, yes,' said Fry.

Cooper consulted the notes Fry had given him. 'John? That would be John Lowther, your brother-in-law?'

'Yes.'

Fry noticed a nurse hovering in the background. 'We'll let you rest now, Mr Mullen. I realize you've had a terrible ordeal, and we appreciate your time and co-operation.'

'It's OK. Obviously, I want to help. I mean, it was my wife and kids who got killed in that fire. If some bastard –'

Fry stood up. 'I understand. Well, until we speak again, Mr Mullen, I'd like you to see if you can remember who else you spoke to that night at the Forester's Arms and at the Broken Wheel, and the names of everyone who was there that you knew.'

'*What?*'

'Well, think about it, sir. If that fire *was* started deliberately, it might have been done by someone who knew that you'd be out of the house at the time. Someone who'd seen you partying at the Broken Wheel with your friend Jed, perhaps.'

Mullen nodded silently.

'Still can't think of anyone?'

'No.'

'Well, we'll keep making enquiries.'

'You've talked to Henry and Moira as well, haven't you?'

'Yes, I visited them the day before yesterday.'

'Why did you have to bother them? They're devastated about Lindsay and the children. We all are.'

'There might be some detail that Mr and Mrs Lowther have noticed. A person they've seen near your house, for example.'

Mullen's expression darkened further. 'You're not letting go of this idea that the fire was started deliberately?'

'No, we're not letting go of it, Mr Mullen,' said Fry. 'Is there some reason that you think we should?'

'I just don't see how it's possible.'

'We'll know that better when we get the results of the forensic examination.'

His shoulders sagged at the mention of forensics.

Sometimes, the word seemed to carry a symbolic power, as if it was a scientific magic that human beings were helpless to challenge. And perhaps that was right. Forensic evidence could kick-start a process that was impossible to stop until the criminal justice juggernaut had crushed everyone in its way.

'Leave me alone,' he said. 'Leave us alone. Someone has got to look after Luanne.'

'I thought you were a bit rough on Mr Mullen,' said Cooper as they left the hospital and walked to the car park.

'Yes, I was. And wouldn't you have expected him to complain a bit more?'

'But if he *had* complained more, then you'd be saying he protested too much, and that was a sure sign of guilt.'

Fry laughed. 'Look, you know the husband is by far the likeliest candidate in a case like this.'

'Statistically speaking, yes.'

'So we have to look at him thoroughly. There shouldn't be any question of letting him get away with conflicting statements, just because he's supposed to be the grieving husband.'

'Conflicting statements?'

'Yes, like when "out with mates" suddenly becomes just one mate when he's pressed. It sounds to me as if good old Jed is the only mate Mr Mullen actually had lined up for an alibi. He had to change his story when he was asked for names. Not enough attention to detail, you see.'

'Diane, you've got him well and truly in the frame already, haven't you?'

'We'll see. What's the betting there are a few more little details Mr Mullen hasn't paid enough attention to?'

'You've given him a chance to work out his story now, though. You warned him you were going to ask for more names.'

'That's right.'

'Well, if Mr Mullen wasn't at the Broken Wheel that night, he wouldn't be able to make up names off the top of his head, would he? So shouldn't we have asked him right there and then?'

'My guess is he'd have said he couldn't remember. And if I tried pushing him, I'd look like a heartless bitch.'

'True.'

'And Mr Mullen would have got all stressed, and a doctor would have come and kicked us out.'

'So . . .?'

'So this way, I've done the caring and considerate bit and given him time to think about it while he's recovering from his injuries. If I've judged him right, the longer he has to think about it, the more anxious he'll get. Then he'll start trying to think up something to give us when we come back. That's where he'll go wrong.'

'Diane, I wouldn't have believed it possible, but I think you're getting more devious than ever.'

'Thank you.'

'You really think these tactics will work on Brian Mullen?'

'Yes. Don't you?'

'Only if he's guilty.'

For once, Keith Wade wasn't out in his garden supervising operations in Darwin Street. Not that there was much to see now, apart from the tent, a few metres of tape outside number 32, and a different member of the chorus from *Pirates* rehearsing his act at the gate.

Cooper had to ring the bell of Wade's house for several minutes before there was a thumping on the stairs in the hallway and the door opened. Wade glared at Cooper, then recognized Fry standing behind him.

'What's happened?' he said. 'What's the panic?'

He was unshaven and bleary-eyed, dressed in tracksuit bottoms and a T-shirt that looked as though it had just been thrown on. Well, at least he didn't sleep in the woolly sweater. And he hadn't said 'where's the fire?', which might have seemed tasteless.

'Sorry, did we wake you up, sir?' said Fry.

'Yes, I told you – I do late shifts.'

'We won't keep you long. This is my colleague, DC Cooper.'

Wade glanced up and down the street. 'You'd better come in a minute.'

His house was pretty much what she would

have expected from a divorced man living on his own. Stale smells of cooking and body odour, mingling with cigarette smoke. He had to move piles of newspapers off chairs to let them sit down, and one glimpse of the kitchen told Fry that its condition wouldn't compare to Lindsay Mullen's, even after a disastrous fire.

'Yes, of course I remember Brian arriving that night,' said Wade when she prompted him. 'How is he, by the way?'

'Physically fine. We hope he'll be discharged today.'

'Great. He's a brave bloke, you know.'

'Did you see how he arrived?'

'No. He was only a couple of houses away by the time I saw him. There was too much else going on, you know. He looked pretty dazed, but he recognized me.'

'What did he say?'

Wade frowned. 'I can't remember exactly. Should I have taken notes? It didn't seem that important.'

'No, I understand. But if you could try . . .'

'Well, he wanted to know if Lindsay and the kids were still in the house,' said Wade. 'That's what he was bothered about, obviously. When I said I thought they were, he went sort of berserk and ran off.'

'And that's when he tried to get into the house?'

'He *did* get in. The firemen had broken the door down by then. Brian ran past them and was in the house before they could stop him. Brave, like I said. I feel really sorry for him, you know. We've always been good friends, and good neighbours. As for little Jack and Liam, they were nice lads. It's such a shame.'

For the second time, Wade seemed to have forgotten that Lindsay Mullen had died in the fire, too. It might be unconscious, but there had to be a reason for the oversight.

'How had Brian and Lindsay been getting on recently?' asked Fry.

'Sorry?'

'You knew them well, and you live right next door. You must have been aware of any problems in their marriage. Domestic arguments tend to get a bit loud, and you're only a few feet away.'

Wade shifted uneasily. 'I don't want to say anything bad about them. It wouldn't be right.'

'In these circumstances, it's not right to keep anything back,' said Fry. 'You must try to be objective if you're going to help us, sir.'

He looked at her, and then at Cooper. Battling with his conscience – if he had one. Or weighing up which approach would be most to his advantage, perhaps. Fry was pleased they'd got him out of bed. His replies might be a little less calculated than if they'd caught him in his guardian-of-the-streets mode.

'OK, I have heard a few rows from next door,' he said. 'But it's normal, isn't it? God knows, I had enough bust-ups with Pat before she left.'

'Did the Mullens' arguments happen recently?' asked Cooper.

'Well, there'd been more of them recently. I could hear the shouting, not what they were arguing about, you understand. I wasn't eavesdropping.'

'Of course not.'

Wade hesitated. 'Come to think of it, I reckon I heard them arguing on Sunday night.'

'The night of the fire?'

'Yes, it must have been before Brian went out. I recall he slammed the front door a bit hard as he left.'

'These arguments, were they getting worse?' asked Fry. 'Do you think they might have been close to breaking up?'

'Breaking up? Why would they?'

'Well, it happened to you, didn't it?'

Wade seemed to consider that. 'Perhaps Lindsay was under stress, with the three children. It can put pressure on a couple, I reckon. But walking away from a marriage doesn't make it better.'

'Do you and your ex-wife have any children, sir?'

'No, we never had kids. Pity – I've always liked children.'

Before they left his house, Fry reminded Wade of his promise to email the photos from his digital camera. 'If you prefer, we could borrow the camera now and return it when we've downloaded the pictures?'

'No, no – I'll do it,' said Wade. 'I've been a bit busy, that's all. But I'll get around to it, I promise.'

Outside, Fry pulled out her phone and called Gavin Murfin.

'How are you getting on, Gavin?'

'I haven't been able to trace the taxi driver yet. Jed Skinner can't remember which firm it was that Brian Mullen used that night. Skinner lives in Lowbridge, so the two of them went off in completely different directions when they left the Broken Wheel. I'm running out of time now, Diane, so it's going to have to wait.'

'OK, Gavin. But otherwise, how was Skinner?'

'A bit oily.'

'Sorry?'

'I found him in the transport department at the distribution centre. He must be their lubrication specialist, by the look of him. Anyway, he confirms Brian Mullen's story to the letter. They went to the Forester's Arms first, then on to the Broken Wheel. They left some time after one. He saw Mullen get into the taxi.'

'Right. Thanks, Gavin.'

Murfin breathed heavily in her ear for a moment before he rang off.

'Jed Skinner was word perfect, Diane,' he said. 'I wish you luck if you're going to try to break *that* alibi.'

16

Fry found a message waiting for her when she got back to the office. *DS Fry, please see the DI. ASAP.* Everything was ASAP around here.

DI Hitchens had strong hands, with clean, carefully trimmed fingernails. He placed them on his desk in his most serious manner. There was still no ring on his finger, though he'd lived with a nurse for a couple of years now, and they'd bought a home together in Dronfield Woodhouse. Fry wondered again about the white scar that crawled across the middle knuckles of his fingers. No one had ever mentioned him getting injured, or being involved in a fight. It looked intriguing. But then, it was probably just the result of something very boring – an accident with a potato peeler, or a hand caught in the blades of a lawn mower.

'Diane,' he said when she entered his office, 'we've had a call from the Forensic Science Service.'

'A result?'

'Well, no. More of a complaint, actually.'

She sat down without waiting to be invited. 'What's the matter with them?'

'Apparently, their fire investigation specialist, a Mr, er . . .'

'Downie.'

'Yes, that's it. He seems to feel you didn't get off on the right foot at Darwin Street. His boss gave me some stuff about co-operation and all pulling in the same direction. Do you know what he's on about?'

'Downie's a bit of a pillock,' said Fry.

Hitchens couldn't help grinning. 'Civilians, eh? Who let them into the equation?'

'Right.'

'Well, could you try to get on a bit better while you have to work with him? It would help relations all round.'

'I can do that.'

'Great. We've got to keep on side with our partners. It doesn't do any good to get "unco-operative" on your record, I can tell you.'

Watching Hitchens, Fry guessed that he was starting to find the job of DI unsatisfactory. The hours were long, the responsibility more and more onerous. And he must be reflecting that the increase in pay from a DS wasn't worth the hassle.

'So how's the fire enquiry going generally, Diane?'

'The dog got a hit, as you know. And this morning

the FSS confirmed the presence of accelerant – butane, just like the lighter fluid can the search team found. It's a triple suspicious death, sir.'

'Oh, brilliant.' Hitchens spun anxiously in his chair. 'Do you have any potential suspects?'

'I favour the husband quite strongly. There's no one else in the picture, so far as I can see. There's a possibility of forced entry, but that could be a blind. The Mullens don't seem like a family anyone would have a grudge against.'

'So once you get a full report from the FSS, you'll be looking to build a case against the husband?'

'Unless he eliminates himself pretty quickly,' said Fry. 'And I'd be surprised if he manages to do that. I'm going to work on his alibi, and take a look at his relationship with his wife. I know there's been at least one public row between them recently.'

'After the meeting, we'll brief the DCI together,' said Hitchens. 'I can tell you, Diane, he won't be thrilled.'

The big news at West Street before the morning briefing was that two enquiry teams were being formed, and the Rose Shepherd shooting was to be a joint operation with A Division. At least the NCOF wasn't getting in on the action.

'A Division?' said Murfin. 'A for Alfreton, Arse End of the Universe? They'll be down to two men and a dog, and not for the first time.'

'There'll be some monthly targets missed, that's for sure,' said Cooper.

'Ah, well. Achieving a lot with a little,' said Murfin cheerfully.

'Gavin, just repeating the Chief Super's catchphrase all the time doesn't help.'

The conference room was packed for the meeting, with many officers pulled in from elsewhere to beef up the enquiry teams. Cooper saw Diane Fry come in and sit on the front row, with Wayne Abbott on one side of her and a CPS prosecutor on the other. From her body language, she seemed not to have noticed either of them. At one point, the lawyer leaned past her to speak to the crime-scene manager. Fry never even blinked, let alone took any part in their conversation. Cooper shook his head, perplexed. Fry's ability to be alone in a crowded room never failed to amaze him.

'First of all, we've had no luck tracing the Vauxhall Astra,' said Hitchens when the briefing got under way. 'Besides, it appears the Astra was never in the field behind the victim's house anyway.'

A scatter of groans and mutterings followed this announcement, as a potential lead seemed to slip away.

'Forensics tell us the tracks were made by something bigger than an Astra. More weight, wider tyres. And four-wheel drive.'

Murfin rolled his eyes towards the ceiling, and

Cooper knew what he was thinking. At one time, someone would have made that assessment at a glance. But now, everyone was cautious. The tests had to be gone through, even if they took two days to reach the same conclusion.

'We don't have any reports of a vehicle like that, do we?' said someone.

'What sort of tyres?' added another voice.

'We'll get a match on the tread,' put in Abbott. 'It just takes a bit more time.'

'Back to the drawing board, then.'

Hitchens was trying not to let his shoulders slump. 'We're starting to get a picture of the victim's movements on the afternoon before she died. We're concentrating on two people that Rose Shepherd met in Matlock Bath. The descriptions from the waitress who served them are pretty vague, but we'll ask her to have a go at some e-fits, and there'll be more appeals in the media. Those two could be important – they're the only people we know of who had contact with Miss Shepherd that day.'

He turned to the board, where photographs of the dead woman were displayed.

'Meanwhile, the victim herself remains a mystery. What we've got here is a woman who kept herself to herself in an extreme way. She had as little contact with people in Foxlow as she could possibly manage, and we've found almost nothing of a personal nature in her house that could lead us to anyone who knew her. That's got to be deliberate.'

'You think so?'

'I can't believe that it's accidental. We've gone through all her papers: bank statements, phone bills, any personal correspondence we can find – which isn't much. We finally located a diary, but it's only one of those little pocket-size appointment diaries. We're checking all the entries in her address book. There's always a possibility that some of the entries are coded or camouflaged in some way. Most of all, we need to trace anyone who ever dealt with Miss Shepherd, particularly if they visited Bain House and actually met her.'

'We're not likely to find a Christmas card list, I suppose?'

'No such luck, sorry. Judging by her phone records, Miss Shepherd doesn't seem to have had many friends – not unless they worked at the local garage or the GP's surgery in Matlock. Those seem to be the places she phoned most often. Apart from that, there are just a couple of puzzlers . . .'

Hitchens paused, perhaps for dramatic effect.

'Firstly, the victim's phone records for the past three weeks show two calls to the same public phone box, which turns out to be in a rural location in Bonsall Dale. Obviously, if you're going to phone someone in an isolated call box, it would have to be by prior arrangement.'

There was a bit of fidgeting around the room, but no one could suggest a reason why Rose Shepherd should have been ringing a call box. A random call, perhaps, hoping to make contact with a complete stranger to talk to? Who could say?

'Does 359 figure in the number of the call box?' asked Cooper.

'Good question. The answer is no. Secondly,' said Hitchens, 'there are a couple of diary entries which refer to someone with the initials SN. There was an entry in her address book too, but it had been crossed out.'

'If we can still read the number . . .'

'It's another unregistered pay-as-you-go mobile.'

'This woman is unnatural.'

'Well, let's not get downhearted. I've saved the good news for last. We do have a couple of possibilities, which will be prioritized today. Number one, there's the victim's GP. He's away at the moment, but at least he should be able to confirm an ID when he gets back, and he might have some information for us, if he ever talked to Miss Shepherd properly. Number two, there's the estate agent who handled the house sale. We found the name of the firm in the victim's phone book – Windsor and Ellis. They're checking their records to see who dealt with Miss Shepherd, and whether that person still works there. Presumably there would have been a solicitor involved, too, when she bought Bain House, though there's no sign of any lawyers in the address book.'

'The estate agents ought to be able to give us that, too.'

'Right. And house-to-house is complete, but as usual we should treat the results with caution.'

'We've done the whole village?'

'Yes, all of it. And we're still getting calls from the public in response to the media appeals. Almost everything we've got so far has been third hand and uncorroborated, unfortunately. Nevertheless, I've asked the incident-room staff to collate the information and hopefully eliminate anything that's been made up on the spot by some eager citizen trying to be too helpful.'

'What are we left with?'

'Well, the consensus in Foxlow is that Rose Shepherd was a retired headmistress who had been working in Scotland but came down here to live after she inherited money from an elderly relative. Some say her father, others an uncle.'

'That would explain the purchase of Bain House, but not her secretiveness.'

'There's more: the word in the village is that she kept her valuables in the house, in some kind of secret stash, and that she was terrified the house might be burgled. There have been a number of break-ins in this area.'

'Yes, that's right.'

'The last tidbit is that Rose Shepherd is said to have a boyfriend back in Scotland. She called him Douglas or Dougie, and he lives near Glasgow.'

'Has Dougie ever been seen in Foxlow?' asked Kessen.

'Not so far as we know.'

'Damn it. This means we're going to have to ask for assistance from Strathclyde Police. If they can track down a Rose Shepherd who was a head-mistress in their area, it might lead us to Dougie. I'll ask them to get Taggart on the job.'

'There's more. The really good news is that we've found someone locally who had direct contact with Miss Shepherd.'

'Hallelujah.'

'It's a chap by the name of Eric Grice, who seems to be some kind of handyman. He doesn't live in Foxlow, but apparently he did occasional work at Bain House. So he's actually spoken to the victim.'

'Perhaps he can tell us why she hardly ever left the house.'

'One suggestion is that she might have been suffering from agoraphobia. An irrational fear of open spaces.'

'But she went into Matlock Bath, didn't she?' said Cooper.

'Yes, and nobody reported her in any distress at being outdoors. We've spoken to her GP's surgery, and she only ever consulted her doctor for insomnia. She seemed to be in good health otherwise, but she hadn't been on his list for very long. Also, the surgery don't have access to her previous medical records. Miss Shepherd told them she'd been living abroad . . .' Hitchens paused. 'Besides, whatever Rose Shepherd was afraid of, it wasn't an irrational fear. The bullets that killed her were real enough.'

'Do we have an update on the bullets?' asked Kessen.

'Well, they've gone to the lab,' said Wayne Abbott. 'The one removed from the wall of the bedroom was too badly damaged to be any use, but the two the pathologist recovered have their surface marks intact. The firearms examiner should be able to give us the make, model and calibre of the weapon, with a bit of luck. And if we manage to locate the weapon, we can match it up to the bullets with a fair degree of certainty.'

'Can't we run the bullets through the ballistics database?'

'You mean IBIS? Well, we could – but what result would you be hoping for?'

'A match that would help us identify the weapon, of course,' said Kessen.

Abbott shook his head. 'I think there might be a misunderstanding of what the database can do. You can only get an identification of a firearm if it's been found somewhere and test fired in the lab. But this weapon is still out there, being used. It won't be recorded in the database.'

'But if the same firearm was used in an earlier incident where the bullets were found, could we establish a link?'

'Perhaps. Provided details from the previous incident have been entered into the database.'

'Ask them to try, then,' said Kessen.

'If you say so.'

'What about the PM report, Paul?'

'Pretty much what we expected. One bullet entered near the victim's left eye and ricocheted around the brain for a bit before lodging behind the right ear. The other penetrated her left lung and was removed from a site close to her spine. A high-powered rifle can do a lot of damage to a human body.'

Hitchens pinned more photographs on the board. From the location of the bullet near the spine, ripples had spread out like a stone dropped in a pond, tearing flesh and crushing soft tissue. The body was almost all water, after all – and the energy of a bullet's impact was converted into hydrostatic force, equivalent to the devastation of a tsunami.

'So far, we can't put anyone else at the scene,' said the DI. 'In fact, we don't even have anyone to perform an official identification until her GP returns. According to the post-mortem report, the victim was medically incapable of conceiving, so there are no children in the picture. Right now, the nearest thing to a next of kin is her part-time handyman.'

After the briefing, Fry went with Hitchens to the DCI's office to report her progress on the Darwin Street fire enquiry.

'When he's well enough, I want to take the husband back to the scene,' she said, after she'd finished bringing her senior officers up to speed. 'Today, if possible. As soon as he's discharged from hospital.'

'Why?'

'For a start, I want to see how he reacts. His response to the deaths of his wife and children has been a bit difficult to judge so far, but that could be the sedatives they're giving him at the hospital. Also, I haven't told him any details of how the fire started. I'd like to see if he's drawn to the seat of the fire, or if he lets slip something that he shouldn't know. Alternatively, if he's innocent, he might be able to point us to some item that doesn't belong in the house, which might indicate an intruder or a visitor that we don't know about.'

'So you fancy the husband for this one, Diane?'

'Yes, sir. The neighbours say there had been problems in the marriage. Mr Mullen even moved out for a while, though it's not known where he went. And his alibi for the time the fire started is a bit suspect – it relies entirely on his best friend, a man by the name of Jed Skinner. I think I might be able to break that alibi down without too much trouble. But I need to do it before Mr Mullen is discharged from hospital, so they can't get together and tighten up their story.'

Kessen looked at her report. 'If Mr Mullen *is* telling the truth, there must be at least one other person who can substantiate his alibi – the taxi driver who brought him home.'

'Admittedly, we haven't traced the driver yet. But even if we do, there was plenty of time for Mr Mullen to start the fire, get clear of the area

249

and catch a taxi back again, arriving when the blaze had taken hold. Then he could draw conspicuous attention to his arrival by doing his tragic hero act in full view of the neighbours. Not to mention the police and firefighters, who were bound to hold him back, so he wouldn't have to be too much of a hero.'

'What if he'd timed it wrong, and arrived before the fire crews?'

'It was a small gamble. Perhaps he had trust in the emergency services. Or perhaps he had more faith in his neighbour spotting the smoke.'

'OK, it's possible.'

'I've also taken possession of the clothes Mr Mullen was wearing on the night in question. With your permission, I'd like to get them to the lab.'

'You're hoping to find traces of accelerant on his clothing?'

'Yes, sir.'

'What about motive?'

'If the marriage was in trouble, I'm thinking it might have come to a head recently. For example, if Mrs Mullen had told him he had to move out, or she was filing for divorce, he might have been upset about her taking the children away. It's happened before.'

Kessen nodded. 'The dog in the manger mentality: "If I can't have the children, you're not having them either." '

'Yes, sir. There's one interesting fact from the

FSS fire investigator, Quinton Downie. He says the fire wasn't started in any of the logical places for a random arson attack. Rather, it began where the children's toys were stored in the sitting room. Apparently, accelerant was poured over them, as well as on the carpet. That might prove to be significant. It makes the attack seem very personal.'

'And it was carried out by someone who was able to get access to the house.'

'Yes. I'm not convinced by the side window being forced. There are no signs of entry inside the room. It's a kitchen window, and I'd expect to find marks on the window ledge or the work surfaces, but nothing's been disturbed. The kitchen looks positively pristine.'

'Footwear impressions outside?'

Fry shook her head. 'Not after the firefighters had done their bit.'

The DCI looked thoughtful for a moment. But he wasn't a man to take long over a decision.

'OK. It sounds as though you've done all the right things, Diane. We'll review the enquiry again as soon as you've got some forensic reports. I'll be your SIO for now, so make sure you keep me up to date with any developments.'

'Thank you, sir.'

'Are you certain the scene was closed down tight from the start, and every bit of potential evidence was preserved? I know you've had the FSS in. That was a good move.'

'Yes, sir,' said Fry. 'Everything by the book.'

'Let's hope your feeling about the husband is correct, then. If we have to eliminate him, it opens up a whole different ball game. A triple murder with no suspects is the last thing we need right now, Diane.'

'What are you lot talking about?' asked Fry when she came back into the CID room and saw Cooper and Murfin deep in conversation with the trainees.

'Mergers,' said Cooper.

'Are you for or against – or do I even need to ask?'

'Well, I was just saying that headquarters in Ripley is already pretty remote for a lot of people. Will it matter that much if we're part of an East Midlands Constabulary? As long as local teams like ours aren't broken up.'

'I'm surprised, Ben. I thought you'd have been fighting for the status quo. In your case, it's your heritage, almost.'

Cooper shrugged. 'I know people think my dad was a real old-fashioned copper, the sort who would always stick to the old ways because he thought they were best. But he never resisted change if he thought it was an improvement. If he knew the problems we have now with serious and organized crime he'd support the idea of a new structure. I think he'd say that it would free us up to concentrate on local issues instead of being distracted by major enquiries all the time. And I feel the same.'

'That scenario sounds pretty boring to me. If you're down at this end of the structure, anyway.'

'I don't agree. Think of the advantages: changes to the rank structure, a shift towards specialization, an increase in non-sworn staff . . .'

'I suppose so.'

Cooper looked at her, trying to digest what she'd said a moment ago. 'Boring? Do you mean that?'

'Yes, I do.'

'What will you do then, if serious crime is taken away from Edendale?'

Faced with the direct question, Fry hesitated, displaying that perennial reluctance to share her private thoughts with anyone. She waited until Murfin and the trainees had moved out of earshot.

'Actually, I've been thinking about applying to SOCA,' she said. 'I've got the experience.'

'They'd jump at you,' said Cooper.

'Do you think so?'

'Yes. If you did that, though, it would be exactly what I said – breaking up the team. That's what I wouldn't want, Diane.'

She looked surprised. 'Thanks.'

'How close are you to making a decision?'

'Not close. Not really. I'm just thinking about it. I'll see how things go.'

Cooper paused before he spoke again. He always had to weigh up his words with Fry, because he hadn't yet learned to predict her reaction.

'Angie?' he said tentatively.

'What?'

'I'm wondering if your sister comes into the decision. Is she the deciding factor whether you move away from Edendale or not?'

'No, she isn't.'

But as soon as Fry said it, she frowned and looked thoughtful. Cooper wondered if it just hadn't occurred to her to look at it that way before.

'Have you thought through the employment implications, though?'

'Ben, thanks for your interest, but if I want to discuss my employment conditions, I'll do it with my DI or Human Resources.'

'Fine, fine.'

Cooper went back to his desk. Like everyone else, he was aware that SOCA had been recruiting. The problem was that officers who joined the new serious crimes agency would lose their unique status. Instead of being classified as constables of the crown, guaranteed a pension and not subject to being sacked, at SOCA they would become agents – ordinary employees. As a result, the agency was struggling to persuade police officers to join.

But he could see Fry going. Promotion possibilities for her were limited in Derbyshire. There were only three DIs in the division, and seven DSs who might hope to succeed them, let alone detectives in other divisions, and uniforms who might want to transfer on their way up the ladder.

'So where are you off to this morning?' asked Fry as Cooper put his jacket on to leave.

'We're talking to the estate agent who sold Bain House to Rose Shepherd.'

'Right.' She watched Hitchens come out of his office and nod to Cooper. 'You're with the DI himself, then?'

'Somebody has to be,' said Cooper.

17

Peter Yates's desk at Windsor and Ellis was modern and tidy, everything carefully arranged. When Cooper sat down in one of the chairs across from the estate agent, he found a polished silver frame facing him. It contained a photograph of a blonde woman and two young children, posing and smiling; a perfect family group.

'Yes, I dealt with Miss Shepherd,' said Yates. 'But most of our business was done on the phone.'

'What address do you have for her before she moved into Bain House?' asked Hitchens.

Yates looked a bit troubled. 'You're sure it's all right for me to give out this sort of personal information?'

'Mr Yates, this is a murder enquiry.'

'Yes, I was just checking. We have a reputation to keep, you know.'

Hitchens raised an eyebrow, but resisted making a comment. Estate agents generally came at the bottom of any popularity polls; neck and neck with used-car salesmen and politicians.

Yates turned to a file that had been waiting on his desk.

'According to our records, Miss Shepherd gave the address of a hotel in London. You can have it, if it's any use to you. I seem to recall that she travelled up by train when we had to meet. Actually, I've got a note here that she came up to Derbyshire only once for the viewing. She signed all the papers at her solicitor's. That was about it, really.'

'Wouldn't you need a permanent address, Mr Yates?'

'No. You might try her solicitors for that, or her bank. She was paying cash, you see.'

'I see.'

'The buyer's solicitors in this case were also in London.'

'So you just met her the one time?'

'It seems so. I'm sorry I'm being so vague, but it was nearly a year ago. We deal with quite a number of prospective purchasers in the course of a year. Many of them we see once, or not at all. It's the vendors we tend to remember – we see much more of them.'

'What do you remember about Miss Shepherd? Anything, no matter how trivial . . .'

'You know, I thought the notes in the file might remind me of something, but there was nothing of interest. It was a very straightforward transaction. She had no particular concerns about the property, nothing but the standard checks that her solicitors did during the conveyance. In fact, it was rather an unmemorable sale, apart from the fact that it was a substantial property on our books.'

Cooper showed him a copy of Rose Shepherd's passport photograph. Neat grey hair and sharp blue eyes. Not the woman he remembered seeing on the floor of her bedroom.

'Was this the person you dealt with, sir?'

'Yes, I believe so. As far as I can recall.'

'Do you know if Miss Shepherd had Bain House redecorated when she moved in?'

Yates looked surprised. 'I couldn't tell you. Why?'

'I was in the house on Tuesday. I saw the sitting room. Off-white and charcoal grey – it seemed out of character, from what little we know of Miss Shepherd. I wouldn't have thought she cared that much about the place to make design statements.'

'Oh, that was the previous owners,' said Yates. 'They had big plans for the property, but I don't think they got any further than the sitting room and the bathroom. They ran out of money.'

'What a shame.'

Yates shrugged. 'It happens.'

'So the electric gates and security systems . . . ?'

'Ah, there was nothing like that. Miss Shepherd must have had it done. Very sensible, too. I would have recommended it, if she'd consulted me.'

They left through the displays of property: prestige homes in one window, compact semis in the other. 'Image,' said Hitchens when they were outside. 'It's very important to some people, Ben.'

'Sir?' said Cooper.

'Did you notice the photograph of the family on Mr Yates' desk?'

'Yes, of course.'

'Good, because you were meant to.'

'What do you mean?'

'Well, he had the photograph facing towards us. *We* could see it, but he couldn't. Doesn't that tell you anything?'

Cooper thought about it. 'If his family were really so important to him, the photo would have been facing the other way, so he could look at it. But it was aimed at his visitors – part of the office décor, designed to impress.'

'Exactly. Mr Yates was sending out a message. He was saying "Look at me, I'm the perfect family man. You can trust me. Give me your business." It only needs a few simple things to create a false image.'

Fry stood over the hospital bed and smiled. 'Mr Mullen, I understand you're about to be discharged. That's good news.'

'Yes, I'm not feeling too bad now. I can't stay in this bed any longer – there are things to sort out. Henry and Moira have been brilliant, but there's Luanne. She needs her dad.'

'I understand. Are you going to stay with Mr and Mrs Lowther in Darley Dale?'

'Yes, until I can get something else arranged.'

'Well, Mr Mullen, we'll need you to come back to Darwin Street as soon as you feel well enough.'

'I'm not going to start sorting the place out yet. I can't face that.'

'No, of course not. But we'd like you to take us over the ground – you're the only person who was familiar with the contents of your house.'

'Contents? Like what?'

'We'll go into all that when we're on site. We also have some photos for you to look at.'

Mullen looked anxious. 'Not –?'

'No.' Fry shook her head. 'Look, I'm sorry, I didn't explain that very well. I meant photographs of items that we recovered near the seat of the fire. It's important for us to establish if there was anything in the sitting room that shouldn't have been there.'

'All right. I see what you're getting at.'

'When do you think you could do that?'

Mullen looked at his bandaged hands. 'As long as you don't expect me to sign anything, I reckon I could do it now. Best to get it over with, eh?'

Fry felt like smiling at him for the first time. 'Thank you, sir. I'll have a word with your doctor. If I can get his agreement, we'll do it today. OK?'

Eric Grice laid down his electric drill and blew stone dust off the wall. As he wiped a film of sweat from his forehead with the back of his hand, he left a small streak of dust on his temple.

'And I suppose you're flummoxed,' he said.

'Flummoxed? That's an interesting word, Mr Grice. People usually say the police are baffled.'

'Aye. But flummoxed is worse.'

Hitchens didn't smile. People like Eric Grice rarely amused him. 'We've been asking around the village since Tuesday for someone who had any contact with Miss Shepherd. It would have helped us if you'd come forward earlier.'

'I don't live in the village,' said Grice. 'My sister does, but she's on her holidays this week. She's in Jersey. Late autumn break.'

'Where do you live yourself, sir?'

'Matlock.'

'It's not a million miles away.'

'In some ways it is.'

Cooper could smell the singed stone from the hole Grice had been drilling into the wall. It looked as though he was planning on erecting some trellis.

'You know, it seems odd that so few people knew anything about Rose Shepherd when she was part of the village for the past year,' he said.

'Ah, well, she only *seems* to have been part of the village. As a matter of fact, Miss Shepherd might as well have been living in a separate universe from the rest of us. A different time and place altogether. That's the impression she gave whenever I saw her, anyway.'

'Did you see her often? She's supposed to have been a bit of a recluse.'

'A what?'

'Everyone else says she didn't go out of the house much.'

'Oh yes, she was a right old hermit, if that's what you mean. But there were some things she couldn't do without.' He shook his head. 'You can't live in this day and age and have no contact with another human being. It just doesn't work.'

'So where did you meet her?'

'At her house, of course.'

'Really?'

'She sent for me to come round now and then. Whenever she needed some odd jobs doing. Not often, though. She tended to save them up – enough jobs for me to do in one visit, like. A dripping tap, a blown fuse, a few tiles off the roof. It seemed as though she could put up with a leak or the lights out for a while, and it didn't bother her. She preferred it to having someone in her house, I reckon.'

'You had the impression she didn't like you being there?'

Grice fingered a set of yellow Rawlplugs, assessing the size of the hole he'd made in the wall. Then he snapped one off and held it for a moment between finger and thumb.

'I was only ever there on tolerance – a necessary evil, you might say. It was like she had to grit her teeth before she even opened the door to let me in. Yes, a very private person, was Miss Shepherd. What name did you call that?'

'A recluse.'

He nodded, as if filing away the word for future use. 'A recluse. Aye.'

'How many times did you go there?'

'I don't know. Five or six, I suppose. The last time was three weeks ago, to clear the guttering and sweep up dead leaves.'

'Mr Grice, did Rose Shepherd ever talk to you while you were at her house? Did she tell you anything about herself?'

'No, not her.'

'Nothing at all?'

'Not a thing.'

'Any little detail that she might have let slip could be useful to us. Why don't you give it some thought –'

'I don't need to give it any thought,' said Grice. 'She never talked to me. She pointed out the jobs that wanted doing, then left me to it. She hid herself away somewhere, went up to her bedroom or something. I thought it was a bit odd at first. The second time I went up to see her, I tried to make conversation. Only to ask whether she wanted me to fix the loose corner of a carpet while I was there. But she didn't want to discuss anything. In fact, she got a bit cross. She told me she'd get somebody else in, if I wanted to ask questions instead of doing the job. I reckon she meant it, too. After that, I didn't even dare ask for a cup of tea.'

'I assume she paid well.'

'Aye, that was it. You do what the customer wants, especially if they're paying over the odds.'

Hitchens was studying him carefully. 'I can't believe you didn't see anything in all the time you were in Bain House, Mr Grice. From what you've just said, you were practically unsupervised. You must have been curious. Well, weren't you?'

'A bit. But I couldn't snoop about the place. I didn't want her to turn up suddenly and catch me at it. I'd have been out of a job definitely then.'

'Even so, you're an observant man, I'm sure. It would be hard to spend time at Bain House, as you did, and not notice anything.'

'OK, there might be something that occurs to me. But I can't imagine how it would be of any use.'

Hitchens smiled at him. 'You'd be surprised. The smallest thing might be significant.'

'All right. Well, like you said, I'll give it some thought.'

'By the way, we'll need to take your finger-prints, sir.'

'Why?'

'For elimination purposes.'

'I don't know what that means.'

'Well, since you visited Bain House several times, your prints will be there. We need to know which ones are yours, so we can discount them.'

'Oh, I see. All right.'

Cooper looked at the work he was doing on

the wall. 'Did you say this house belongs to your sister?'

'No, I just said she lives here.'

'Who does she live with?'

Grice leaned towards him in a conspiratorial manner.

'Can you keep a secret?'

'Yes.'

He leaned a bit closer. 'So can I.'

Brian Mullen hesitated for a long time outside the front door of number 32. Fry gave him space. She reminded herself that it was the first time he'd seen his home since the fire; in fact, the first time he'd seen it in daylight since he left the house for a night out with Jed Skinner.

'Take your time, sir.'

'I'm all right.'

Mullen seemed to regard her consideration as a spur to action. He stepped forward, and was guided into the house via the approach path, through the plastic tape marking the boundary of the crime scene. He almost stumbled in the hallway, as if he was suddenly lost and didn't know which doorway to turn into.

Fry wondered if he even recognized the place as his own home. There was almost nothing left of the original décor now. The wallpaper was blackened, the furniture charred embers. Items that would have been familiar to Mullen had been removed completely during the forensic examination. Instead, the rooms contained these strange, colourful little displays. Crime-scene flags and disposable photo markers, dozens of white squares with reference codes written on them. The old film set was in the middle of being transformed for a new production.

One of the SOCOs went by carrying another pack of markers. Had they used a hundred in here already? Fry watched him unpack the flat, heavy-duty card, folding and locking the pieces into shape for use with the flags.

'There were some toys and other items near the source of the fire,' she said. 'Could you identify them for us, sir?'

Fry showed him the photographs and the exact locations where the items had been found. They included the melted Barbie doll and the remains of the PlayStation console. Then there was the blackened Monopoly board – charred piles of fake money, and red and green blobs that had once been hotels and houses.

She knew this would be painful for him. But Mullen did as he was asked, fingering the photos as if they were mementoes of a holiday he vaguely remembered. He stood in the middle of the sitting room, balancing uneasily on the stepping plates because he'd been told not to touch anything or stand on the carpet.

'I've never seen this before,' he said.

'What is it, sir?'

He tapped one of the photographs with a finger. 'This thing. It looks like a kangaroo.'

Fry took it from him and checked the scene inventory.

'It was logged in as a wooden dinosaur.'

'It doesn't belong here.'

'Are you sure? It's been damaged by the fire.'

'A wooden dinosaur, you say?'

'According to the crime-scene examiners, it's made from varnished walnut, with leather ears. It would have stood about six inches tall in its original condition.'

Mullen shook his head. 'No, the kids didn't have anything like that. They were more into PlayStations and video games. Well, Luanne had her baby toys, too. But wooden dinosaurs? No.'

'So where did it come from?'

'I couldn't tell you.' He looked at the photos again. 'Where *would* you buy this kind of thing?'

'Who else might be in the habit of buying toys for your children?'

'Their grandparents, of course. Or my brother-in-law, John. He and Lindsay saw a lot of each other – John might have picked the thing up somewhere, I suppose.'

Fry put the photos back in the file. The toy wasn't important, really. Many fathers would be vague about what their children played with.

'Let's leave that for a moment then, sir. Just walk this way, would you? And mind where you tread. Stick to the stepping plates.'

Offering up a small piece of information seemed

to have given Mullen confidence. At least he was doing something positive.

'What do you want me to see now?'

'The hallway, sir. The hallway is important. Although the fire started in the sitting room, it was the smoke filling the hallway and rising up the stairs that caused the real problem.'

'I know about this. I tried to get into the house, if you remember. The smoke was so bad that I couldn't see anything, or even breathe.'

'Quite right. If the firefighters hadn't pulled you back, you might well have been more seriously injured.'

'So what do you want to know?'

'I was wondering who left the door open from the sitting room into the hall. That was what provided enough air for the fire to get a hold. It was also what allowed the smoke to spread through the rest of the house. If the fire had been contained in the sitting room a bit longer, the alarm might have been raised soon enough for lives to be saved.'

Mullen said nothing, but stood gazing at the stairs. Behind him, his family liaison officer appeared, grimacing at Fry. But she took no notice.

'Were the doors downstairs normally left closed at night, Mr Mullen?'

'Which doors?'

'From the sitting room to the kitchen, for example?'

'Yes.'

'And what about this door, the one into the hall?'

'Well, maybe. But Lindsay might have left that one open. She sometimes did, if I was out. She knew I'd close it when I came home and went to bed. Only I didn't . . .'

'I know. I'm sorry if this distresses you, sir. Just one last thing. Were you aware of anyone hanging around near the house in the days before the fire? Did any of the neighbours mention someone asking questions about you and your family?'

'No, nothing like that.'

Fry nodded at the liaison officer, who came forward and put an arm round Mullen's shoulders.

'I tested the smoke alarm every month,' said Mullen, with some difficulty.

'By pressing the button?'

'Yes.'

'Did you realize that it only tests the sound of the alarm, not whether the detector itself is functioning?'

Mullen looked paler than ever. 'No, I didn't know that.'

Fry watched him for a few moments, but felt no nearer to getting inside his mind.

'I'll give you a lift to Darley Dale,' she said. 'That's where you want to go, isn't it?'

'Yes, to my parents-in-law.'

When she'd got him in the car, Fry let him sit quietly for a while as they drove across

Edendale. Many people would feel uncomfortable with the silence and want to make conversation. But not Brian Mullen. She left him to stew until they were out of town and heading towards the A6.

'Tell me about the arguments you'd been having with your wife,' she said.

'What arguments?' said Mullen.

'According to your neighbours, there had been several rows between the two of you in recent weeks.'

He shook his head. 'We had a row about the new carpet, that's all. I didn't think it was the most practical thing with three kids in the house. And I didn't like the idea of Henry buying things for us all the time, either. I told Lindsay I could support my own family without his help.'

'Yes?'

'But she got her own way in the end. She could never say no to Daddy when he wanted to give her something. So it wasn't much of an argument.' Mullen twisted in his seat to look at her. 'Is that what you meant?'

'And the rest.'

'No, no. We never had rows, as a rule.'

'That's not what I heard.'

'Well, you've got it wrong.'

They entered Bakewell, and Fry had to concentrate as she negotiated the narrow streets and the busy roundabout in the middle of town. She was able to relax again as they approached the entrance

270

to Haddon Hall. But there were only a few miles left now.

'You told me earlier that Lindsay and her brother were very close,' she said. 'That can be a difficult relationship for a husband to deal with sometimes. How do you get on with John Lowther?'

'Fine. Just fine.'

'Not even a hint of jealousy, perhaps? If John bought presents for your children, it would be natural for a bit of resentment to creep in.'

'Any resentment wasn't on my side,' said Mullen.

'Ah. So you think your brother-in-law begrudged someone coming between him and the sister he was so close to? I can see how that might cause friction in the household. Did your arguments concern John?'

'You've still got it wrong. And whoever told you that has got it wrong, too.'

And that was the last thing she got out of him. Mullen remained silent and sullen all the way to Darley Dale. Now and then, he glanced anxiously out of the window at people passing on the pavement, and once he gave a sudden start when a car pulled alongside them at the traffic lights. Fry had no idea what he was so worried about, but she didn't think it could be her driving.

Finally, she dropped him off outside the Lowthers' gate, and he thanked her ungraciously. Fry watched as Moira Lowther came out of the bungalow and hugged Brian near the chiminea. That was just like Mrs Lowther. Very keen on hugging people.

Instead of heading straight back to West Street, Fry decided to call at the mortuary to collect the pathologist's report. Mrs van Doon was in her office and greeted her visitor personally.

'Yes, all three of your victims had carboxy-haemoglobin levels over fifty per cent – which is sufficient in itself to account for death. Levels of up to ten per cent would be normal, anything more indicates inhalation of carbon monoxide. I believe there might also have been hydrogen cyanide present in the fumes from the fire. That's a particularly potent toxin, with a rapid action.'

'Where would that come from?' asked Fry.

'Hydrogen cyanide? It's produced by materials which contain nitrogen – wool, silk. And polyurethane.'

'Polyurethane, as in furniture foam?'

'Yes, possibly.'

'Which of those would explain why three people failed to escape from a house fire when they were woken by the smoke?'

'Hypoxia resulting from high carbon monoxide levels. At the levels present in these individuals, I'd say they would certainly have been feeling ill and disorientated at the least. They might even have been unconscious.'

'But we're sure they died as a result of the fire?'

272

'Yes. Soot particles can stain the mouth and pharynx of a person who's already dead, but if soot is present beyond the vocal cords it means the victim was alive during the fire.'

The pathologist produced a photograph. It was meaningless to Fry, which was probably for the best.

'All three post-mortems showed evidence of soot in the airways. The two children also had it in the oesophagus and stomach. Those black streaks on the mucus of the trachea indicate that your victims were alive at the start of the fire. Alive, but not necessarily conscious.'

The waitress from the Riber Tea Rooms had arrived at West Street to be guided through the process of producing some e-fit pictures of the people Rose Shepherd had met in Matlock Bath the day before she died. She did her best, but she wasn't sure about the details.

'Thank you for coming in anyway, Tina,' Murfin was saying as Fry walked in.

'It's not much use, is it?'

'You did your best.'

'I'm really sorry. I wanted to help.'

'Don't worry about it. But if you happen to remember anything else, you will let us know, won't you?'

Fry turned, and saw Cooper, watching the waitress leave.

'Didn't she give us much?' she asked.

'I've only just got back myself. But Gavin says we ended up with something as vague as her descriptions were: a woman in her thirties, a man who could have been any age, because she hadn't really taken much notice of him. It was Rose Shepherd herself that Tina remembers best.'

'Two adults – one male, one female. Who could they have been? There aren't many possibilities cropping up in the Shepherd enquiry so far. I suppose there's either set of next-door neighbours, the Birtlands or the Ridgeways . . .'

'Frances Birtland works in Matlock Bath,' said Cooper. 'She has a part-time job at the Masson Mill shopping village. But she's well past her thirties.'

'Still, it's a connection of a kind. How far is it from Masson Mill to the tea rooms?'

'Half a mile or so.'

'Close enough for her to have nipped out for an hour.'

'Her employer would have to cover for her, in that case.'

Fry nodded. 'True. It's getting a bit complicated for a chat over the teacups. And we'd have to place her husband in Matlock Bath, too. According to your interview report, his health isn't too good.'

'There *is* another couple we might consider,' said Cooper. 'Though we've only had contact with one of them so far.'

'Who do you mean?'

'Eric Grice and his sister. She lives in Foxlow.

And Grice is the one person who knew Miss Shepherd and has actually been inside Bain House.'

'You're right,' said Fry. 'We ought to ask one or both of them what they were doing on Saturday, if only so we can eliminate them.'

'We'll have to wait to speak to the sister. Grice says she's in Jersey.'

'What did you make of this handyman? Do you think he was telling the truth?'

'Of course not. I bet he was all over that house like a rash, given half a chance. Imagine – the whole village is speculating about the mysterious occupant of Bain House, and our Eric is the only one with access to the place and the chance to talk to her. There must have been all kinds of things he noticed.'

'He's just not ready to tell us yet, right?'

'But he will,' said Cooper.

'Do you think he could have seen something relevant to the shooting?'

Cooper hesitated. 'Well, he might be able to point us in the direction of a motive. Or of somebody with a connection to Rose Shepherd, at least. That's what we're lacking right now, isn't it?'

'If it was any of the people from Foxlow who met Rose Shepherd in the tea rooms, it means they've been lying to us.'

'Yes. But it seems more likely that it was someone else entirely. Two people that we just haven't come across yet.'

Fry could see that Murfin was on his way back from showing the waitress out, and she needed to speak to him. But Cooper hadn't finished yet.

'Diane, there's a lot of effort going into the Shepherd enquiry,' he said. 'But you're not getting much support in the Mullen case, are you?'

'I don't need it. As long as they leave me alone and don't throw me too many distractions.'

'A triple death? Two of them children?'

'These are two very different crimes, Ben. The Shepherd killing was a ruthless, professional act by a very dangerous individual, but someone who might have no direct connection to the victim. He'll take a lot of effort to track down, and even more work to build a successful case against. But the Mullen enquiry – those killings were personal. The answer will be much closer to home. And that's the big difference.'

18

Later, at her desk, Fry finished reading the patholo-gist's report on the Mullen family. She could hear Mrs van Doon's voice in her head, describing how the hot gases had damaged the lining of the airways and lungs, leaving the tongue, pharynx, and glottis scorched and inflamed. Damage to the lungs had precipitated pulmonary oedema. Inhalation of carbon particles blocked the air passages with mucus. Any burns on the victims were post-mortem. They had been alive, but not necessarily conscious.

Finally, she put the report aside. Forensics would have to give her something to build a case on. It was difficult not to get impatient, though, when Brian Mullen was out of hospital and walking around. She pictured him sitting in the conservatory at the Lowthers' bungalow, with his mother-in-law fussing round him, bringing him cups of tea, giving him a hug when he needed it.

Hesitating only for a moment, Fry picked up the phone and called Wayne Abbott.

'There's a lot of stuff to get through, you know. And the Darwin Street enquiry isn't the only one we're dealing with.'

'I realize that, Wayne, but I need to know whether you found any fingerprints in the sitting room.'

'The only ones we could retrieve came from members of the family. We were lucky to get what we did, considering the fire and smoke damage, and the amount of waterlogging.'

'Did you lift any from the wooden toy – the dinosaur?'

'I'm afraid not. It was too badly charred.'

'And the lighter fluid can?'

'That's gone to the lab at Wetherby. They're giving it the works, but it takes time.'

'Is that our best hope, Wayne?'

'Right now, yes. Unless you can produce a likely suspect.'

'Thanks.'

She finished the call and looked around the office. Everyone was busy with tasks connected to the Rose Shepherd enquiry. Everyone. But that didn't mean she couldn't demand a bit of their time.

'Hey, Ben, would you take a look at this?'

'What have you got?' said Cooper from across the room.

But before Fry could show him the photo of the toy dinosaur, her phone rang. It was pretty much a one-way conversation: 'Great, OK . . . I see. Yes, sir, right away.'

Cooper was still hovering at his desk when she finished. 'What's up?'

'The DCI wants us in for a meeting, right now. HOLMES has finished processing Rose Shepherd's diary, address book and the other documents found in her house. Remember the mysterious "SN" mentioned in the diary? There's only one name in her papers with matching initials: Simon Nichols.'

'Simon Nichols . . .' said Cooper, responding to a vague familiarity.

'That's it. Does it mean anything to you?'

'Isn't he in Fairport Convention?'

'In what?'

'It's a band. Folk rock.'

'Oh, right. You think Rose Shepherd might have been a folk rock groupie?'

'No, it must be another Simon Nichols.'

'HOLMES can't give us any clues as to who this Simon Nichols is, or where we can find him. But the incident room are checking all the usual intelligence. There's also a team going through all other sources: phone directory, electoral roll, DVLC . . . We need to track down any Nichols in the area.'

'In the area?' said Cooper. 'He isn't necessarily –'

'I know. But we've got to start somewhere. We should start getting results soon. Meanwhile, does anybody have any thoughts?'

'Whoever killed Rose Shepherd didn't enter the house, so far as we can tell,' said Hitchens. 'So we can conclude that he wasn't worried about there being evidence in the house that would lead us to him.'

'That assumes the crime was carefully thought out beforehand.'

'It looks that way.'

'Of course, it might only have been the shooting and the getaway that were planned,' suggested Cooper. 'If he thought of killing Rose Shepherd as a way of solving some problem, he might have overlooked what would happen once her body was found.'

'Perhaps he knew there was nothing in the house that could lead back to him,' said Hitchens. 'If Miss Shepherd didn't know him, if he was a hired professional, there'd be no direct connection between him and his victim.'

'That's logical,' said Kessen. 'But there's one other alternative.'

'Yes?'

'What if he'd already searched the house and removed anything incriminating? Then he'd feel able to carry out the killing from a safe distance.'

'Well, it could explain why there are no personal letters in the house. But who would have the opportunity to do that? The security at Bain House was too tight, and Miss Shepherd was rarely off the premises.'

'What we need is a motive to narrow the field a bit. Any suggestions? I suppose we can discount robbery, since there was no attempt to enter the house.'

'Money could still be a motive,' said Hitchens. 'If there's a will –'

'There doesn't seem to be one in the house. It's possible there's a solicitor somewhere with a will, but the London firm who handled the house purchase say they have no knowledge of it.'

Fry smiled. 'If there's someone out there who planned this murder in order to inherit Rose Shepherd's money, they'll come forward eventually, won't they?'

'Eventually? That won't do. We need to be able to show some progress on this enquiry pretty quickly,' snapped Kessen.

'OK, what other motives might we consider?'

'Jealousy? Revenge? Perhaps Rose Shepherd was a threat to someone?' suggested Fry.

'Jealousy requires some kind of close personal relationship,' said Hitchens. 'Miss Shepherd doesn't seem to have had any of those. Not recently, anyway.'

'What about this Eric Grice?'

'Grice, the handyman? What about him?'

'He seems to be the only person who was allowed into Bain House, the only one who had any contact with Miss Shepherd. I wonder if there was more to their relationship than a bit of odd-jobbing.'

'Well, they were both unmarried, so that shouldn't have been a problem. A bit on the mature side, perhaps, but I'm told that doesn't necessarily make any difference.'

'Judging by her obsession with keeping herself

to herself, she would probably have rejected any attempts at intimacy out of hand. For all we know of Grice, he might not be the type to take that calmly,' said Fry.

'But if he crossed the line in some way, Miss Shepherd would have kicked him out, surely. Yet she let him keep coming to the house, didn't she?'

'Did she? How do we know that?'

'Only from Grice himself,' admitted Cooper.

'When does he say he was last at Bain House?'

'Three weeks ago, to clear the guttering and sweep up dead leaves.'

'Well, we know for a fact that he had contact with Rose Shepherd, which puts him in a very small minority for now. And he must have known which room she slept in. What sort of vehicle does he drive?' said Hitchens.

'He has an old Land Rover that he carries his tools around in.'

'Four-wheel drive?'

'Of course. But Grice says he was always restricted to certain parts of the house. It sounded convincing,' said Cooper.

'Maybe,' said Fry. 'But that just means he was limited to one area per visit. How many times did he go to Bain House?'

'Five or six times, he says.'

'Enough opportunity to work his way through the whole house?'

'I suppose so.'

'Besides, we only have his word for how

restricted his movements were. Miss Shepherd isn't available to confirm his story.'

'Right,' said Kessen. 'Let's take a closer look at Mr Grice. Get a detailed account of his last visit to Rose Shepherd. And check whether the tyres on his Land Rover are a match for the tracks from the field.'

'We don't actually have any evidence against Grice,' pointed out Cooper.

'If he isn't implicated in the shooting, he won't mind co-operating, will he?'

'It doesn't always work like that.'

'His other clients won't feel happy about the police asking questions. He must understand that co-operation is in his own best interests.' Kessen seemed to think this settled the problem. 'All right, I want Grice to list every single room he's visited in Bain House. Then we can match up his account with the prints we lifted. In particular, I want to know whether he was ever in that master bedroom.'

Before he could move on, the phone rang, and Hitchens took the call. A smile came over his face.

'It seems Mr Grice's fingerprints were found in two of the bedrooms at Bain House, including the one where the victim slept. So if he says he was never in those rooms, he's lying.'

Kessen looked around the group. 'DS Fry. I know you've got a lot on, but perhaps you'd like to have a go at our Mr Grice this time.'

'With pleasure.'

*   *   *

283

'And who the heck are you?' said Eric Grice, winding the orange cord around the handle of his power drill.

'Detective Sergeant Fry.'

'Oh, aye? Reckon you can get more out of me than your mates did? I don't have anything more to tell, you know.'

'Well, let's see, shall we?'

'You might have time to waste, but I haven't. There's work to do.'

'Mr Grice, you've given us a list of the rooms you visited in Bain House. Are you sure this is a comprehensive list? You haven't left any rooms out?'

'No, it's right,' he said. 'A lot of the work I did was on the outside, like.'

'So the only room upstairs that you were ever present in is the bathroom – is that right?'

'Yes.'

'In that case, Mr Grice, how do you explain the fact that we recovered your fingerprints from two of the bedrooms?'

'The bedrooms?'

'The master bedroom, where Rose Shepherd slept, and the second bedroom, just along the landing, where she kept her desk.'

'I don't know anything about that.'

'You never did any jobs for her in those rooms?'

He shook his head. 'She wouldn't have wanted me going in her bedrooms. Like I told you, she was a very private person, Miss Shepherd. She kept me at arm's length, so far as she could. I always knew the house was out of bounds, except for when I had to be somewhere to get a job done. I never even went upstairs to use the bathroom. She had a downstairs cloakroom, you know.'

'I don't think you understand, Mr Grice. I'm telling you that we found your fingerprints in two of the bedrooms at Bain House. Are you still denying that you went into those rooms?'

'Well, like I said –'

Fry could feel herself starting to get impatient. Did the man think that he could alter the facts just by continuing to deny them? She leaned across the table, startling him in mid-sentence.

'What were you doing in Miss Shepherd's bedroom?' she said. 'And before you answer, think about this, Mr Grice: a murdered woman's body was found in one of those bedrooms, and you're the only person whose presence we can prove there. If you don't have any explanation, how do you think that's going to look when we charge you and prove to a court that you're lying?'

Grice blinked. He seemed bothered to be scrutinized so closely. But Fry waited, not moving or relaxing her stare while she gave him time to process the implications. Finally, his eyes flickered to the side to avoid her gaze.

'It was my sister, Beryl,' he said.

Fry frowned. 'What was?'

'There's always been a lot of talk in the village about Miss Shepherd, you know. Nobody knew anything about her, but that didn't stop them talking. You know what it's like – everyone had their own ideas.'

'In other words, it was all speculation?'

'Well, yes. There were a lot of half-baked stories. None of them were true, of course. You know what it's like – a lot of biddies who watch too much telly.'

'So what relevance is this?'

'Beryl kept on and on about it. She knew I was the only person who Miss Shepherd let into Bain House, so she thought I ought to know all about the woman. I told her I didn't know a thing, but she kept pestering me. Pestering and pestering. Of course, she wanted to show off to her pals in the village, and tell the other biddies that she knew the proper facts, all the stuff they didn't.'

'The inside information.'

'Yes, that's it. She wanted to show off, like. I thought it was a lot of daft nonsense. I told her they all ought to find something better to talk about. But she wouldn't let up. So next time I was in Bain House, I took a chance to have a bit of a nosy about. To see what I could see. Just to find a bit of something to keep Beryl quiet, that's all.'

'So you managed to get into the bedrooms?'

'Yes. Only for a quick look round. To see if she had any dead bodies or mad relatives hidden away in there, you know.'

Grice gave her a tentative smile, but Fry refused to acknowledge the joke.

'But you said Miss Shepherd didn't like you

going upstairs. How did you get into the bedrooms without her noticing?'

'I was mending a joint on a pipe in the kitchen, and I told her I had to turn off the water at the stopcock in the bathroom. She didn't know any better, you see.'

'Where was Miss Shepherd while you were nosing around in the bedrooms?'

'She was downstairs, in her sitting room. She went in there to be away from me, I suppose. So I didn't go in the front bedroom, because I thought she might hear my footsteps.'

'And did you find anything interesting to tell your sister?'

'Not really. Well, nothing at all, as a matter of fact. It was boring.' He shrugged his shoulders. 'So I had to make some stuff up.'

'Hold on – you made things up about Miss Shepherd to tell your sister?'

'Well, yes. Otherwise she would have kept pestering me. I had to get her off my back.'

'And no doubt your sister would have spread this false information around her friends in Foxlow?'

'That was the general idea. I didn't think there'd be any harm in it. None of the stuff was ever likely to get back to Miss Shepherd herself, because she didn't talk to anyone in the village. See what I mean? So it was harmless.'

Fry caught her breath. 'What false information did you make up, Mr Grice?'

'I can't remember now.'

'I can't believe it was anything too complicated. You don't have the imagination.'

He glowered at her. 'I don't know. It was just what came to mind.'

'Let me have a guess, then. Did you tell your sister Miss Shepherd had a hidden safe in the house where she kept all her valuables?'

Grice pulled his face. 'Yes, probably.'

'Did you tell your sister Miss Shepherd was a retired teacher from Scotland?'

'Yes, I think so. I couldn't really tell –'

'And, Mr Grice, this is very important – did you tell your sister that Rose Shepherd had a friend called Dougie in Glasgow?'

Eric Grice nodded slowly, but said nothing.

Fry sat back. 'Well, sir, for a man who thought he wasn't doing any harm, you've certainly wasted a lot of people's time.'

'God damn the man,' said DI Hitchens. 'I could cheerfully strangle him with his own drill cord.'

'At least he's talking now. I've got someone taking a statement from him, and we'll speak to his sister, too, to see if their accounts tally. But I believe he's telling us the truth now.'

'Meanwhile, it's back to square one in our picture of Rose Shepherd. When we ignore all the stuff that Grice made up to keep the gossips happy, the information we have about her now amounts to what?'

'Nothing.'

'It can't do.'

'Sweet FA, if you prefer.'

'No, no. We do have some verifiable facts. We've *got* to have some.'

'If you say so, sir.'

Hitchens looked at the board, scrubbed off some of the details and studied what was left. 'She's a British passport holder, born in London. And we've got her age – she was born in 1944.'

'A wartime baby.'

'Yes. Maybe her parents were killed in the Blitz or something.'

'I thought we were looking at the verifiable facts.'

'OK. Well, we've got her name, age, place of birth. And her physical details – height, weight, hair colour. She moved to Foxlow ten months ago, and she came here from London. She had plenty of funds, because Bain House wasn't cheap, and she was a cash buyer.'

'And apart from that . . . ?'

Hitchens tilted his head on one side to look at the photograph of the victim from a different angle. It didn't seem to tell him anything new.

'That's about it,' he said. 'We're no nearer to filling in her past history. Or to tracing any personal contacts, now the famous Dougie from Glasgow has proved mythical.'

'Have we talked to everyone in her address book?'

'Almost everyone. One or two companies that are listed have gone out of business. The odd thing is that her book only dates from the day she moved into Bain House. Apart from the solicitor and the estate agent, nobody we've spoken to had any contact with her before November last year.'

'Did any of these individuals detect an accent?'

'Only those who were offered a leading question by the officer interviewing them. In other words, if they were asked whether Miss Shepherd had a Scottish accent, they agreed she might have done. Otherwise, they had no suggestions to offer.'

'Grice has a lot to answer for.'

'Agreed. But I don't think it would make much difference in this case. None of them could really agree on her appearance or manner either. One said Miss Shepherd had a nice smile, another said she was very reserved and never smiled at all. We've had a lot of different estimates of her age, too. You'd hardly think they'd met the same person.'

'Well, a harmless middle-aged woman – who'd take much notice of her, unless she did something to draw attention to herself?'

'And she didn't do that.'

Hitchens spun round and looked at Fry. 'A harmless middle-aged woman that no one takes any notice of. Do you think you'll end up like that one day, Diane?'

'Hardly.'

'Why not? We all get middle-aged, don't we?'

'The key word is "harmless",' said Fry.

The DI laughed. 'You're right. I can't see anyone not noticing you, no matter how old you get.'

'Did we get anything from her contacts list?'

'Well, her dentist can tell us that Rose Shepherd had a few previous fillings. Her GP prescribed her Nitrazepam for her sleeping problems. And the garage can tell us what the emissions were like on her Volvo. Pick the bones out of that, if you can.'

'Why did she have trouble sleeping, I wonder?'

'Who can say?'

'Well, at least we have a confirmation of her ID from the dental records. We don't have to wait for the GP to get back.'

Hitchens opened the file. 'One thing we did find in the house was the receipt for her car. It was bought from a Volvo dealer in Chesterfield and delivered to Bain House a few days after Miss Shepherd moved in. The receipt gives the recorded mileage at the time of sale, and we checked it against the current reading. She did about three hundred miles in a year. She was the proverbial careful lady owner.'

'My God, she hardly went anywhere,' said Fry.

'She had no one to visit, did she?'

'Apparently not.'

He raised his face to drink in the sounds. Cars and motorbikes; thumping music from the pub, the thud of a diesel exhaust. There were loud voices as a crowd of youths and girls queued to get into Brody's nightclub on the top floor of the Pavilion. Laughing, shrieking, squealing. The noise echoed off the front of the building, allowing him to bathe in the clamour.

He was waiting in the bus pull-in near the tufa foun-
tain, talking to the fish as they popped up to see if he'd
brought them any food. Hissing, splashing, plopping.
But he mustn't stay here too long, or a policeman would
come his way, suspecting that he planned to stalk some
ridiculous teenage girl in a short skirt. Now, then. Now
then. Move along.

He laughed. It was so funny, the image of the
policeman, thumping about in his boots, creaking in his
yellow plastic jacket, the radio squawking constantly in
his ear, sending him messages, messages, more messages,
telling him where to go and not to go, instructions and
orders, comments and commands, barking and babbling.
How did he stand it? The policeman must be deaf. Deaf
in his mind. It was so funny that he laughed again.
Chuckle, chortle, snigger.

But he knew immediately he'd laughed out loud. He
could tell by the faces of the nightclub queue, turned
towards him in a glare of light. Derisive, hostile. Someone
tittered, someone jeered. Something jabbered and muttered
at the back of his brain. It was time to be elsewhere.

He turned, hunching his shoulders inside his over-
coat, and walked towards the Promenade Fish Bar. He
was following the lure of a rumbling motorcycle engine,
a two-tone horn on a car racing up the road. Further
on, he could hear the sounds of an amusement arcade.
Rattle, crash, boom. They wouldn't let him in, but he
could stand outside and enjoy the buzz of the traffic, too.

Night-time was the most difficult. There was too little
noise. Always too little. He was sure he wasn't alone in
feeling most vulnerable at night. Darkness could hide

anything, couldn't it? It was populated with fantasies and horrors, ghosts and demons, and all the other fears that chattered like monkeys in the corners of his mind. Not to mention the burglars and rapists, the crazed axemen muttering in the alleys, drawn to the sound of human breathing like moths to a flame.

Every time he went to sleep, he knew he might wake up to a presence in the room, a voice congealed into reality. He pictured the moment when the breathing he could hear was not his own, when the shadow behind the door began to move, when an arm brushed against the wall, a whisper of fabric in the silence and a hoarse mumble of his name, before the final lunge of the knife. He imagined those last moments so often that he could feel his limbs tangle in the sheets as he thrashed to escape the blade. Slash, stab, rip. There, what did I tell you?

A hospital room was no better. The sounds that drifted down corridors during the night were strange and incomprehensible. Like bedlam, the music of the madhouse. Howl, roar, bark at the moon. And not only sounds, but smells. They could blend in the mind like a thick soup, swirling and forming pictures that he'd rather not see inside his head. There were half-spoken memories that he'd carry for ever, recollections of unseen people discussing him, their voices hushed and murmuring, commenting on his state of health, using words that were unknown to him. Planning his disposal, as if he were an animal.

Of course, it was stupid to fear the unknown. People who did that were just projecting their own ugly thoughts on to a blank mask, like throwing handfuls of mud at a marble statue. Why live in terror of the unfamiliar?

Why let the silent, dripping darkness of the imagination displace the wicked reality?

Those were the things that made other people afraid, but he knew he wasn't like them. He'd been made differently from the rest of humanity; his mind was constructed of a glittering, fragile crystal instead of some greasy clay, scooped from the earth. His consciousness rang like a bell, echoing and tinkling, speaking his name, calling him softly, tolling with disdain.

Some of these places would be closing for the night soon. Matlock Bath would empty, and he'd have to go home. He'd have to face another night, counting to himself to fill the silent hours, reciting the alphabet, and cursing, cursing . . . One, two, three, and DAMN, DAMN, DAMN!

He didn't care about the unknown. Not in the least. He knew exactly what to be afraid of, and it was something all too real. He heard it wailing in the distance. It was difficult to drown out, even now. He knew how dangerous it could be, and where it would come from. He just didn't know when it would finally draw near and speak.

19

Early next morning, an officer from the incident room entered DCI Kessen's office at West Street, and placed several slim files on the desk. Watched by Hitchens, Kessen thumbed through the files.

'Well, it looks as though we've got the first hits from our Nichols trawl,' he said.

'Any Simons?' asked Hitchens.

'Oh, yes. Three. One of them lives in Ashbourne, and he's ten years old.'

'Damn it.'

'Well, maybe we shouldn't eliminate him out of hand. Kids are given mobile phones at a very young age these days.'

'And high-powered semi-automatics?'

'Let's hope not. Get Ashbourne section to talk to the parents anyway, check there isn't some remote connection with Rose Shepherd. It seems pretty unlikely, but we'd best rule it out.'

'And the others?'

'The second Simon Nichols is eighty-five years old. Actually, his full name is Edward Simon Nichols, so strictly speaking he's ESN. He's in a residential care home in Alfreton, but he could have some connection with Rose Shepherd.'

'We need to spread the net wider, don't we?'

'Nichols isn't an uncommon name,' said Kessen. 'There could be hundreds of Simons around the country. But unfortunately, these seem to be the only leads we have at the moment. Do you want to allocate them, Paul?'

Hitchens took the files into the CID room and passed on the news to the officers on the early shift.

'Is there one for me?' asked Cooper.

'Yes, I saved this one for you specially, Ben. This Nichols lives on a farm, so it'll suit you down to the ground. The address we have for him is Lea Farm, near Uppertown – wherever the heck that is.'

'I know Uppertown. It's near Bonsall.'

'Bonsall?' said Hitchens. 'Just a minute –'

'Yes, Rose Shepherd made calls to a phone box in that area, didn't she?'

Hitchens smiled as he handed Cooper the file.

'Off you go, then. There's no time to waste.'

When Fry arrived at West Street, it seemed unnaturally quiet. She made her way to the DCI's office, where she found Kessen and Hitchens frowning over a document written in a language she didn't recognize. She leaned over the desk and looked closer. No – it was the alphabet she didn't recognize. Some kind of Cyrillic script?

'Morning, Diane. Take a look,' said Hitchens. 'This could be a whole new angle on the Shepherd enquiry.'

Fry picked out a photograph from the file. It showed the rear view of a red Ford Escort with a foreign registration number and a shattered back window. The car was parked in a garage, with wooden double doors left half open and a padlock hanging from the hasp. The only other thing she noticed was the international plate – BG. Before she could work out what country the initials referred to, she'd unfolded a label attached to the back of the photo and found it was headed in English. The Bulgarian Interior Ministry.

She raised an eyebrow at Kessen, and he took the photo from her. 'OK. A year ago, there was a double murder in a city in northern Bulgaria – a place called Pleven. This car was found by the roadside outside the city. The bodies of two people were in it.'

'Who were they?'

'Their names were Dimitar Iliev, aged forty-three, and Piya Yotova, forty. Iliev had been shot in the head, and Yotova had bullet wounds in the back and arms.'

'Was it some kind of execution?'

Kessen shrugged. 'The Pleven police examined the scene for evidence, but they found nothing to help them identify the assailants.'

'What has this got to do with Rose Shepherd?' said Fry.

'We're not sure yet. But it could have something to do with Simon Nichols. We got a hit on the name from Europol. They're building up a lot of intelligence on cross-border organized crime these days. According to their database, Simon Nichols is an alias for a Bulgarian criminal called Simcho Nikolov. They're sending the complete file on him ASAP.'

Fry tapped the photograph. 'He's a suspect for this shooting in Pleven?'

'He was a known associate of Yotova's, and he disappeared about the time of the shooting. The Bulgarian police have been looking for him ever since.'

'So he could be a professional hit man,' said Hitchens.

'It looks that way,' said Kessen. 'Europol intelligence has come up with two more associates of Nikolov's: the Zhivko brothers – Anton and Lazar. It appears they were members of a criminal gang that got involved in some kind of turf war. The older brother, Anton, was badly injured. He got a bullet lodged in his spine and was left paralysed from the waist down. The Zhivkos had enough money stashed away from their criminal activities that they were able to do a runner and get clear of the country.'

'Don't tell me they're here?'

'Yes, right here in Derbyshire. Two years ago, the Zhivko brothers opened an electrical shop in Chesterfield. It's possible Nikolov came here to join them. So far, they've behaved themselves, but Europol have passed on a tip-off that the Zhivkos are expecting a visitor from their own country – a visitor they might not welcome. An organized crime surveillance unit has been set up in Chesterfield to keep an eye on things.'

'An East European feud happening on our territory?' Hitchens ran a hand through his hair. He was starting to look less elegant than he had when the week started. 'We'd better find out if we have any more Bulgarians in the area. I'll run a check on the dispersal facilities, for a start.'

Kessen studied Fry. 'There's a job for you, Diane. Europol have arranged for an English-speaking officer to liaise with us from Pleven. He'll be calling this morning. And I want you to deal with him.'

Fry was aghast. 'With respect, sir, I've got far more important things to do than become involved in international liaison – especially on the basis of such a tenuous connection.'

'Not quite so tenuous,' said Kessen calmly. 'DC Cooper is following up a potential lead to Simon Nichols in the exact area where Rose Shepherd made calls to a public phone box. And don't forget that the victim had the international dialling code for Bulgaria in her address book – the magic 359.'

Still fuming, Fry went back to her own desk. Bulgaria. The Balkans, right? A former Soviet bloc country, a bastion of Communism during the Cold War era. But what else did she know about it? Nothing.

Fry was still trying to picture what a Bulgarian might actually look like, when her phone rang.

'Hello, DS Fry.'

'*Alo*. My name is Sergeant Georgi Kotsev. I'm calling from Pleven Police Department, on behalf of the Bulgarian Ministry of the Interior.'

Fry tried to mask her sigh. 'Oh, Sergeant Kotsev. Hello. Thank you for sparing the time to talk to us.'

'It's a pleasure to co-operate with our colleagues in the United Kingdom.'

His voice was deep and only slightly accented, not what Fry had expected at all. It didn't fit the Slavic stereotype that had been lurking at the back of her mind – some hatchet-faced villain out of a James Bond film. Kotsev sounded like the man they saved for PR work, smooth and articulate, with excellent English.

'I have your fax about the two shooting victims in Pleven,' said Fry. 'I wonder if you have any further information?'

'We know that they were both shot with an assault rifle, probably a Kalashnikov AK47.'

'Are AK47s commonly available in Bulgaria?'

'If you know the right people, of course.'

Fry grunted, unsurprised. Kalashnikovs were everywhere. They'd become legendary around the world's trouble spots.

'We manufacture a great many Kalashnikovs in Bulgaria,' said Kotsev, perhaps misinterpreting her silence. 'Yes, even now.'

'And they're used by criminal gangs, Sergeant?'

Kotsev laughed. '*Da, razbira se*. Of course. But, you know, the United States government bought many thousands of Kalashnikovs for use in Iraq. Those guns were also made in Bulgaria. They operate better than the American M-16 in dusty conditions, so our manufacturers produce a weapon to NATO standards. Kalashnikovs travel well, like our wine.'

Fry could have listened to him talk for a while, his voice was so interesting. She guessed he'd be one of those people who were terribly disappointing when you met them in person, because their faces didn't match the picture their voices conjured up. Probably he *was* hatchet-faced, after all.

'Any idea of a motive for these killings?' she asked.

'Certainly. People want money. Sometimes they see a way of filling their pockets and getting away with it.' From the tone of his voice, she could almost hear Kotsev shrug. 'And then they get drawn in to events. They mix with the wrong people.'

'And the law catches up with them.'

'The law? Not so often.'

Fry didn't feel able to join in with his chuckle. She turned back to the report on the shooting. 'Dimitar Iliev was involved in organized crime, is that right?'

'Yes, we believe so. But Iliev was a very small player in the game, who became greedy, we think. He and Yotova were found in their car on the E83 highway outside Pleven. We don't know where they were heading.'

'Tell me what you know about Simcho Nikolov.'

'Nikolov is aged fifty-five, a native of the Rhodope Mountains. An army veteran. He was a companion of Iliev's for many years – indeed, they served together as soldiers, but fell on bad times after release from the army. Like so many, these two men turned to crime. For a long time, they were protected from prosecution by their connection with powerful criminal bosses.'

'But their luck ran out,' said Fry.

'Iliev's did, at least. Simcho Nikolov has been sought ever since. We have had no news of him.'

'The shooting was a year ago. You don't seem to have made a lot of progress.'

'Sadly, that is not unusual in this type of investigation.'

'Well, could you keep us updated?'

'I'll fax you any relevant information if we have new developments. Would that be suitable?'

'Yes, excellent.'

Kotsev paused. She thought she heard him drinking, and imagined a cup of decent coffee in his hand. Did they have good coffee in Bulgaria? Just the idea of it was making her mouth dry.

'And what about you, Sergeant Fry?' he said. 'What is your situation?'

'One of my colleagues is following up a possible lead to Nikolov. In fact, he's on his way to the address right now. And we've identified some associates of Nikolov's living in the area. Two brothers by the name of Zhivko.'

Sergeant Kotsev seemed to choke over his coffee. 'Zhivko? Anton and Lazar?'

'Yes.'

'Is one of them disabled? In a wheelchair?'

'I believe so.'

'You should arrest them immediately.'

Surprised by the sudden urgency in his tone, Fry raised her eyebrows at her colleagues in the office, the way they all did when they had someone strange on the phone.

'They don't appear to have committed any crimes here, Sergeant,' she said. 'But we've got them under surveillance.'

'They're dangerous people. And so are their associates. Anton Zhivko was almost killed in an assassination attempt by a rival gang. That was why they left the country.'

'We're aware of that. But they seem to be running a legitimate business so far.'

'That is a joke.'

'No.'

'The Zhivkos are desperate men. In fear of their lives, and therefore dangerous.'

'I'll mention your concerns to my senior officers.'

There was silence at the other end of the phone for a moment. The line to Pleven was so good that she could hear Kotsev breathing, and even the faint buzz of background conversation, and a door closing somewhere.

'If you would like for someone to travel to England, it can be arranged,' he said.

'Why?'

'To assist in your investigation. We very much wish to help. Co-operation with our European colleagues is encouraged at the highest level.'

'Well, I don't think that will be necessary for now, but I'll pass on your offer.'

'It's been a pleasure to liaise with you, Sergeant Fry. I hope we'll speak again soon.'

'Goodbye, then.'

'*Ciao*.'

Fry put the phone down. *Ciao*. Was that a Bulgarian word?

Then she noticed Murfin making frantic gestures at her with his phone.

'What is it, Gavin?'

'I've got that waitress on the phone – the one from Matlock Bath, who came in to do the photofits. I think you'd better speak to her.'

'OK, put her on.'

Murfin transferred the call, and Fry picked up.

'Good morning, Miss Rawson. I understand you have some new information for us. What is it? Have you remembered something?'

'Well, I've just seen something really. That woman I saw on Saturday – it's the one who's in the papers. The one who was killed.'

Fry was disappointed. 'Yes, Rose Shepherd. We know that, Tina. It's the other two people we're trying to identify.'

'No, no. That's what I'm trying to tell you. She's

right here in the paper. I mean the woman she was meeting, the younger one.'

'Who's in the paper, Tina? I don't understand what you're saying.'

'Listen, I'm telling you. The woman that Miss Shepherd met at the tea rooms, the one you wanted me to give you a description of – I've seen a photograph of her in the paper. It's her, it's definitely her.'

Tina took a deep breath, as if realizing that she wasn't going to make herself understood unless she spoke more slowly.

'I'm looking at her photograph right now, Sergeant. She's the woman who was killed in the house fire in Edendale. It says here her name is Lindsay Mullen.'

Almost all the houses in the Bonsall area were built in the local style – limestone walls with contrasting sandstone quoins and door and window surrounds. Derbyshire limestone was notoriously hard to work, so in some places the builders had laid rough stone without any attempt to form courses. Cooper could see small stone buildings scattered across the landscape here. Most of these were field barns, used for storing feed and equipment, or sheltering animals. But some of them were probably disused coes, the huts built by lead miners near their mine shafts.

With a clatter of wings, a flock of racing pigeons took off from a loft and circled Cooper's car. Pigeon lofts seemed to be a feature of Bonsall, too. And that phone box outside the Barley Mow pub – wasn't that supposed to have been designed by the same architect who built Liverpool Cathedral and Waterloo Bridge?

Through Bonsall, the road became single track, with a few passing places tucked into the stone walls. The farm where Simon Nichols worked lay on the plateau to the west of Masson Hill. Cooper had to pass through Uppertown, then follow a couple of B roads before abandoning tarmac altogether for a route the maps would call 'unclassified'. There were no helpful signs, and many of the tracks were old miners' roads that led past the remains of disused lead workings and took you back to where you'd started from. You had to know where you were going in an area like this.

Despite what he'd told the DI, Cooper didn't really know where he was going. This meant he had to stop to consult his OS map, and try to interpret the spider's web of black and green lines that crammed the spaces between the B roads. To his left he could see the curious bumps in the landscape that indicated the covered shafts and overgrown spoil heaps of a long-abandoned mine. But he had no idea whether it was Low Mine, Whitelow Mine, or Beans and Bacon Mine. Or even one of half a dozen sites marked on the map simply as *Mine (disused)*.

Finally he found himself driving down a stony track, looking for a farmhouse that had been promised by a worn sign half a mile back. But before he found Lea Farm, he came across a pick-up truck and a middle-aged farmer unloading posts for fence repairs.

'Good morning. DC Cooper, Edendale Police. I'm looking for a Mr Simon Nichols.'

'Simon? He's not here. He'll probably be holed up in his caravan.'

'He lives in a caravan?'

'Yes, down at the bottom of the big field there.'

'Do you own this farm, sir?'

'Yes, the name's Finney. Michael Finney.'

'So you employ Mr Nichols?'

The farmer grunted as he heaved aside two more posts. 'I suppose so.'

'When did you last see him?'

'Not for a few days, as a matter of fact.'

'Is that normal? I mean, if he's supposed to be employed here.'

Finney straightened his cap and turned to look at Cooper, weighing him up with a shrewd glance.

'Well, the thing about Simon is, he tends to drink quite a lot. Sometimes he goes on a bender and stays away for a couple of days. Other times, he just sleeps it off in the caravan. But he turns up eventually. He's a good worker, when he's sober. That's why I keep him on.'

'And he's cheap, I expect?'

The farmer shrugged. 'This is unskilled work. He's never complained about the wages.'

'Can I take a look at the caravan?'

'If you like. Let me get the last of this stuff off the truck, and I'll show you.'

307

The caravan stood in a corner of a field, almost hidden by weeds and a copse of trees. Cooper had to park his Toyota in a gateway and walk into the field. The eel post of the gate was new enough to swing smoothly on its hinges, but the clap post it closed against was a chunk of weathered timber so black and hard that it almost seemed to have turned to stone.

'Keep him well out of the way, don't you, Mr Finney?'

The farmer shrugged. 'Simon prefers it down here. He likes to keep himself to himself.'

'There's often a reason for that.'

'I don't know what you're getting at.'

Behind the caravan, a row of silage bags glistened in black plastic wrappings, pools of water reflecting the branches of the trees. Overhead, the upper boughs were full of dark, untidy shapes – the nest of the rooks Cooper could see flapping restlessly against the sky.

'Just that some people prefer not to get visitors . . .' he said.

'Oh, I feel that way myself some days.'

'. . . and it usually means they have something to hide.'

Finney sniffed sceptically, but trailed after Cooper as he approached the trees. The nearer he came to the caravan, the more Cooper became aware of the silence in this corner of the field. Apart from the rustling of the birds, there was no sound or movement, no sign of life. Surely someone who didn't like visitors would be alert for a stranger approaching, or the sound of a car parking in the lane.

Cooper stopped and looked around. The field was full of tussocky grass and outcrops of flat, pale limestone. It was enclosed by two walls that snaked across the landscape until they crested a rise. Halfway up the slope, a section of wall had bulged and fallen. The dislodged stones lay on the ground, grass growing over them. This land hadn't been used to contain livestock for a while – not unless Mr Finney was happy for his animals to scramble over the damaged wall.

'I don't suppose Mr Nichols has a car, sir?'

'A car? No. I give him a lift into town now and then, if he needs to go to the doctor's or something,' said Finney. 'Otherwise, he gets around on that –'

The farmer pointed to an old motorbike propped against one end of the caravan. Cooper hadn't noticed it until now. It was so decrepit that it seemed to have grown out of the weeds.

'He uses the bike to get around? Even when he's out drinking?'

'Sometimes.'

'But he isn't out on it now, is he?'

'I reckon not.'

With a sinking feeling, Cooper knocked on the door of the caravan. 'Mr Nichols? Are you in there?' He knocked again, a metallic clanging as if he was hitting a big tin can. A big, empty tin can. 'Anyone home?'

'He might be asleep,' said Finney.

Faded curtains were drawn across the windows. A pattern of orange flowers, speckled with black dots. By pressing his face close to the glass, Cooper could see a small slice of the interior through a narrow gap where the curtains didn't meet. He saw the edge of a folding wooden table, a scatter of papers, and two beer cans. Orange cans, to match the curtains. Probably Stone's Bitter from the supermarket in Matlock. One of the cans had been knocked over, and beer was spilt on the table.

'Police! Open up!' called Cooper, more loudly. And he gave the door a couple of good thumps that shook the caravan on its chassis. 'Mr Finney, the occupant appears to be absent. Do I have your permission to enter this caravan?'

'Eh? Well, I suppose so – if you really want to. It won't be very nice in there, you know. Old Simon, he isn't the cleanest of folk.'

'It doesn't matter. I don't suppose you have a key, sir?'

'I might have one back at the house. But we probably don't need one. You could just try –'

But Cooper had already tried. The handle turned in his fingers with a faint scrape of metal. 'You're right, we don't need one.'

He gave the door a yank, but it jammed in the frame where it had warped out of shape. Cooper braced his foot against the step and pulled harder. The soft aluminium began to bend in his hands, and the door screeched as it was forced open.

Cooper flinched at the noise, his teeth suddenly set on edge, his muscles tensing instinctively.

With the door open, the two men were frozen for a moment, suddenly reluctant to enter the caravan, or even take a step closer. A fat blue-bottle buzzed through the gap and zigzagged slowly past them, too tired and bloated to escape.

Finney drew in a sharp breath, as if he'd been punched in the stomach. His involuntary cry of disgust sent a flock of rooks clattering into the air, cawing with alarm, their black feathers rattling through the branches. Then the farmer made a choking, gurgling sound and staggered towards the wall. He hadn't reached it before he doubled over and vomited into the grass.

Standing in the doorway of the caravan, Cooper covered his mouth and nose with a hand as he watched a pool of dark, sticky liquid hover on the edge of the step before trickling slowly towards the ground, forming an oily pool on the earth. The sweet smell of it was like a finger pushed down his throat, making him swallow as he fought a surge of nausea.

Cooper didn't have to look very far to find the source of the smell. He didn't even have to enter the caravan, which was a relief. Because Mr Finney had been right about another thing. It really wasn't very nice in there.

20

'She must have been a stranger,' said Brian Mullen. 'I can't think who else this person would have been.'

Mullen was in the conservatory at the Lowthers' house in Darley Dale. His father-in-law sat near him, perhaps for moral support. Occasionally, Mullen glanced into the house, where his mother-in-law was keeping Luanne entertained. Fry didn't have much interest in babies, but this one seemed reasonably civilized and quiet.

'Did your wife mention meeting her, sir?'

'No. I knew she'd been out on Saturday, of course. Lindsay left me with the children for a couple of hours. She said she wanted to do some early Christmas shopping, that was all. That was the way she was, you know – she liked to plan ahead.'

'Which shops did she go to?' asked Fry.

'I don't know. She wouldn't have told me that.'

'And she didn't say anything afterwards?'

Mullen considered it.

'Come to think of it, I think Lindsay did say she'd chatted to a couple of strangers in a café. I've no idea who they were.'

'Did she mention any names?'

'No. Of course, she probably didn't ask them their names, if it was just a casual conversation.'

'Possibly.'

'You know what it's like. You don't necessarily want to strike up an instant relationship with complete strangers. You've no idea what sort of crooks they might be these days. People pretend to be friendly, and they turn out to be con artists after your money.'

'Did she describe these people at all?'

'No, why should she? It was only a passing remark, that she'd been chatting to a couple of people. I expect they were just talking about the weather, or the difficulty in finding somewhere to park, or whether the tea was any good. Why would she describe them? It's as if you're suggesting it's Lindsay's fault she didn't say anything.'

Seeing Mr Mullen becoming agitated, Fry paused and let him subside.

'I can't remember any more than that,' he said. 'Do you think these people might have been responsible for the fire?'

'We don't know, sir. But it's very important that you try to remember anything your wife might have said. If it occurs to you who she might have been meeting, or any little details she let slip, please inform us straightaway.'

'All right. Of course.'

Fry stood up to go. She hadn't achieved anything by the visit. In fact, she wondered if she'd just given Brian Mullen a get-out for the arson. Mysterious strangers didn't fit into her scenario.

A pool of light ran slowly over the corpse. It started at the feet and travelled up the legs to a distended stomach. Pale skin showed through burst shirt buttons. The hand holding the Maglite tilted, and the beam moved across the chest, paused at the throat, and finally hovered over the face.

'Was there a fight in here?'

'I don't know. I think this might have been its normal condition.'

The light focused on Ben Cooper's face. He blinked in the glare and smiled uncertainly.

'Is it possible to tell how he died?' he asked. 'There's a bruise on his cheekbone, but I suppose he could have got it when he fell.'

The pathologist ran her torch over the face of the corpse again. 'I'll be able to confirm that after the PM. It depends what damage I find underneath the tissue. If the bone is fractured, it might suggest blunt-force trauma – an injury caused by a greater impact than a simple fall.'

'A blow to the head?'

'Possibly. It might not be as plain as that in my report.'

'He's been lying here a while. He's already starting to smell a bit.'

314

'Yes, he's been dead a couple of days. That might make it more difficult. Post-mortem changes can mask small injuries. There's a very strong smell of alcohol, too.'

'Yes, I noticed that.'

Nichols's body lay wedged between a bench seat and a fold-up table. The angle of his limbs gave the impression he'd been struggling, but whether against an attacker or just to get up, it wasn't clear. He was face-up, and had vomited at some time – well, a couple of days ago, at least. His stomach was white and bloated where it was exposed, but his face and hands looked thin to the point of gauntness. He was unshaven, and his dark hair was receding.

The interior of the caravan was strewn with clothes, and a number of empty lager cans stood on the drainer by the tiny sink. A scatter of papers and magazines lay on the table next to a little portable TV set, but Cooper was afraid to touch them. Best to let the SOCOs sort them out after the body had been removed.

'I presume he lived on his own,' said Hitchens later, as he stood well clear of the smell.

'Yes, I think it would be safe to say that, sir.'

'What else have we got, Ben?'

Cooper flicked open his notebook. 'He's known as Simon Nichols, but that's probably not his real name. He's aged about fifty-five, and he'd lived here for eight months. The caravan belongs to the farmer, who doesn't seem to have asked many questions.'

'I hope he didn't pay too much rent. I've never seen such a dump.'

'I gather it was in exchange for his work on the farm. Free accommodation and probably less than the minimum wage. It was originally used for accommodating foreign students who came over in the summer to help with the harvest. But this farm hasn't produced a decent crop for years.'

'How can you tell?'

'Didn't you notice the field on the way in? It's full of bracken and ragwort. The place has been neglected.'

'OK. And this is Nikolov?'

'Well, Nichols certainly wasn't his real name. Mr Finney admits that his worker wasn't British. He never asked him about his nationality, but guessed he might be Polish. Nichols didn't speak much English, only what he needed to get by.'

'I bet "beer" was a word he knew,' said Hitchens.

A Scientific Support van crawled into the field and parked next to the silage bags. Wayne Abbott got out.

'My God, this took some finding.'

'Better get the masks out, Wayne,' said Hitchens. 'We're going to need you to take this caravan apart.'

Flood lamps were already up, and a crime-scene tent was going over the caravan.

'I asked Wayne to bring a gunshot residue kit,' said Hitchens. 'I don't know how this man is connected to Rose Shepherd, but we're not going to miss anything.'

The latest GSR kit was designed for a presumptive test at the scene, and another in the lab later. Previous tests had involved swabbing the hands of a suspect and sending the swabs to a lab. Since results from the scanning electron microscope took weeks or even months, many officers had saved time by just not bothering with GSR.

'Negative. Sorry,' said Abbott a few minutes later.

'Damn.'

'There's hardly any food in this caravan,' said Cooper. 'Just cans of beer and half a bottle of vodka. He looks ill, too.'

'Dead people usually do,' said Hitchens.

'Not always.'

The DI ran a hand across his forehead. 'No, you're right, Ben.'

Cooper took a walk around the field where the caravan was sited. There were lots of gaps in the drystone walls, easy enough for anyone to get in or out of the area without having to come down the track or past the farmhouse.

'If the farmer can be believed, Simon Nichols lived a quiet, reclusive life and was hardly seen in daylight, except when he was working.'

'Great,' said Hitchens. 'He's already starting to sound like Rose Shepherd.'

21

'You see what I meant about not being able to cut yourself off completely?' Fry said later, when she had Cooper and Murfin together in the CID room.

'Miss Shepherd, you mean?' said Cooper.

'Of course. She not only had the postman, the meter reader, and God knows who else coming by the house, but she was forced to have Eric Grice in to do a few odd jobs, the repairs she couldn't manage.'

'I wonder if he was handy for a few *really* odd jobs,' said Murfin.

Fry gave him a look. 'She had to take a gamble on Eric, didn't she?' she said. 'It must have been a toss-up whether to get a complete stranger in every time she needed something doing, or to stick to one local man. She must have known Eric would talk about her in the village, but she decided a bit of gossip was preferable to having people in the house she knew nothing about. At least she could be sure that Eric was the genuine article.'

'Yes, she had to let someone a little way into her life,' said Cooper. 'I wonder if Mr Grice realizes how privileged he was.'

'Privileged, right.' Fry began to count on her fingers. 'Then there was the estate agent and the solicitor. She wasn't in a position to buy a property without professional help, and they had to know something about her. Her bank account details, for a start.'

'And –'

Fry held up another finger. 'And then she met Lindsay Mullen in Matlock Bath.'

'But do you think that was entirely by chance, Diane? A random encounter between strangers? Or could there have been some connection between them?'

'Maybe she wanted to give Lindsay something?' said Murfin.

'Why, Gavin?'

'Miss Shepherd seems to have known that she was in danger and people were trying to find her. What if she had an item in her possession that she didn't want anyone to get hold of? Why not pass it on to someone entirely unconnected? A stranger, in fact.'

Fry began to move restlessly around the office. She walked to the window and back again towards her desk, as if a change in the direction of the light might help her to see things more clearly.

'If she did that, she was sealing Lindsay Mullen's fate,' she said. 'It looks as though Rose Shepherd

319

was already being watched when she went into Matlock Bath that day, doesn't it? And whoever was watching her must also have followed Lindsay home.'

'Why would Miss Shepherd pick on Lindsay to talk to?'

'Why pick on anybody? For heaven's sake, who buttonholes complete strangers in cafés and engages them in conversation?'

'Drunks and nutters,' said Murfin.

'Exactly. And Rose Shepherd was neither of those.'

'Well, she had to be a bit odd. This woman was a hermit with a secrecy obsession.'

'That's right. You don't have to be a complete nutter,' said Cooper. 'Rose Shepherd had cut herself off for so long, perhaps she just wanted a few minutes of ordinary conversation, even with a complete stranger. In fact, a stranger is a better choice. They don't know anything about you, or your past. So they don't start off with preconceptions about you.'

'If she was that desperate, why didn't she talk to Eric Grice? Whenever he came to Bain House, Miss Shepherd kept herself out of the way and refused to engage in conversation.'

'Maybe she was afraid that, once she started talking, she wouldn't be able to stop. She couldn't risk it.' Cooper looked up at her. 'You know what it's like yourself. When you've got something preying on your mind and you find someone easy to talk to, it all comes spilling out.'

'Really?'

'Oh, well – maybe not you, Diane.'

'Thanks,' she said, and meant it.

'But take it from me, it works that way with a lot of people. You can find yourself telling everything to some sympathetic stranger who's prepared to listen. I think Rose Shepherd was so scared of giving away clues about herself that talking to people was too much of a risk. So she avoided it. Simple as that. A bit like a recovered alcoholic avoids taking the first drink. It's not the one drink that's the problem – it's what he knows it will lead to.'

Fry began to pace the room again. 'OK. So what was she hiding?'

'Well, that,' said Cooper, 'I don't know. I can't imagine what it's like to be so alone, to cut yourself off from everyone that way. How could anyone do that?'

'Why are you asking *me*?'

Cooper raised an eyebrow at her tone and looked around the room. 'Apart from Gavin, there's no one else here, Diane.'

Fry was silent for a while, staring down at the floor. 'This is getting us nowhere. Instead of all these what ifs, we need to start finding some answers.'

'Sounds good to me,' said Murfin. 'So when do we start?'

'Gavin –'

'Sorry.'

'Well, I know one thing,' said Cooper. 'It's difficult to see a connection between the fire and the shooting. And now Simon Nichols – how does he fit in? I suppose if he didn't die until Tuesday, he could have been involved in both incidents.'

'Hold on,' said Fry. 'So far as we can tell, there were nearly twenty-four hours between the two. In Rose Shepherd's case, the medical examiner gave us a pretty wide range for time of death – between thirty and forty hours. But let's get this straight – the Foxlow shooting came first. It's just that the victim wasn't discovered until after the fire.'

'Maybe Lindsay Mullen was in the wrong place at the wrong time, then. She must somehow have got a look at Nichols, or whoever was watching Rose Shepherd. A good enough look to be able to identify him later.'

'So he decided to take her out before she could give anyone a description?'

Cooper nodded. 'Before she even knew that Miss Shepherd had been killed. The body wasn't discovered until Monday afternoon.'

'Somebody wasn't taking any chances, were they?'

'It's because they're –'

'Yes, I know. Professionals,' said Fry. 'That's another factor against Nichols. If he wasn't a professional himself, he had the right contacts.'

'Well, we'll have to wait for the PM results before we know more about Nichols.'

Fry stared at the ceiling for a few moments. 'You know, you were right – the Shepherd enquiry is becoming a big distraction for me. I should be focusing on the arson.'

'What do you mean?' said Cooper.

'Well, there *are* easier ways to kill somebody, don't you think? Easier than breaking into their house and setting fire to their sitting room. More guaranteed to get the right results, too – because, if the smoke alarm had been working properly, the Mullens might have escaped.'

'Perhaps not that much easier, if you want to make it look like an accident.'

'An accident?' Fry tapped the Rose Shepherd file. 'That doesn't sound like the Foxlow suspect, does it? There was certainly no attempt to make Miss Shepherd's death look like an accident. Quite the opposite – it was done openly and audaciously, like some kind of warning: "Look, we can get to anyone, anywhere."'

'Ye-es,' said Cooper.

Fry looked at him sharply. 'I take it you've formed a different opinion, Ben?'

'Well, just because there was that difference it doesn't necessarily follow that they weren't connected, does it? Our suspects might have had some reason for wanting to make the fire look accidental, but not the shooting of Rose Shepherd.'

'What reason?'

Cooper shook his head. 'I don't know . . .'

'No. But what we do know at the moment is

323

that Rose Shepherd had connections with a Bulgarian criminal, who's also been found dead. We don't have any more information on Nikolov until we get PM results and the intelligence files from Sofia.'

'You almost make that sound like a good thing, Diane.'

'Well, it means I can focus on the Darwin Street fire for a while. Unrelated, or not.'

A few minutes later, Fry finished reading the post-mortem reports on the Mullen family for the second time. She put the report aside, then recalled what Mrs van Doon had said about the victims being confused and disorientated by the inhalation of smoke.

She picked up the phone and rang Scientific Support. Wayne Abbott, one of her favourite people.

'Wayne, you know you said the fingerprints in the house at Darwin Street all belonged to members of the family?'

'Yes?'

'Which members of the family did you mean specifically?'

'Hold on . . .' She heard the rustling of paper as he found the right file. 'Here we go. Well, as you might expect, there were prints from the householders everywhere – that's Mr Brian Mullen and Mrs Lindsay Mullen. And the children, of course. They were easy to differentiate because of their size.'

'OK.'

'Right. Those prints were mostly from the relatively undamaged parts of the house, you understand.'

'Like the kitchen?'

'Exactly. I mention that because we lifted a couple of prints belonging to the grandmother, Mrs Moira Lowther. We asked all the family to give their prints for elimination purposes, of course. But hers were only in the kitchen. Nice, smooth surfaces for us to dust, you see. We found none from her husband, though. That doesn't necessarily mean anything. There was so much damage in the sitting room –'

'Anyone else on the list?'

'Yes, the dead woman's brother, Mr John Lowther.'

'Where were his prints?'

'Oh, kitchen, bathroom, sitting room. Some of his were on the children's toys that we salvaged. I expect he used to spend some time playing uncle with the kids, don't you think?'

'Yes,' said Fry. 'That's probably it.'

The engaged sign was showing on the door of Interview One. Inside, John Lowther seemed to be sweating. Damp patches had appeared under his armpits, and his glasses were slipping on his nose. He looked like a man caught performing some shameful act. Yet all he was doing was sitting in a police interview room, waiting for the questions.

With Cooper sitting in to observe, Fry began by asking Lowther to confirm his name, age and address. Then she looked at him, momentarily unsure how to approach the interview, to get him talking.

'I gather your address is an apartment, sir?'

'Yes, it's a new development in Matlock. They converted an old will, I mean mill. It's rather nice.'

'I see. Do you own the apartment, Mr Lowther?'

'It's a nine-hundred-and-ninety-nine-year lease. With nine hundred and ninety-seven years left to run. Less two years, you see. But it's no loss.'

Fry frowned. 'Right. And you're an actuary by profession?'

'– confession? Yes, I have very intensive experience in the field.'

'Do you?'

'I worked in Leeds, in West Yorkshire, for three years. But I left that job a year ago.'

'So you're not employed at the moment?'

He smiled. 'You might say I'm resting. There's not so much work for actuaries around these ports.'

'I see.'

Fry had never felt so unsure of anyone before. She could hear herself saying 'I see' too much, a clear indication to anyone listening that she hardly understood a thing that Lowther was saying. Did he recognize that, too? Was it a deliberate ploy on his part to disrupt her interview technique? If so, it was very subtle. But it was working.

Suddenly, Lowther seemed to stare past her at something on the wall.

'Is there a dog here somewhere?'

Fry didn't know what to say. She looked at Cooper to see how he was reacting, but he was quite still, watching carefully.

She paused to gather her thoughts before her next question. But Lowther wouldn't allow a pause.

'One of my neighbours has a dog. A cross-bred Alsatian. Long-haired, shaggy – you know? All the time I've lived in the apartment, I've never heard it bark. Not even when the binmen come in through the back gate.'

'Why does that worry you, sir?'

'How do you know what's a dog, and what isn't? Dogs are domesticated wolves. But wolves don't bark. So if a dog doesn't bark, is it actually a wolf? It's a question of identity, you see.'

'Mr Lowther, when did you last see your sister?'

'Oh, Lindsay? Last week. It could have been the week before.'

'Did you visit the house in Darwin Street on that occasion?'

He hesitated, contorting his mouth as if trying to work around some words that he couldn't pronounce.

'I can't remember.'

'Surely you can remember where you last saw your sister.'

Lowther stared at her. She noticed that the

327

focus of his eyes was shifting back and forth, like someone trying to get a fix on a constantly moving object. Fry began to feel as though she wasn't really there to him. Not all of the time, anyway.

'I can't remember. Did I say that already?'

Fry deliberately shifted her position, made a show of moving her notes on the table, gestured with her hands in front of her face. Anything to make sure she had John Lowther's full attention.

'I know you were very close to your sister, sir. But what sort of relationship do you have with your brother-in-law, Brian Mullen? Would you say there was some resentment between you?'

But Lowther barely seemed to have heard her. He made that chewing movement with his mouth again. Fry decided he wasn't trying to pronounce the words, but to swallow them, to suck them back into his mouth before they reached the air.

Then, astonishingly, he smiled at her. It was a charming smile, friendly and guileless. *What a nice conversation we're having* his expression seemed to say.

'Is there another question?'

Fry sighed. 'Yes. Mr Lowther, have you ever seen this before?'

She showed him a photograph of the wooden dinosaur.

'Tyrannosaurus.'

'Have you seen it before?'

'No. Is it from abroad?'

'We don't know.'

328

'Some people go abroad, hunting for whores. No, for babies.'

'What?'

'I'm sorry, I get confused sometimes. I'm not sure what you're asking me. Is it time?'

Fry automatically looked at her watch. 'Time?'

'Time to leave.'

'Do you want to leave, sir? You're only here voluntarily, so you can leave whenever you want. We can't keep you against your will. But we only want to ask you some questions, Mr Lowther. We're trying to find out how your sister and her children died.'

'What are they saying?' said Lowther.

Again, he seemed to be looking at something behind her. Or perhaps not looking at something, but listening.

'Are you all right, sir?' she asked.

'You don't have to believe what people are saying, you know.'

'I'm sorry, sir, I don't quite follow –'

'The things they say,' he insisted. 'They aren't always right. You don't have to believe them.'

'Which people do you mean particularly?'

Lowther looked anxious. A bead of sweat formed at his temple and trickled slowly towards his jaw.

'Whoever it is that you're listening to. *I* don't know who they are. I don't know who any of them are.'

'What have people been saying to you, sir? Have

you been hearing rumours? Please share any information you have.'

Lowther tilted his head. 'I've got exceptional hearing, I'm told. I can hear the people in the next room now.'

Fry tried for a while longer, probing for information about his feelings towards Brian Mullen, and about the last time he'd visited the Mullens' house in Darwin Street. But she could feel that she was getting nowhere. The conversation seemed to veer off in directions that she had no control over, and she didn't know how to bring it back under control. She just didn't have anything of substance to use against Lowther and pin him down.

When the interview was finally over, they watched John Lowther leave. Then Fry walked back and checked Interview Room Two.

'There wasn't anyone in the next room,' she said.

'So what was he hearing?' asked Cooper.

'I don't know.'

'Something outside? Someone chatting in the corridor?'

'Maybe.'

'Some people do have particularly good hearing. They say blind people develop their other senses to compensate.'

'So what is John Lowther compensating for?' said Fry. 'Let's face it, he's unbalanced.'

'Hang on, Diane. He could be faking it.'

'Faking it?'

'Well, all that stuff was verbal. It was like a smokescreen. He didn't actually answer any of your questions, as I'm sure you noticed.'

'A bit of a teacake,' said Fry thoughtfully.

'What?'

'It was something Gavin said.'

'Well, we shouldn't underestimate Gavin's judgement.'

'I think I'll get John Lowther's background looked into,' said Fry. 'Faking it, or not.'

Listening to the interview tapes afterwards, Cooper noticed a pattern to John Lowther's answers. Sometimes he spoke quickly, the words spilling out with no prompting. At other times, he was hesitant, leaving long pauses before he answered. During these periods, he seemed to ramble and go off at tangents, often failing to address the question altogether.

At other times, Lowther seemed eager to anticipate what his interviewer was going to say, and tried to complete her sentences for her, often guessing the wrong word from its initial letter or sound. It sounded like a verbal equivalent to the predictive text function on his mobile phone. Both produced gibberish too often to be any real use.

Cooper had heard this kind of language before. The sound of it brought back so many unpleasant memories that he knew he was reacting on an emotional level. He tried to suppress the response, to smother assumptions that might prevent him from being objective. These days, his antennae twitched at the first sign of aberrant behaviour in those around him. Right now, he was even more touchy on the subject, thanks to Matt and his obsessions. But not every eccentricity or verbal quirk was a sign of mental illness.

He looked around for Fry. 'I wonder if Lowther might have had experience of police interviews before,' he said.

But Fry shook her head. 'Not according to the PNC. He doesn't have any previous.'

'No previous convictions, yes. But he might have been questioned and not charged. Should I follow it up?'

'Yes. And don't forget Lowther was on West Yorkshire's patch for three years.'

'OK. Have you done a PNC check on Brian Mullen, by the way?'

'He has no record, not even any driving offences. There's no local intelligence on him either, so he has no known criminal associates.'

'No one he could call on for a competent arson job, then?'

'I don't think he needed to. This was a personal affair.'

'Right.'

Fry watched Cooper put on his jacket and check his mobile phone, ready to leave.

'Are you in Matlock Bath later this afternoon, Ben?'

'Yes. I've got to go back to the shopping village.'

'Do me a favour – keep an eye out for some-where you might buy a wooden dinosaur.'

Cooper stopped. 'What? Oh, the photo that you showed Lowther.'

'I want to find out where this came from. It must be fairly unusual. I've never seen anything like it myself, and Brian Mullen tells me he's never seen it before either. If it was a gift for one of the Mullen children, it might have been from a recent visitor to the house.'

Cooper studied the wooden toy closely. 'Hang on – I think I did see something like this in Matlock Bath on Tuesday. Not exactly the same, perhaps – but similar.' He shook his head. 'I'm sorry, Diane, I should have taken more notice.'

'That's OK, Ben. But check it out for me, will you?'

Cooper handed the photos back. 'The Rose Shepherd enquiry isn't getting anywhere, is it? It's too unfocused.'

'I agree. What we need is someone to point us in the right direction.'

'Oh, I nearly forgot – there was a message from Sergeant Kotsev,' said Cooper.

'Oh? What does he say?'

'He says his flight from Sofia will land at Manchester Airport at twenty minutes to five.'

'What? He's coming *here*? For God's sake, why weren't we told about this?'

'I don't know. Maybe there was another message that we missed.'

'And maybe not,' said Fry bitterly. 'Twenty to five? Does he mean *today*?'

'I suppose so.'

'Damn it, he must have been phoning me from the check-in desk. He must have been practically on board the plane already.'

'Do you want to hear the rest of the message?'

'No, but you'd better give it me anyway.'

'Well, he sends his respects to Sergeant Fry. And he wonders if you'd be free to pick him up from the airport.'

22

Cooper decided to drive down through Cromford to reach Matlock Bath. It was a relief to get out into the countryside again. This was his natural environment, not the stuffy meetings to discuss assassinations and organized crime, where he felt uneasy and out of his depth. Let Diane Fry have that side of the job, if she wanted it.

Emerging from the canopy of trees on the Via Gellia, he passed a little tufa cottage. This was one of the area's most photographed buildings, and it looked just the way he remembered it – a house made of grey, spongy stone, with wisteria growing up the wall and geraniums in the window boxes, like something out of a fairy tale.

A few yards further on, the road swung to the right by the old Pig of Lead pub and the mills nestling in Bonsall Hollow, below Ball Eye Quarry. There was a quirky little bookshop opposite the pond in Cromford – the type of place that had vanished from most high streets, but still lurked in corners of the

Peak District. Cooper could see it across the water as he entered the village. On a day like this, he'd have liked to be free to spend an hour or so browsing the shelves, making discoveries, drinking a cup of freshly ground coffee. Maybe there'd be home-made homity pie on the menu.

But he had to drive on, filtering left at the cross-roads on to the A6. After the tightly clustered cottages of Cromford, Masson Mill looked enormous in its position between the road and the river. This stretch of the Derwent Valley had been classified as a world heritage site a few years ago. When the centre of the cotton industry moved to Manchester, the mills and millworkers' villages of Derbyshire had been left almost intact in their rural backwater.

Some of the old millworkers said that the ghost of Arkwright himself still trod the creaking floor-boards at Masson Mill. It was easy to believe that he wasn't long gone when you saw the dusty boxes stacked on the shelves in the spinning room. '*Return to Sir Richard Arkwright*'. Of course, everyone knew he was buried down the road at Cromford. The mansion he'd built, but never lived in, stood directly across the river from the mill, among trees that he'd planted but never seen grown to maturity.

The back wall of the mill overlooked the river. Its five storeys were full of windows – long ranks of them separated into pairs by stone mullions. They were spaced with Victorian precision, but so small and dark that nothing was visible behind the glass. Those windows stared out across the rushing water like blank eyes. There were scores of them, a hundred pairs of eyes – a high, brick wall full of dead faces.

Upstream, a fallen tree trunk was caught on the edge of the weir. It jerked from side to side as the flow of water hit it, dead boughs thrashing like a man drowning in the foam. It must have been drawn into the current from the opposite bank, or it would have been carried away into the water channel that fed the mill wheel.

Inside the shopping village, Frances Birtland had just arrived and was taking off her coat.

'My neighbour?' she said. 'Rose Shepherd?'

'You don't remember your neighbour coming in on Saturday?'

'No. Did she come in? How embarrassing. But I saw so little of her, that I suppose I didn't recognize her.'

'Your colleague Mrs Hooper recognized her from her photograph in the papers.'

Mrs Birtland shook her head. 'I don't read the papers very much. They're always so depressing, aren't they?'

'But you were definitely here all that afternoon?'

'Of course. Did Eva say different?'

'No.'

A customer was hovering behind him, and Cooper stood back for a moment. He took the opportunity to check out the stock on the central display units. He prided himself on his observation, but he'd completely missed the wooden toys last time he was here.

Cooper picked one up. It wasn't a dinosaur, but the wood looked the same as the toy that Fry had shown him, and the style of carving was identical.

He looked at Frances Birtland, who was smiling at him, hoping for a sale.

'Where are these from?' he said.

'Eva has them imported direct from Bulgaria. Traditionally crafted and ecologically friendly. I think they're lovely, don't you?'

'Is there a dinosaur in the range?'

'Yes, but I'm afraid we sold the last one.'

Darren Turnbull pulled his Astra on to the grass verge, waited until a tractor went past, then nipped into the phone box. He never liked using his mobile to ring Magpie Cottage, in case Fiona got hold of the phone and checked his calls.

'You've got to come and meet me outside the village,' he said when Stella answered.

'So you know it's you they're looking for, don't you?' she said. 'You're scared, Darren.'

'I just don't think it's sensible to make a free gift of some gossip to those nosy buggers that live near you.'

'You know what I think – you've got to go to the police.'

'I can't, Stell.'

'They're trying to catch someone who committed a murder.'

'I know, but –'

'So you don't care? You don't care that there's a murderer walking about right in my village, murdering women who live on their own?'

'Oh, Stella, you'll be all right.'

'You ought to be here looking after me and making *sure* I'm all right.'

'Meet me in Wirksworth or Cromford or somewhere,' he pleaded. 'That's not far to go.'

'And then what, eh?'

'Well –'

'If you think I'm doing it in the back of a car at my age, Darren Turnbull, you've got another think coming. Especially in your bloody Astra, with the police looking for it everywhere. I don't want some copper banging on the window and catching me with my knickers off.'

'We'll go somewhere quiet. There's lots of places we could find.'

'No. Darren, either you go to the police like you should, or I'll phone them myself and tell them who that car belongs to.'

'Stella –'

'Yes, I will. And then they'll come round to your house to pick you up. How would your precious Fiona like that, eh?'

Darren went cold at the thought. He glanced guiltily out of the phone box, but no one was around to see him.

'Look, Stell, there's no need for that. I'll come round to the cottage as usual tonight, and we'll have a talk about it, OK?'

'Fine. See you, then. And don't forget the booze.'

Before she left West Street, Fry knocked on the door of the DI's office to report her movements. She found Hitchens staring at a passport that lay on his desk in a clear plastic wallet. Its cover was the familiar burgundy red, with the royal crest embossed in gold. The lion and the unicorn, *dieu et mon droit.*

'Is that Rose Shepherd's passport?' she asked.

'Yes. Don't you think it's weird to have a French motto on the front of a British passport? I bet most people don't understand what it means.'

'We're in the European Union now,' said Fry. 'We're not supposed to understand what anything means. So why is it here?'

'The HOLMES team checked the passport number. It seems that no such passport was ever issued by the UK authorities. We're going to send it to the FSS for their document examiners to have a look at, but the conclusion seems pretty clear. Rose Shepherd's passport is a forgery. A very good one – but still a forgery.'

'But that means –'

Hitchens swivelled his chair to face her.

'Yes, Diane. It means we have absolutely no idea who she really was.'

* * *

It was five thirty-eight in the evening when Lazar Zhivko tapped the numbers into the keypad and locked the door of his electrical shop in Stephenson Place, Chesterfield. He rattled the handle to make certain it was secure and looked over his shoulder, as if afraid that a mugger might choose this moment to strike. Lazar's eyes were dark with anxiety as he scanned the pavement and the cars parked in front of the shop.

While Lazar hesitated in the shop doorway, his brother Anton was already waiting at the kerb, drumming his fingers impatiently on the arms of his wheelchair, fidgeting with the rug on his knees. He stared straight ahead, taking no notice of the people passing by, even though they barely had enough room to get past him without stepping into the road.

When he glanced in the direction of the Rutland pub, the streetlights seemed to form even deeper shadows among the lines etched like knife marks in his face.

The camera recording Lazar Zhivko's movements had captured that expression on his face many times before. It was immortalized in the stills pinned to copies of his file and handed out to officers on surveillance shifts. One observer had described it as the look of a man who'd learned always to expect the worst.

'I wish I knew what the hell the brother was looking at.'

The two surveillance officers were starting to

feel drowsy. The store room was stuffy, and specks of dust drifted in the air whenever either of them moved from the cardboard box he was sitting on. All afternoon they hadn't dared to open the sash even an inch, in case they drew attention to their position. Even now that it was getting dark, they were being careful.

'It's not us he's looking at, anyway.'

'Are you sure?'

'Don't worry, he hasn't seen us.'

'Maybe he's spotted somebody on the pavement this side of the road. We ought to get someone in the street to check.'

'No, I don't think so.'

'Well, he must be looking at the menswear shop next door, then. I know their window display is pretty weird, but I wouldn't have thought it was bad enough to make him look like that.'

Anton Zhivko's expression was much more difficult to interpret than his brother's. Anton looked resigned, yet contemptuous, as if he could see a threat approaching and had resolved not to run, but to face it without fear.

The angle of the camera was adjusted as Lazar Zhivko finally left the door of the shop. Stepping on to the pavement, Lazar gripped the handles of his brother's wheelchair and kicked off the foot-brake. The camera panned slowly to follow him as the two men headed towards the white Renault Kangoo parked outside the bakery.

'He's lost sight of whatever it was. Now, he just

looks pissed off. He's saying something to Lazar. That's the trouble with making silent movies like this – you need subtitles. It's a pity Technical Support couldn't have got a microphone on to the wheelchair to pick up sound.'

'How would they have done that? Anton is only ever out of the thing when he goes to bed or to the toilet. Besides, how good is your Bulgarian?'

By now, Lazar had stopped at the rear of the Kangoo and applied the brake on the chair. He thumbed an electronic key from his pocket and the lights on the vehicle flashed.

The Kangoo had an electrically operated folding ramp and a power winch to load the wheelchair through the rear doors. Someone with too much time on his hands had added a note in the file to say it was a Bekker conversion. Lazar didn't look strong enough to have helped his brother out of his chair and into the van without the winch. And there was no doubt the Zhivkos could afford an extra thousand pounds or so for the technology.

'Well, business is over for the day. I reckon we can knock off and claim our Oscars.'

'Not until they're clear of the area. Let's do the job properly.'

'OK. But all this on account of some dodgy intelligence? I hope Europol appreciate what we're going through on their behalf.'

The camera's field of view covered the

Zhivkos' vehicle and three cars parked in front of it on the north side of Stephenson Place. Surveillance had confirmed that the brothers always arrived early to make sure they got a space for the Kangoo near their shop. To the west, there were double yellow lines along the kerb all the way to the lights at the corner of Knifesmithgate, so the position of the camera had pretty much decided itself. The first-floor store room above the charity shop provided a decent vantage point, at the right angle to catch the face of anyone leaving the shop. Even better, there were bars on the store-room window and stacks of boxes already in place to disguise the camera's outline.

A radio crackled. 'Have they left the shop?'

'Yes, they're in the street, about to load the wheelchair into the van. It looks like they're heading for home.'

'A wash-out, then.'

The monitor showed that Lazar Zhivko had positioned his brother's chair behind the Renault and left him there while he went to the driver's door. There was still time for a contact, but not much. The brothers would be gone from the scene in the next couple of minutes.

'A couple of lads are walking towards the shop from Knifesmithgate.'

'Lads?'

'Sorry. Two white males, aged eighteen to twenty, wearing jeans and sweatshirts. They're slowing a bit as they get to the vehicle. No, they're just admiring the van.'

'They're not interested in the Zhivkos?'

'They're passing on. No contact. We got them on film anyway.'

'Nothing. As soon as the brothers move out of the street, we'll call it a day here. Team Two can pick them up at home.'

The aluminium ramp was unfolding itself from the rear doors of the Kangoo. Lazar leaned in to press a button under the dashboard, and the lift lowered slowly towards the road. The roof of the vehicle was high enough to take both Anton and his wheelchair without any undignified heaving to transfer his body to a van seat. It wasn't the most stylish mode of transport, but it was convenient for the Zhivkos, and so distinctive that it was a gift for surveillance.

From this distance, it wasn't possible to hear the hum of the electric motor that drove the ramp. But because it was too loud, or for some other reason, the brothers didn't try to speak to each other over the noise. Lazar was by the driver's door, waiting for the platform to touch the road so he could connect the winch. Anton looked exhausted, his eyes cast down at his lap. He wasn't watching the ramp. He must have seen its operation many times before, perhaps regarded it with resentment. It was one more mechanical aid that he shouldn't have needed but for the damage done to his legs.

Anton could have a weapon concealed under the rug across his knees. The nervous plucking of his fingers at the edges could be his way of keeping a handgun within easy reach, yet out of sight.

But nothing in the intelligence reports had indicated the Zhivkos might be armed. In any case, there was no intention to arrest the brothers, not right there in the street with dozens of passers-by getting in the way. If an arrest ever happened, it would be done in the privacy of the brothers' home at dawn, with the advantage of surprise and force of numbers, a hydraulic ram through the front door and officers in body armour dragging them from their beds before they were even awake.

Before the surveillance officers had turned away from the monitor, something strange happened. Both the Zhivko brothers reacted to something simultaneously. Their heads came up sharply, as if they'd been startled by a sudden noise. Their eyes met across the roof of the Kangoo, and for the first time Anton opened his mouth to speak. No – not to speak, but to shout, to yell. To scream.

It was a scream that never came. If Anton made any sound at all, it was the last one of his life. The force of the explosion hurled him across the bonnet of a taxi and into the middle of the road. His chair was crushed by a bus, but Anton's body broke away from the wreckage and bounced across the tarmac until he crumpled into a smouldering heap in the gutter. There was just one glimpse of his motionless figure before it disappeared in the cloud of black smoke that surged from the blazing Kangoo.

Lazar Zhivko had been luckier. The blast had blown him backwards against the wing mirror of a parked Volvo. The mirror snapped and a three-inch steel shard pierced his back, penetrating his left kidney. Glass fragments from the Kangoo's shattered windscreen ripped into Lazar's face and hands, and shredded his clothes. Flames from the burning vehicle spread rapidly to nearby cars and the smoke dipped and swirled in a sudden breeze.

The window of the store room had blown out, and the shop's alarms were ringing. The two officers had ducked and thrown their arms over their heads, but it was already too late. Smoke billowed across the window and surged through the gaps in the glass. Debris spattered on the cardboard boxes and showered the floor in a layer of grit.

'Jesus, what was that?'

The radio was already calling for fire appliances and ambulances. The microphones in the shop would be picking up the sound of the explosion and shattering glass.

Even inside the store room they could feel the heat of the flames. The blast had seemed to happen in slow motion, following a blinding flash of light powerful enough to etch the startled faces of the two victims into the retinas of watching eyes. Their

347

faces would be there for days, forever staring, shocked and frightened, opening their mouths to speak, but never uttering a word.

'It looks as though someone visited the Zhivko brothers after all.'

23

At Manchester Terminal One, Fry stood in front of W. H. Smith's, waiting for passengers to emerge from baggage reclaim into the arrivals hall. In the amusement arcade, two teenage boys were playing a grand prix driving game, and the flashing lights were distracting Fry's attention. She was afraid she'd miss her visitor. But on the other hand, she knew he'd stand out all too well when she saw him.

She recalled Cooper's comments as she'd left the office to collect Sergeant Kotsev.

'How will you recognize him?' he'd asked. 'He won't be in uniform, surely.'

'Well, he's six foot two inches tall, with black hair, dark brown eyes and a neatly trimmed moustache.'

'How do you know that? Did his brown eyes just come up in conversation?'

'Yes.'

But, in fact, the description had been in an email he'd sent her. Fry had discovered it in her inbox immediately after receiving the phone message. Sergeant Kotsev was already in the air by then.

So when he came in sight, Fry recognized him straightaway. He was towing a large black suitcase with four wheels. It seemed to trundle on behind him effortlessly, like the animated luggage in a Terry Pratchett story.

Georgi Kotsev was definitely tall and dark. He had good bone structure, and a slight tan, but not too much. A recent holiday in one of those Black Sea resorts, perhaps? He wore a black leather jacket, quite new, though probably a cut-price copy of a designer label. Fry thought he'd have looked pretty good in a well-cut suit, too. His hair was black, trimmed short, but combed back to reveal a hint of waviness.

He also looked vaguely angry as he came down the ramp. But his expression cleared quickly when Fry introduced herself.

'Welcome to England, Sergeant.'

Kotsev smiled. '*Blagodariya*. Thank you.'

'If you'll follow me, I've got a car waiting.'

She ought to say something else, but she'd always found small talk difficult. All the way from Edendale to the airport, she'd been worrying about the prospect of making stilted conversation with a stranger. But as Fry led her visitor across the walkway to the short-stay car park, she found there'd been no need to worry. He began to talk without any prompting.

'I came by Lufthansa,' he said. 'The German airline, you know it? Only four hours and fifty-five minutes, including one stop at Frankfurt. Very quick, very efficient. A British Airways flight is two hours longer – and yet more expensive.'

'You know, your English is very good, Sergeant Kotsev.'

'Ah, *merci*. Thank you. And German aircraft have three inches more leg room. Did you know? That is important, too. For me, at least. Are the British less tall than Germans? No, I don't think so. Oh, and then there is Czech Airways. A joke, of course.'

'You're an admirer of German efficiency, then?'

'We have to give them credit for what they achieve,' he said.

Her Peugeot was fortunately close to the entrance. She was anxious to get in the car and be under way.

'Wasn't Bulgaria invaded by the Germans during the last war?' she said as she opened the boot for his suitcase.

The question had come out of her mouth before it had even occurred to her she might sound too much like a character out of a *Fawlty Towers* episode. Well, that was the danger of making small talk. The pressure to say something that would fill the silence led to stupid comments.

Kotsev started to nod his head, then seemed to change his mind and shook it vigorously instead.

'No, no – we were on their side. It was the Russians who invaded us.'

'Really?'

He folded the handle of his case and loaded it into the car. 'Sadly, there is some ignorance here about our history.'

Fry thought of the people Kotsev might meet back at Edendale. 'I can't promise you anything else.'

He politely remained silent while she exited the car park and negotiated her way out of the airport, following the signs back to the motorway. When the silence began to feel uncomfortable, she searched her mind for something else to say. What *did* you say in these circumstances? *What the hell are you doing here? Why don't you just go back home where you belong?*

'So where did you learn to speak English so well, Sergeant Kotsev?'

'Ah, I attended a good school in our capital, Sofia, and later at university. Regrettably, there are still very few police officers in my country who speak English well. You could visit many provincial police stations in Bulgaria and find no officers who speak English at all.'

Fry laughed. 'It's nothing to be ashamed of. How many police officers do you think we have in Edendale who speak Bulgarian?'

Kotsev smiled. 'It's different. It will be necessary for many more of us to speak your tongue when we enter the European Union.'

'Still, it must be very irritating to have us all coming to your country and expecting you to speak to us in English.'

'Ah, but ours is an unimportant little language.'

It was intriguing to hear Kotsev say that without sarcasm or bitterness, as if he actually meant it. She would normally have expected at least a small chip on the shoulder.

'Well, it's true that Bulgarian wasn't offered as a course option when I was a student,' she said.

Her visitor seemed to take in everything they passed on the journey from the airport. Not that there was much to see on the M60 orbital. He'd pushed the passenger seat as far back as it would go to accommodate his long legs, and Fry was conscious of the fact that he could watch her from that angle without her knowing it. She stood the uncertainty for as long as she could, then she turned to meet his eyes. Kotsev had been right about how brown they were. They made her think of dark chocolate. Thornton's apricot parfait.

'So you are a graduate, Sergeant Fry?' said Kotsev. 'What is your degree, a Bachelor of Arts or a Bachelor of Science? Police officers should have a good education, I believe. It's very important, if we are to have the respect of the people. Myself, I attended the University Saint Kliment Ohridski in Sofia.'

'I was at the University of Central England in Birmingham. We called it UCE. As a comedian said once, it isn't named after its initials, but the grades you need to get in.'

He regarded her quizzically, perhaps not fully understanding what she'd said, but recognizing the self-deprecating tone. Fry immediately felt embarrassed. She didn't know what had made her say that about her old university. She had no reason to denigrate it. At the time, UCE had been exactly what she needed – a route to escape into a different world, where opportunities were available for the grasping. She was sure it had been a lifeline for many who'd gone there before her, and since. Some said that institutions like UCE served a more useful purpose in society than any number of Oxbridge colleges, with their dreaming spires and drunken hoorays throwing themselves off bridges.

'It's kind of you to escort me,' said Kotsev. 'You must be very busy, I'm sure. A shooting enquiry for you to pursue. Connections to organized crime. Worrying complications for a small police department.'

'Yes, it *is* a bit hectic.'

He fell silent until they were out of Glossop and travelling southwards along the ridge through Hayfield and past Chapel-en-le-Frith.

'So this is the county of Derbyshire,' he said. 'Very pretty.'

Fry didn't respond. She generally tried to avert her gaze from the view whenever there was a steep drop away from the road.

'What are these hills called?' asked Kotsev.

'Er . . . I'm not sure.'

'And this valley? The river?'

'I forget. But if you really want to know, I'll introduce you to one of my colleagues when we get to Edendale. He knows everything about the area.'

His eyes were on her again, she could feel it. It was making her tense. *Watch the countryside going by, why don't you?*

'So what sort of place is Pleven?' she said, trying to sound as though she was interested in the answer.

'Pleven is located in the agricultural region of Miziya, in the north of Bulgaria. It's surrounded by limestone hills. You might feel at home if you visited there.'

'Might I? Why?'

'Those are limestone quarries I can see ahead of us, if I'm not mistaken.'

'Oh. Probably.'

'So the hills are very much like these. But the city of Pleven has a population of a hundred and forty-three thousand persons. Not like this.'

'That's all right, I'm used to big cities,' said Fry. 'I don't really belong in this area.'

'I see. Myself, I'm a city person too – though I was born in a village in a rural district. My family moved to Sofia, where I received my education. Later, as a police officer, I was assigned by the ministry to Pleven.'

'And you developed an expertise in organized crime?'

'Yes, indeed. Recently I have been working in co-operation with the Organized Crime Groups Unit at Europol. We formed a Joint Investigation Team – Europol officers and Bulgarian law enforcement. It's very interesting work. We have had some great successes, of which we are very proud.'

'You mean pro-active operations? Disrupting the activities of organized crime?'

'More than disrupting. Two years ago, we broke a major organized crime network which was spreading counterfeit euro notes into Western Europe. More than four hundred officers carried out raids in several cities. Four illegal print facilities were closed. Fake documents, credit cards and tourist visas were seized, in addition to many counterfeit euros. Believe me, General Borisov of the Bulgarian Police and Europol Director Storbeck were very happy to present the results of that co-operation.'

Fry didn't know what to say. She was too busy suppressing an overwhelming surge of envy. This guy was from some place in Eastern Europe that she'd never even heard of, yet he was leading the sort of life she dreamed of. He was enjoying a useful and exciting career, while she was stuck in this backwater that she was almost ashamed to let him see.

She put her foot down on the straight stretch of road over the plateau towards Edendale. There weren't any villages to speak of up here, only scattered farms with tumbledown outbuildings and abandoned tractors. There were more sheep than people, by a factor of about five hundred to one.

'Not far now,' she said.

Kotsev nodded amicably. 'You know, when Bulgaria joins the EU, I would be interested in transferring to Europol. There are often vacancies for a First Officer. Then I could live in The Hague. Do you know The Hague? It's a good city. Very pleasant. Very civilized.'

Fry turned to look at him, to see if he was laughing at her. But she met his eyes, and she could tell that he wasn't.

Fry delivered Kotsev to the new Holiday Inn off Edendale's relief road and made sure he managed to get checked in all right. Not that he seemed to need any help. The girl behind the reception desk practically fell over herself to offer him wake-up calls and restaurant reservations.

'I hope you'll be comfortable here,' said Fry when he'd collected his room key. 'Our divisional commander has asked if you'll take part in a briefing in the morning. Will that be all right?'

'*Dobre*. That's OK.'

'I'll see you tomorrow then, Sergeant.'

'Thank you for everything, Sergeant Fry.'

'That's all right. Goodnight.'

'*Ciao*.'

He picked up his bag to go to his room, but

instead of leaving through the revolving doors Fry found herself hesitating. Kotsev smiled at her politely, his dark eyes crinkling at the edges.

'Was there something else?'

'Well, I was just going to say . . . The thing is, I know what it's like arriving in a strange place where you don't know anyone. Eating meals alone is the worst thing, isn't it? It's too embarrassing going into a restaurant on your own.'

'I will ask for room service and watch some English television while I eat,' he said.

'Oh.'

'Unless you were about to suggest a better idea?'

Fry took the cue. 'Well, if you like, I'd be happy to take you to dinner tonight and show you a bit of Edendale. As it happens, I'm free.' He opened his mouth to reply, but she rushed on. 'Well, it's preferable to sitting on your own, isn't it?'

Kotsev bowed slightly. 'A great deal better, Sergeant. Thank you, I would be delighted.'

She let out the breath that she hadn't realized she was holding until then.

'I'll pick you up here at about seven thirty, then.'

'Seven thirty. Excellent. Goodbye for now.'

He insisted on shaking hands again. Then Fry watched him walk to the lift, rolling his shoulders a little under his leather jacket as he shifted the weight of his case. Kotsev pressed the button, and glanced back while he waited. Fry was surprised to find herself still standing there like an idiot. She waved self-consciously. But he was already turning to enter the lift, and he probably didn't see it.

'*Ciao*,' she said quietly, as the doors closed behind him.

'The device was taped under the chassis and wired into the electric motor for the ramp. Unloading the ramp closed the circuit and detonated the device. Click, boom. Simple, but effective.'

The army bomb squad captain looked pleased with himself, as if the device had been his own design and he'd scored top marks in his assessment. In his fatigues, he looked alarmingly young to be in charge of the combined briefing at Chesterfield police headquarters.

'How big a device?' said Hitchens. 'I mean, how much explosive?'

The captain shrugged. 'Twenty pounds or so. We can give you a better estimate later. But, to be honest, it didn't need to be any bigger to achieve its primary purpose.'

'Which was?'

'Well, it looks pretty clear to me. I'd say the purpose was to take out the owners of the vehicle – not to maximize casualties or cause general devastation. This wasn't al-Qaeda, you know. We're not talking terrorism here.'

'We're not?'

'In my opinion, the attack was targeted too precisely. But that's your province, I suppose. You and our friends from Special Branch, anyway. I expect they'll have their own ideas.'

Kessen didn't look pleased at the mention of Special Branch.

'How long would it take somebody to attach a device like that to the vehicle?'

'If it was someone who knew what they were doing, no more than a few minutes. There's nothing clever about the device itself. It's the method of detonation that's a bit smarter than usual. Whoever attached the explosive must have worked out his method pretty well beforehand. It's not something you'd be able to improvise on the spot. So, if you want my opinion, it wasn't just some opportunist assassin slapping a bit of Semtex under the chassis when no one was looking.'

'They needed access to the interior of the vehicle?'

'Oh, yes.'

'And they had to know in advance what they were dealing with?'

'Exactly.' The captain smiled. 'Personally, I think that should make your job a lot easier. There can't be many people around here with that sort of expertise.'

'Well, we hope not.'

'We've all heard such a lot about Semtex,' said Hitchens. 'I suppose it must be easy to get hold of if you know the right people?'

'It used to be. Especially if you had contacts in Libya, which is where most of the stuff went to.

It became the terrorists' explosive of choice, because it was difficult to detect, easily obtained – and as little as two hundred and fifty grams could bring down an airliner.'

'Two hundred and fifty?'

'Slightly over half a pound. Think of a packet of butter.'

'Are you sure? It doesn't seem enough to bring down an airliner.'

'Ask the people on board Pan Am 103, or the residents of Lockerbie. The device in that case was estimated to contain three hundred and twelve grams. It made a pretty thorough job, wouldn't you say?'

'You said it *used* to be easy to get hold of,' said Hitchens. 'Only used to be?'

'For the last four years, all sales of Semtex have been under the control of the Czech government. They've added ethylene glycol dinitrate to produce a distinctive odour and aid detection. They've also tried to reduce the shelf-life; all new supplies contain an identifying code.'

'So Semtex is more difficult to obtain now, and easier to detect?'

'If it's newly manufactured. The trouble is, there's still a lot of the old stuff around. The security services reckon the IRA has about ten tonnes of it, for a start. They'd probably be willing to share it around if they're paid enough.'

'Could this be the sort of explosive used by quarrying companies?'

The expert looked at him pityingly.

'Well, there are a lot of quarries around here,' said Hitchens. 'There are blasting operations going on all the time. If they were using this stuff –'

'I doubt it. Plastic explosives are much more expensive than other materials that perform just as well for ordinary blasting. On the other hand, if you have a major demolition project in the area, that might be a different matter.'

'I've tested the water upstairs,' said Kessen as the group of E Division officers walked back to the car park after the meeting.

Hitchens stared at him as if he'd suddenly starting speaking a foreign language. 'Sorry, sir?'

'Upstairs. They're happy for us to run with the Rose Shepherd enquiry for now, but I have to keep everyone in the loop. Fully informed of developments.'

'Right. And who's everyone?'

'I've got quite a list. As you might imagine, MI5 and Special Branch are too busy with other things right now, and SOCA isn't up and running properly. But they all want to keep tabs on what we're doing anyway.'

'In case we mess up completely.'

'That's about the size of it.'

'You know, sir, a cynic might think they were actually hoping we'd mess up, just to prove a point. Sort of "Give them enough rope and they'll hang themselves."'

Kessen sighed. 'You could be right. But we have to get on with the job and achieve the best outcome we can. Let's get a copy of the report sent round to Sergeant Kotsev at the Holiday Inn, so he'll be up to speed for tomorrow morning. C Division will want to borrow him tomorrow, too, so he can fill them in on the Zhivkos' background.'

'I've just called DS Fry to keep her informed,' said Hitchens. 'Apparently, she's seeing Kotsev later this evening.'

'Oh? Well, I'm glad we're being hospitable,' said Kessen.

24

Fry was on her way home through Edendale when she took the call from Hitchens. Turning off Meadow Road, she bumped her Peugeot over a patch of rough ground in front of the old cattle market, wincing as a front wheel bounced into a deep pot hole and muddy water splashed over her offside wing.

'Yes, I heard about the explosion in Chesterfield. What's our interest in it? Oh, really?'

While she listened, Fry stared at the ruined buildings that had once been the premises of Pilkington & Son, livestock auctioneers. The demolition workers had left two rows of sheep pens standing outside, exposed to the weather. Rusty gates were falling off their hinges, iron bars had been bent out of shape by vandals, or by panicking animals.

'The Zhivko brothers? That's more than a co-incidence . . . yes, I bet they are.'

Fry felt suddenly tired, and an inexplicable

tremor of fear ran through her. Not at the thought of the explosion that had killed the Zhivkos in a Chesterfield street. The fear was caused by something else, closer to home.

'Yes, of course, sir. I'll liaise with Sergeant Kotsev.'

She ended the call, and glanced at herself in the rearview mirror, seeking a trace of that fear in her own eyes.

'Oh, yes – liaise. That's what I'll do.'

Fry sat in her car for a few moments longer. A section of the main cattle market building remained, gaunt and roofless. Through the chain link fence with its *Keep Out* signs, she could just see the edge of the sale ring. Almost nothing was left of the tiers of wooden seats that had once formed an amphitheatre into which frightened animals had been driven for auction.

The closure of Pilkington & Son meant that half of the town centre was no longer brought to a halt on market days by trailers and cattle transporters. Ben Cooper said that a vital element had been taken away from Edendale. Something about its long history as a rural market town, a dislocation from its agricultural hinterland.

But the cattle market had another meaning for Fry. This was a place she had once thought she was going to die.

Instinctively, she raised a hand to her face and touched the faint bump under her skin, the remains of a scar that everyone assured was no longer visible. Maybe they were right. Yet whenever she looked in the mirror, she could see it for herself.

Fry looked at her watch, remembering how little time she had to reach home and get changed before she was due to go out again. She rolled the car slowly along the fence, strangely reluctant to tear herself away from a crowd of unpleasant memories, compelled to scan the derelict buildings for familiar doorways and walls.

Beyond the main building, she glimpsed a tangle of trees over a tunnel of dark shadows. The cattle market had been built close to the railway station, in the days before road transport became the norm. But the overgrown tracks where cattle wagons were once unloaded had been torn up now, leaving a secret back lane through this part of town.

That was something everyone needed now and then, wasn't it? A glance down a hidden, private road that might lead to a new life.

Angie was due at her job tonight, working behind the bar at The Feathers in New Street. Yet she had that secret little smile on her face as she pulled a denim jacket over her T-shirt.

Diane was glad her sister looked so much better than when she first moved in. But there was something still there, below the surface, that she didn't know how to deal with. It was the main reason that she sometimes had to nerve herself to enter her own flat, the way she had tonight. Yes, she had to brace herself to face her own sister. And then she had to suppress the guilt, of course.

At least the job meant Angie wasn't sponging any more. Or not so much, at any rate. With her wages and a few tips, she ought to be able to afford some new clothes. But clothes seemed to be the last thing Angie was interested in.

The other problem was that the flat had only one bedroom. The sitting room had become a second bedroom where her sister had been sleeping for months now. Actually, quite a few months. It was funny how some people's homes could feel *too* lived in.

While Angie got ready to go out, Diane looked at the wallpaper, striped in a faded shade of brown that she'd barely noticed.

'Hey, Sis, would you like to help me re-decorate?' she asked.

'What?'

'It's long overdue. I was thinking of something modern. Off-white and charcoal grey. What would you say to that?'

Angie groaned. 'What the hell's wrong with you, Di? Are you turning into Carol Smillie? If so, you might as well shoot me now, because I can't live with you any longer.'

'Who's Carol Smillie?'

'Are you kidding? She used to do those TV makeover shows, re-decorating people's houses.'

'Why would she do that?'

'It's entertainment.'

Fry paced around the flat. 'So you wouldn't be able to live with the idea, then? A couple of off-white walls here, and a charcoal grey one there. Maybe one abstract picture in a chrome frame.'

'It would drive me mad,' said Angie. 'It sounds totally cold and soulless. I couldn't stand it for more than a day.'

'Yes, that's what I thought,' said Diane.

'You're not really going to do it, are you?'

'One day. One day I might.'

When Angie had left, Diane stalked the flat for a while, restless and dissatisfied with something. She seemed to have been dissatisfied ever since she came to Derbyshire.

She gave the wallpaper another glare, then realized how hungry she was. Then she thought about Ben Cooper. She imagined he was a proper little domestic god when he was tucked up securely in his home in Welbeck Street.

Later that evening, Georgi Kotsev leaned across a table at Caesar's restaurant and raised his glass. 'We say *Nazdrave*.'

'Cheers.'

'Yes. Cheers.'

'Is the wine all right?' asked Fry. 'There isn't much choice of places to eat in Edendale.'

'*Losho nyama*. No problem.'

The last time Fry had eaten in Caesar's, she'd been with Angie. It had been one of those futile attempts at re-creating the bond between them.

She remembered that she'd only ended up feeling embarrassed by her sister. No, a bit ashamed – and therefore guilty, too.

It was the only place she'd been able to think of at short notice to bring Sergeant Kotsev. Inexplicably, she'd felt the need to give him a good impression of Edendale. As if it mattered – to him, or to her. They were both strangers passing through, except that Kotsev would be gone a bit sooner.

Though it was supposed to be an Italian restaurant, Fry had a suspicion that the waiters were East European. Judging by the shouted exchanges she overheard occasionally, probably the kitchen staff were too. It hadn't occurred to her when she chose the restaurant and booked the table. But now she wondered whether an idea had been in the back of her mind to make Kotsev feel more at home, give him a little bit of Eastern Europe right here in this strange, foreign town.

But then, as they'd entered the restaurant, she had a momentary panic at the thought that he might be offended instead. The waiter who'd served her last time could have been Albanian or something. There were a lot of old territorial disputes and ethnic conflicts in the Balkans. Didn't Bulgarians and Albanians have some kind of long-standing hatred between them? Might Kotsev refuse to be served by an Albanian waiter and make a terrible scene?

Oh, God. And all she'd wanted to do was make

life a bit easier for someone. That would teach her to keep out of other people's lives.

But Kotsev behaved impeccably. And she was relieved she'd chosen somewhere smart, because her guest was turned out nicely for the evening. She was glad she'd made a bit of an effort herself. Come to think of it, she might have been wearing the same cord blazer and hand-knitted alpaca cotton top that she'd put on tonight when she came here with Angie. She didn't get many opportunities to wear them, and nothing else in her wardrobe had seemed suitable.

Kotsev looked at the menu. 'Could you recommend anything?'

'The confit of duck is excellent,' she said, since it was the only thing she'd ever eaten here.

'I think I will try a steak,' he said.

Fry wondered if he'd read her ignorance so effortlessly.

'What would you normally drink in Bulgaria?'

'Our national drink is *rakia* – grape brandy. Or wine. People of this country are acquainted with Bulgarian red wine?'

'Yes, of course.'

'Our white wine is also delicious. But Bulgarian folklore presents a lot of songs about red wine and only one about white, which goes: "Oh, white wine, why are you not red?"'

Fry laughed. 'You said you were born in a village. So your parents were country people, Sergeant Kotsev?'

370

'Please. Call me Georgi.'

'I'm Diane.'

'Yes, I know.'

Kotsev's brown eyes were rather sad when you came to look closely. The dark hairs on his wrist curled over the band of a gold watch, and his shirt cuffs were white and crisp. His clothes surely hadn't come out of his suitcase like that. Fry could picture him ironing his shirts in his hotel room. Not many men could use an iron properly, but she bet that Kotsev did it very well.

'You know, there were many different types of people in my family in the past,' he said. 'But mostly they were shepherds, goat chasers. Peasants, in other words. Sometimes men would come to our village from the city. If they wore long leather coats and had moustaches, we knew they were from the police, from the local administration or from the Party. The law was theirs. One word from them could have changed our lives. It's difficult for you to understand the way we lived.'

Kotsev's English wasn't quite perfect, after all. She was starting to detect a tendency to pronounce the past tense of certain verbs as if there was an extra syllable on the end. Liv-*ed*. Chang-*ed*. She put it down to a lack of opportunity to practise conversation with native English speakers. It was understandable, too – since sometimes there *was* an extra syllable. Fry wondered whether she should correct him when he did it, or if he'd be offended. She decided not to mention it, unless he asked. It wasn't a problem. In fact, she found it rather appealing.

'Was this near Pleven?' she said.

'No, in the far south of our country, near the border with Greece. Quite a remote region of Bulgaria. No one spoke English there. Generally, it seems that all Bulgarians learn Russian, and a few learn German. But outside of Sofia, English is not commonly spoken. I was glad to go to the capital with my family. Otherwise, I might still be living with the goats.' He put down the menu. 'Have you chosen?'

'Yes, I think so.'

Kotsev looked at the waiter across the restaurant. That was all he seemed to do, yet the man was instantly at their table to take their order.

'But it's good to know a little of your family history,' he said a few minutes later. 'My grandfather worked in a macaroni factory. When we were living in the countryside, my father used to talk of a girl, the daughter of a jeweller. I think he fell in love with her, you know. But they could never have married. Her family were bourgeois exiles from Sofia.'

'Bourgeois?'

'Yes. You understand what that means?'

'Of course.'

Fry hadn't heard the expression 'bourgeois' for a long time. Not since her student days, when there were still some old-fashioned Socialists around in Birmingham. It sounded rather quaint now.

'Sadly, my mother died when I was very young,' said Kotsev. 'I don't remember much of her. Only a green scarf with glittering threads woven through it. And I remember she had beautiful teeth. As white as Greek cheese, my father used to say.'

'Good grief, what sort of compliment is that?'

'A simple one, but honestly meant.'

A bottle of wine arrived, and Kotsev waited while it was poured.

'As for my father,' he said. 'The memory from my childhood is a smell – a Soviet aftershave, which I think was called *Tachanka*.' He smiled. 'And you, Diane?'

'Me?'

'You say you don't belong in this rural area?'

'No, I'm from the Black Country. That's near the city of Birmingham. An urban area, with a lot of people. Over a million.'

'I see.' He took a drink of wine. 'And what of your parents?'

'My parents?' said Fry. 'Like you, I remember almost nothing of them.'

'Nothing?'

'Almost nothing.'

Kotsev waited patiently, but realized she wasn't going to say any more. When the waiter returned, they ate quietly for a few moments. Fry supposed she ought to ask him what he thought of the food.

But food didn't interest her much as a topic of conversation.

'What exactly is your role in Pleven now, Georgi?'

'Oh, you wish to talk business?' he said.

'I'd like to know how the Zhivko brothers might fit in to our present enquiry. Can you fill me in on some background?'

'Ah, the Zhivkos – our dear friends Anton and Lazar. They were previously suspected of being engaged in a great number of criminal activities in my own country.'

'Yes?'

Kotsev's smile became quizzical as he hesitated under her expectant gaze.

'There are many issues involved, Diane.'

'Tell me some of them, at least.'

He nodded. 'Well, as I mentioned, I've been working in co-operation with our colleagues at Europol for some time. Bulgaria is not a member of the European Union yet, you understand, but we co-operate nevertheless. We value their expertise in organized crime. A lot of events have been happening in my country, because of the EU.'

'What sort of things?'

'Our government has been given conditions to meet before we will be allowed to join the EU. "Clean up your act," they say. One of the things the EU does not like is our organized crime, our Mafia.'

'Is organized crime such a big problem in Bulgaria?'

'A big problem?' Kotsev laughed. 'You might say that. There are certain people who have become very rich running crime in my country. They grow so rich that they buy football clubs, or casinos in Sunny Beach. They rule their kingdoms by violence – punishment beatings, shootings. These are very ruthless men, and very powerful. The *mutras*, we call them. Clever and cruel killers.'

'*Mutras*?'

'In Bulgarian, *mutra* means "ugly face". If you saw these people, you would understand. Many of them were out-of-work body builders or wrestlers who had to look for alternative employment. So they learned to shoot guns and joined forces with shady businessmen to exploit Bulgaria after the Change. You know what I mean by the Change? The events of 1989?'

'Oh, the end of Communism.'

Kotsev nodded. 'Well, these people made a big name for themselves by offering security to businesses – for a monthly fee, you understand. Owners who refused to pay fell victim to repeated robberies. You would call it the protection racket. Now *mutra* daddies drive around in armed convoys, and the only way we can get rid of them is if one of their own does it for us. These people behave as if they're living in a Hollywood movie. We have Anton "The Beak" and Vassil "The Scalp". Until now, they have been untouchable.'

'Why untouchable, Georgi?'

Kotsev tapped his nose. 'Connections. It is said that some of our highest government officials owe their positions to an association with these gangsters. And now they're in a difficult position. Our government wants to join the European Union. The European Union says we must get rid of our Mafia. "If the police are issuing traffic tickets but turning their backs on major organized crime," they say, "it raises a question over how democratic your country is." Would you agree?'

'Well, yes.'

'*Dobre*. There you have our problem. Sadly, if we don't make progress in this area, it will delay our entry. A very big problem.'

'I see.'

'But, ah!' said Kotsev, throwing out a hand. 'Not such a problem, after all. Suddenly we have a miracle! And now, things are going our way.'

'A miracle?'

'In the past two years some of the most powerful Mafia bosses have been eliminated. One of them is shot leaving a casino after celebrating a victory by his football team. Another is gunned down with his bodyguards outside a bar. Sometimes, an entire family is murdered, as was often the case in blood feuds. All these killings appear to have been carried out by an expert shot. Perhaps more than one, we do not know. The suspects have never been caught, or even identified. The official theory concerns a war between rival gangs, who have employed hit men to do their dirty work.'

'That sounds feasible.'

'Yes, of course.' He waited expectantly.

'Are you suggesting the Zhivkos died in this way?' asked Fry.

Kotsev spread his hands apologetically. 'You understand there is much I can't say.'

'I'm too junior, is that it?'

'My apologies, Sergeant. But, you see, the Zhivko brothers found themselves in the middle of all this. First on one side, as the agents of a leading *mutra* chief. Then, suddenly, they are on the losing side of the game. The Zhivkos are in danger of their lives, and they must leave the country. Yet even here, in Britain, they were not safe.'

Fry knew there was something else that he wasn't telling her. His silence invited another question, if only she could work out what it was.

'Wait a minute – you said that was the *official* theory. What's the unofficial one?'

Kotsev smiled. 'You may know, Sergeant Fry, that we have a highly efficient secret service in Bulgaria, the Darzavna Sigurnost. They were trained by the KGB in the old days, and many of them have remained in their employment. Their usefulness did not disappear with Communism.'

'I'm not sure what you're saying, Georgi.'

'Some of these people have a talent for conveni- ent assassinations. What more efficient way could there be to remove annoying criminals and save the difficulty of a trial, where embarrassing facts about government officials might emerge? A few extra *stotinki* in the pockets of a Darzavna Sigurnost operative. Boom, boom. Problem solved. Now it's, "See, Mr EU Commissioner, we don't have the nasty Mafia any more. How lucky. Now you can let us into your club." '

Fry put down her fork. 'No, that's too incredible,' she said.

Kotsev's eyes crinkled as he held up a forkful of steak.

'To you, perhaps. But you're not in Kansas now.'

25

Cooper took his brother's call at home in the middle of the evening, just as he was settling down to watch a good film with a bottle of beer in his hand and the cat on his knee.

'Ben, it says here that older fathers are more liable to have kids with schizophrenia. If you're between forty-five and forty-nine, you're twice as likely to have a child with the illness as a man of twenty-five.'

'Matt, you're only thirty-five now. You were still in your twenties when you had the girls.'

'Yes, well. I've written down all the facts to talk to the doctor about. Did you know schizophrenia can start at any age, but most people are affected in their late teens or early twenties? In their *teens*, Ben.'

'Considering the average teenager, I wonder how they can tell.'

Matt had taken a breath to continue, but came to an abrupt halt as if his brother had made a rude noise down the phone.

379

'It's not funny, Ben.'

Ben found himself standing in front of the fireplace in the sitting room. The framed photograph on the wall was one of the few things he'd brought with him when he moved out of Bridge End Farm. It was both reassuring and somehow disturbing to have his father's eyes watching him as he listened to his brother.

'You know something?' he said. 'Mum would have found it funny.'

Matt sighed. 'For heaven's sake, Ben.'

And the strange thing was that Matt was so similar to their father in many ways. Even this conversation sounded like one of those occasions when Joe Cooper would sit his sons down and give them advice. *A few words of caution* . . . It had been one of his favourite phrases.

'Matt, have you thought of joining one of the support groups? There's one called Rethink. It used to be the National Schizophrenia Fellowship.'

'Why would I do that?'

'So you could talk to people with similar experiences and get some reassurance. That's what those organizations are for.'

'You're not being very helpful, are you?'

'Actually, I think that's exactly what I'm being.'

Ben was glaring at his phone now. But he couldn't keep it up. He had to smile when he pictured his brother doing the same at the other end. This was the way their arguments always started.

'I can tell you're not in the right frame of mind at the moment,' said Matt. 'You must have had a bad day, or something.'

'As a matter of fact, it wasn't such a bad day – until now.'

Of course, he didn't really mean that, but there was almost a set script between them when they got to this stage. Matt knew it as well as he did.

'Oh, right. Sorry to have bothered you, I'm sure. I suppose that means you won't want me to share any information I manage to find out from Dr Joyce tomorrow?'

'You'll suit yourself, Matt. It doesn't matter what I say.'

There was a muttered swear word, a crash of something falling over, and silence. His brother had gone.

Ben found his eyes focusing straight ahead. And there was Sergeant Joe Cooper, gazing out from his place in the second row, among all those other solemn-faced police officers lined up in their best uniforms to have their photograph taken.

It was odd, really. He'd spent so much time thinking that his life had been dictated and over-shadowed by the legacy of Joe Cooper. Everyone who'd known his father said how alike they were. Here he was doing a similar job, in the same place, and often dealing with the same individuals that Joe Cooper had encountered.

Sometimes it had made Ben feel as if he was a clone, a walking carrier of his father's gene pattern. He hadn't seriously considered what he might have inherited from his mother's side, or which of her chromosomes he'd been allocated during conception. Her hair colouring, yes. The eyes, maybe. But what else was lurking in his DNA that he'd never been aware of? What genetic predispositions might he be carrying, that he risked passing on to future generations? Both of his parents were part of his nature. And he didn't regret it. But the feelings stirred up by that thought had become equivocal.

He switched his attention away from the photograph to the Richard Martin print of Win Hill on the adjacent wall. The landscape normally brought him back to earth when he got too preoccupied. Literally back to earth.

Then Ben laughed to himself. All of this anxiety presumed he would ever get married or find a permanent partner. He didn't have any such intentions at the moment, and maybe that was for the best. He'd really hate to be in Matt's position, discovering the awful possibilities when it was already too late.

'This is pretty, but I still prefer cities,' said Kotsev as they walked by the river after dinner. 'At ten o'clock at night in Sofia, the streets would be full, even though it's a Thursday. People would be selling sunflower seeds or salted sweetcorn. They would be buying books from fold-up tables. There would be loud music from stalls dealing in pirated CDs. A few counterfeit Rolex watches or Levi jeans, perhaps. Beggars and street artists, and pickpockets and prostitutes. It would be like a party. Here, there is nothing.'

Fry studied him, wondering whether he was joking. It was difficult to tell sometimes. She could only get a clue by watching his eyes. Then, when he saw her staring, Kotsev laughed.

'You like living in Sofia?' she said.

'In some ways.'

'It isn't all one big party, then?'

'Let me tell you something, Diane. In a suburb of Sofia where I used to live as a young police officer, we were in an old apartment block from the Soviet era. Very grey, very ugly. We had a two-bedroom apartment for the family. But we were lucky. Some of our neighbours had many more children – they had to put mattresses in the kitchen, in the sitting room, on the balcony. Every shop in the neighbourhood had brightly coloured stickers on the door, to show which Mafia protection agency they were insured with. This was normal. It was the way everyone lived, and we understood it.'

'I don't think *I* would understand it, Georgi. A situation like that wouldn't be tolerated here, even in our worst neighbourhoods.'

'Some people say the power of the Mafia is a necessary phase in the progress towards a capitalist economy,' said Kotsev, with a questioning tilt of his head.

'I think that's rubbish.'

He stopped, teetering on the stone ledge bordering the river. It occurred to Fry that she might be considered foolhardy to be alone at night in a quiet spot with a man she'd met only a few hours ago. But she didn't feel uneasy at all. Big as he was, she could probably disable Kotsev easily. She hadn't lost her skills completely.

'You ought to know how the KGB operated in the old days,' he said, peering into the dark water. 'They used the secret service organizations of East European countries as their tools. In Bulgaria, the Darzavna Sigurnost specialized in "wet" operations – contract killings. Do you remember the Markov case? It took place some years ago, at the height of the Cold War. Before your time, perhaps.'

'Thank you, Georgi. But I've heard of the case. A Bulgarian defector, wasn't he?'

'Yes. And after he defected, he was assassinated. In daylight, in a London street. They say he was injected with the poison ricin from the tip of an umbrella. They also say it was the Bulgarian secret service who carried out the assassination. No one in Bulgaria would contradict that report.'

'Yes, but even so –'

'Another dissident was shot in the back with a poisoned bullet near the Arc de Triomphe in Paris. Ricin was used in that incident, too.'

'But –'

Kotsev held up a hand. 'Wait. There was the attempted assassination of Pope John Paul II in

1981. You remember? It was alleged that Darzavna Sigurnost recruited the hit men who carried out the shooting – two Turks. When one of them was captured by the Italians, he made allegations against our secret service. But he retracted them after a spell in the Rebibbia jail in Rome, where he was allegedly threatened by Bulgarian agents. Afterwards, he blamed the plot on the Vatican itself.'

'Even so, Georgi –'

Kotsev laughed. 'Yes, you're right. Even so. Like you, Sergeant, I do not believe our beloved secret service was involved in the killing of Dimitar Iliev.'

'Who was it, then? Simcho Nikolov?'

'Well, these killings were probably carried out by a local person, a paid assassin. Someone like Simcho Nikolov, perhaps. But it's possible they were ordered by a major Bulgarian crime boss, one of the remaining Mafia. A very powerful man, particularly now that some of his leading rivals have been . . . eliminated. A man with friends in high places.'

Fry fought a brief internal battle between her own ambition and what she knew to be the proper protocol. Finally, she sighed. 'This is really a matter for Special Branch or MI5 – they're our lead bodies for organized crime. You're scheduled to meet with them tomorrow in Chesterfield for a briefing on the Zhivko brothers.'

'The Zhivkos are not a loss,' said Kotsev, with a faint air of disappointment.

They had arrived at the point where water poured over a weir and the river formed little wooded islands populated by sleeping birds. Even at this time of the evening there were people by the river, enjoying an oasis of peace under the shadow of St Mark's Church. Kotsev paused again.

'We have our tourist attractions in Pleven, also,' he said, admiring the reflection of the illuminated church spire in the water.

'Really?'

'Oh, yes. If you ever visit our city, you must see our famous Pleven Panorama – the largest structure of its kind in the world. Larger, even, than the Borodino Panorama in Moscow.'

'Wonderful.'

Fry wasn't sure she knew what a panorama was. She'd always thought it was one of those views of the countryside from the top of a hill that Ben Cooper loved so much. But that didn't sound like what Georgi was talking about.

'The Pleven Panorama tells a great story. The tragic destiny of our people, their dramatic fight, the compassion in the hearts of our Russian brothers. Within the Panorama, the spectator sees a charge of the Turkish cavalry, smoking shells, burning fires in the city, the Russian General Skobelev attacking a Turkish fortification. This attraction causes a great deal of interest in our city.'

'As you said yourself, we don't know much about Bulgarian history here.'

'No, of course.' Kotsev smiled. 'But its construction might be of interest to you.'

He looked at her, as if expecting a reaction. But she still didn't know quite what he was telling her.

'I don't think so,' she said.

'Ah, well.'

He began to walk on again, but Fry stopped him.

'Georgi, who should we be looking for? If the Zhivkos and Simcho Nikolov came, then who else is here?'

'Here?' He laughed. 'Here in the United Kingdom? You could start with seven thousand Bulgarian entrepreneurs. Including, perhaps, a one-legged roofer.'

The breeze was turning cool down by the river. Fry shivered a little, wishing she'd brought something warmer to put on. Apart from when she was at the office, she always seemed to make the wrong decisions about what to wear.

'You've lost me,' she said. 'It was all making sense, right up until the bit about the one-legged roofer.'

Kotsev easily kept pace with her as she headed along the river towards the bridge. A few minutes' brisk walking, and she could be back in her car with the heater turned up.

'You don't recall?' he said. 'A few years ago, your government introduced a so-called visa fast-track system. The purpose was to encourage entrepreneurs from Eastern Europe to come to the UK and set up business. Sadly, this system went badly wrong. Applications were not checked efficiently – many were not checked at all. Seven thousand unskilled Bulgarians and Romanians were allowed into your country on visas meant for entrepreneurs.'

'Yes, I remember now. But the one-legged roofer?'

'Ah, I bent the truth a little. He was actually a Romanian. But, you see, at that time there was an organized fraud in operation. One person submitted seventy identical business plans to support visa applications from Bulgarian individuals. They made a mockery of your entry control procedures, Diane.'

'So you're saying that pretty much anybody could have come into this country?'

Kotsev shrugged. 'If they could afford it. Yes, it was easy to beat British immigration controls. But this was expensive for a Bulgarian worker. Fraudulent papers might cost up to three thousand pounds. It's funny, you know – that was about the same amount of money that many British people were spending at that time on buying up cheap homes in my country, to spend a summer month by the Black Sea. Would you consider that irony, Diane?'

'Yes, that's irony, Georgi.'

Their feet echoed on the bridge. Fry had been thinking that she'd welcome the lights and the sight of people in the street. But instead she felt suddenly reluctant to leave the darkness and the quietness of the river. She stopped halfway across the bridge and leaned on the parapet. Kotsev came to stand next to her, sharing that mysterious attraction to water.

'You understand, the process for applying for a visa as a self-employed person became a very nice loophole,' he said. 'But there always had to be an invitation of some kind. There were plenty of people who wanted to bend the rules, but they needed a partner in Britain. An individual in your country could set up a company, offer a Bulgarian worker a job, and then look the other way when he slipped off – in exchange for cash, of course. You see, the corruption and greed is not all in Bulgaria.'

'There must have been risks, though.'

'Any risks were worth taking. You try to get a hundred individuals into the country and succeed only with forty? You've still made a hundred thousand pounds. That's a great many *stotinki* for a Bulgarian.'

'This all blew up into a scandal a couple of years ago, didn't it? I remember the immigration minister having to resign, and visa applications from Bulgaria were suspended. But it was too late by then, I suppose?'

'Indeed. Too late.'

'The words "horse", "stable door" and "bolted" come to mind.'

'Now you're making as much sense as my one-legged roofer.'

'I'm sorry.'

Kotsev smiled at her, his eyes crinkling again. 'You appreciate, there is a lot of information I do not have myself. But I'm sharing with you what I know – because I think we understand each other.'

Any answer would have felt awkward, so a moment of silence developed. For a few seconds, it was just the two of them, surrounded by darkness and silence, gazing into the water. Fry looked down at their hands, hers and Georgi's. They were so close on the rail that they were almost touching. She felt as if she was an inch away from something unexpected, a contact she could so easily reach out for, and hold on to.

Then a young couple appeared on the opposite bank and began to walk slowly across the bridge. Kotsev moved back from the parapet when he heard the footsteps. He brushed against her as he turned, and Fry caught a whiff of his scent when he touched her. She inhaled instinctively, trying to read some elusive meaning in a smell.

'*Kalina Tet-a-tet*,' he said quietly. 'It's Russian.'

Fry met his gaze for a moment, wondering how he'd known what she was thinking.

Cooper retrieved his beer and switched on the TV. But the film had already started, and it didn't look quite so interesting after all. In fact, he thought

390

he'd probably seen it before, and just forgotten the title. So he disentangled himself from the cat and picked up his phone again. He dialled a number from his phone book.

'Hi, it's me. What are you doing?'

And immediately it was as if he'd been sucked into some kind of time slip. Time went by without him being aware of it, because he was in a world when time didn't really exist. When he next looked at his watch, the call seemed to have lasted for nearly an hour. He'd finished his beer, walked into the kitchen, opened the fridge, and come back with another bottle, all without breaking concentration. It was a miracle the way the mind could focus on the important things.

'Better go. Are you on duty tomorrow . . .? I'll see you, then.'

Finishing the call, he decided to go to bed early. But he lay awake for a while with the cat lying on his duvet, purring like a mobile generator. He always thought a feline in the bedroom was appropriate, in a way. A cat was the Celtic equivalent to the dog Cerberus – the guardian at the entrance to the Underworld. Randy could watch over him as he slipped across the vulnerable threshold between waking and sleep.

Tonight, his brain was already wandering out of his control, following its own path. He was remembering random incidents from his past when reality might have been different from what he'd perceived. There had been moments, of course. There'd been times when he thought he saw things that didn't exist, when he'd woken to a voice in the night and realized it was only a dream. There had been entire periods of his life when everything had been dark and twisted, and out of proportion. As a teenager, his whole world had seemed out of kilter. But you could only recognize that later, couldn't you? Reality was a matter of perspective.

Finally, he drifted to sleep recalling how many times his mother had spoken to him when he knew she wasn't there. He could hear her voice plainly, even now. It was a reality he couldn't deny, a truth that defied logic. It was a sound snatched from the past, and trapped inside his head.

Four hours later, Cooper woke in a panic. He felt as though he couldn't move. A great weight was pressing on his chest, pinning him to the bed. He knew he was in that indefinable place between sleeping and waking, and he wanted to cry out, but he couldn't make his lungs work. Somewhere nearby a voice was speaking to him, but it was mumbling too indistinctly for him to hear the message.

And then suddenly he broke through a barrier, and shot upright in bed with a wordless shout. Randy flew off his chest, a resentful yowl filling the bedroom.

Cooper found he was sweating, and his heart was thumping. There was a burning pain in his arm, too. Was this what it was like when you had a heart attack? Should he phone for an ambulance, or wait and see what happened? He was only thirty, too young to die of heart failure.

It took him a few minutes to calm down. When he was breathing more slowly, he put on the light and checked his arm. He discovered it was covered with little claw marks, where the cat had been mauling him during the night. If the skin was broken, the scratches would get infected. A cat's claws were never entirely clean.

The mumbling he'd heard might have been the cat, too. Or it might have been the rain he could hear hitting the roof of the conservatory. It must have started while he was asleep.

Half an hour later, the rain eased off, and finally stopped. By then, Cooper was sitting in his kitchen with a cup of coffee on the table, waiting for the light to seep through the windows.

It was barely dark when he got the call. 'You know what you have to do, Johnny. It's time.'

He didn't need to ask any questions. He recognized the voice straightaway, and he knew the instruction was something he had to act on. And he had to do it now. 'Yes, it's time. It's time.'

There had been a train of thought in his mind that he couldn't quite grasp. Too many distractions and distortions, that was the trouble. At moments, he almost got a clear view of some mental will-o'-the-wisp that ought to be followed and interpreted. His thoughts were connected, but the connections were slippery, so they escaped his groping fingers. At other times, he knew the illusion of meaningfulness was just that – an illusion. It was like a blurred or shifting picture puzzle. The content seemed to change the more you tried to define it, or get it into focus.

Someone had explained it to him once. They said that incoherence resulted from a loosening of associations, a dysfunction at the neuro-cognitive level. He had no idea why he should remember that, when he couldn't recall things that had happened the day before. Especially when he didn't understand some of the words that were used.

Or perhaps that was the reason – he remembered because he didn't understand. Yes, that could be it. There was no solid meaning in the words to escape him. No soft, slippery undertones, no blurry significance. Only letters and sounds, and nothing else. Like bare earth, with no life in it. No humanity or feeling behind the words to confuse him. No voices at all, only noise.

But it was a voice that had distracted him again. He had no idea what he'd been thinking about before it came. That was the way his thoughts were – always shifting. Forever flitting this way and that. The flight of ideas. He liked the sound of that phrase. The flight of ideas. It sounded exciting and creative. It made him sound like some kind of genius whose mind soared above everyone else's, light and fragile, a crystal bird. Reflecting the light like a prism, riding the currents of the wind, dipping and soaring. Never following the same direction for more than five minutes at a time.

He waited as long as he could, resisting the urgent whisper until it became intolerable. Then he left the apartment at about two a.m., rolled his car quietly on to the street and started the engine. All the people in their houses were asleep by now, except for those sleeping alone, afraid what might be out there in the dark, the burglars and rapists, and the crazed axemen.

'You know what you have to do, Johnny.'

26

Fry was early for the briefing next morning. The room filled up around her, but she let the increasing level of noise wash over her. When Cooper arrived, he looked flustered and dishevelled, as if he'd only just got out of bed. But that was his normal style: His hair fell untidily across his forehead, there was a scuff mark on his jacket, and his tie needed straightening, as usual. Casual was OK, but on Cooper it made him look disorganized. She had an urge to tell him to tidy himself up before he met the public. Most of all, she couldn't help reflecting on the contrast between Cooper and Georgi Kotsev.

The divisional commander, Chief uperintendent Jepson, had made an appearance to greet Sergeant Kotsev.

'I've emailed Captain Pirinski to thank him for loaning your services, Sergeant. It shows a very

396

positive attitude on the part of the Bulgarian authorities.'

Kotsev shook his hand. 'Thank you, sir.'

'I'm very glad you came. It's so useful to have a translator; not to mention your experience in the field of cross-border organized crime.'

'I'm pleased to help.'

The Chief Super took DCI Kessen aside and put a hand on his shoulder.

'Special Branch and C Division are taking the Zhivko bombing – it's their pigeon, after all. But they'll liaise with us on any connections to Rose Shepherd or Simon Nichols.'

'Very good, sir.'

'It's the best way, Oliver.'

'Yes, I know.'

When he took the floor at the briefing, Kotsev turned out to be an excellent speaker, showing no signs of nervousness. He'd obviously had practice at presentations, and his almost perfect English and smart appearance commanded attention, even from this jaded bunch.

'First a little background,' he said. 'Your colleague Sergeant Fry assures me that not all of you are experts on Bulgarian history.'

Behind him, the chief superintendent chuckled, and almost seemed about to nudge Kessen to share the joke.

'In the last fifteen years, organized crime has thrived in Bulgaria, its influence reaching all parts of our society. Sadly, the state apparatus has been too weak to deal with this problem. Too corrupt also, you might say. But no longer. Now, anti-corruption is a byword in our ministries.'

Kotsev paused and looked around the room. Fry wondered if he'd made another joke. But even the chief super didn't get it this time.

'You're talking about a kind of Mafia, Sergeant?' prompted someone.

'A kind of Mafia, yes. However, our organized crime groups are becoming more sophisticated, and they are developing their own areas of expertise. In addition to trafficking women into the international sex trade, Bulgarian criminals are skilled at counterfeiting currencies, forging credit cards and identity documents. Their enter-prises are said to account for a third of the Bulgarian economy. They control tourism on the Black Sea coast, the ports, construction, agricul-ture. They seek power, and their influence runs very deep. But recent efforts of our authorities have put pressure on these criminals and created competition for a shrinking market. That is why there are currently so many murders – they are struggling to keep their influence.'

Kotsev spoke for a few minutes, outlining the issues he'd explained to Fry the previous night, but in less detail, skating round the more alarming possibilities. Listening to him, Fry wasn't sure how she should feel about having been privileged to share inside information. It was flattering in a way, perhaps. But it put her in an odd position, knowing more than her senior officers, or at least having a fuller picture.

When Kotsev paused again, a hand went up. 'If these individuals have so much power and influence, is it difficult to mount a successful prosecution?'

'Yes, we have a tough time making charges stick. Witnesses deny their testimony or have accidents, lawyers back out of cases, evidence disappears.'

'You said "various counterfeiting activities" – would that include passports and identity cards?'

'Yes. The counterfeiters' main area of business is forging euro banknotes. However, the United Kingdom is not a market for counterfeit euros – yet. Groups operating here are more likely to be employing their skills in the production of false identity documents.'

'What about the couple who were killed in their car? Were they involved in organized crime?'

'Yes, we believe this was the case, based on the known associations of Dimitar Iliev and the nature of the assassination. But there are also ethnic problems in Bulgaria, and Piya Yotova was a Romani woman. We do not know for certain who pulled the trigger, but Iliev and Yotova were shot with a Kalashnikov automatic rifle.' Kotsev smiled sadly. 'Kalashnikovs are causing some embarrassment. These weapons have been illegally exported to many war zones, and are therefore damaging our international image.'

'And Simon Nichols? How was he connected?'

'Simcho Nikolov? We are convinced from our intelligence sources that he was a major participant in counterfeiting operations. That was his particular area of expertise. Unlike the Zhivko brothers, we do not believe he was engaged in enforcement activities.'

There was a moment of silence when Kotsev had finished. Hitchens stood up to take over.

'It might be worth mentioning a bit of news at this point,' he said. 'The firearms examiners have identified the weapon that killed Rose Shepherd.'

'A Kalashnikov?'

'No. Turns out it's a fairly unusual item. This took some research on the lab's part, so I think we owe them a favour. But they say it's a Romanian military sniper rifle, the Pusca Semiautomata cu Luneta, or PSL. It might be considered to belong to the Kalashnikov family, but it's different in appearance.'

'Well, one thing's for sure. Nobody's going to admit to owning such a gun. There's a mandatory five-year prison sentence for the possession of an illegal firearm.'

'It's probably a clean weapon anyway. It won't be easily traced back to its origin.'

Hitchens nodded. 'As for Simon Nichols – or Simcho Nikolov, I should call him – we haven't yet received the full post-mortem report, but so far there is no evidence that his death was due to anything but natural causes, or an accident.'

'So he probably isn't a victim? In that case . . .?'

'Yes,' said Hitchens. 'We should be regarding him as a potential suspect for the Rose Shepherd killing. We need to find some way of establishing his movements in the last few days before he died.'

After the briefing, Cooper found himself standing in the corridor with Liz Petty. Some mysterious force seemed to place them together at unexpected moments. Or perhaps that was only the way it seemed.

'Are you OK?' he asked.

'Yes, fine. Thanks, Ben.'

When he spoke to Liz on the phone her voice always sounded so warm that it took him by surprise, almost knocked the feet from under him. Many female police officers formed a hard exterior, but not SOCOs, it seemed. He'd have to be careful not to make a nuisance of himself phoning her too often, just to hear her voice.

Petty seemed about to touch his arm, but drew back suddenly and looked past him, over his shoulder.

'Uh-oh.'

'I was asking Liz about the search at the caravan,' said Cooper when he saw Fry approaching.

'That's OK.'

'She just happened to be passing, and I –'

'It's all right,' said Fry as she drifted by. 'I don't care. See you later.'

They both watched her disappear down the corridor.

'What's up with her?' said Petty.

'I've no idea.'

'Perhaps she's turning human.'

'I'd better get on anyway,' said Cooper uneasily. 'There was one thing I wanted to ask you.'

'Yes?'

'Do you think it would be possible to find out more about this weapon that fired the shots at Bain House, the PSL sniper rifle? I know the lab have pulled out the stops for us, but could you have a word with Wayne?'

'I'm not sure, Ben. What do you want to know?'

'Whether there are non-military versions of it.'

'OK,' said Petty. 'I'll see what we can find out.'

Diane Fry sat at her desk and watched Georgi Kotsev talking to Hitchens and DCI Kessen. But she wasn't thinking about Kotsev. She was thinking about Europol.

Fry hadn't really considered it before. She'd been aware of Europol, of course, as one of the organizations continually being spawned by the integration of European Union countries. But it had never occurred to her until now that it was a possible career move.

Since Kotsev's arrival seemed to be causing some distraction for her senior officers, she decided to take the opportunity to check their website. Yes, Europol was looking for employees who were creative, self-reliant, energetic and willing to take up challenges. It wanted candidates who were able to work in a dynamic, fast-moving environment that required a high level of flexibility.

Fry nodded. She could do that, couldn't she?

The bad news was that job opportunities were now open to nationals of twenty-five EU states, including all the new members, such as the Czech Republic, Poland, Estonia, Latvia and Lithuania. And probably Bulgaria and Romania too, before long. The good news was that balanced gender representation was a priority, so Europol particularly encouraged applications from women.

She found half a dozen jobs currently available for law enforcement personnel. Counter Terrorism and Serious Crime. If interested, contact your Europol National Unit.

Fry felt an almost physical surge of excitement. It was one of those rare moments when a vista of future possibilities seemed to open up; opportunities to change her life, to make it better.

She remembered what Georgi had said about working for Europol: *I could live in The Hague.* The idea seemed both astonishingly unlikely and perfectly feasible. She'd never been to Holland. In fact, the only places she'd been to on the Continent were Calais, Paris and Naxos. But she could live in The Hague. She was as European as anyone else, wasn't she?

Where were those Europol job descriptions again? Fry was sure she must meet all the criteria

403

for potential applicants. And now, thanks to Georgi Kotsev, she even knew something about cross-border organized crime.

'Anybody know where the Europol National Unit is based?'

'Yes, at the NCIS in London,' said Cooper, without looking up. 'Their HQ is in Vauxhall Bridge, near MI6. I think you can see it in some of the James Bond films.'

'Thanks.'

Fry waited to see if anyone enquired why she was interested in Europol. But there wasn't a murmur. Well, that didn't surprise her. No one cared what she did, or where she went.

There was a seminar she'd attended recently on the use of Sirene, a new data system linked to the Police National Computer. The system was designed to give access to information from all the Schengen countries, and get an alert placed against the details of anyone suspected of involvement in organized crime. That would be useful – when it came in. It had been mentioned during the seminar that the British part of the system would be administered by the Sirene UK Bureau. Based at the NCIS. Fancy that.

'We're still not up to speed on organized crime, are we?' said Fry, when Cooper got to his feet and passed her desk.

'That's one of the reasons we're going to end up being merged, isn't it? That, and our neighbours' problems.'

'We can't blame it on Nottinghamshire.'

'We can try.'

Fry sighed. 'You're so parochial,' she said. 'You're all so parochial.'

On the DI's desk, the plastic wallet was now labelled as evidence examined by the documents section at the forensics laboratory.

'The passport has been confirmed as a forgery,' said Hitchens. 'Likewise Rose Shepherd's driving licence. With those two items, you can build an identity for yourself in no time.'

'Pity there was no sign of a birth certificate,' said Fry.

'You don't need a birth certificate unless you're applying for a genuine passport. People who supply forged identity documents don't care where or when your birth was registered. So the person called Rose Shepherd won't have a birth certificate.'

'What about her DNA and fingerprints?' said Fry.

'We're running them through the database.'

'No wonder she got that shredder installed. If you had a fraudulent identity yourself, you'd know about taking precautions. But, despite her East European connections, she's not your typical terrorist suspect, is she?'

'True. But she'd need the right contacts to change her identity so effectively. Nikolov looks likely. But there are plenty of possibilities, given her links to organized crime. When we discover her real identity, we'll find the motive for her murder. There must be something she did in the past that she was trying to conceal.'

Cooper nodded, but he was doubtful. He found he couldn't reconcile the picture he'd built up of Miss Shepherd with the idea of her being a criminal with a background full of sordid secrets. If she liked cats, she can't have been all that bad.

Of course, when this woman took on a new identity, she'd done a pretty good job of it. But it was never going to be perfect. It wasn't really possible to start life all over again with the totally blank slate Rose Shepherd seemed to have craved. There were always a few threads that remained unbroken somewhere in any person's life. No matter who she was, or where she came from, this woman was a product of all the experiences she'd gone through in sixty years of existence.

And in Miss Shepherd's case, there must have been people in her life who she couldn't entirely leave behind. Despite her change of identity, one of them had been bound to catch up with her some day. It was just a question of finding the right thread – the one that remained unbroken.

'Did I tell you?' said Cooper. 'I think I might have found where the wooden dinosaur came from.'

During the briefing, Gavin Murfin had seemed fascinated by the shine on Kotsev's shoes. He'd sat with his eyes permanently directed downwards, as if he'd been hypnotized.

'What do you think of him, Gavin?' asked Fry.

'His shoes are very shiny.'

'Are they?'

'Yes, very military-looking. I bet he feels much more at home in uniform.'

'All part of his professional manner, wouldn't you say?'

Murfin sniffed, but didn't take the bait. 'By the way, West Yorkshire Police have no record of John Lowther on their local intelligence systems. But I tracked down a former colleague from the building society where he worked – a Mr Barrington. Apparently, the word around the office was that after Lowther left the company he was in hospital for quite some time.'

'What for?'

'Nobody ever knew. It was only a rumour that went round. Lowther's resignation had come as a bit of a surprise, so there was some speculation about a mystery illness. You know the sort of thing. In those circumstances, people tend to assume cancer. In fact, Mr Barrington was surprised to hear that John Lowther was still alive.'

'See if you can find out what was wrong with him, will you?'

'That's going to be difficult,' said Murfin. 'Even if the rumours are true, I don't know what hospital he was in. I might be able to get the name of his GP in Leeds from the company's personnel records, but you know what doctors are like . . .'

'The rumour must have come from somewhere, though.'

'Office rumours? That's like catching feathers. People put two and two together and make them add up to whatever they want. It's the same round here, in case you hadn't noticed.' Murfin shook his head. 'There was *one* person Mr Barrington mentioned. Not a friend exactly, but someone John Lowther might have talked to a bit more than his other colleagues.'

'Does he still work there?'

'It's a she. And she moved to a rival firm a few months ago.'

'But you could find her, though, if you tried.'

'I suppose so.' Murfin paused. 'Diane, surely we could ask Lowther's parents? They must know about his hospital stay.'

'Yes, I'm going to ask them,' said Fry. 'But I don't trust them to tell me the truth. I want to make sure I have an independent account.'

'I can't promise anything. There's such a lot on right now.'

'OK, Gavin. Just try, will you?'

Fry seemed to have heard herself saying that far too often recently. Was she the only one these things occurred to? Or was she obsessing too much over irrelevant details?

'Where's your Bulgarian?' asked Murfin.

'C Division. He's assisting on the Zhivko bombing, too.'

'Busy man.'

'When he comes back, I'm taking him down to Foxlow. He wants to see Rose Shepherd's house.'

'Does he know anything about her?'

'I don't think so.'

Murfin answered the phone and held it out to Fry.

'Speak of the devil,' he said. 'It's Boris.'

Fry took the phone. 'Hi, Georgi.'

'Diane, *alo*. I'm returning to Edendale. I need to talk to you.'

'Has something come up?'

'I have to talk to you about the assassination of Rosica Savova.'

'The assassination of who?'

'The woman you know as Rose Shepherd.'

27

Standing in the sitting room at Bain House, Fry thought of the heaps of flowers and cards piling up outside the Mullens' house in Darwin Street. Last time she'd been there, teddy bears and other children's toys had been added to the pile. There was talk of opening a memorial book at the community centre. This morning, the local papers had been full of photographs of the Mullens, tributes from people who'd known them, and poems from children at the school Jack had attended.

But there was none of that for Rose Shepherd. No one in Foxlow had left flowers at her gate. No one had talked to the papers about her. Even Eric Grice had decided against that.

'So who was Rose Shepherd really?' asked Fry.

'She was a woman by the name of Rosica Savova,' said Georgi Kotsev, staring at the grey walls. 'She had a Bulgarian father, but her mother was an Irish national, from County Galway.'

'She could put on an Irish accent, if she felt like it?'

'It might have been natural. We don't know much about her past history, so which country she spent most of her time in is unclear. But she had been working in Bulgaria for several years before she came here. Our police department has an intelligence file on her, due to her association with Simcho Nikolov and Dimitar Iliev.'

'What crime was she involved in?'

'None that we know of,' said Kotsev. 'There has never been any evidence against her. However, Savova was connected with the wrong people. That in itself causes us suspicion.'

'Did she have a job?'

'She worked as an advisor for an adoption agency.'

'And you're quite sure she and Rose Shepherd were the same person?'

'I noticed the photographs of her in your incident room. I wasn't entirely sure then – I had to do a little checking.'

'I see.'

Kotsev admired the TV set and the stereo. 'What money did she have? You've examined her financial affairs?'

'We've been through all her bank statements. Rose Shepherd had one current account and three savings accounts.'

'But not much cash in them, perhaps?'

'No, but –'

'It's not surprising. Rosica Savova must have

411

lived in Bulgaria through the time of the 1996 bank collapse. That was when more than a third of our banks closed down, and much of our money simply disappeared.'

'Disappeared?'

Kotsev shrugged. 'Who knows where it went? Many say it was sent to Switzerland for a holiday and returned after a nice rest. Like a faithful dog, the money came straight back to the pockets of the people who looked after it before, and those people became suddenly wealthy again. Our beloved credit millionaires.'

'What has that to do with Miss Shepherd?'

'Everyone who lost their money in 1996 also lost their faith in banks. Have your people searched the house properly?'

'What do you mean by "properly"?' said Fry, bridling.

'Inside the walls, under the floorboards? The chimney?'

'Why would we do that?'

Kotsev turned slowly. 'To find her money.'

Fry took a call on her mobile. When she'd finished, she discovered Kotsev upstairs, tapping the walls of the main bedroom.

'Good news, Georgi. The blue Vauxhall Astra we're looking for was seen again in Foxlow last night. This time we have a registration number, and the PNC gave us a name and address to go with it. The vehicle is registered to a Mr Darren Turnbull, of South Wingfield.'

'Is that nearby?'

'Not too far. But we wouldn't get there first, Georgi.'

'We could try.'

'There's no point. DI Hitchens is already on his way there.'

'Pity.' He tapped the wall again. 'It sounds hollow here. But it could just be the chimney. You should get your people back to examine the structure of the house.'

'Oh, I don't know about that, Georgi. It sounds like a major exercise. I can't see how we'd justify ripping the house apart.'

'You need Savova's personal information? Her private contacts? Where else would she keep them, but in her secret safe, with her money?'

'She used the internet, Georgi. We think she might have had some free web storage space that she used for information like that. We just haven't found it yet.'

'The internet? *Gluposti*. Find her money, you find her heart and soul.'

'That's very cynical.'

'Take a look at the real world, Diane.'

Fry was thoughtful as they returned to the car and drove out of Foxlow.

'Georgi, what do you think of our methods so far?' she said.

'Very interesting. But your enquiries are in the wrong direction, Diane.'

'What do you mean?'

He waved a hand out of the window at the cottages they were passing. 'You are wasting your time with these *Albanski reotani*.'

'Who?'

'These . . . slow-witted country people.'

'Hold on, I've got another call.'

This time, it was Hitchens himself. 'Where are you, Diane?'

'Just approaching Matlock.'

'Great. We're at Darren Turnbull's house in South Wingfield, but his wife says he's driven down into Matlock to go to the bank. His car should be parked by the railway station.'

'OK, we'll be there in a couple of minutes.'

'It's a blue Astra. You've got the reg?'

'Yes, leave it to us.'

A few minutes later, Fry coasted her Peugeot into the station car park at the bottom of Dale Road. They found the Astra almost immediately.

'OK, now we have to wait for him to come back.'

She parked where they had a clear view of the vehicle, looking along a line of parked cars towards the station.

'Tell me again why we want to talk to this man,' said Kotsev.

'Darren Turnbull's car was seen in Foxlow on Saturday night, at about the time Rose Shepherd was shot. I mean –'

'Rosica Savova.'

'Yes. Well, Turnbull doesn't live in the village,

414

so we need to know what he was doing there, and what he might have seen. And why he didn't come forward in response to our appeals.'

Kotsev eased his legs with a sigh. 'If I had seen Rosica Savova's assassin, perhaps I would not come forward and tell the police either.'

'Why, Georgi?'

'It could be dangerous.'

Fry looked at him, surprised all over again. He was like some oversized alien sitting in her car, a visitor from another world.

'He can't possibly have known it might be dangerous,' she said. 'Turnbull is just an engineer in an aircraft engine factory.'

'It depends what he saw,' said Kotsev. 'In my experience, many people see things that they keep quiet about, for their own safety.'

'Maybe.'

Kotsev suddenly sat up straight. 'Is this the man?'

'Let's see which car he goes back to.'

A man was strolling along the line of vehicles. He was in his thirties, sandy-haired, wearing a black parka. The hood was down, which gave them a good look at his face. He stopped, hesitated as if he wasn't quite sure which was his car, then pulled a key from his pocket and approached the blue Vauxhall.

'Yes, that's him. Let's go.'

Turnbull looked up nervously and saw them coming. He mouthed a curse, then turned and began to run towards the station. God knew where he thought he was going.

Fry broke into a sprint, but Kotsev easily outpaced her, his long legs covering the ground in seconds.

'*Politsia!* Police!'

Catching up with him, Kotsev took hold of Turnbull's arm and twisted it sharply behind his back, pushing his face into a wall.

'My friend, you shouldn't try to escape. You have to tell us what we want to know.'

Fry was frozen for a moment, shocked by Kotsev's action. 'Georgi!'

He looked at her, his eyes glinting, his jaw set as if he intended to face her down. She was glad Kotsev wasn't wearing his gun.

'Sergeant Kotsev, you don't have any jurisdiction here. This isn't Bulgaria.'

Slowly, he relaxed his grip on Turnbull's arm, but didn't let go completely. Nor did he stand back, so Turnbull's face remained pressed against the stones.

'You're right, of course. You do things a little differently, Sergeant Fry. But I know the methods that work with these people.'

'Let go of him,' hissed Fry.

Another moment passed. Finally, Kotsev stood back, and smiled.

'I apologize. I have no jurisdiction. This is your suspect.' He turned Turnbull gently away from the wall and pretended to dust down his clothes. 'I apologize to you, too, my friend. I intended you no harm. I hope you feel comfortable, and that you are well enough to be questioned by my colleague.'

Turnbull didn't look reassured. In fact, he looked more frightened than ever at the sudden change. Now, he had no idea what was happening.

'What the hell is this?'

'You *are* Mr Darren Turnbull?' said Fry.

'Yes.'

'Are you the owner of a blue Vauxhall Astra hatchback, X registration?'

'Yes, why?'

'Were you in the village of Foxlow on Saturday night?'

Turnbull's mouth dropped open. His brain still seemed to be working, but so slowly that no connection was being made with his vocal cords.

'Sir?'

'I can't tell you,' he said.

Kotsev had been standing by quietly, but now made a sudden gesture. It might only have been impatience he couldn't restrain, but the suggestion of imminent violence communicated itself to Turnbull.

'No, I really can't tell you,' he said. 'I'd be in big trouble. Big, big trouble.'

'Let's all go back to the station, then,' said Fry. 'And we'll talk about which sort of trouble you'd rather be in, Mr Turnbull.'

*   *   *

417

In the mortuary, the pathologist turned to Kessen and Cooper. 'The bruise on his temple was the only physical injury. It wasn't enough to kill him, but it could have caused mild concussion.'

'There's a little more to it than that,' said Kessen.

'Well, I found exceptionally high levels of alcohol in the bloodstream – and that *would* have been enough to kill most people. But tolerance varies, you know.' Mrs van Doon raised an eyebrow. 'If he was an experienced drinker, he could have survived the alcohol poisoning. Short-term, anyway.'

'It sounds as though he was very experienced,' said Cooper.

'I thought so. Well, here's an unwise combination for you – the victim was also malnourished. I'd say he hadn't eaten properly for some time.'

'So that combination was the cause of death?'

'Not directly. My conclusion is that he fell on his back, suffering a blow to the head on the way down. It's a pity he couldn't have turned on to his side. It might have saved him.'

'There wasn't room where he fell in his caravan,' said Cooper. 'He was lying wedged between a table and the bed.'

The pathologist nodded. 'Well, that explains it. While he lay unconscious, or in an alcoholic stupor, he choked on his own vomit.'

Darren Turnbull sat in Interview Room One. 'I suppose this is about the shooting, isn't it? The old lady who got shot in Foxlow.'

'Would you like to tell us something about that, Darren?' said Hitchens in his friendliest manner.

'I don't know anything about the bloody shooting,' said Turnbull, apparently missing the friendliness.

'Oh, really? So why did you mention it?'

Turnbull twisted his hands restlessly, but his voice seemed to be failing him again.

'I mean, you must know *something* about it. You raised the subject, Darren, not us.'

This time, Hitchens let the silence develop. He was prepared to wait for Turnbull to fill the silence.

'I saw it on the telly,' he said. 'That's all. I read about it in the papers. That's how I know about the murder, just like everyone else. So what does that mean, eh?'

'That you're admirably conscientious about keeping up with the news, I suppose,' said Hitchens, opening the file in front of him. He made a show of reading the top page for a few moments, as if he was seeing it for the first time. He raised an eyebrow as he looked at Turnbull again.

'Your car – this blue X-reg Astra. It was seen in Foxlow on Saturday night. Well, the early hours of Sunday, actually. It was remarkably near the scene of the murder, Darren.'

'Maybe.'

'And having diligently watched all those TV reports and read the items in the newspapers, which all mentioned that we were appealing for the owner of a blue X-reg Vauxhall Astra to come forward, you nevertheless stayed away, and failed to contact us. Why was that, Darren?'

'I'm going to be in *big* trouble,' said Turnbull.

'Darren, this is a police station. You're being interviewed in connection with a murder enquiry. We have reason to believe that you were in the vicinity around the time the murder occurred, and yet you've failed to come forward voluntarily as a potential witness. Believe me, you're already in big trouble. It would be a lot better if you're honest with us now. Otherwise, things could get . . . well, complicated for you.'

Turnbull sighed deeply. 'I suppose I knew it would come to this in the end. I was visiting a friend. A girlfriend, all right?'

'In Foxlow?'

'Yes.'

'And this was Saturday night, extending into the early hours of Sunday morning?'

'Yes. So if some old nosy parker saw me or my car, that's what I was doing. OK?'

'Name?' said Hitchens, with his pen poised.

'What?'

'Your girlfriend's name, please.'

'I can't tell you.'

'We need to substantiate your story, Darren. What time did you leave Foxlow?'

'About three a.m.'

'And your friend would be able to confirm that?'

'Of course she would.'

'So what's the problem?'

Turnbull didn't answer. He looked at the table between them, torn by some difficulty that he was unable to resolve into words.

Hitchens looked at the file again. 'You're married, Darren.'

'Yes, I am.'

'I met your wife. Fiona, is that right? Happy together are you?'

'Yes, of course we are.'

'That's good. We don't like to see marriages break up.'

'Now you're taking the piss.'

Hitchens laid the file down. 'Let's get this straight, Darren. You're having an affair with a woman who lives in Foxlow, and you don't want your wife to know about it. Is that about right?'

'Yes,' said Turnbull grudgingly.

'OK, I understand that. But look at it this way, Darren. You're a potential witness in our enquiry. All we want is to ask you a few questions about anything you might have seen or heard that night. And we'll want to speak to your girlfriend to corroborate your story, as I said. And that will be it. Provided it all checks out, we'll thank you for helping us with our enquiries, and there won't be any need for us to speak to Fiona.'

Turnbull nodded cautiously.

'On the other hand, if you continue to refuse to account fully for your movements that night, we'll be obliged to ask questions about your background and circumstances, find out who your associates are . . . Your wife would be the obvious place to start.'

'I hear what you're saying.' Turnbull hung his head. 'Would I have to go to court to give evidence?'

'That depends. But I think it'll be unlikely. All we want to do at the moment is eliminate you from our enquiries, Darren. And it would be nice if you could help us to establish any fresh leads. We'd feel quite appreciative.'

'All right.'

'I presume you must have told your wife some story about where you were, by the way?'

'I told her I was putting in an extra shift at the factory. I work for Rolls Royce in Derby, and she doesn't really have any idea what we do there, so I can just say we have a rush job on.'

'Fine.'

Hitchens opened the file again and picked up his pen. 'Do you want to give me the name of your girlfriend now?'

'Stella Searle. She lives at Magpie Cottage, right next to the churchyard in Foxlow.'

'Now we're getting somewhere.'

'Stella's divorced. She lives in that cottage on her own.'

'I'm sure that makes it better.'

'You know what I mean.'

'So what time did the night shift start?' asked Hitchens.

'Sorry?'

'I mean, what time did you arrive in Foxlow to visit your divorcée?'

'Oh, about half past eleven. I don't go there until it's dark – people who live in villages are so nosy they want to know everything about you. I park the car on a lane behind the churchyard. There are no lights there, but there's a back gate into Stell's garden.'

'Very handy. This Magpie Cottage – it would be right on the corner of Foxlow High Street and Pinfold Lane, am I right?'

'That's it.'

'So what time did you leave on Sunday morning? Be as accurate as you can, please.'

'It was close to three o'clock. I always leave at that time. That's when the late shift ends, so I get home about the right time.'

'OK, now we get to the bit where you might be able to help us, Darren. Did you see or hear anything as you were leaving the cottage? At three o'clock in the morning, it ought to have been very quiet. I'm hoping you were alert enough to notice any activity, even after your visit.'

Turnbull lowered his voice. 'Yes, I did see something.'

'What did you see?'

'A black car. Big four-by-four, it was. Japanese. Tinted windows. Smart motor.'

'Japanese? Did you recognize the make?'

'Mmm, I'm not sure. Some of them are a bit similar, aren't they? Toyota, Mitsubishi?'

Hitchens sighed. 'Did you happen to see any part of the registration number?'

'No, sorry.'

'But you're sure of the colour? Even though it was dark?'

'I saw it pass under a streetlamp – the one by the phone box. It's the nearest one to Stella's house.'

'How many occupants?'

'One in the front, at least. I couldn't tell if there was anyone in the back because of the tinted windows. Sorry.'

'And this vehicle was heading in the direction of Bain House?'

'If that's the big house with the gates at the top of Pinfold Lane, it definitely went that way, then came back towards the High Street.'

'All right, Darren. If you wait here, we'll get someone to show you some photos, and we'll see if you can identify the make and model of the car you saw.'

'What? Can't I go yet?'

'Not yet.'

'I had no connection with that woman at all, you know,' said Turnbull. 'Except that I was in the village when she died.'

Having given this information, Turnbull suddenly regained confidence and turned belligerent.

'I could put in a complaint about the foreign bloke,' he said. 'He hurt my arm in Matlock. And

424

I've got a scratch on my face. He's not supposed to do that, is he? I wasn't even under arrest – you said so.'

'We could soon change that, Darren.'

'It's not right.'

'If you want to make a formal complaint about the conduct of any police officers, speak to the custody sergeant and he'll give you a form to fill in.'

When they were alone in the corridor, Hitchens looked at Fry quizzically. 'Foreign bloke? Sergeant Kotsev?'

'He isn't quite used to our procedures yet,' said Fry.

'Kotsev is only here as an observer, Diane. You're responsible for him. If Turnbull does put in a complaint –'

'I don't think he will,' said Fry. 'Do you? Too much chance of publicity.'

'No, you're right. But be careful.'

When she was alone, Fry spent some time browsing the Europol website again, checking the location of the organization's headquarters and how to get there. It was just idle curiosity, of course. No more than that.

But now she had formed a picture in her mind. She could see herself catching the number 9 tram in the direction of Scheveningen, getting off at Riouwstraat and crossing the footbridge over the canal to reach the Europol building. If she worked there, she would find a little apartment some-where fashionable, but central for the city. Overlooking another canal, probably. Or maybe the same canal.

Actually, she wasn't sure how many canals there were in The Hague. She might be getting it mixed up with Amsterdam in her mind. That was easy to do, when she'd never visited either city. She didn't even know the country. Put that way, it sounded a mad thing to do, to contemplate working in a totally foreign country. But then, why would anyone want to live in a place that they knew every little bit of?

Finally, Hitchens appeared and gestured to her, and she followed him into the DCI's office.

'We got Darren Turnbull to look at the motors file for us,' said Hitchens. 'He's not a happy man, but looking at pictures of cars seemed to calm him down a bit.'

'And?'

'He thinks it was probably a Mitsubishi Shogun that he saw in Foxlow that night.'

'Excellent,' said Kessen.

'We've checked the incident logs, and nothing is missing locally. But South Yorkshire have a hit. On Saturday evening, a black Shogun was stolen from the car park of the Church of Free Worship in Totley. That's on the outskirts of Sheffield.'

'Even better.'

'Wait, there's more. Traffic already have a report of a Shogun abandoned under a disused railway bridge near Wirksworth. Burnt out, of course. And it's been there since Monday at least.'

'Our suspects made a switch, then.'

'It looks like it, sir.'

'What's happened to the Shogun?'

'It's still there at the moment. DC Cooper's on his way to take a look.'

Kessen was looking a bit happier. 'I don't suppose we have any idea what kind of vehicle they might have transferred to?'

'No. But we haven't even started making enquiries in that area yet. We'll give the car the works *in situ*, then fetch it in for the vehicle examiners.'

'Good work, Paul. But make sure any more stolen vehicles that are found get the once-over before they're returned to their owners. They could have made a second switch at some point. Let's pass that request to South Yorkshire, too. Chances are they doubled back towards Sheffield from Wirksworth. These weren't our local joy riders.'

'Yes, sir.'

'Not that we'll get anything useful, even if we find another vehicle. We're looking at a professional job.'

'You know, if they're professionals, we won't get DNA profiles from any of these scenes. Pros make sure they keep up to date. Even joy riders don't go out at night until they've watched *CSI*.'

'We might get lucky.'

427

Hitchens shrugged. They all knew that the risk of leaving DNA was becoming familiar to career criminals. With the national database throwing up a thousand matches a week, how could it be otherwise?

'So much for the famous village surveillance experts,' said Fry. 'They spotted Darren Turnbull's Astra twice, but they never saw the Shogun.'

Hitchens looked at her. 'What have you done with Sergeant Kotsev, by the way?'

'I've given him to Ben Cooper to look after for a while.'

28

Georgi Kotsev didn't seem at all disturbed to have left civilization behind. He waited patiently for Cooper to re-fold the map, gazing around the landscape as if he expected a few peasants to appear and direct them to the right place.

'We're nearly there,' said Cooper.

'*Dobre*. OK.'

It seemed to Cooper that traces of pagan legacy were still there to be seen at every turn in this area, though few people noticed. They didn't see them because their attention was focused on shop windows and traffic, the obsessions of modern society that overlaid history and pushed ancestral beliefs into the background. Now it was as if these ancient objects existed in an extra dimension, where they were only visible if you knew they were there and you looked straight at them.

There was a representation of Sheela-na-Gig incorporated into the stonework of St Helen's Church at Darley Dale. The goddess of creation and destruction. Few people noticed it, surely, or understood its meaning. If they did, they'd be campaigning for its removal.

A couple of miles down the road, a display cabinet in Matlock church still contained a set of crantsies. Time-darkened maiden's garlands, each one commemorating the death of an unmarried woman. Their wickerwork frames were decorated with symbols of purity – ribbons, roses, flowers of folded white paper – set around a centrepiece of a collar, a pair of gloves or a handkerchief, something that had belonged to the woman.

'Is folklore important in Bulgaria, Georgi? I imagine it is.'

'Yes, certainly. When I was very young, my grandmother gave me a book of Bulgarian fairy tales. The stories had many supernatural characters – werewolves, vampires, wood-nymphs. Lots of pictures. They stay in your mind when you're a child.'

'Yes, that's right.'

'I remember one fairy tale in particular. It told about a man who finds himself on another earth, in a different world. The only way he can get back to his own world is by riding on the backs of two eagles. But he has to feed the eagles with his own flesh so that they will carry him.'

Fairy tales weren't really Cooper's thing. But he knew some of them were supposed to have profound symbolic meanings, if you could manage to figure them out.

'And what did that story teach you, Georgi?'

'That sometimes it is necessary to sacrifice everything, in order to get to where you have to be. Even to sacrifice your own flesh and blood.'

'I see.'

Then Kotsev smiled, his dark eyes glittering. 'Also, that you should never trust eagles. Even when they say they're doing you a favour.'

The Shogun had been abandoned under a bridge that was left over from a disused mineral line. It wasn't even a bridge any more, because the central section had been removed. But it had only crossed a farm track anyway. By the looks of the deep tread on the wheel tracks in the mud, the farmer had probably passed the Shogun several times this week without bothering to report it.

A Traffic car stood guard on the road side of the bridge. But someone had done a good job of torching the Shogun. It was difficult to tell what colour the scorched paintwork had been, but for a few streaks left on the boot and around the front wings. The interior, though, looked relatively undamaged.

Cooper looked around the area. The last glance at the map had given him an idea.

'There's not much we can get from the car until the SOCOs arrive,' he said. 'I'd like to take a look up this way, Georgi.'

'Very well. Your sergeant says you know everything about this area.'

'She does?'

'Yes, indeed. Sergeant Fry must regard you very highly.'

Cooper laughed. 'I don't think you've known her long enough. It probably wasn't a compliment.'

Though Kotsev's stride was longer, he obviously wasn't used to walking over rough terrain, and definitely not uphill. He was panting in minutes. That was a sign of too much city living, in Cooper's view. No matter how big their muscles were, a forty-five-degree slope always sorted the men from the boys.

'Where are we going?' gasped Kotsev, stopping to rest and watching Cooper moving steadily away from him.

'Just to the top of this rise.'

'*Chaga, chaga*. Wait.'

'What's the matter, Georgi?'

'I think the air is a little thin here.'

'We're not even a thousand feet above sea level.'

Kotsev began to move again, but awkwardly, planting his feet with great deliberation on the rough grass. His knees were probably hurting by now, if he never used the right muscles.

A moment later, Cooper was standing at the top of the slope, letting the breeze cool his forehead. To the north east, he could see a drystone wall running along the skyline, marking the road between Wirksworth and Middleton. He followed the wall a little further north – and there was the distinctive outline of a red phone box.

He smiled. When public phone boxes were first designed, they were painted bright red to stand out from a distance. For decades, it had been important to know where the nearest phone was, and these old kiosks would have been a welcome sight. They weren't used a lot nowadays. But they were such an integral part of the landscape that they were kept in the countryside as a conservation measure, as much as for emergency use.

Finally, Kotsev struggled the last few yards and arrived alongside him, breathing heavily and wiping sweat from his forehead.

'Georgi, how many people in Bulgaria have mobile phones?' asked Cooper.

Kotsev stared at him. 'Everybody, except for those who are too poor. And the very old, who don't understand them.'

'Yes, it's the same here. And even if you don't own a mobile, you have a phone in your house. Not many people are too poor or too old for that.'

'What are you saying?'

'Well, it's different, of course,' said Cooper, 'if you happen to live in a caravan.'

If he could have seen over the next hill, he might have been able to make out the red blob of a similar phone box in Bonsall Dale. That was the one Rose Shepherd had made two calls to. According to the map, it must be the nearest one to Lea Farm, where Simcho Nikolov had lived. Calls to the phone box by prior arrangement. Miss Shepherd had been in contact with Nikolov in the past three weeks.

Their connection supported speculation in the Bulgarian intelligence reports, a theory that Nikolov and Savova had been friends, or even lovers. Here was a link that had been more difficult to break than a mere business relationship.

Well, it was handy that rural phone boxes were marked on Ordnance Survey maps. But the box wasn't what Cooper had noticed first. His eye had been drawn to the contour lines showing the steepness of the slope and the footpath above the bridge. It was funny the way things worked out sometimes.

He was turning to tell Kotsev that they might as well go back down to the burnt-out car, when two shots echoed across the hillside, one following quickly after the other. The flat *smack* of the first discharge sent birds scattering from the trees.

Kotsev looked around anxiously, and his hand went to his hip. 'It's stupid not to be armed. Why don't they let you have guns?'

'We don't need them,' said Cooper. 'Most of the time.'

'And the times when you do?'

'We try to keep out of the way of the bullets.'

Kotsev snorted. 'It's stupid. You know this is the only police service in the world whose officers aren't armed?'

'No, there's New Zealand too.'

'New Zealand? But all they have to deal with are kangaroos. Here, you have armed gangsters, and terrorists. The IRA. Yardies. al-Qaeda. It's stupid.'

Cooper laughed, and Kotsev glared at him.

'Why are you laughing?'

'I think you just don't understand us, Georgi.'

There was a movement in the field ahead, and two figures appeared, walking rapidly down from the direction of the phone box. When they passed a stretch of fallen wall, the figures became identifiable as two men wearing peaked caps and quilted body warmers. Both of them had double-barrelled shotguns tucked under their arms.

'So,' said Kotsev. 'Do we run away?'

As soon as Cooper walked back into the office at West Street, Fry slammed the phone down and glared at him. 'See, I took my attention off Brian Mullen. I let him know he was under suspicion, and then allowed him the chance to do a runner. I should have been completing the case against him by now so we could make an arrest. But I was distracted. Too much attention on the Rose Shepherd enquiry. How can anyone be expected to do two jobs at once, and do them properly?'

Fry paused, and looked at Cooper. He didn't answer her, but she didn't expect him to. He was only there for her to have someone to sound off at. Fortunately, he was good at that.

'What's happened, Diane?'

'I need to talk to Brian Mullen again,' she said. 'He should be with his parents-in-law in Darley Dale, but they say they don't know where he is today. And he has Luanne with him.'

'That's bad news.'

'Bad news? It's a total disaster. I'm sending Gavin out to speak to John Lowther, and to anyone else who might know where Mullen is. But I've a nasty feeling he's done a runner.'

'Are you still fancying Mullen for the arson? What would his motive have been?'

'He and Lindsay had been having blazing rows. Loud ones, by all accounts. Their neighbour Keith Wade heard them arguing earlier that evening. The parents are being cagey on this one, so I don't know how serious their marital problems were, but they could have been on the point of splitting up. Lindsay might have threatened to walk out on Brian, and told him he'd lose the children. That would have hit him pretty hard, I think.'

'Oh, so he killed them?'

'It happens, you know – some distraught dad decides to end it all, and take the family down with him.'

'But Brian Mullen didn't do that, did he? He was the one who survived.'

'Well, he could have chickened out at the last minute. Once he saw the flames and felt the heat, and realized what he was doing.'

'I suppose that's possible.'

'You sound doubtful. Tell me – you always seem to have some theory of your own that doesn't fit with anyone else's. Are you going to share it with me, Ben?'

Cooper shook his head. 'I don't have a theory. It's just that . . .'

'Yes?'

'Well, if what you're saying was really the case, I'd expect Mr Mullen to be consumed with guilt right now. He'd be thinking that he ought to have died in the fire with his family, and blaming himself for his cowardice in not going through with it.'

'That would explain his present attitude, wouldn't it?'

'No, I don't think so, Diane. It doesn't feel right.'

But Fry had stopped listening to him. She was staring at the photograph of the Mullen family – Lindsay and the two boys, with Brian holding baby Luanne. Three of them were dead, and two still survived.

But that wasn't the way it was running through her head. The words she couldn't get out of her mind were slightly different, a phrase she'd learned a long time ago in the playground.

Three down, two to go.

Fry could almost hear children's voices chanting it in the distance, their tone a mixture of triumph and challenge. They summed up the feeling of a task half done, and the determination to complete it.

Three down, two to go.

The phrase filled her with a sudden sense of urgency, a conviction that an awful disaster could be taking place right under her nose while she was distracted by irrelevant detail.

437

'Ben,' she said, 'you know what? Right now, I bet Brian Mullen is thinking just one thing. That he ought to get on and finish the job.'

Of course, it was possible that the Lowthers were lying when they said they didn't know where Brian was. They might only be trying to protect their son-in-law from further distress. Very admirable, but not when it got in the way of her enquiry.

Fry decided she would go straight to Darley Dale, to take the Lowthers by surprise. They wouldn't find it easy to hide the fact that Brian and the baby were in the house if someone turned up on their doorstep.

First, she found the photograph again – the one of the whole Mullen family, Brian and Lindsay, the two boys and Luanne. This might have been one of the last pictures they had taken together. And they did look like a happy family, didn't they? At least the Mullen children had been given a secure start in life, protected and safe, if only for a few years. It might seem the wrong way to be thinking. But there were a lot of kids who never experienced that sort of life at all, and Fry had been one of them.

There were sixty thousand children in foster care or local authority homes. It was hard for Fry to think of herself as part of a huge, anonymous mass. But that's exactly what she'd once been – just another statistic in a depressing flow of unwanted children, shuttling to and fro through the back alleys of society; kids destined never to have a real family, or a real home.

At least for a while it had been Angie and Diane together. That had made fostering a bit more tolerable. But even that had come to an abrupt end.

Fry shut her eyes against the sudden stab of pain. It was a memory that tormented her, even now. That moment she'd realized the unbelievable: Angie had left for good, walked out of their foster home in Warley and disappeared. Ever since then, Diane had thought that she'd make things right by finding Angie. But perhaps the truth was that she had never forgiven her sister for that betrayal, and never could. It was a truth she hadn't acknowledged until now.

Sixty thousand children. Fry knew the statistics. Half of those sixty thousand wouldn't get a single GCSE, and would leave school with no qualifications, barely able to read or write, destined for dead-end jobs, if not a permanent place on the dole queue. Fry was one of the measly two per cent who made it to university. Many were consigned to a life on the street, holed up in a filthy squat or crack house, pissing away their existence. Some care-home children felt unwanted and unvalued for the whole of their lives. Many never formed a normal relationship, because they didn't know how. They'd never been shown.

Two thirds of those children were in care because they'd already suffered abuse or neglect.

One in eight moved foster homes more than once a year. And that was a problem, when there was already a shortfall of foster carers. Too many kids, and not enough places for them to go. Fostering was a tough job. Now she'd heard that the government was considering putting vulnerable children in boarding schools and paying their fees.

Fry turned back to the photograph of the Mullen family. But it wasn't Lindsay Mullen and the two boys she was looking at now. They were dead, and past saving. Her focus had shifted.

She held the print up to the light from the window, trying to bring out the depth of colour that suddenly seemed so important. She was studying Brian Mullen and the carefully wrapped bundle in his arms. Luanne Mullen, aged about twelve months at the time the photo was taken. It was unusual, perhaps, for a child of that age to be held by the father in a family group. She might have expected Lindsay to be the one showing off the baby, with the father proudly flanked by his two sons. But that wasn't the way the Mullens had posed.

That detail might have been what drew Fry's attention. It was like a tiny fly twitching its wings in the ointment, a flaw in the normal expectations. Insignificant in itself, but still . . .

As she stared at the child's face, Fry suddenly realized how extraordinarily beautiful Luanne Mullen was. She wasn't the type to fall into a gooey heap every time she saw some unprepossessing infant with jowls like Winston Churchill. Not at all. Most babies were ugly as sin, except to the poor benighted parents, who couldn't see the reality in front of them because their eyes were glued shut with bewilderment and exhaustion. But not Luanne. Churchill had never looked like this. In fact, Luanne Mullen was the most beautiful child she'd ever seen.

Then Fry was struck by the contrast between Luanne and her father. Not that Brian was repulsive, exactly, but he was fair-haired, angular and pale. Luanne, on the other hand, had black hair – so black that it was startling in a child of her age. Her eyes were dark, too, like little pools of black ink.

And there was another thing – the child's skin was surely several shades more Mediterranean than Brian's English pallor. So what about the mother? Well, there she was – blonde hair, showing light brown at the roots. And green eyes.

Of course, it was perfectly possible that the couple had produced a child who looked like that. English people weren't exactly pure-bred Anglo-Saxons, after all. They were mongrels to a man, a mixture of Celts and Vikings, Saxons and Normans, and more exotic arrivals. In the North West of England, almost everyone had an Irish migrant or two lurking in their family tree. This child's conception might simply have thrown up the genes of some Gaelic or Huguenot ancestor. Or her looks could result from a more recent influence – a Jewish refugee grandfather, or a Middle Eastern immigrant.

Yes, all of those things were possible. But none of them was the first thought that sprang to Fry's mind when she looked at Luanne Mullen.

29

When Fry looked down at the A6 that afternoon, she didn't know what to expect. A stagecoach with four grey horses, or two of them drawing a landau. Maybe Dick Turpin on Black Bess. Who knew what went on in this area?

She passed the Lowthers' car standing on the drive. A white Rover, nice and clean. A couple of years old, though, so it was probably time Mr Lowther had a new one.

Once she was sitting in the Lowthers' conservatory, Fry lifted the photograph of Brian and Lindsay and their three children off the corner table. No pussyfooting around any more. Not at this point.

'Luanne is a very attractive child, Mrs Lowther,' she said.

'Yes, isn't she?'

'She doesn't look a bit like either of her parents, though. Her colouring is very dark.'

'It happens. There's no accounting for genes.'

'I know what you mean,' said Fry. 'But you can account for the genes in this case, can't you? Luanne is definitely your daughter's child?'

Henry Lowther had remained impassive so far, trying to smile politely, but not quite managing it. Mrs Lowther fidgeted, reluctant to answer. But Fry was prepared to wait.

'No, she's adopted,' said Mrs Lowther at last.

'Ah, finally,' said Fry. 'And this adoption was how you came to know Rose Shepherd, am I right?'

'Yes, it's true.'

'And the meeting in Matlock Bath on Saturday? Whose idea was that?'

The Lowthers looked at each other. 'I suppose I suggested it to Lindsay,' said Henry. 'It was just a casual remark, really. "It would be nice to see Rose Shepherd again and say thank you, wouldn't it?" Something like that. That was weeks ago. And Lindsay didn't say anything at the time. But the idea must have taken root in her mind, because a few days later she spoke about organizing a meeting as if it was already a *fait accompli*.'

Mr Lowther's self-conscious use of the French phrase made Fry think of Georgi Kotsev's *ciao* and *merci*. But then, Georgi rightly took pride in his command of languages. How many could Henry Lowther hold a conversation in? Until now, he hadn't even made a good fist of English. Not if you defined conversation as an exchange of information.

'You're going to have to be more forthcoming with us, sir.'

Lowther got up from his chair and moved restlessly around the conservatory. He was a big man – much too heavy round the waist, of course, but intimidating when he stood over you like that.

'You have to realize that they went through a difficult experience together,' he said. 'The adoption process in Bulgaria wasn't easy. Not at all what we expected. It was quite a shock to arrive at that orphanage. We had never seen anything like it.'

'Tell us how it came about.'

'I have some business contacts in Bulgaria,' said Lowther. 'They came over here a few years ago to talk about forming trade links, possibly even a joint venture. They were very impressed with our set-up, and we made sure they had a good time while they were here, of course. They invited me over to Bulgaria for a little jaunt in return for our hospitality.'

'And did they show you a good time?'

'Oh, there was some vodka, and a lot of red wine. We explored the country a little.'

'Where did you go? Pleven?'

Lowther hesitated slightly. 'Dounav.'

'Vodka and red wine? Didn't you drink any *rakia*?'

'I tried it, but I'm not too fond of brandy.'

'And Rose Shepherd?'

'I was put in touch with her through one of

my business contacts. He knew someone who'd used her services previously. The advantages of networking, you see. You can get hold of pretty much anything if you know the right people.'

'Was it you who suggested the adoption to your daughter?'

'I mentioned it as an option.'

'I see.'

'It worked quite well, in the end,' said Mr Lowther defensively. 'We were desperate for a girl – or at least, Lindsay was. But after Liam's birth, the doctors told Lindsay and Brian they couldn't have any more children. Adoption is such a chancy process in this country, and it takes so long. In any case, you can't get babies to adopt here any more. And Lindsay didn't want a child the same age as the boys. We'd read about orphanages in Eastern Europe where all these babies needed parents. Once Lindsay heard about that – well, you can imagine what she was like.'

'Not really, I'm afraid.'

'Well, it was all we could do to stop her catching the next flight to Romania. We knew there wouldn't be any peace until she'd gone to look for herself. But we read up on it a bit – on the internet, you know. And we found that Bulgaria was the place to go these days. So that's where we went. It seemed as simple as that, at first.'

'You keep saying "we".'

'I couldn't let Lindsay go out there on her own.'

'No, but it might seem more natural for her husband to have gone with her.'

Lowther paced the length of the room. 'It's difficult for Brian. He has his job, and he can't just take time off whenever he wants to. But I can organize my time however I like. I've got people I can delegate to. And my daughter came before my business, anyway. I was ready and willing to go to Bulgaria with her.'

'And Rose Shepherd helped you arrange an adoption?'

'She worked with the people at the orphanage.'

'Oh, of course. The orphanage.'

He stopped pacing and stared out of the window at the traffic. His shoulders seemed to sag as he was forced to bring back the memories.

'It was in a small town about thirty miles from Pleven. When we found the place, it was a run-down building with peeling paint, full of chipped wooden cots and thin mattresses. It was awful. Lindsay nearly cried when she saw outside. The thing I remember most is the smell of bleach – it was the first thing that hit us when we went in. But it got worse after that. We could see that the children all slept in cots, regardless of their age. And some of them looked to be more than four years old. We discovered that they were expected to share clothes, and even toothbrushes. Food seemed to be in short supply, too. It was so depressing. Personally, I would have turned round and come home immediately. But then there was Zlatka . . .'

'Sorry? Did you say Zlatka?'

'Lindsay and Brian decided to call her Luanne, but her Bulgarian name was Zlatka Shishkov. She was so small and frail, with big eyes and dark, wispy hair. No one could have resisted her.'

'And that was the child the orphanage offered you?'

'Not at first. There was another child they wanted us to take. A girl who was already past her third birthday then, yet she spoke no more than a few words of what the people at the orphanage called "baby Bulgarian". She still wore nappies, too. Her records said that she'd been neglected by her mother for at least the first year of her life, and she had limited interaction with adults. So she didn't develop all the normal emotional responses or social skills, you see. When anyone reached out to touch her, she flinched away. She was happy to have visitors, but only because it meant being out of her cot for a while. She had no idea who these strange people were that had come to see her.'

'It was you and your daughter who visited the orphanage?'

'Yes. When we went there, I was told that the children might not react to me well. Most Bulgarian orphanage workers are female, so the children had limited experience with men. And, of course, Zlatka had never known her father.'

'Go on.'

'Well, the first time we saw Zlatka, we were in

448

the director's office, the only freshly painted room in the orphanage. A carer brought her in and put her down on a rug for us to look at her. Lindsay said afterwards that she instantly felt a sort of gaping emptiness in her stomach filling up with love. She said in that moment, she became Zlatka's mother.'

Fry said nothing. She didn't personally understand the urges being described.

'I never questioned her about that,' said Lowther, interpreting her sceptical expression. 'There are some things we can't understand about each other, we just have to take them on faith. That instinct was something I could never feel myself. But I didn't doubt it in Lindsay. It was the most powerful emotion I'd ever seen in her. Stronger than when she had either of the boys. It doesn't make sense, does it? But that was the way it was.'

He looked questioningly at his wife, who nodded slowly but didn't speak.

'There were some really bad times after that first occasion, you know,' he said. 'But Lindsay said she could always bring back the feeling of that moment she saw Zlatka. She said it was sometimes the only thing that stopped her from giving up.'

'What do you mean by bad times, sir?'

Lowther didn't seem to hear her, and she had to ask the question again. He stirred from the window, staring at her vaguely.

'Oh, there were so many difficulties. Bulgarian adoptions require court approval – a notoriously slow process. It took months even to set a date for a hearing, and we were told that many adoptions required more than one hearing. Miss Shepherd was a great help, giving us advice all along the line, helping us to understand the rules, explaining all the bureaucracy. But at the first hearing, the judge refused our application. He said there were minor problems in the paperwork. We had to hire a Bulgarian attorney to correct the errors, then the court had to schedule another date. The process seemed to go on for ever. I remember there was a sort of prosecuting attorney, who was employed to point out legal problems. He was a tall man with black hair and broad shoulders, and he wore a bright red robe. We started to refer to him as Satan.'

'All right. But this must have been, what – twelve months ago?'

'Yes, that's right. Luanne was six months old when we brought her out of Bulgaria.'

'She's been slow to develop in a lot of ways,' said Mrs Lowther. 'But that's because of her background. When we got her, she could just about grasp a rattle, and her head still flopped about when we sat her up. She had no idea how to feed herself.'

'The boys were much more advanced than that, so it was a bit of a shock for Lindsay,' added her husband.

Mrs Lowther smiled sadly. 'Luanne's eighteen months old now, and she babbles to herself all the time, but she has difficulty forming words, even "mummy" and "daddy". She tends to repeat the last word of anything that people say to her. She's very restless physically, isn't she, Henry?'

'She certainly is. And she can be very emotional, too – she laughs and cries almost at the same time.'

'And she's still having trouble sleeping through the night, I believe, sir?' said Fry.

Lowther hesitated. 'Oh?'

'Your son-in-law said that's why Luanne was staying here on the night of the fire, to give Lindsay a bit of respite.'

'Oh, that's right,' said Lowther. 'Luanne is still suffering from separation anxiety. Lindsay and Brian should have learned how to let her cry before now, but they couldn't. It's always a difficult thing to do, of course. As a parent, you can't ignore your child when it's calling for you.'

Fry wasn't impressed. Henry Lowther didn't look like a man who'd get up in the middle of the night to attend to a crying baby, but she might be misjudging him.

'So explain to me again how you came to meet with Rose Shepherd in Matlock Bath last weekend.'

'Oh, that was a mistake. I ought to have known it was a mistake from the start. But Lindsay seized on the idea so eagerly, you see. She wanted to say thank you to Miss Shepherd for helping her to get Luanne. I told Lindsay that she should be thankful for what she had and put all the stuff in Bulgaria behind her. But it became almost an obsession with her. You know what women can be like. Well, that was what our daughter was like, anyway. Once she got an idea into her head, it couldn't be shifted.'

'So you set up a meeting?'

'Yes.'

'You must have had some way of getting in touch with Miss Shepherd, then.'

'There was an email address. It was one of those free web-based accounts where you don't have to give any details of your identity to sign up. You only have to provide a name, but you can make that up. Everyone does it.'

'I see. Well, we'd like that email address, please, sir.'

'I'll find it for you. You know, I don't think she can have checked her email very often. It took her some weeks to reply to my message. In fact, I suspected she wasn't going to respond at all. I thought she must have changed her email account, or died even. I didn't know, at the time.'

'You weren't aware that Miss Shepherd was living nearby?'

Lowther laughed. 'No, that was the amazing thing. But she didn't know Britain very well, so this might have been the first place she thought of. Ironic, isn't it? I was stunned when she suggested meeting in Matlock Bath. In my own mind, I'd been thinking of a city somewhere, maybe even London. The anonymity of crowds, you know. But apparently she didn't travel very far once she got into that house at Foxlow.'

'She told you where she lived, then? Was that information in her email, or did she tell you when you met her in the Riber Tea Rooms?'

'Neither,' said Lowther. 'No, she didn't give away anything like that. I read about the house in Foxlow in the papers, and then saw it on the TV news. As I said, I was stunned. To think Miss Shepherd was only a few miles away from us. Do you think it *was* deliberate on her part, to move into Derbyshire?'

'We don't know. But there are a lot of things we don't know about Rose Shepherd.'

'I can't help you very much, I'm afraid. She didn't share any information about her private life.'

'Talking about sharing information – Mr Lowther, why didn't you come forward and tell us you knew Rose Shepherd when you heard the news about her death?'

'Why? Good God, don't you think we've been a bit too busy with our own concerns to pay attention to the news? The last four days have been a complete blur.' Lowther started to go red in the face as he warmed to the subject. 'Our lives have been turned upside down by the fire, you know. We've been backwards and forwards to the hospital and the mortuary, visiting Brian, identifying the bodies of our daughter and our grandchildren, making statements to the police, taking calls from our family and friends, fending off the press, doing our best to look after Brian and Luanne. Not to mention John. My wife has been exhausted with it all. She's cried herself to sleep every night. And you think we've just been sitting around watching TV?'

'All right.'

Fry waited for him to calm down. Perhaps she'd been a bit unreasonable. But after the experience with Darren Turnbull, this silence about Rose Shepherd on the part of the public was starting to feel like a conspiracy.

'Besides,' said Lowther, 'nothing happened at our meeting. Nothing of any significance.'

'You just made small talk?'

'It was all a bit awkward, really. Once we'd said what we'd gone to say, there was nothing else to talk about. After a while, Miss Shepherd gave Lindsay a gift for Luanne, then she left. She seemed quite nervous, glad to get away.'

'This gift, sir . . .?'

'A sort of wooden toy.'

'A dinosaur?'

'Yes. I believe so.'

That detail confirmed, Fry decided to try a different tack.

'What about a man called Simon Nichols? Did you have any dealings with him, Mr Lowther?'

'Nichols? No, the name means nothing to me. Who is he?'

'Somebody else Miss Shepherd was in contact with.'

Lowther screwed up his eyes thoughtfully. 'I always had the impression she had an associate of some kind. Perhaps more than one.'

'Did she never mention any names? What about Simcho Nikolov?'

'No, no. She was very careful, you know.'

'Not careful enough, in the end.'

He grimaced. 'I think she must have lost touch during these last few months. It's easy to lose contact with the real world when you cut yourself off like that. Poor Miss Shepherd.'

'I don't really understand why Brian and Lindsay were so desperate to adopt,' said Fry.

'As I said, Lindsay really, really wanted a girl. It was *so* important to her.'

'But, still – they could have waited a bit longer, couldn't they?'

Lowther coughed and shifted uncomfortably. 'Well, as I said . . . there was a problem. About three years ago, Brian had mumps. When you get them as an adult, it's a very serious condition. It can cause infertility.'

'And that's what happened to your son-in-law?'

'Yes.'

'Were you aware of any problems in your daughter's marriage?'

'Problems?'

'Between Lindsay and Brian. Had they been having arguments recently?'

'Most married couples do have disagreements,' said Lowther stiffly. 'As I said, we all went through a bad period during the adoption, which put a bit of pressure on everybody. Tensions spill over now and then. But recently . . . ?'

He looked at his wife, who seemed even more reluctant. 'If they had problems, then it was a personal matter between themselves. Young women don't tell their mothers everything these days, I'm afraid.'

'Mr and Mrs Lowther, where is your son-in-law?'

Neither of them answered her, and she began to get angry.

'And your granddaughter? She isn't here today. So where is she? Where are Brian and Luanne?'

The Lowthers looked at each other again.

'We don't know.'

Fry's mobile rang, and she saw from the display that the call was from Gavin Murfin.

'Excuse me a moment.'

She stepped outside on to the terrace to take the call, while the Lowthers sat and watched her.

'Diane, you'll want to know this straightaway,' said Murfin. 'I persuaded someone in West Yorkshire to make a few enquiries into John Lowther's spell there.'

'Well done, Gavin.'

'Well, I didn't have time myself. So that's another favour I'll have to repay.'

'Did they turn anything up?'

'I got a call a few minutes ago. They say John Lowther was a psychiatric patient in Leeds for three months. That's why he had to leave his job.'

'Did you go to Matlock to speak to him?'

'I'm at his apartment now. But John's not home. And the neighbours say they haven't seen him since yesterday.'

'Oh, great,' said Fry. 'The Lowthers are really, really going to love me.'

Moira Lowther was in her garden when Fry returned to the house. Perhaps she went out there to escape from the plants. When she heard what Fry wanted to talk about now, she sat down unsteadily in one of the chairs set out on the decking.

'John is psychotic, not a psychopath,' she said. 'There's a big difference.'

'Yes, I'm sure.'

Her husband stepped out of the sliding doors from the conservatory, and stood next to his wife, his jaw stiff with emotion.

'People don't understand that they're entirely different things,' said Mrs Lowther. 'Psychosis isn't characterized by a tendency to violence towards others. They're a risk to themselves, but no one else. Psychotics aren't manipulative either, the way psychopaths are. But how many people do you think register that difference? To them, it's all the same.'

Her husband leaned forward to put in his own comment. 'But then, we're talking about the sort of person who can't distinguish a paedophile from a paediatrician. It's sheer ignorance. Some people wallow in it.'

Mrs Lowther looked up at Fry. 'So our son is psychotic,' she repeated. 'Not a psychopath.'

'Yes, I understand.'

'Do you?'

'Actually, yes. I do.'

Moira Lowther looked at her differently then. Letting your own emotions come through was normally a sign of weakness in this job. But Fry realized it might actually help with the Lowthers. An unrelentingly professional approach wasn't always the best thing, after all.

'Tell me about it, then,' she said.

'We will, if you like,' said Mrs Lowther. 'But you should talk to his specialist. Dr Sinclair can explain it a lot better than we can. You might say that we're too biased. Too emotionally involved.'

Fry opened her mouth to comment, but changed her mind. That was another thing she didn't like – people predicting exactly what she was going to say.

30

Fry hadn't realized there were loft apartments in Matlock. They certainly hadn't reached Edendale yet. But John Lowther's home was on the fourth floor of a converted mill complex on The Cliff, high above Matlock Green, overlooking a conservation area. Lifts had been installed, and an entry system with coded access from the communal areas.

Yes, some of the original features had been retained in the conversion, but not too many. Enough to make 'period character' a selling point, probably. Judging by Lowther's place, the interiors had been given a very modern feel. This was open-plan living – a walkthrough from a study hall to the kitchen under exposed roof timbers and diagonal supports. The apartment was all chrome and glass, pastel shades and a tiny dining table set for two, looking as if it ought to be standing in an intimate corner of a fashionable restaurant. One problem, though. There was a high central ceiling, but if you wanted to walk close to the walls and look out of the windows, you'd better be a midget, or not mind a few bruises. The pitch of the roof was steep. Really steep.

Fry stood in the middle of the living area and checked out the doors off the hallway. Two bedrooms, even. It was all wasted on a single man, which John Lowther plainly was. She guessed he hadn't chosen the décor himself, either.

'There's nothing of immediate interest,' said Murfin. 'But we did find a bottle of tablets on his bedside table. Orphenadrine.'

'Never heard of it.'

'It's probably not important.'

'No . . .'

Fry began to move away, then stopped and came back.

'What's the matter?' said Murfin.

'That phrase – "it's probably not important". Those sound like famous last words to me. You'd better check it out, Gavin.'

'OK, if you think so.'

She had a feeling about this apartment. There was something she couldn't see. Inside any home, there were public places and private places. In the rooms where strangers might be expected to intrude, the contents were carefully chosen to present an image: highbrow books, artwork, the collection of expensive porcelain. But take a peek into the bedroom on your way to the loo, and you might find the truth behind the façade – the trashy novels, the S&M gear, the Prozac on the bedside table. Or in this case, perhaps, the Orphenadrine.

Fry wondered what lurked behind the foliage in a house full of plants, what a conservatory stuffed with fuchsias and tree ferns ought to be telling her. On the way down to Matlock, she'd phoned in and asked them to check the details of Luanne's adoption with the authorities in Bulgaria. A link might emerge, or an inconsistency.

Cooper walked in clutching a bottle of Buxton Spring water, as if he was taking a break at home in his own sitting room.

'What are you thinking about, Diane?' he asked.

'Henry Lowther.'

'Not pleasant thoughts, judging by your expression.'

'I was just wondering . . .'

'Don't keep it to yourself, then.'

'Well, Brian Mullen said the reason Luanne wasn't in the house at Darwin Street on the night of the fire was because she was staying at her grandparents'. She wasn't sleeping through the night, and the Lowthers had taken the child to give him and Lindsay a rest, to let them get a night's sleep. That's what he said.'

'Sounds fair enough.'

'Mr Lowther didn't seem to know that, though.'

'What makes you think that?'

'Oh, I might be mistaken,' said Fry. 'It was only an impression, because of the way he hesitated when I mentioned it. And that was my own fault – I prompted him with Mullen's version of events, instead of asking him outright. I didn't think it was important at the time, you see.'

'Probably it isn't.'

'I expect you're right. Brian and Luanne were the only two members of the family who weren't at home when the fire started. But it must have been by chance, mustn't it?'

'So where do we go from here, Diane?' asked Cooper.

'I've no idea.'

'What leads do we have that can be followed up?'

'None that I know of.'

'Have we got any clues at all?'

'No.'

Cooper tipped the last of the water into his mouth and tossed the empty bottle into a bin.

'We're really getting on top of this enquiry, then,' he said.

Fry didn't react. Let him think she was mellowing with age, if he wanted to. Or that she just didn't care any more.

'You know, John Lowther reminded me a bit of that story you told me,' she said.

Cooper looked round. 'Story?'

'The one about the woman who lived in a cottage near your farm when you were a child.'

'Old Annie?' said Cooper. 'Well, I can't see the similarity myself.'

'You said she didn't speak to anyone for weeks on end, then talked far too much when she was in company. As if she had to prove that she could still hold a conversation.'

Cooper looked surprised. 'Yes, I did say that.'

'Also, you mentioned finding her frightening. A slightly hysterical tone to her voice, you said. *That's* what John Lowther reminded me of.'

'I know what you mean.'

'Well, there's a job for you to do, Ben. I'll call ahead and get the interview cleared with the hospital.'

'Hospital?'

Fry explained to him. As Cooper prepared to leave, she listened to the silence of the apartment, well insulated and far enough away from the main road to deaden the sounds of traffic.

'We've got to find John Lowther,' she said. 'He could be a lot more dangerous than Brian Mullen.'

Fry dialled the number of the bungalow in Darley Dale, where she had been only half an hour before.

'Mrs Lowther, where would your son go? What place might he be heading for right now?'

She could picture the Lowthers looking at each other, deciding what answer to give. Fry half expected the phone to be handed to the husband, but it was Moira who spoke.

'When John wants to be alone, he likes to go up to the Heights of Abraham.'

*   *   *

463

An hour later, Dr Alexander Sinclair took off his white coat and put on a suit jacket, transforming himself from a clinical psychologist into a business executive. He sat down at his desk, opened a file and put on his glasses.

'You appreciate this is very exceptional, Detective Constable.'

'The circumstances are exceptional, too,' said Cooper. 'We wouldn't have asked you for this information otherwise.'

'Yes, so I've been persuaded by your senior officers. I'm only agreeing to this conversation on the understanding that I'm acting in the interests of my patient, and no further.'

Sinclair peered over the top of his glasses, a mannerism that Cooper hated. It made him look like a disapproving schoolteacher.

'We're extremely concerned for Mr Lowther's safety,' he said. 'Not to mention the safety of others that he might come into contact with.'

'Very well. There are some specific details of this patient's history that I can't go into, but I can answer general questions about his condition, which might help you.'

'Well, we already know that John Lowther spent three months in a psychiatric unit in Leeds.'

'That's correct.'

'Was he sectioned?'

'No, he admitted himself voluntarily, following a series of psychotic episodes.'

'What sort of episodes?'

'Mr Lowther was experiencing auditory and visual hallucinations.'

'Auditory – ?'

'He heard voices,' said Sinclair impatiently. 'And "visual" means he was seeing things.'

'Thank you.'

He sighed and looked down at the file. 'At the time, Mr Lowther appeared to be suffering hallucinations of increasing frequency and severity. Admitting himself to the unit was a very sensible decision on his part. He had good insight at that point, so he knew that he was ill.'

'I'm not sure what you mean by insight, Doctor.'

The glasses came off, making Sinclair human again for a few moments. His eyes were pale blue. He was probably capable of projecting a reassuring bedside manner, when he thought it was necessary.

'One puzzling feature of psychosis is that the affected individual doesn't recognize the strange or bizarre nature of his own experiences. Even in the case of acute psychosis, a patient might be unaware that his hallucinations and delusions are in any way unrealistic.'

'Yes, I see.'

'However, the level of insight can vary from one case to another. There can be quite good insight in some instances. Of course, this makes the psychotic experience even more terrifying. It means, you see, that the sufferer knows exactly what's going on. To put it bluntly, he knows he shouldn't be seeing demons and angels, or hearing voices – but he sees and hears them nevertheless. He can't stop himself. Try to imagine being aware that you're not in control of your own mind any more. You'd have to accept that some of your everyday perceptions are real, but others are illusory.'

'It's difficult to put myself in that position.'

'Of course it is. Believe me, when a patient is aware that he's losing control of his own thoughts, it strikes to the very core of self-belief, and can have an extremely destructive effect on his relationship with the world around him. It undermines the concept of identity, you see. I can imagine nothing more devastating, or more terrifying.'

Sinclair put his glasses back on and peered at his visitor, assessing his reaction. Cooper was surprised by his sudden departure from the script, or rather from the notes in his file. For a few seconds, he'd spoken with real conviction. It struck Cooper that Alexander Sinclair had actually seen this happen to people he knew well – not just patients, but friends or family. Perhaps that was why he'd agreed to talk, despite the constraints of confidentiality.

'Can you tell me what John Lowther's auditory and visual hallucinations consisted of? Is it possible to say?'

'In general. He heard voices that commented on his behaviour, and told him to do certain things.

That's why he admitted himself. He was frightened of what the voices might make him do, and he wanted us to stop them.'

'And did you?'

Sinclair smiled. 'Psychosis is only a symptom of mental illness, Detective Constable. The subsequent diagnosis was bipolar disorder. Mr Lowther was treated with anti-psychotic drugs until the episodes receded, and then we adjusted his medication until he was stable enough to be discharged.'

'So the medication made the voices go away?'

'Well . . .'

Cooper watched him hesitate.

'But only as long as he kept taking the tablets?' he said.

'Of course. Anti-psychotic drugs work by changing the activity of chemicals that transmit messages in the brain. It's very important to take the medication regularly, and at the prescribed doses.'

'So when was John Lowther discharged from the unit?'

'In April. He was in good spirits by then. He said he was going to tell everyone that he'd been away on holiday. Somewhere nice, like the Caribbean. Except that it couldn't be the Caribbean, because he didn't have a sun tan. I dare say his family didn't let anyone know the truth either. That's perfectly usual. There's still a lot of stigma attached to mental illness, I'm afraid.'

'He'd have to be on anti-psychotic drugs for some time, I imagine.'

'Yes. But his records do show that he was worried about the side effects. Mr Lowther complained that he put on weight. And he twitched a lot, which he found distressing. Also, he said the medication made him impotent.'

'He was very restless when we saw him last week.'

'But no twitching?'

'No.'

Sinclair fiddled with his glasses. 'Mr Lowther was prescribed Orphenadrine for the side effects, but he didn't like the idea of taking more tablets. So instead . . .' He hesitated again.

'You think he might have stopped taking his anti-psychotic drugs?'

'Yes, it's possible. Dealing with side effects is always a bit of a trade-off. It's a question of striking the right balance for each individual. Mr Lowther said once or twice that the effects of the drugs were worse than a few harmless delusions. He thought he'd return to his old self if he stopped taking the medication – he'd become slimmer, stop twitching, regain sexual function. It's a common response. Patients feel an overwhelming desire to go back to a time when they felt happy and safe.'

'Hold on a minute – "a few harmless delu-sions"?' said Cooper, picking out the most remark-able phrase in what he'd just heard.

Sinclair fixed him with a sad gaze from his pale

eyes. 'That would be the way it seemed to him, at this particular stage. I think Mr Lowther had probably forgotten the nature of his auditory hallucinations.'

'How is it possible to forget something like that?'

'It's a normal function of the brain to filter out negative experiences and retain the positive ones. This applies to psychotic episodes as much as to anything else.'

'I can't see anything positive in what you've described, sir.'

'Then I haven't described it properly. The fact is, not everyone finds psychosis a negative experience. While some patients suffer persecutory or self-blaming delusions, others develop grandiose fantasies or have an experience of deep religious significance. This can appear very positive and life-affirming.'

'Are you serious?'

'Absolutely. I've known some individuals describe a psychotic episode as a revelation, a wonderful and exciting new way of seeing the world – in fact, the sort of experience that people seek from hallucinogenic drugs. You know, a surprisingly large percentage of the population have undergone a psychotic episode of some kind, without being disturbed by the experience. At the end of the day, a hallucination is merely the misattribution of internal events to an external source.'

Cooper shook his head, trying to throw off a

sudden, unwelcome burst of insight, a glimpse of how it might feel if the reality of his own world became suspect. He was sure *he* would find it disturbing.

'Could we get back to the question of John Lowther's condition, and how he was being treated?'

'Well, when Mr Lowther was discharged, he returned to the community. He has family members in Derbyshire. It's normal practice to ensure that the family are fully aware of the importance of maintaining medication. We can't be there standing over every patient personally, to make sure they take their drugs.'

'Who was supposed to do that? His parents?'

Dr Sinclair frowned at the file. 'According to his records, there's a sister.'

'She's dead.'

'Oh.'

'And I think she might have been too preoccupied recently to worry about her brother.'

'Mr Lowther must have been due for a review,' said Sinclair. 'Perhaps his GP had examined him recently.'

They looked at each other for a moment, conscious of the futility of trying to work out where and when the system had gone wrong.

'Basically, a dangerous psychotic was allowed out into society unsupervised,' said Cooper.

'No, no, you don't understand. Once a patient is discharged and living at home, clinicians are helpless. Even if we know they might be a risk to themselves and others, we can't force an individual to continue medication. Not at present.'

'But you'd like to be able to compel people to take their drugs?'

'Detective Constable, fifty thousand patients are detained by psychiatrists every year. If we can't compel people to continue medication when they're back in the community, all that happens is that some of them get very ill again and have to be detained a second time, or a third. It just goes on and on.'

'The revolving door approach. We see it often enough in the courts.'

'I'm sure you do,' said Sinclair. 'Besides, John Lowther isn't dangerous unless he *has* stopped taking his medication. And even then, he's only a risk to himself. You say his sister died? The trauma of her death might have disrupted his normal routine anyway. It would be easy for him to slip. I hope he hasn't gone beyond caring for himself.'

'Doctor, if John Lowther's psychotic episodes returned, would the hallucinations be as powerful as they were previously?'

'Possibly more so. To be honest, in my next consultation with him, I might have been moving towards a conclusion that he was suffering from a treatment-resistant condition.'

'What would you have done then?'

'Tried another drug. Probably Clozapine.'

Sinclair took a tissue from a box on his desk and wiped a drop of sweat from his temple. 'There's one other thing that might be relevant . . .'

'Go on, sir.'

'At the time he was admitted to the unit, Mr Lowther was also suffering from night terrors.'

'You mean nightmares?'

'No, night terrors. Nightmares occur during REM sleep, terrors are experienced in stage four sleep. In practice, the distinction is that you remember nightmares, but you don't remember terrors. They're subconscious phenomena – but no less stressful, psychologically and emotionally.'

'And those might have returned, too?'

'It's possible.'

'In John Lowther's case, would his deteriorating condition be noticeable in the way he talks?'

'Yes, Mr Lowther suffers from thought disorder, another symptom of psychosis. It can lead the patient to speak quickly and incessantly, or to switch topic in mid-sentence. He could eventually become incoherent, using inappropriate words or mispronouncing them, or making up new words altogether.'

Cooper had been trying to make notes as the psychiatrist talked. But his pen paused, and he looked up.

'Would you be willing to listen to a tape of an interview we conducted with Mr Lowther, and give us your opinion on it?'

'Certainly, if you think it would help.'

472

'How do you think John Lowther is likely to react in the present circumstances?'

'It's difficult to say. He'll be in a rather unpredictable state. But one thing I'm sure of: he must be a very frightened man.'

'Frightened of what? Of us?'

Sinclair smiled. 'Hardly. At the moment, you're the least of his problems.'

'What, then?'

He put his glasses down and closed the file. Then he toyed with the items on his desk, teasing them into a more satisfactory arrangement.

'Most of all, John Lowther will be frightened of himself,' he said. 'Of his own inner demons, if you like. Whatever form those demons might be taking.'

'I don't understand.'

'I'm doing my best to explain. You see, Mr Lowther knows about the voices from past experience, though he'll have tried to suppress the knowledge. If he's off the medication, his auditory hallucinations will return. They might have returned already.'

'What will that mean to him?'

'At this stage, he should be lucid enough to understand what's going on, and to be aware that it will get worse. He'll be facing up to the horror of what he might do at the urging of those voices, and the options he has left to save himself, to avoid turning back into the evil monster he once considered himself to be.'

'I can think of one option,' said Cooper, holding his eye. 'He might feel the only way he can prevent himself from turning into that monster is to end his own life.'

Sinclair nodded. 'Yes, you're right. John Lowther is a much greater risk to himself than to anyone else.'

'Thank you.'

As Cooper stood up to leave, Sinclair seemed to slip from the script again, just for a moment. 'A grasp of Mr Lowther's thought process is essential, you know, Detective Constable.'

'Why, sir?'

'Because it's counter-intuitive.' The psychiatrist made a weary gesture. 'I realize it's difficult to understand. Most of us know what it means to be afraid to die. But it's rare to meet someone who's scared to live.'

Fry burst into the office anxious to know whether Cooper had returned from his visit to Dr Sinclair. But Murfin was taking a call as she walked through the door. His eyes were wide, and she watched him expectantly when he put the phone down.

'According to the authorities in Pleven, the Mullens' adoption application was never fully processed,' he said.

'What does that mean?'

'It means they didn't complete the adoption procedures. There were some legal problems with the papers, apparently, and their application was rejected by the court.'

'And what happened to Zlatka Shishkov?'

'They say they can't tell us that, for reasons of confidentiality. But one thing's for certain – she wasn't adopted by the Mullens.'

Fry stared at him in amazement, wondering whether she'd heard him right.

'So where did their baby come from?' she said. 'And who the hell is Luanne?'

31

The bar of the Mulberry Tree in West Street was deserted in the afternoon, once the lunchtime rush was over. It was hardly worth staying open, except as a matter of principle. This afternoon, there were only two customers – and one of them was there reluctantly.

For a moment, Georgi Kotsev smiled at Diane Fry and placed a strong, brown hand on the table between them, like an offering.

'Baby smuggling,' he said. 'It's very regrettable.'

'Is that the word you'd use?'

'Forgive me. My English is not adequate, perhaps.'

'It's just fine, Georgi.'

Fry couldn't remember when she'd last sat in a bar with so little atmosphere. The walls were subdued pastel colours, designed in a mock Georgian style, but with ornate chandeliers. The armchairs were imitation leather and so deep that she had to sit forward on the edge of her chair to remain upright. Kotsev had left his glass of vodka untouched in front of him out of politeness, though she'd refused his offer of a drink.

'Until the year 2004, baby selling wasn't a crime in Bulgaria,' he said. 'Even now, a woman who sells her baby has committed no offence. By law, she is regarded as a victim.'

'But what about the dealers? The middle men?'

'Yes, their activities are now a criminal offence. If they're caught, they might face a year in prison.'

'*A year*? Are you kidding?'

He shook his head slowly. 'Things are changing. But perhaps not quickly enough for some.'

'Why would a mother sell her baby, Georgi?'

'Ah, babies are a valuable commodity. A mother might sell one to buy a house, or to feed the rest of her family for a little while.'

'It can't be so easy to smuggle babies out of the country, can it?'

'What? Bulgaria has five borders – Romania, Serbia, Macedonia, Greece, Turkey – and all of them leaky, like a sieve. And we have the Black Sea coast, with little ports where you can sail a boat across. Yes, our country has become a corridor for smuggling of all kinds. Drugs, cigarettes, vegetables, people . . .' Kotsev fingered his drink. 'A while ago, our authorities broke a kidney-trafficking ring. Six people had been taken to a clinic in Istanbul, where their kidneys were sold to transplant patients. This is a rich business for someone – kidneys are worth between two and five thousand dollars each. It depends on the blood type, you see.'

'Did you say vegetables just now, Georgi?'

'Ah, yes. Potatoes, for example. Also apples. Any kind of food that is scarce. In Sofia, the police arrested a smuggler known as Nick the Chicken, on account of his speciality.'

Fry sat back, fighting the feeling that she'd stepped into some kind of Russian farce. The armchair squeaked at her movement. Taped music played somewhere, and a barman appeared to wipe glasses that hadn't been used.

Kotsev couldn't resist a sip of vodka. 'The main interest to us might be in the connection with the victims of the double shooting in Pleven. It seems they not only had a personal relationship, but they were also colleagues.'

'That's not unusual.'

'No. But guess where Dimitar Iliev and Piya Yotova worked.'

Fry didn't like being asked to guess. Someone who asked you to guess expected you to be wrong, and she usually was. But as she remembered the photo of Iliev's red Ford Escort with its shattered back window and BG plates, Fry thought she heard distant screams, and the voices of children. And she realized she didn't have to guess. 'An orphanage,' she said.

'You are almost correct. Iliev and Yotova were employed by an official organization which places children in state orphanages.'

478

'So they had a lot of power in deciding the fate of those children?'

'*Da, razbira se.*'

'And perhaps they were in a position to falsify paperwork, remove records, take illegal payments –'

Kotsev threw out an arm dramatically. 'Where money is involved, someone will become corrupt. But perhaps they thought they were doing good work too.'

'Doing good? How?'

'At one time, our Bulgarian orphanages were not very pleasant places to be. Some children stayed in them for many years, without ever finding homes. Who can say whether it might not have been better to find a child a home, even if illegally?'

'Somehow, Georgi, I suspect these people aren't too scrupulous about checking where children are going to end up.'

He bowed his head slightly. 'Perhaps you're right. It's possible some of those orphans went to a bad fate.'

'Why hasn't this trade been exposed?'

'Well, there are political ramifications . . .'

'Oh, the European Union,' said Fry. The phrase had begun to sound like the kiss of death to rationality.

'Yes, indeed.'

'I suppose what it boils down to is that the Bulgarian authorities wouldn't want evidence of large-scale baby smuggling to come to light right now.'

'Especially if other EU member states are involved. It would cause quite a scandal. Worse, it would give ammunition to those who do not want Bulgaria to join the EU.'

Fry felt suddenly exhausted. No matter how hard you tried to achieve some kind of justice, there were occasions when it was obvious you were wasting your time. The realities lined up against you were insurmountable. And this was the way it always would be. Human nature would never change.

'So we're looking at a baby selling ring, with at least four people involved. Is that right? The two people killed in the shooting in Pleven, plus Rose Shepherd and Simon Nichols. Or, rather, Rosica Savova and Simcho Nikolov. And what about the Zhivko brothers?'

'There are connections between them, certainly.'

'Were Dimitar Iliev and Piya Yotova wealthy?'

'No, not all. They had an ordinary home in an apartment block in Pleven. They drove an aged Ford Escort, as you saw. They had no money hidden away, that we could find.'

'And Nikolov was pretty much destitute.' Fry thought of the electronic gates guarding Bain House in Foxlow. 'So it appears that Savova made all the money from the enterprise.'

'*Da*. It would seem so.'

'Do you think there was a falling-out between

the principal players? Was it Nikolov that Rose Shepherd was afraid of? Did he come to Derbyshire looking for her?'

'I do not know, Diane.'

'Well, someone did. And the Mullens got innocently mixed up in this?'

'It depends what you mean by "innocently". They must have removed the baby from Bulgaria illegally.'

'True. We know that much, at least. But why would the Mullens' adoption have failed?'

'Who can tell? Adoption has become very difficult for foreigners.'

'But Bulgaria was supposed to be *the* place to go to adopt a baby. According to Henry Lowther, anyway.'

'No longer,' said Kotsev. 'Since Bulgaria wishes to join the EU, it has signed the Hague Treaty. As a consequence, our new laws say that orphans or abandoned children become available after having no contact with their family for six months. I understand there are now fifteen thousand children in our orphanages, but only a very few legally adoptable.'

'So the Lowthers fell foul of that change?'

'I would say so. It is a legacy of the Soviet mentality – let the state do everything for you, from cradle to grave. And this is the result. The state can look after your unwanted child, why not? So yes, it is difficult. It costs many thousands of dollars.'

'So they went for the illegal option. They must have been desperate by then.'

Kotsev nodded. 'Is there a photograph of this child?' he asked.

'Yes, here –'

He looked at the photo of Luanne for several minutes. Then he muttered under his breath something Fry didn't catch. For the first time, she thought she saw his confident exterior dented.

'She looks to me as though she might be a Roma,' said Fry.

Kotsev sighed deeply. 'Yes, you're right. I had a suspicion, but no more.'

'Suspicion?'

He waved a hand, as if he were swatting away a fly. 'I understand if you're angry at this, but there is some information that is difficult to share.'

'Oh, really? I thought you were sharing everything with me, so we could work together as colleagues.'

'Very well.' He shrugged. 'It's possible that this child belongs to one of our leading criminals, the Mafia boss I mentioned. A very unpleasant gangster.'

'What do you mean "belongs to"?'

'They say he had a child, born to a young Romani woman. The woman ran away from him when the baby was born. It took him a little while to catch up with her.'

'What happened to the woman? Is she dead?'

'People who upset *mutra* chiefs don't survive

very long. But her body has never been found, that's all I can say.'

'And she sold the baby?'

'It is possible,' said Kotsev. 'Her concern might have been to save the child, to get her out of the way of danger. That is how it is with mothers, I understand. But fathers want their children, too. Some want them very badly.'

'How would he have tracked her down here, to Derbyshire? Could his influence reach here so easily?'

'Yes. In fact, he might have preferred it. It's not so easy in Bulgaria for the *mutras* now. As I said, the country is changing. There's no place for those who grew up in the old ways.'

'The old ways, Georgi? You mean bribery and corruption?'

Kotsev shrugged. 'After the Change, that was the way things worked. It was the system.'

'But the system didn't work equally for everybody, did it? Isn't that important?'

He smiled. 'Ah, now you sound like a Communist.'

But Fry didn't return his smile. 'In particular, it didn't work for Zlatka Shishkov.'

'This is true.'

'Georgi, would a father really go so far to get his child back? Would he go to *any* lengths?'

Kotsev took a drink, started to shake his head, then nodded instead. 'I can't answer that question, Diane.'

Fry looked at him, wanting to ask him whether

he was a father himself. But she was afraid it would sound too personal.

Kotsev shrugged. 'We might have expected the child to be taken – to be returned to her father. But that hasn't happened.'

'Not yet,' said Fry. 'It hasn't happened *yet*.'

Fry updated her colleagues at West Street with the news, and they considered the theory suggested by the latest information.

'You know, I never thought the fire made sense myself,' she said. 'And it still doesn't.'

'No? What do you mean?' asked Cooper.

'Well, starting that fire was a very dangerous thing to do, wasn't it? It doesn't fit the same pattern as the killing of Rose Shepherd. Apart from the effectiveness of the technique, there are no signs that it's a professional job. Where's the planning, the cool calculation?'

'Perhaps you're right, but I'm not sure why.'

'Ben, look. For a start, they must have known Luanne wasn't in the house with the rest of the family, or they wouldn't have risked it. Not if they wanted to get her back so badly.'

'Yes, I agree.'

'And I'm not even sure what they hoped to achieve by starting the fire. Did they mean for the Mullens to be killed?'

'Maybe they just made a mistake. If they acted recklessly and failed to make sure that Luanne Mullen wasn't in the house –'

'They'd be in big trouble, wouldn't they?'

'But now it's Luanne who's at risk again, isn't it? These people will stop at nothing. So forget the fire – the living are most important. We have to save that child.'

'If Brian Mullen is thinking straight, he ought to realize the risk,' said Cooper.

Fry shook her head. 'This case has been the same all the way round. No one has behaved in a rational way. Everyone involved seems to have gone headlong towards their fate with blinkers on. You'd think they were a lot of lemmings throwing themselves off a cliff.'

'Emotions,' said Cooper. 'Emotions always interfere with rational behaviour.'

Fry began to put together her notes to update the DI and Mr Kessen.

'Do you want someone to check on the Heights of Abraham later, Diane?' asked Cooper. 'The Lowthers said that's where John is likely to go.'

'Yes, thanks.'

As she was on her way out of the room, Cooper remembered one more thing. 'By the way, I've asked Dr Sinclair to listen to the interview we did with John Lowther. He'll be coming in any time now.'

'Good idea. It'll be interesting to hear what he has to say.'

'Would *you* be worried if you had hallucinations, Diane?'

Fry frowned. 'I suppose so.'

485

'Apparently a lot of people aren't troubled by them and don't seek psychiatric help.'

'Really?'

'Yes. It's strange, isn't it?'

Cooper felt he was putting it mildly. Of course, he only had his experience with his mother to go by. She'd certainly been troubled by the hallucinations caused by her schizophrenia, and so had everyone else around her. But his experience might be a narrow one.

'What sort of hallucinations are we talking about, though?' said Fry.

'According to Dr Sinclair, the misattribution of internal events to an external source.'

Fry laughed. 'Oh, those sort.'

After she'd been interrogated for twenty minutes by Hitchens and Kessen, Fry felt exhausted. Her eyes were dry and her skin felt grimy. She nipped down the corridor to the ladies', where she splashed cold water on her face and practised controlled breathing for a while until she felt calmer.

Then she looked at herself in the mirror over the washbasin. Some days, it wasn't a good idea to do that too often. If she wasn't careful, she could suddenly get a glimpse of a person she'd almost forgotten – the girl who'd lived in those foster homes back in the Black Country. Sometimes it seemed like a million years ago. But at other times, she knew it was really just yesterday.

Fry had once seen a newspaper article that began: 'Kate Adie, Marilyn Monroe, Jim Bowen, Larry Grayson, Edgar Allan Poe, Bill Clinton and Steve Jobs . . . What do they all have in common?'

The journalist's answer, of course, was that they were all adopted or fostered. It made Fry want to rip the newspaper into shreds and stuff it up the feature writer's backside. As if she might aspire to make it on to a list that included Larry Grayson and Bill Clinton. It didn't fill her with positive emotions to know that she shared something in common with Jim Bowen. And Edgar Allan Poe? Wasn't he stark, raving bonkers?

Fry dried her face, combed her hair, and brushed her jacket. There was no reason for her to look as untidy as Ben Cooper.

Of course, there were a lot of bad reasons for adopting children. Adoption was often a selfish act, but some of the reasons were selfish in particular ways. Some couples thought it would save their marriage, others wanted to replace an infant who'd died, or provide a companion for an only child. They might do it because all their friends had babies, or because they saw a child as a fashion accessory, or a political statement. They thought adoption would provide company in their old age, or a pension plan, a successor in the family business, or just someone to carry on the name. All of those reasons were essentially exploitative. None of them focused on the child for its own sake. So what had Lindsay Mullen's reason been? Could she believe what Henry Lowther said?

Adoption was always tough. But it seemed evident that the Mullens loved Luanne. If her natural father succeeded in getting her back, there was no knowing what her fate might be.

Fry stared at her reflection and shook her head. She was starting to feel better. She was thinking again, instead of just reacting. She needed expert advice really, but it was difficult to know where to go for expertise in baby trafficking. Not every agency was forthcoming with information.

She remembered that there was a South Yorkshire Police unit called Operation Reflex, set up to combat human trafficking. An officer from the Immigration Service worked with the team to provide information on individuals who might be involved in immigration crime.

But Reflex were interested in women being trafficked for the sex trade. They'd scored a success in Sheffield a little while ago, with the case of a fifteen-year-old Lithuanian girl sold into prostitution. The girl had arrived at Heathrow Terminal Three to take up a job selling ice cream, and had herself been sold for the price of a second-hand car. Before she arrived in South Yorkshire, the girl had been passed around from hand to hand, gradually losing her value when she was no longer a virgin and had suffered damage from regular beatings. It was probably what the car trade called depreciation.

Fry watched her face change in the mirror. That was better. Now she looked more like someone who was in control.

'Fear is a very interesting emotion,' said Dr Sinclair. 'You can't be afraid retrospectively. You can only fear something that hasn't happened yet.'

Setting up the tape for him, Cooper paused before pressing the 'play' button. Damn right, he thought. That was why there were so many things to be afraid of.

'Scared to live,' he said. 'That's the way you described Mr Lowther's current state of mind.'

'That's correct.' Sinclair looked up. 'If you don't understand that concept, then you haven't learned to glimpse what goes on in other people's minds. Some individuals find life unbearable, every day a torment. They become convinced that continuing to live will be such an ordeal that dying is the only possible escape.'

Cooper couldn't think of an answer to that. He started the tape, and they listened to John Lowther's interview in silence for a few minutes.

'Yes, some people go abroad, hunting for whores. No – for babies.'

'Sorry?'

'I'm not sure what you're asking me. Is it time?'

'He's conflating two subjects in his mind here, I think,' said Sinclair. 'The whores and babies thing, I mean.'

'I wondered if John Lowther could be a paedophile. What do you think, Doctor?'

Sinclair shook his head vigorously. 'No, there's no indication of that.'

'Are you sure? I'm no psychiatrist, but *babies* and *whores* sounds a very dubious association of ideas to me. I understand that Mr Lowther doesn't quite know what he's saying, but isn't that sort of thing called a Freudian slip?'

'Freud has nothing to do with it. You don't understand how this works. What we're dealing with here is not an association of thoughts, but a disassociation. Mr Lowther's brain is skipping so quickly to an unrelated subject that there appears to be no distinction or separation between them, as far as the listener is concerned. That's *not* the way it is in the patient's mind – his brain just isn't making normal connections, the way ours would. Mr Lowther is probably saying words that *sound* like the ones he's thinking.'

'OK. Anything else?'

Cooper pressed the 'play' button again, and they listened to the rest of the interview. Sinclair jotted a few notes.

'Yes, in this interview, I think we can hear pressure of speech, where the patient speaks quickly and incessantly. Also derailment, or flight of ideas, when he switches topic, sometimes in mid-sentence. That can be in response to an outside stimulus.'

'I like your tie.'

'Yes, that sort of thing. You might also detect a degree of tangentiality, when he replies to questions in an oblique or irrelevant manner. To you, in your profession, that would probably sound very suspicious and evasive, I imagine.'

Cooper nodded. Evasive was the exact word that he'd used about John Lowther after his interview.

'In this form of speech, he reaches conclusions that don't follow logically, or his thoughts might have no conclusion at all. Sometimes the individual words are correct, but the manner they're put together is wrong, resulting in what some clinicians call *word salad*. Sounds rather than meanings govern the connection between words – a *clang association*. He might also repeat a word over and over, or echo other people's speech.'

'That confusion in his speech was already evident a few days ago.'

'Really?' Sinclair frowned. 'It varies with the individual patient, of course. But perhaps he had stopped taking the medication earlier than we thought.'

'Will this get worse?'

'Yes, as his condition deteriorates, he might become incoherent, using inappropriate words or mispronouncing them, or making up new words altogether.'

'*Hunting for whores. No – for babies.*'

Sinclair shrugged. 'It's impossible to interpret his real meaning without having Mr Lowther here for a proper interview.'

Cooper bristled. 'A *what*?'

'My apologies. I meant a properly structured clinical interview.'

Cooper watched Sinclair gather up his notes, plucking up the courage to say what was on his mind.

'Doctor, you said that many people who have psychotic episodes find them a positive experience.'

'Yes. Many of them are non-clinical individuals, of course.'

'Non-clinical?'

'Individuals who have hallucinations but aren't troubled by them, so they don't seek treatment.'

'But if they have psychiatric problems, they *should* be receiving treatment, shouldn't they?'

'Unless it's a troubling experience, it wouldn't be what we term a psychiatric problem.'

'I don't understand.'

Sinclair leaned back in his chair and looked at Cooper. 'Do you believe in the supernatural?'

'Well, I'm not sure –'

'No, of course not. Many of us aren't sure. But, you see, from a neurological point of view, people with a tendency to psychotic experiences show increased activation in the right hemisphere of the brain. The same increase has been found in perfectly healthy people with high levels of paranormal belief, or mystical experiences. Even creative individuals can show a similar pattern.'

Cooper opened his mouth to ask whether that

meant people who believed in the paranormal were mad, but Sinclair shook his head.

'No, supernatural experiences aren't themselves a symptom of mental illness. But people with different views of reality or unusual opinions have always held a rather complex role in society. Some are considered mad, while others are treated as prophets and visionaries. At the end of the day, the difference comes down to a question of contemporary social attitudes.'

'You seem to be suggesting that almost anyone might suffer from psychosis of some kind.'

Sinclair closed the clasps on his briefcase with a click. 'Well, it has been argued that patients with psychotic illness are simply at one end of a spectrum. Some practitioners say that psychosis is merely another way of constructing reality, and not necessarily a sign of illness at all. Only a small proportion of people who experience hallucinations are actually troubled by them.'

The psychiatrist smiled past Cooper, who turned to see Gavin Murfin hovering near the desk.

'Well, I suppose police officers have to be feet-on-the-ground sort of people. No time for the imagination, eh? But most hallucinations are quite neutral, you know. They might simply take the form of a voice commenting on what you're doing. People get used to that. In fact, for some individuals it's rather comforting, as if they have a permanent, invisible companion, perhaps a loved one who's died. Believe me, it's not uncommon.'

'I can imagine that.'

'Well, now – instead of something neutral or reassuring, think of a voice that constantly makes negative comments about you and your actions. That's the troubling sort of hallucination experienced by people in clinical groups, who need psychiatric help to deal with them. Treatment isn't necessary unless the experience is disturbing.'

They walked down the corridor towards the stairs, passing the busy incident room on their way towards the reception area. By the front desk, the psychiatrist paused to shake hands. He held Cooper's hand a little too long, giving him an appraising stare.

'You know, many hallucinations occur in the phases of consciousness between waking and sleeping. You might hear your name being spoken, or get a feeling of someone being in the room, or of falling into an abyss. All of those are common. There's a sort of paralysis that occurs in the hypnopompic stage just before waking – a sensation like a heavy weight on your chest that prevents you from moving or calling out for help.'

'Oh, yes?' said Cooper, wondering what he might be giving away by his expression.

Sinclair smiled reassuringly. 'Generally, people write those experiences off as dreams, DC Cooper. They wake up. And then they get on with their lives.'

Cooper walked slowly back to the CID room,

and found Murfin already at his desk, watching Fry heading towards him.

'You know this voice that constantly makes negative comments about me and my actions,' said Murfin.

Cooper looked up in surprise. 'Yes, Gavin?'

'It's a relief to know it's only a hallucination. I thought it was my DS.'

When Cooper had briefed her and left for the Heights of Abraham, Fry thought about John Lowther's confusion of speech. He hadn't seemed to mix up his words when she'd seen him on Wednesday – not the way he had later, when he was interviewed. He'd been more vague and confused than anything else. Dr Sinclair might be right. But it was rather more like a description someone else had given her recently.

Ignoring the glances of Cooper and Murfin, Fry picked up the phone and called Juliana van Doon at the mortuary.

'Mrs van Doon, what would be the effects on a person who'd suffered only slightly from smoke inhalation?'

'Mild hypoxia? Well, there might be effects on the voice. Coughing, hoarseness, stridor – that's a high-pitched sound, like croup. You could look for singed eyebrows, moustache, or other facial hair. Also traces of soot in the nose or mouth, slight burns to the face.'

'Yes, but what about their behaviour?'

'Their behaviour?' The pathologist hesitated. 'This is just an informal opinion?'

'Of course.'

'Well, I'd say a person suffering from mild hypoxia would appear distracted, and probably clumsy in both their speech and manner. Is that what you were thinking of, Sergeant?'

'Yes,' said Fry, nodding gratefully. 'That's exactly what I was thinking of.'

32

He'd forgotten the other voices. Somehow, he'd managed to put them out of his mind, until they started to come back. It was so strange, the way the brain could shut out things that it didn't want to know about, drawing curtains across the darkest corners, no matter how terrible the secrets that lay behind them.

These were *the* voices. The voices that told him to do things. He'd remembered them too late. Much too late.

John Lowther's hands trembled as he drove his Hyundai down the A6. His palms felt slippery on the steering wheel, and the windows steamed up so badly that he had to turn the fan on full to clear the condensation from the windscreen. For a moment, he considered letting the glass stay steamed up and driving blind through Matlock, letting fate take its course. But in the next second, he knew the idea had come from one of his voices, whispered almost imperceptibly into his ear. His defensive measures were failing.

He switched on the radio, let the tuner find a music station, and turned up the volume. It was Peak FM, playing the Stones – 'Paint it Black'. Perfect. He belted out the words along with Jagger as he passed through the square and over the bridge into Dale Road, oblivious to the stares and laughter of pedestrians when he halted in traffic. They couldn't hear him, and all he could hear was the music. The best of all worlds.

In Matlock Bath, he crossed the Derwent and parked near the old railway station, with its little cowled chimneys, mock timbering and herring-bone brickwork. Though the Derwent Valley line was still open to Derby, Matlock Bath's ticket office and waiting room had been converted into a wildlife gift shop. From here, it was possible to walk across the track and follow a footpath to the cable car station.

He passed a compound full of spare cable cars. Actually, half cars. They looked as though they'd been cut open to reveal their interiors. The hum of motors and the creak of cables over wheels increased to a rapid whir as a string of cars swung out of their station, dipping and bobbing as they rose. Two strings passed each other high over the village, half-hidden by the trees. In the roof of the station building, a huge steel wheel turned the cables. He saw with relief that all the cars were empty. There wasn't much business for the Heights of Abraham at this time of year, with the kids back at school.

Arriving at the Treetops Centre, he found a sign that said *Where to go next.* Good question. Near the High Falls shop were a woodland family, carved by someone with a chainsaw and power file. The elm girl, the daughter of the family, was a young sapling crowned by a giant squirrel clutching an acorn, waiting to chew her bones.

A narrow doorway gave access to the base of the Prospect Tower. Halfway up the steps, there was no light from the opening at the top, just the faint glow of a bulkhead light on the wall below the handrail. The outer stones were worn smooth by the feet of thousands of visitors, but the inner steps still bore the mason's tool marks, where they were too narrow to walk on.

This tower had been built to take advantage of the views and provide work for the unemployed. But it also contained a rare thing – a true spiral staircase. There was no central column, and the steps tapered sharply, so they were only wide enough to walk on if you stayed close to the outside wall and clung to the rail.

Finally, he stood at the top of the tower, with its three-hundred-and-sixty-degree view. It was so misty today that it was like a steady drizzle falling on him when he stood at the top of the tower. Spider's webs in the hawthorn bushes had collected the moisture and shone like silver handkerchiefs draped between the branches.

Lowther looked over the parapet. Matlock Bath was below him, with the A6 and the Derwent snaking their way from the north beneath the crags of High Tor. Masson Hill and High Tor had split apart at some time. A fissure in the tor was a continuation of the same mineral vein that formed Masson Cave, which now lay on the opposite side of the valley. He could hear the traffic on the road, the clank of machinery working somewhere, a flock of jackdaws on the hill. Then the cables whirred into life as another set of cars began their descent.

The cable cars stopped automatically near the top of their climb, to allow visitors to admire the view and take photographs. He'd hung there himself on the way up, alone in his bubble high above the ground. Where to go next? The answer was too tempting. He'd imagined his cable car breaking loose and dropping towards the A6, the wind whistling through the sides as it fell, turning slowly in the air. The sound of the wind might drown out the voices. The impact with the ground might stop the world whirling round his head, scare away the colours and shapes that crept closer to the corners of his vision like spiders in his brain.

Southwards, he was looking at the dome of the Pavilion and the Fishpond Hotel. At the south end of the village, high among the trees, was Gulliver's Kingdom, with its towers and turrets and the screams of children riding the switchback. That was where most of the voices came from. The voices of children. They were difficult for him to ignore, and even harder to understand.

If he put twenty pence in the telescope, he might be able to see right into the theme park. He might make out the pirate ship on Bourbon Street, or the singing frogs and a talking apple in the Palais Royale. Further away, there'd be the Rio Grande Train Ride chugging its way through fake cacti and replica Indians, and imitation vintage cars that ran on tracks, like trams. Kids didn't need much to spark their imaginations, if they were young enough – if they hadn't reached the age when they were taught to fear anything that wasn't quite real.

He didn't go to Gulliver's Kingdom any more. He hadn't been there for over three months, not since that day in July. But he could still picture himself wandering away from the Music House, through the Millennium Maze and across the Stepping Stones to reach Lilliput Land Castle. There was a mirror room in the castle. He loved the distortions there, enjoyed knowing that this was one place in the world where everyone saw a distorted version of reality, and not just him. He would stand looking at the fragmented images for a while, not focusing on any one detail, but letting the shapes blur and tremble on the edge of his vision as he swayed gently from side to side. Then he would move on, past the giant chess set to Fantasy Terrace.

They'd asked him to stop coming to Gulliver's

Kingdom. They said he frightened the children. But there was nothing to be frightened of, was there? His hallucinations were fully under control now. He could hold them in his hand and spin them, watching the light play on their colours, turning on their sound for as long as he wanted to listen, then turning them off again.

It was good to give himself a little glimpse into that world, knowing he had the power to switch it off whenever he liked. It was as if he possessed the key to a door that allowed him a glimpse of a strange, enticing universe. It was far too tempting not to take a peek now and then, wasn't it?

Dr Sinclair had explained it was simply another way of seeing reality, and it was nothing to be frightened of. Well, as long as it was all under control, it was fine. And it was, right now. It was all under control.

33

By the station car park in Matlock Bath, a laurel hedge had dropped its big, black berries all over the path, where they'd been squashed by passing feet. No one picked these berries – well, not if they had any sense. Laurel berries looked very appealing, but they were poisonous.

'We can go up on a cable car,' said Cooper. 'It's a lot quicker.'

The alpine-style cable cars had replaced the zig-zag paths up the hillside as the easiest way to get to the Heights of Abraham estate. The tower was visible on the summit near the cable-car station, its flag fluttering in the wind.

'Oh, I don't think so.'

Cooper laughed. He'd bumped into Kotsev on the way out of the office at West Street, and the Bulgarian had somehow tagged along, promising not to be in the way. Sergeant Fry had told him to make sure he behaved properly, he'd said.

'It's fine, Georgi. You're not scared?'

'No, no. It's no problem.'

They climbed into one of the cars. It was big enough to hold six people, but it was a quiet day. The doors closed, and the cars rotated slowly before suddenly swinging out of the station, into the light. They immediately began to climb steeply up the cable, soaring high over the river and the rapidly dwindling traffic on the A6. The sides of the car were clear perspex from ceiling to floor level, so it was possible to look straight down at the ground, already hundreds of feet below and getting further away by the second.

'*Dyavol da go vzeme*. Oh, God.' Kotsev covered his eyes and gripped the edge of the seat tightly.

'Are you sure heights aren't a problem for you?'

'I'll be OK. OK, OK.' He risked a peep through his fingers. '*Mamka mu!*'

By the time they had reached the highest point above the valley, Kotsev was sweating and breathing deeply to calm himself. This was the point on the journey where the cars slowed down and hung stationary for a minute or two, high above the valley floor.

'Are we broken?' said Kotsev nervously. 'Do we need rescue?'

But then the wheels whirred again, and the cars approached Masson Hill through an avenue of trees as the cable passed over the first gantry. From there, it was an easy coast in, past the base of the stone tower to the hilltop station.

'You can look now,' said Cooper.

Kotsev took his hand away and opened his eyes. 'Yes, OK. It was a little too high.'

Fry found Jed Skinner in the garage at the distribution centre outside Edendale, where he worked as a mechanic. He was wearing disposable gloves like a scenes of crime officer as he worked on the engine of a large van. No more dirty rags and oily hands for car mechanics these days, then. Gavin Murfin had been exaggerating.

'Do you happen to know where your friend Brian Mullen is right now?' asked Fry when they'd taken him into the supervisor's office.

'He's staying with his parents-in-law. They live at Darley Dale.'

'He's not there any more.'

'Oh?'

'When were you last in contact with him?'

'Yesterday. They wouldn't let me visit him while he was in hospital, but Brian rang me yesterday afternoon to say he was out. He was pretty fed up, so I went to see him in the evening.'

'At Darley Dale?'

'Yes.'

'Did he say anything to you about leaving to stay somewhere else?'

'No, not a thing.'

'You live at Lowbridge, don't you, Mr Skinner?'

'Yes, but you won't find Brian there. He could have come and stayed with me, if he'd asked, because we're mates. But he didn't ask.'

'All right.'

'Phone my wife if you don't believe me.'

'We might do that,' said Fry.

Skinner gazed out of the window of the office at a truck being backed out, its reversing alarm echoing inside the garage.

'Has Brian got the baby with him? Luanne?' he said.

'We believe so, sir.'

'Shit. I hope you find them.'

'So do we.' Fry paused. 'Speaking of Luanne, we know about the adoption. Mr Mullen's father-in-law has explained to us that Brian and Lindsay couldn't have any more children, because Brian was infertile after a bout of mumps.'

'Mumps?' said Skinner. 'Is that what he told you?'

'Certainly. He said the illness caused physical damage that made Brian become infertile.'

'Well, it's not what Brian told me at the time. Mumps had nothing to do with it.'

'So what was it, then?'

'STD.'

'A sexually transmitted disease?'

'That's right. I can't remember the exact name, though. Something with "clam" in it.'

'Do you mean chlamydia?'

'Yes, that's what Brian had. And it wasn't the first time, either. Chlamydia was what caused the damage. He told me all about it. If you get it too often, it causes scarring and blocks the – you know, the passage.'

Fry stared at him, her mind adjusting to a series of new possibilities. 'Not mumps?'

'I wonder if mumps was what he told his in-laws,' said Skinner. 'I met Henry Lowther once. He's the sort of bloke who likes everything to seem right and proper. Even his son-in-law – since he's stuck with him.'

'Does Brian not get on with the Lowthers?'

'Well, you know what it's like. He wasn't really good enough for their daughter from the start. They'd have preferred Lindsay to marry someone loaded. A step up on the social scale, if you know what I mean. Not a few steps down, like Brian.'

'Mr Skinner, were you aware of any problems in the Mullens' marriage? Was there any trouble between Brian and Lindsay?'

'Trouble? Why should there be?'

'Well, for a start, I presume Lindsay knew about the chlamydia? That would make quite a difference to their relationship, I think.'

The idea seemed to strike Skinner for the first time. 'You think she might have blamed Brian for the fact that they couldn't have another child naturally? Lindsay really, really wanted a daughter, you know.'

'Yes, I know that.'

Skinner nodded. 'That would make her a bit upset with him, I suppose.'

'Well, yes,' said Fry. 'And there are other things that might have upset her, too – like where her husband picked up an STD in the first place.'

'Hey, you're right. I imagine there were a few words exchanged.'

'But Brian never mentioned anything like that to you?'

'Do you know, there were times when he was a bit pissed off, and I reckoned he might have had problems at home. But he never explained why – we didn't talk about things like that.'

Fry cursed to herself as she left Jed Skinner and got back in the car. Male friends, what a waste of time. To learn anything about the state of the Mullens' marriage, she needed to talk to Lindsay's mother. But she didn't give much for her chances of getting information out of Mrs Lowther right now.

With a frown, Fry turned to her notes from the interviews with Brian Mullen, seeking the smallest clue. After a few minutes, she picked up the phone and called Cooper.

When his phone rang, Cooper was standing by the lid of a shaft into the hillside that had been sealed by a steel grille. A bush rustled, showering drops of moisture, and a small, grey shape slipped along a branch, stopping to pull off the berries.

'Ben, what are these illuminations that Brian Mullen mentioned?'

'Illuminations?'

'I'm sure he said they were in Matlock Bath. The only illuminations I know of are in Blackpool.'

'Well, they're not quite the same. In Matlock

Bath, there are some lights along the promenade and across the river, but when people talk about the illuminations they mean the parade of boats.'

'Boats?'

'They create designs out of lights and mount them on rowing boats. Then they parade up the river – when it's dark, of course. So what you see isn't the boat but something like, say . . . an illuminated London bus floating on the water. There's other stuff, too – fireworks, entertainment. You can see it all from the pleasure grounds in Derwent Gardens.'

'OK. So when does this happen?'

'September and October, but only at weekends. They call them Venetian Nights. I don't know why, it must be something to do with the boats. But they always attract big crowds. Why, what are you thinking?'

'Brian Mullen. When I interviewed him in hospital, he said that he and Lindsay had promised to take Luanne and the other children to see the illuminations in Matlock Bath. It was supposed to be a special treat.'

'Yes, but surely he'd have more sense than to . . .'

Cooper stopped speaking, and Fry laughed. 'What was it you were saying earlier, Ben? About people acting in an irrational way?'

'Emotions interfere with rational behaviour.'

'That was it.'

'Diane, why were you so sure about Mr Mullen being involved in the fire?'

'He never seemed particularly grief stricken to me. Some of those people leaving flowers outside the house looked more upset than Brian Mullen did.'

'He was probably in shock, Diane. Besides, a public show of emotion is unnatural for some people. He could well have been suppressing it while he was in hospital. Being discharged and coming home would be the time when the truth hit him hardest, don't you think? I mean, finding just Luanne waiting for him, and knowing that he'd never see the rest of his family again. There must have been a moment when he couldn't suppress the knowledge any longer. That would be when his world caved in, I imagine. If he talked to a counsellor at the hospital, he was probably warned about that.' Cooper gazed down at the cap of the mine shaft thoughtfully. 'Although I'm not sure when that moment would be – because Mr Mullen didn't actually go home, did he? He went to his in-laws' house when he left hospital.'

'No, you're wrong. He did go home,' said Fry. 'I took him there.'

Cooper paused. 'Oh. So you did.'

'I wanted him to see the house after the fire.'

He hesitated for a moment, wondering what the right thing was to say. 'Well, it wasn't your fault, Diane.'

She was silent for so long that Cooper thought her mind must have switched to a different subject altogether, the way it sometimes did. And when

Fry did speak, he still wasn't sure whether that was the case, or not.

'Thanks a lot, Ben,' she said at last.

And then she was gone, and Cooper was listening to the faint hiss of his phone.

A second later, Georgi Kotsev emerged from a summer house a few yards up the steep path. The building was made of tufa, with a thatched roof.

'I don't see him,' said Kotsev. 'What is this place anyway?'

'A tourist attraction.'

'OK, I believe you.'

'When we've finished, we can walk back to the village, if you're too scared of the cable car. All we have to do is press a button to release an automated gate near West Lodge.'

'Let's keep looking.'

Cooper followed Kotsev up the path. Next summer, he ought to bring Liz up here. They could have a goat's cheese panini or a tuna melt in the Hi Café, or sit on the terrace of the Summit Bar with a table among the flowers, overlooking Matlock Bath.

That was assuming they were still together next summer, of course. He'd never gone out with anyone for as long as twelve months before.

For a moment, Cooper turned to look back through the trees at the view down into the valley. He recalled that the white building near the tavern was Upper Towers, where beer had once been served to lead miners. Inside, it had round rooms, so they said.

'Hey, here!'

Cooper spun round and found Kotsev standing with a Heights of Abraham employee in a high-vis jacket.

'Have you got something?'

Kotsev pointed up the hill. 'He's at the tower.'

The burnt-out Shogun was in the garage, covered in a tarpaulin. Wayne Abbott greeted Fry and Hitchens with a clipboard in his hand.

'Yes, this is definitely the vehicle that was driven into the field at Foxlow. The tread pattern is an exact fit with the impressions we lifted. We matched soil from the tyres and the wheel arches. Luckily, the interior escaped the worst effects of the fire, and we found traces of gunshot residue on the seat covers. The fabric retains barium and antimony residue better than human skin.'

'Well, that's a positive development,' said Hitchens. 'We've got a definite lead at last.'

'There's more,' said Abbott. 'I didn't expect this, but we got some prints off the underside of the dashboard, where it hadn't been burned too badly. They're in the system, too. Somebody's been in this car who has previous form.'

Hitchens took the print-out. 'Brilliant.'

Fry leaned closer to look. 'Anyone we know?'

'The name means nothing to me. Anthony

512

Donnelly, aged thirty-seven, with an address in Swanwick.'

'Never heard of him.'

'He has several past convictions for theft from a vehicle and taking without consent, plus all the usual extras – no insurance, driving while disqualified, et cetera, et cetera.'

'Just an average car thief,' said Fry, feeling unreasonably disappointed.

'Mmm, maybe. The most recent charge on his record was in connection with an organized lorry-jacking scheme. Truckloads of white goods diverted to new owners via a lay-by on the A1. I remember that case – five or six people went down for it. But it seems Donnelly was acquitted.'

'So it could be that he's gradually moving up in the world, getting involved with more serious operators.'

'Driver for a professional hit man?' said Hitchens. 'Well, let's go and ask him, Diane.'

'If that information is from the PNC, then the first thing we have to hope for is that the address is accurate for once.'

The wheels and cables were still humming and rattling, but it no longer seemed to be merely the whir of machinery, the hiss of high-tension steel passing through the air. The noises formed words, murmuring and whispering, mumbling and chattering.

And then John Lowther looked down into the

valley again. The fragile crystal of his mind had cracked. He could see the fragments lying on the ground, fading and turning brown, as if they were mere ordinary clay. Through the fracture in his consciousness, he heard the final voice. It was still faint, but he recognized it. Oh, he recognized it all right. In the past, this voice had forced him to do things that he had never wanted to do. And now the voice was back. He had no idea what it would make him do next.

'Johnny, you know what you have to do.'

They would come for him soon. They would scent him out, sniffing the fear in his sweat. They would use dogs to listen for his voices when they became too loud. And they'd follow him when he left the house, track his movements wherever he went. And one day the searchlights would catch him on the corner of a street, and the lights would probe deep into his mind and see what was there. And the whole world would know his evil.

Cooper could see John Lowther on the platform at the top of the stone tower, leaning over the parapet. Even from this distance, he could tell that Lowther was trembling violently, as if he was no more than a leaf shaken by the wind blowing across the hillside. Strands of hair fell over his forehead, and his eyes were fixed on the horizon. He might have been listening for some distant call that would summon him away, an echo that would reach him from far in the south.

Lowther seemed completely oblivious to the knot of people beginning to cluster round the base of the tower. Their heads were tilted back to stare up at his silhouette, black against the sky. But not once did Lowther look down at the ground.

'He's been up there for some time now,' said the staff member. 'A visitor started to get uneasy about him. She said he was behaving oddly.'

'All right. Thank you.'

'Is there anything else I can do?'

Cooper looked at the concrete apron the tower stood on, and the rough boulders built into the base. 'Right now, you could help us most by keeping everyone clear of the tower. Well clear – back as far as the play area.'

The man followed Cooper's gaze, and turned pale. 'You don't think he might . . .?'

But Cooper put a hand on his shoulder. 'If you could just move these people back, sir.'

'Of course.'

Georgi Kotsev was examining the doorway to the tower. It was arched, like the entrance to a church, but so narrow that Kotsev looked as though he'd hardly be able to squeeze through it. Signs either side of the doorway warned visitors to take care on the steps. And they gave the building's name – the Victoria Prospect Tower. Right now, it seemed ironic. Cooper wasn't looking forward to the prospect at the top.

'A tricky location,' said Kotsev.

'It couldn't be worse.'

As he'd approached the tower, Cooper had called Control to report the situation. Help would be on the way, and it looked as though he might need it. But it would take time.

When Cooper looked up at the parapet again, a fine mist fell on his face and trickled into his collar. Lowther must be getting cold and uncomfortable up there by now. He wasn't even dressed for the rain.

'OK, let's go and talk to him.'

Rain had blown in through the doorway, creating a dark patch in the stairwell. Inside, the view upwards was dizzying. Stone steps curled away into the tower, with bare tree trunks zigzagging overhead from wall to wall. Cooper could see both the outer and inner surfaces of the staircase at once, which seemed entirely wrong. His instincts were telling him that it was impossible to walk on stairs that coiled so tightly and rose so steeply.

Standing close to the wall, Cooper took hold of the handrail and began to ascend. Mounting the spiral staircase was like walking up a twisted ribbon, or climbing a strand of DNA. It was a sort of stone helix, cold to the touch and smelling of earth. You had to be careful on these steps, or you could fall right through the spiral and plummet to the base of the tower.

Just before the last turn, the bulkhead lights on the wall ended, and Cooper stopped when he saw daylight from the platform. He jumped when he became aware of Kotsev's breathing below and behind him on the steps. His mind had been so distracted that he'd forgotten his companion.

'Georgi, you'd better stay back out of sight. We don't want to frighten him too much.'

'*Dobre*. I'll be right here, behind you.'

Cooper's heart was beating harder after his climb. All the way up the tower, he'd been conscious of the narrowness of the steps, and the drop through the spiral. One slip could be disastrous.

Slowly now, he eased himself the last few feet on to the platform, trying not to make any sudden noises. Leaving the stairwell was like emerging into a different world, with light and air and an awareness of the valley all around him – banks of trees whispering in the breeze, the cables hissing as they pulled another string of swaying cars across the river. Lowther was standing nearby, his hands resting on the parapet.

'Mr Lowther, do you remember me? Detective Constable Cooper.'

Lowther seemed to become aware of him for the first time. He tried to back away, but he was already pressed hard against the parapet and could only scrape slowly around the platform until he was on the eastern side. He stood with the Heights of Abraham behind him, birds swooping through the woods, water dripping from branch to branch, cable cars descending to the base station.

Cooper took a step backwards, trying to judge

a safe distance that wouldn't make Lowther feel under too much pressure. At the same time, he had to find some way to keep the man's attention on him. At the moment, his concentration seemed to be wandering, his eyes darting around the landscape, distracted by the whir of cables and the voices of people on the ground below.

'Just take it easy, sir. There's nothing to worry about.'

He felt faintly ridiculous as soon as he said it. He could see from the expression on Lowther's face that the man had plenty to worry about. Real or imagined, it was all there in his eyes and in the twist of his mouth. Fear, verging on panic.

'You're quite safe, Mr Lowther. I'm here to help you.'

Trying to inject a calmness into his voice that he didn't feel himself, Cooper spread his hands in a reassuring gesture. His fingers touched the edge of the parapet, and he saw the stone was yellow with encrusted lichen.

'Is there a dog here somewhere?' said Lowther.

Cooper smiled then. Bizarrely, it sounded like progress. 'You recognize me, don't you, sir? You remember me? I'm DC Cooper. We talked yesterday. I was with a colleague, and you told us about your neighbour's Alsatian.'

'Tyrannosaurus.'

'And we showed you a wooden dinosaur, that's right.'

'You don't have to believe what they're saying.'

A gust of wind brought the sound of children's voices up the valley from Gulliver's Kingdom. Laughter and screams. Kids hurtling over the switchback, plunging into the log flume, their mouths open, their clothes flying.

Lowther inclined his head. 'They're there,' he said. 'Not far away now.'

Cooper was concentrating so hard on the other man, tensed for a sudden movement, that he was hardly aware of movements on the edge of his vision, the increasing number of sounds around him. He reminded himself that John Lowther saw the world differently, and was probably already in an entirely abnormal state of mind where he saw things that didn't exist and heard voices that Cooper couldn't.

For some reason, Cooper couldn't stop his thoughts wandering. He remembered thinking about the indoor area at Gulliver's Kingdom, the place his nieces wanted so much to visit. The Wild West, an ice palace, jungle adventures. It was just there, in the distance, prominent among the trees. He could see it without taking his eyes from Lowther's. Right now, Cooper could imagine himself in the middle of a Wild West shoot-out, that nerve-jangling moment when two men waited for each other to make the fatal first move. Or maybe that wasn't it. Perhaps he was in the ice palace. Skating on very thin ice indeed.

'There's nothing to worry about, sir,' he repeated. 'Let's just go down to the bottom of the tower, and we can talk. We can talk about whatever you like.'

Lowther shook his head. 'It'll soon be Monday,' he said.

'Monday?'

Frowning, Cooper found the lines of a song going through his head. An old Boomtown Rats classic.

'So what don't you like about Mondays?'

'Not Mondays,' said Lowther. 'Next Monday. The thirty-first of October.'

'Oh.'

Of course. Halloween. The time when the forces of evil were at their most powerful, the night when the doors to the underworld stood open and it was possible to communicate with the dead. Another belief that died hard, despite the efforts to make it all about pumpkins and apple bobbing.

'I can't be alive by then,' said Lowther. 'I can't.'

'All we need to do,' said Cooper, 'is get you down from here and take you to see a doctor. They can stop the voices, John. You know they can. They've done it before.'

'You don't understand,' said Lowther, shaking with agitation. 'Mum said you understood, but you don't. When people talk to me now it's like a different kind of language. It's too much to hold in my mind at once. My head is overloaded and I can't understand what they say. It makes me forget what I've just heard because I can't hear it for long enough. It's all in different bits, you see, which I have to put together again in my head. Until I do that, it's all words in the air. I have to try to figure it out from people's faces. But their faces always say something different from their voices.'

'Mr Lowther, please calm down and stop talking for a minute.'

'I have to keep talking, to drown out the voices.'

'We'll get you some treatment, to make the voices go away.'

'They'll never go away – not completely. They'll always be there . . .' He seemed to be listening to something. Whatever he heard terrified him, and he shouted the next few words. 'It's Lindsay's voice. Lindsay – and the children. I heard them scream. I'll always hear them scream.'

'Look –'

What happened next, Cooper wasn't quite sure. He'd been trying to concentrate on what John Lowther was saying, so he could respond and re-establish a connection. He'd been trying to maintain eye contact, to hold the man's attention and keep him talking. But something had spooked him. Lowther jerked backwards against the parapet as if he'd been shoved in the chest or pulled back by an invisible hand.

Then he was going over, and Cooper was diving forward to grab hold of him. He found only clothes to clutch at, smooth material that slipped through his fingers and left him nothing to grip. He felt Lowther's weight shifting inexorably outwards as gravity seized him and dragged him over the edge.

'Georgi! Help me, quick!'

Kotsev came thumping up the steps, gasping as he reached the top.

'*Dyavol da go vzeme!* Oh hell!'

But Kotsev was too late. Cooper felt his muscles scream against the effort of holding on to Lowther's coat, fabric stretching and tearing between his fingers. Lowther was doing nothing to help himself. Before Georgi could reach over the parapet to help, Lowther slipped out of Cooper's hands. His arms and legs flailed in the air, and his body bounced once off the stones of the tower as he fell, his mouth open, his jacket flying.

It was only in the final second that John Lowther's screams joined those of the children that he could hear. A second of screaming, and then the impact. And all the voices were silenced for ever.

34

When the call came in, the helicopter unit had been responding to a Casevac request, the recovery of a paraglider who'd made a heavy landing on the slopes of Kinder Scout and broken his ankle. By the time the casualty had been evacuated to a hospital in Chesterfield and the aircraft was free to be re-tasked, the suspect vehicle was already on the M1 and heading south.

Anthony Donnelly was on the run in his beige C-class Mercedes. The first sign of a police car in his street in Swanwick, and he'd legged it. A sign of experience, that, having the car warmed up and ready to go, facing the right direction. Without the helicopter, he might have got clean away before he even reached the motorway.

Normally, Oscar Hotel 88 could be airborne in three minutes from a call, with an average transit time to an incident of seven minutes. It took far longer for officers dealing with an incident on the ground to decide they needed the helicopter deployed.

But now the helicopter unit was airborne a mile west of the M1. On board, the observer was following the Mercedes on his video camera, the zoom facility picking the car out easily from the surrounding traffic. Even the officers following at a distance in an unmarked Omega had no idea the helicopter was there, until its call sign cropped up on their talk group.

If he's heading for the airport, we need to intercept him before he enters the terminal.

We don't have units in place yet. We're waiting for Firearms Support.

How long are we going to wait?

As long as it takes. We have to assume the suspect is armed.

Understood.

Listening to the exchange, Fry could detect the underlying anxiety at the prospect of an armed confrontation in a public place. And it would be a very public place, if the suspect got as far as the concourse in the airport terminal building.

She checked her map. Coming south from Sheffield, the M1 passed through part of Derbyshire, entered Nottinghamshire near Pinxton, then crossed back over the border again for the last stretch towards the airport. The confusion of jurisdictions made no sense in policing terms. It was an anomaly that someone always pointed out when the subject of merging police forces came up.

524

East Midlands Airport lay right by the M1, between junctions 24 and 23A. From the north, the Mercedes would take 24 if it was heading for the airport. Right now, it was approaching the slip road into Trowell Services.

Watch for him pulling off.

Have we alerted our neighbours?

Control rooms are in the loop.

One result of the M1's waywardness was that Trowell Services lay over the border in Nottinghamshire, despite being within two miles of Ilkeston nick. Permission had to be obtained for an operation on neighbouring territory, and officers would have to keep the control room at Sherwood Lodge informed as well as their own at Ripley.

But the Mercedes went past the services and drove another eight miles down the motorway. The helicopter's observer kept up a running commentary to guide the units converging on the suspect.

Leaving the motorway now.

The vehicle came off at junction 24 and took the fourth exit at the roundabout on to the A453 in the Donington Park area. At the next round-about, it would have to stay on the same road and bear right at the lights into the airport. But it didn't do that.

Turning into the Travelodge. It looks as though he's parking up.

OK, take up positions and await FSU.

Fifteen minutes later, Hitchens gave Fry the thumbs-up, and a big grin. Their suspect was in custody.

'So you don't want to tell us about Rose Shepherd,' said Hitchens, watching Tony Donnelly across the interview-room table.

'I've got nothing to say.'

They'd been trying for a long time, struggling through the kind of interview that Fry hated – the kind that made her think of banging her head repeatedly against a wall. Good only when it stopped. In fact, she had a suspicion the average wall would crack long before this suspect.

Donnelly and the duty solicitor stared back at the detectives across the table. They had an air of being two visitors at a zoo, wondering when these strange creatures were going to do something more interesting.

'What about Lindsay Mullen, then?' said Hitchens.

Donnelly hesitated slightly before he answered. 'No comment.'

'Where did you first see Mrs Mullen?'

'No comment.'

'Did you even know her name, Tony?'

'No comment.'

Fry could see Hitchens gathering his thoughts before the next question. Like her, he'd seen the expression that had briefly passed across Donnelly's face when Lindsay Mullen's name had been mentioned. Surprise, incomprehension. A lack of recognition. Just for a moment, before he'd trotted out the standard response.

'You saw Lindsay Mullen meet Rose Shepherd at the Riber Tea Rooms in Matlock Bath, didn't you?' said Hitchens.

'No comment.'

But the answer came more quickly this time, more confidently. Donnelly knew who they were talking about again. It seemed to Fry that he hadn't known Lindsay Mullen's name until then. Somehow, that made her killing worse. It appeared even more cold and merciless. She had been an anonymous woman eliminated without a second thought. And the two children? What about them? They'd just been in the wrong place at the wrong time.

'There's one thing that really puzzles me,' said Hitchens. 'How did you know who Lindsay Mullen was?'

Donnelly smiled. 'No comment.'

'I mean, did you have advance information about the meeting taking place? Did you have a description of Mrs Mullen that enabled you to identify her? Or did you listen in to their conversation somehow?'

A shake of the head. 'No comment.'

'Whichever it was, the organization seems to have been exceptionally good, very well planned.'

Donnelly gazed down at the table, but Fry could see the smile on his face. If his eyes had been visible, she guessed that she'd see in them that he was laughing – laughing inwardly at the stupidity of the police.

'Or was it only luck, Tony?'

His head came up then, and his eyes narrowed at Hitchens. 'I don't know what you're talking about.'

'It was Rose Shepherd you were looking for, wasn't it? And you stumbled on Lindsay Mullen at the same time. That must have been very convenient for you. It made the job a lot easier, I imagine. What would you have done otherwise? Were you planning on breaking into Miss Shepherd's house and interrogating her until she gave you the information you wanted?'

Donnelly glared at his solicitor. 'What's this shit?' he said.

'Detective Inspector Hitchens, could you clarify what my client is accused of? We don't understand this line of questioning.'

'We're conducting enquiries into the murder of Miss Rose Shepherd, who was shot and killed in Foxlow in the early hours of Sunday morning. We're also investigating the deaths of Mrs Lindsay Mullen and her two children, who died in a fire at their home in Edendale on the following night. And we'd like to know from your client the names of his associates in these offences.'

There was quite a long silence after Hitchens' statement. When Donnelly responded, it was with a smirk that would have got him a punch in the mouth at one time, before interview rooms were equipped with tape recorders and video cameras.

'No comment,' he said.

Fry fetched two coffees into the DI's office. It was something she wouldn't normally let herself be caught doing. But they both needed some caffeine. Even so, she took care to avoid the door of the CID room, in case anyone saw her.

'Thanks, Diane,' said Hitchens.

He was spinning his swivel chair from side to side, making it squeal at the end of each turn. It was a habit he had when he was angry or stressed.

'What's the plan, sir?'

'I'll let Donnelly stew for a while, then I'll have another go at him later.'

'He'd never heard Lindsay Mullen's name before,' said Fry. 'I could tell from his face when you asked him about her.'

'Do you think so, Diane?'

'Yes, I do.'

Hitchens stared out of the window as he took a sip of coffee and put the cup down quickly. It was too hot, as usual.

'I'm inclined to agree with you. It was almost the only time we got a genuine reaction out of him. He was surprised. And then he thought it was funny. It makes things more difficult for us, doesn't it? It suggests there were more people involved than we first thought.'

Fry sat down, balancing her own cup on her knee. 'What do you mean?'

'If Donnelly doesn't know anything about Lindsay Mullen, it means the Darwin Street job must have been given to someone else.'

'Really?'

'Well, it's good practice. Separate teams, with no contact between them. Neither team knowing what job the other is doing. There'd be much less chance of them implicating each other that way. That would explain why Tony Donnelly doesn't even know Lindsay Mullen's name. He probably only read about her in the papers, like everyone else.'

'I suppose it could also be the reason why the arson seemed so much less professionally executed. There were always too many differences in approach for them to fit together comfortably. So we have a second suspect, you think?'

'At least.'

'Nikolov?'

'I don't see how. There's no indication that he left the farm during the last couple of days before he died. More likely, he picked up a newspaper, or turned on the radio, and heard about Rose Shepherd's killing. Then he drank himself to death.'

'He followed her to Derbyshire, then followed her into death?'

Hitchens blinked a little. 'Well, Nikolov was no hit man.'

'Who, then? I wonder if that could have been someone recruited at short notice. They can't have expected to identify the Mullens so quickly after finding Rose Shepherd. There'd have to be a last-minute change to their plans.'

'A local villain, dragged off the street for a one-off job, cash in the pocket?' said Hitchens, brightening noticeably.

'He'd be easier to find, wouldn't he?'

'Easier to find? If he'd left us some DNA, we'd have him banged up already.'

'But, as it stands, we have no evidence to charge Tony Donnelly in connection with the Mullen killings.'

'No, none at all. But he's not going anywhere, since we have his prints from the Shogun. So we can worry about that later.'

Fry stood up, abandoning her untouched coffee on a corner of the DI's desk. No matter how hot it seemed at first, coffee from the machine always turned cold and undrinkable with unnatural speed.

'But the case against him for Rose Shepherd will be tight enough, won't it?'

'If forensics come through,' said Hitchens. 'With luck, we'll get a DNA match from the car, gunshot residue from his clothes, footwear impressions from the track where the Shogun was abandoned. There'll be something, don't worry. We'll build a tight enough case. In fact, it'll be a headline grabber when it comes to trial.'

Fry still hesitated. 'I wouldn't want the Mullens

to get forgotten in all the excitement. In a way, the arson was a far worse crime.'

The DI nodded. 'They won't get forgotten, Diane, I promise you. Why don't you get on with that line of enquiry now, and start sifting out some possibles from intelligence? The IU ought to be able to suggest a few names you'd go to if you wanted a nice house fire in a hurry.'

There was one other subject they weren't mentioning. It had all been gone through already, and no doubt it would be thrashed out again before long.

'And the Lowthers?'

'They're coming in tomorrow,' said Hitchens. 'And I'm not looking forward to it one bit.'

'Ben Cooper has gone home, by the way,' said Fry, though the DI hadn't asked her.

Hitchens looked hurt, as if she'd accused him of not caring about his officers. 'Yes, I know. But he seemed OK, don't you think?'

'As far as I could tell. He gave a clear enough statement, but that's just training. It was a hell of a thing to happen. Ben was right there, and he did his best. John Lowther was always going to do it, one way or another.'

'But knowing Ben . . .' said Hitchens.

'He'll be blaming himself. Right.'

At home that night, Cooper was going automatically through his routine – feeding the cat, taking a shower, checking the fridge, remembering he had no food in the flat. That was the great thing about routines – you didn't need to think. You could switch off the brain and freewheel.

Then he switched on his PC and opened Outlook. The evening's crop of email included a series of George W. Bush jokes, sent by his friend Rakki from his office address. It looked as though he'd forwarded them to everyone he knew, so the jokes would be doing the rounds for a while yet. In fact, Cooper was sure he'd seen most of them already.

He read them anyway. Not because he was interested, but because it stopped him thinking about anything else. It stopped him re-running the images and sounds from a couple of hours before – the terrified expression on a face falling through air, a sickening crunch, and a voice suddenly cut off, stopped short as if someone had turned the 'off' switch of a radio. And the awful silence that followed. Worse – the singing of the birds and the whirring of cables, as life carried on as normal, undisturbed by the moment of death. It was as if they were mocking him for his failure.

Oh, wait. That was the stuff he wasn't going to think about.

Cooper surprised the cat by picking him up and rubbing the fur behind his ears. Randy gave him a hostile look. This wasn't in the routine. There was still food to be eaten.

'OK, OK. It's not your problem, I know.'

But it had done the trick, and broken his train

of thought. He put the cat down again and turned back to his email. *How many is a brazillion?* That was a good one.

Of course, there was more to think about yet. It was Friday, the day of Matt's appointment with Dr Joyce, their GP. Matt knew his brother would be home at this time of the evening, but he'd have no idea what Ben had been through during the day.

As if their minds were already making a connection, the phone rang. Ben had no doubt who it was. He could picture Matt in the office at Bridge End Farm, and he could imagine his expression changing with each unanswered ring. He could just decide to ignore the call, of course. Would Matt give up and go away, and never mention the subject again? No, he wouldn't.

'Hi, Matt.'

There was a second of silence. 'How did you know it was me?'

'It figured.'

'I keep forgetting. You're a detective.'

Matt sounded calmer than when they'd spoken last night. Was that a good sign, or not?

'You had the appointment today, right?'

'Yes, I did.'

'Was it any use?' asked Ben.

'Well, actually – yes.'

'What did he tell you?'

'Nothing. He just listened.'

'Right. So . . . ?'

'He's a smart bloke, that doctor,' said Matt. 'That's all I needed, really – somebody to listen. I felt a lot better afterwards.'

'Well, that's good.'

Ben reflected that it was perhaps what he'd refused to do himself, to listen. He hadn't wanted to hear what Matt was saying.

'Do you know what I reckon?' said Matt. 'I think I was getting worked up about this business over Mum's problem so that I didn't have to worry about the real stuff.'

So they were back to the euphemisms. Back to the family collusion, the maintenance of the pretence. That was quite normal.

'Anyway, I thought you'd want to know. Was I right to call?'

'Yes, you were right, Matt. Thanks. I'll see you at the weekend, probably.'

A moment of silence again. The sound of Matt thinking. 'Are you OK, Ben?'

'Yes, I'm fine.'

Finishing the call, Ben went back to his PC. There was an offer of fake Rolex watches that hadn't been caught by his junk-mail filter, and an advert for the latest bargains at an online CD shop he'd used once. And there was an email from Liz. It was only a short one, but it meant a lot more than all the others put together. It finished with a little smiley face formed by a colon, a dash and a bracket.

It was odd to think that this might have been

Rose Shepherd's means of communicating with the world. Emails were a deceptive form of communication at the best of times. Without hearing the intonation in someone's voice, or getting clues from their facial expression or body language, it was easy to misinterpret the meaning of their words. Irony could be taken literally, a joke could be read as an insult, and ferocious arguments could develop for no reason. Conversation was transmitted through a filter that got half of it wrong, like some unfinished translation program.

But at least it was communication, of a kind. Cooper remembered his mother's attitude after she'd begun to get really ill and almost never left the house. Lying in her bed at Bridge End Farm, she had once said to him in a lucid moment that she wasn't sure the world existed any more. When he asked her why, she explained that she had no evidence it was really out there still. Other people talked about it sometimes, but she never actually saw it for herself.

It had been pointless for him to argue with her. Of course, her family and friends often sent her postcards from the places they visited. Cheerful, colourful pictures of sandy beaches and historic buildings. France, Italy, Florida, Skorpios. Bulgaria, even. But Isabel Cooper didn't believe in those places, any more than she believed in the people she saw on TV. For her, the outside world had become a series of images on a screen, and a set of postcards in a box. Just another illusion.

Maybe she had come to believe, like Bishop Berkeley, that nothing existed unless she perceived it for herself. Cooper didn't know much about philosophy, only what he'd learned in a sort of slogan form during General Studies lessons at Edendale High School – *esse est percipi*, the principle of existence through perception. So he wasn't sure what else Berkeley's theory said. Was the opposite true? If you perceived something, did that mean it existed? Or could perception be an illusion, too?

35

When the Lowthers arrived at West Street next day, Fry showed them into the DI's office, where they sat in an uncomfortable silence. Hitchens swivelled his chair once, then stopped when he heard the squeal and looked embarrassed.

Fry found a seat to one side, out of the Lowthers' immediate view. But it was her that Moira Lowther was looking at when she spoke. 'You weren't listening, were you? I told you John wasn't a danger to anyone but himself. He was psychotic, not a psychopath. I told you, but you didn't listen.'

Fry didn't know how to answer her. According to Cooper, Dr Sinclair had said the same thing. And it seemed they had both been right.

'Our officers did their best to save your son's life,' said Hitchens with a placatory gesture. 'It was a very difficult situation.'

'You were pursuing him.'

'No, Mrs Lowther.'

'*She* was.'

The jerk of the head was insulting, but Fry stayed calm.

'DS Fry wasn't even at the scene when the incident happened,' said Hitchens.

'What about the officers who *were* there? Why can't we speak to them?'

'There'll be a full enquiry into the circumstances, I assure you.'

Fry and Hitchens exchanged glances. The enquiry wouldn't be comfortable, and these things often left a sour taste – personal grievances, doubts about where loyalties lay, and whether officers could depend on the support of their chiefs. But it all had to be done properly and above board.

'We'll keep you to that promise,' said Mrs Lowther.

'Of course.'

Fry could still feel herself being glared at. 'We questioned John as part of the investigation into your daughter's death,' she said. 'We were trying to cover every possibility, that's all.'

'It's ridiculous. John would never do anything like that. They were so close. As close as a brother and sister could be.' Mrs Lowther choked on the last word. 'And now we've lost both of them.'

Cringing at the onset of tears and the threat of full-blown hysterics lurking below the surface, Fry looked at Hitchens for support. In a storm, you clutched at any straw.

'Mr and Mrs Lowther, I can't tell you how sorry we are,' he said. 'Believe me, if there's anything at all we can do –'

Henry Lowther had been sitting rigid and furious, his tension showing only in the trembling of his hands and the throbbing of a small vein in his temple.

'Anything you can do?' he said, his voice an ominous whisper. 'Don't you think you've done enough to us already?'

Cooper couldn't help looking for the Lowthers' Rover in the visitors' car park that morning. Sure enough, they'd already arrived. He could see their car in front of the main entrance as he pulled up to the gates of the compound.

It was impossible to imagine how Henry and Moira Lowther would be feeling now. Cooper wondered if he ought to offer to talk to them, and whether it would do any good.

As he locked up the Toyota and walked towards the building, he tried to analyse his own feeling, too. That was difficult enough, God knew. One part of him wanted to talk to the Lowthers in the hope that it might make some sense of their son's death. But another part of him was afraid – afraid of what too much emotion could do. That was the shallower side of his character, he supposed; the scared and defensive side.

In the CID room, he found Gavin Murfin already at his desk. That was unusual in itself.

Gavin never arrived at work before him, especially on a Saturday.

'You know that the what's-their-names are here?' said Murfin when he saw Cooper. 'The Lowthers.'

'Yes, I do.'

'They're in with Diane and the DI.'

'There haven't been any messages then?'

'Not yet. If I were you, Ben, I'd find a reason to get out of the office as soon as possible. The DI can deal with it.'

'Maybe.'

But Cooper took off his jacket and sat at his desk to see what he had to catch up with. There was nothing from Scenes of Crime, so no new information on the gun. But there was a copy of the full post-mortem report on Simon Nichols, alias Simcho Nikolov, complete with a set of photographs. He hadn't really looked at Nichols too closely before, but guessed that he hadn't been much prettier in life than he was in death. Not for the past few years, anyway. The marks left by the man's lifestyle were etched deep into his face, just as surely as they'd ruined the interior of the caravan. Too much alcohol and not enough food. Too many cigarettes and not enough attention to hygiene.

Yet, when he studied Nichols' face, Cooper could see that there was still a vestige of the man he'd once been. The bone structure was still there, broad and well-proportioned. A Bulgarian face, of course. He was Nikolov, not Nichols.

Cooper remembered the red phone box on the roadside in Bonsall Dale. It seemed likely that Nikolov had phoned Rose Shepherd from there. And then there had been that final phone call, made from an assassin's mobile to lead her into his sights. So, in a way, John Lowther wasn't the only one who'd heard voices. Miss Shepherd had been hearing them, too – voices that had led her to her death.

Suddenly aware of someone standing at his desk, Cooper gave a start and looked up guiltily, not knowing who to expect. But it was Gavin Murfin.

'I brought you a cup of coffee,' he said. 'Since you're obviously not going to take my advice.'

'Thanks, Gavin.'

'No worries. You look as though you could use it.'

At the sound of voices and footsteps, they both turned towards the door. But the voices went further away, down the corridor somewhere. After a minute or two, footsteps returned and the DI's door closed again.

'I think they've gone,' said Murfin.

Cooper nodded. 'But Diane is still in there.'

'Looks like it. I suppose we'll find out what's going on eventually.' Then Murfin sighed deeply. 'Or maybe not.'

The squeak of the chair in the DI's office was really starting to get on Fry's nerves now. Yet the noise seemed to give Hitchens some perverse pleasure, especially as he'd physically prevented a maintenance man from oiling the thing when she'd suggested it.

'So do you have any evidence that Luanne Mullen is in imminent danger, Diane?' he asked when she put her proposal to him after the departure of the Lowthers.

'Well, no.'

'Has she ever been mistreated by her father? Has he ever threatened to harm her?'

'Not that we know of.'

'What about Brian Mullen himself? A few days ago, you were convinced he was responsible for the fire that killed his family. Have you managed to substantiate a case against him?'

'No.'

'So we've no cause to arrest him, have we?'

'No.'

'And we don't actually have the slightest bit of proof that he's done anything wrong.'

'No. But we should also consider Georgi Kotsev's theory that Luanne Mullen's natural father is trying to get her back'

'Yes, we'd have to take that seriously, if there was evidence,' said Hitchens. 'Is there evidence, Diane?'

'I can't produce any right now.'

'You see the problem. No evidence. It's all supposition.'

'That might be true, sir. But the fact that Brian Mullen has gone AWOL with the surviving child looks very suspicious to me.'

'Sadly, he's not legally obliged to keep us informed of his whereabouts. If he's taken the child for a trip somewhere, then there's nothing we can do about it. Nothing at all.'

'But the Lowthers are being equally secretive. I'm sure they know where Brian is.'

'Have you asked them?'

'Of course.'

'And what do they say?'

'They say their son-in-law is distressed and needs some time away from being hassled by us.'

Hitchens smiled. 'I suppose that could be true, too, couldn't it?'

Fry wasn't amused. 'I assure you, sir, I don't hassle members of the public.'

'Of course not, Diane. You're a model of respect and discretion.'

She felt her jaw tighten, and tried to relax her muscles in case she looked too tense or aggressive.

'But it's hardly surprising the family feel that way, is it?' said Hitchens. 'Let's not forget that they've lost both their children and two of their grandchildren in the course of a week. And now you want to hunt down their son-in-law and their remaining grandchild.'

'It's not like that at all.'

'But that's the way it's going to seem to the

Lowthers. Let me tell you, I never want to experience as uncomfortable a half hour as I spent with those two people this morning.'

'I'm certain Brian Mullen is going to turn up at the Matlock Bath illuminations tonight,' said Fry. 'As certain as I can be.'

'Your grounds for that belief seem to be very tenuous, to say the least. Why would he risk taking the child to Matlock Bath?'

'It was something he'd promised the family. Even with only Luanne left, I think he'll follow through on the promise. *Especially* with only Luanne left.'

'I see.'

'There's more. I'm concerned that this visit could be the prelude to a significant act on his part. I think Mr Mullen is planning to do something rash and desperate.'

'What do you mean?'

'My feeling is that, unless we find him tonight, it could be too late.'

The DI swivelled his chair again, making Fry grind her teeth with frustration.

'It's not like you to base your reactions entirely on gut instinct, Diane. Have you got a personal problem with this case?'

'No, sir.'

Hitchens watched her, waiting to hear more, perhaps hoping she could give him some solid justification. But Fry had already exhausted what she had to say, and stayed silent.

The DI looked disappointed. 'Well, I'm sorry, but I can't authorize an operation to apprehend Mr Mullen at this event in Matlock Bath tonight. I've heard nothing to justify the use of resources for such a wild-goose chase. Let alone the effect on the family, which you don't seem to be taking into consideration. You could land us with an even bigger public relations disaster than we already have.'

Fry stood up to leave. 'Thank you, sir.'

Hitchens held up a hand to keep her back. 'You haven't asked me about Tony Donnelly.'

'Is there any point?'

'I re-interviewed him this morning.'

'How many "no comments" did you get?'

'A few,' admitted Hitchens. 'We're going to have to put some effort in on Donnelly, interviewing his family, friends, neighbours. His background will have to be looked at, his whereabouts checked, alibis pursued . . .'

This time, nothing would keep Fry from leaving the DI's office.

'Are you sure there's nothing else you want to talk about, Diane?' he said.

'Yes, thank you. Quite sure.'

Cooper saw that he'd been right. There were so many visitors trying to get into Matlock Bath that by five o'clock all the car parks in the village were full. Police officers in yellow jackets were directing long queues of motorists to a park-and-ride facility at the rugby club a mile down the road. The pavements were packed with people queuing at the fish-and-chip shops or eating out of paper packages as they leaned over the railings to gaze at the river, throwing their last few chips to the ducks. Many of the crowd were family groups, young children sitting in pushchairs or strapped to the parents in carriers.

It had already been gloomy enough by half past four to use sidelights as they drove down from Edendale. On the way here, the mood had been sombre. Dead leaves had filled the lay-bys like a yellow tide.

'I have to remind you that we're here unofficially,' said Fry. 'Strictly speaking, you're off duty.'

Cooper nodded. 'We understand that, Diane.'

'No overtime, then?' said Murfin.

'No overtime, Gavin. Sorry.'

Murfin shrugged. 'It gets me out of the house. And it means you can't tell me not to eat fish and chips while I'm working, right?'

'Right.' Fry looked at Kotsev. 'Georgi? There's no obligation on you to be here at all.'

'What else would I be doing? Sitting in my hotel watching English television? I wish to be part of the team.'

'Thanks, Georgi.'

'And I'm not to beat up any suspects, OK?'

Fry glanced at him, seemed to recognize that he was joking, and let it pass.

'I've told the inspector in charge of the

547

uniformed operation that we're here, but I didn't give him any more details than he needs to know. He's far too busy to bother about us, anyway. He's expecting a crowd of six thousand people and a lot of traffic problems. All he's got to handle it are a dozen bobbies and a few CSOs.'

'So what are we looking for exactly?' said Murfin.

'Brian Mullen. And, I hope, Luanne.'

Cooper coughed uneasily. 'Diane, if your theory about Brian Mullen is right, what will happen to the child? Will she be sent back to Bulgaria? Surely she wouldn't have to go back to her real father after all?'

But Fry's face was hard, giving nothing away. 'That won't be our decision to make. All we have to do is find them.'

'So our responsibility stops there, does it?'

'Ben, I hope you're not going all social worker on me again.'

'But don't you sometimes wonder what happens to people afterwards – I mean, when we've done our job and the courts have done theirs? Don't you worry that all you've done is make a whole lot of people's lives even worse? Do you always sleep properly at night, Diane?'

'Yes, like a log.'

'I'm not sure I believe you.'

Fry looked at Cooper more closely. 'Are you all right, Ben? Look, don't worry too much about John Lowther's death. You did your best to help him. It was the system that let him down, not you.'

'There'll be an enquiry. It might decide that I did the wrong thing. There's only my word for what happened.'

'You have a witness,' said Fry. 'Georgi was there.'

'No, he didn't see what happened,' said Cooper. 'I told him to stay back on the stairs.'

Fry looked at Kotsev, who gazed back at her impassively.

'On the contrary,' he said. 'I saw everything.'

'You can't have done,' said Cooper. 'Georgi, there's no need –'

'I will tell the story, if I'm called upon. Ben acted well. He was a hero.'

Cooper flushed, uncomfortable with both the sentiment and what seemed to be Kotsev's misguided loyalty.

'Let's get on with it, shall we?' he said.

He couldn't help being sceptical about what Fry hoped to achieve in Matlock Bath tonight. A suspect loose among the crowds, strolling through Derwent Gardens with all these families? It didn't bear thinking about. The risk to the public represented an operational nightmare.

DI Hitchens had made the right decision, in Cooper's view. No responsible senior officer would authorize an attempt to carry out an arrest in these circumstances. The most they could do safely was to keep Mullen under surveillance – and even then it would be at a distance. So no heroics. Follow him until he was in a location where the situation could be safely contained. Oh, yes. And pray he didn't get away again.

'Oh, and make sure you all stay in touch,' said Fry. 'That's what the radios are for.'

'Yes, how come you manage to get these radios and ear pieces issued, if we're here unofficially?' asked Murfin.

'Gavin, haven't you learned when not to ask questions?'

They started from the northern end of the village and separated, taking the riverside walk and the parade of shops in pairs. The village really was getting packed. This was the last night of the illuminations, and the night would climax with a fireworks display from the top of High Tor.

Tomorrow, the Heights of Abraham would close for the winter. The cable cars would stop running, the gift shops would shut, and the terraces of the Hi Café and Summit Bar would be left empty. The clocks went back an hour in the morning, and winter would have arrived.

Actually, Cooper knew he should be glad of something to do tonight. He needed to occupy his mind. Ever since the incident on the tower, he'd been aware of a deep ache that he was reluctant to explore, a doubt that he'd never have the answer to. Could he have done more to save John Lowther? If he'd acted differently, if he'd stayed back, if he'd made a grab for the man sooner . . .

Despite telling his story three or four times since the tragedy had happened, he didn't know whether he'd done the right thing or not. He supposed it would be for other people to judge him.

'This is more like home,' said Kotsev, watching the crowds.

'What?'

'A big party in the street. People having fun. Give me a few stalls selling sunflower seeds, and I would be happy.'

'You'll have to make do with fish and chips.'

Kotsev laughed. '*Mnogo vkusno*. Delicious.'

They walked slowly through the beer garden behind the Midland Hotel, overlooking the river. Clusters of people were gathered at the Bikers' Well near the war memorial. Here, the shallow river was bordered by horse chestnuts, branches skimming the surface of the water. Disused, ivy-covered steps led down to the water's edge. Tilted beds of rock formed multi-coloured cliffs on the opposite bank. An old ceramic drainage pipe lay embedded in the mud near a scattering of shingle.

The illuminated boats were due to parade from New Bridge at the southern end of the village as far as the Pavilion, passing along the length of Derwent Gardens. On a map showing the start and finish, some comedian had drawn in a black shape halfway along the route and marked it 'Bermuda Triangle'.

Cooper looked across the road. Fry and Murfin

were standing in front of the chop house at the bottom of Holme Road, watching the crowds using a pedestrian crossing opposite the Thyme Restaurant.

Behind the Riverside Fish Restaurant was a boating jetty, then a row of shops leading to the Pavilion. Hulley's buses were ferrying people from the park-and-ride area to the Pavilion car park, which had been reserved for emergency vehicles. Scores of motorbikes now lined the kerb on South Parade, all the way from the ice-cream parlour up to the aquarium. A girl was selling ice cream and slush puppies from a kiosk. A pair of mallard ducks stood hopefully on the pavement outside a fish shop.

There was no sign of Brian Mullen, and Derwent Gardens weren't open to the crowds yet. Cooper crossed the road to the corner of Temple Road. The car park here was full, too. He and Kotsev walked along the rows of cars, looking for Mullen's red Citroën without success.

Cooper turned at the end of a row, and Kotsev touched his arm.

'Ben, it's OK.'

'What do you mean?'

'You shouldn't worry about such things. About such people.'

For a moment, Cooper thought he was going to lose control. He felt as though he might let all the stress out in a burst of anger against the wrong person.

'Look, just give me a minute, Georgi.'

Just below the car park, he found a pond. It lay in a circular hollow near the road, overhung by bay trees. In the middle of the water, a fountain sprayed over a column of tufa. Dozens of the black beetles called waterboatmen sculled on the surface among floating lilies, perhaps fooled by the strings of coloured lights into thinking it was still daytime. In fact, the column looked to be more moss than tufa. But on the bank behind it were patches already turning to stone. The vegetation looked normal from a distance, except for its colour. But it was already dead and hard, retaining only the appearance of life.

'It looks as though the gardens are being opened up,' said Fry through his ear piece. 'The crowds are starting to move that way.'

'Well, at least they'll all be in one place. There are thousands of them. And they're still coming in. There's another busload arriving now.'

'I've asked for a car to cruise through the rugby ground to see if they can spot Mullen's car at the park-and-ride.'

'Good idea.'

Kotsev was waiting for him on the pavement. Most of the police officers deployed in Matlock Bath tonight were on traffic duty, keeping the lines of cars moving. Across the road, the gardens themselves were being patrolled by security staff and stewards in yellow jackets. As soon as the fairground and fast-food stalls had set up, the barriers were taken down and people began to filter past the volunteers standing by with buckets for donations.

'There are so many people,' said Cooper. 'We'd better split up from here. You know what Brian Mullen looks like, Georgi?'

'I have the photograph. And there's the child with him –'

'Yes, probably.'

Cooper worked his way past the St John Ambulance, the Venetian Boat Builders Association, stalls for the Cats Protection League and a Chernobyl children's charity. A woman who looked like a gypsy pulled a scarf across her face and turned away from the light. A fortune teller, or perhaps a pickpocket. Well, it wasn't his business tonight.

It was dark now, and all the children were carrying rainbow spinners, yellow light sticks or flashing fish. One by one, they stopped and pointed at the illuminated butterflies and dragons in the trees. Cooper came to a central area lined with fast-food vans. The local radio station, Peak FM, had set up its roadshow in the bandstand, where an ageing Elvis in a black outfit was belting out songs from a cloud of green artificial smoke.

Further on was the fairground. An old-fashioned ferris wheel, a mini waltzer, a set of dodgem cars and a train ride. Down at this end of the gardens, the mixture of smells was enough to make your head swim: diesel fumes from the generator running the dodgems, chemicals from a row of portaloos, hot dogs and onions from a fast-food van.

He stood between the boom of rap music blasting across the dodgems circuit and the sound of a teenage rock band performing 'Layla' in a cloud of green smoke at the Peak FM roadshow. Around him were the screams of children on the pirate boat, the constant clang of a bell on the train ride. A would-be Eric Clapton launched into a dramatic guitar solo.

'Even if they're here, there's no way we'll spot them in this crush. We don't stand a chance.'

'Stay near the front of the crowd. He won't have Luanne at the back, if he wants her to see the boats.'

'OK.'

The strings of coloured lights were reflected and elongated in the water, and across the river the trees on the hillside were lit by patches of brilliant colour – blue, green, red. Seven thirty came and went. By the time announcements over the PA system warned of the impending boat parade, people were already jostling for the best positions along both banks of the river and on the new bridge. Above the gardens, a bus passed behind the illuminated trees. In the distance, Upper Towers was lit up on the Heights of Abraham. It floated in the sky like some airborne castle.

'There are people standing three deep on the bridge. I don't know how it can take the weight.'

'That's nothing. They're about five deep this side of the river. It looks pretty much the same across the other side.'

'At least they're standing in one place now, instead of moving about. Let's try and get round the crowd while the boats keep their attention.'

The commentary was almost impossible to make out from here. It was a loud blare, an indistinguishable voice echoing among the trees, only the occasional word emerging from the babble. The announcer seemed to be telling the crowd that the winning boat was called American Express.

The boats drifted out one at a time from the boat jetty until they were in the middle of the current. When they were midstream, each one lit up suddenly, to a cheer from the children on the bank. So the Empire State Building and the White House appeared all at once in the darkness, drifting above the water, glittering in multi-coloured lights that reflected on the surface.

The winner was followed by more boats. A steam engine rode magically on the river, a miniature paddle steamer floated in a pool of its own light. There was a vintage car, a carousel, a biplane, a Viking longboat. As they came by, it was impossible to distinguish the boats from their reflections, red cascades bursting and rippling across the surface in the splash of oars.

'It's hopeless, Diane.'

'Keep trying.'

Cooper worked his way through the crowds on the bank. People were so tightly packed that it was impossible to walk normally. He found it uncomfortable to move with such short steps, squeezing his way between the backs of strangers. Some of the faces were too close to make out. People were standing on the slopes to see over the crowd. Some were under the lights, and some were in darkness. Underfoot, it was impossible to see if you were treading in mud or a puddle. A light drizzle had begun to fall, adding a mist to the blur of coloured lights above the heads of the crowd.

Soon after eight o'clock, people began to drift out of the gardens again, and Cooper made his way back across the bridge. The raised areas of grass had been trodden into mud and people slipped on damp tree roots. Fast-food cartons crunched underfoot. The rock band was still playing, but had moved on to 'Sweet Child of Mine'.

'Where are you, Ben?'

'I'm near the bandstand. Look for the Dinky Donuts van. You can't miss it – there's a big pink thing on the roof, like an inflated condom.'

'OK, I see it.'

Cooper waited, the crowds separating around him, music blasting his ears. Teenagers walked by with their mobile phones held out in front of them to take photographs of each other. He thought he caught a glimpse of the gypsy woman again, a blue scarf flashing briefly in the lights. When the band finished playing, the announcer started trying to persuade everyone to move across to the west bank of the river for the fireworks display.

'I'm still here, Diane. I can't see you yet.'

His ear piece was silent. And for a moment, Cooper remembered that you didn't have to be a recluse to be alone. It was possible to feel desperately alone even in the middle of the biggest crowd.

36

An air of anticipation developed again as nine o'clock approached. Streams of people came back over the bridge to the gardens, or stood on the pavements outside the Pavilion and the Fishpond pub. Their faces were turned up towards the rock face of High Tor. The hill rose into the night sky above the swathes of multi-coloured trees. An expectant hush gradually developed, but for a little chatter here and there.

Then the crowd was silenced by a terrific bang that hit the village like a huge hand had been slapped down on the landscape. It punched eardrums and stopped a few hearts, judging by the expressions on the faces around him. It was the maroon, the single loud report that signalled the start of the display.

The maroon was followed by flares, fountains and rockets, candles. Brilliant white star bursts and red blossoms. They produced a barrage of bangs and whistles, whizzes and crackles, intense light and smoke. Glittering, coloured fire hung over the tor. A canopy of colour exploded into sparks, bangs, crackles and whistles. He saw the characteristic sparkling tail of a rocket on its way up. Screamers and screechers chased each other into the sky. Small stars and balls of fire changed colour in flight, finishing with a series of bangs. Comets grew brighter, their tails splitting into small fragments. Serpents snaked and wriggled through the air.

'Hold on. Diane, I can see him.'

'Brian Mullen?'

'Yes.'

'Are you sure?'

'It's him and Luanne. They're right down the north end of the gardens, near where the boats are docking after the parade.'

'Can you get to them, Ben?'

'I'm on the wrong side of the river. The nearest crossing is the footbridge. I'll have to go back and cross over.'

'Which way is Mullen heading?'

'He's standing still at the moment. No, wait – he's moving.'

'Has he seen you, do you think?'

'I don't think so. I'm on the darkest part of the bank over here. But he's moving all right. God, he's running. Diane, he's started to run. He'll be on the road in a minute.'

'I'll get back to the car and drive down. Gavin, where are you?'

'By the ice-cream kiosk in the Pavilion car park.'

'Get to the road, and I'll pick you up.'

There was no way of spotting Brian Mullen again, once he'd disappeared into the crowd. There were too many paths up there in the trees, too many dark corners, too many members of the public in the way. And too many of them were parents with small children.

'I'm pretty sure there's no way out at the other end of the gardens,' said Cooper. 'Not unless you're fit enough to scramble up the slope and get over that wall. Mullen couldn't do it with a small child in tow.'

'So he'll have to come back this way?'

'The nearest way out on to the road is by the netball court. I left my car at this end, Diane – opposite the church.'

'OK, we'll catch you up. Don't worry, he hasn't got a big start on us.'

But the police on traffic duty had closed off the entire stretch of road when the fireworks started, and Fry found lines of traffic were already backing up in both directions.

'Oh, shit.'

'Did Mullen get through?' asked Cooper when she told him.

'A CSO up here says a red Citroën went through like a bat out of hell just before they closed the road.'

'It's lucky I was on this side of the gardens. Georgi's with me now, and we're nearly at my car. Where do you suppose he's going?'

'He isn't going anywhere, as far as I'm concerned. His car will be stopped when it reaches Cromford. There are two officers posted at the junction, with manual control of the traffic lights.'

Kotsev followed Cooper into his Toyota, and it bounced off the kerb as Cooper accelerated down the empty roadway.

'He's definitely heading south, Diane?'

'Yes. There's nothing else that way, is there? No other roads? No way he can dodge us?'

'There's just Masson Mill. It's only three hundred and fifty yards downstream from the gardens, but he'll be able to see the Cromford junction from there. He's not an idiot – if he sees the uniforms standing at the lights, he'll know what's going on.'

'Masson Mill? The shopping village?'

'That's it. He could turn into the car park at the mill – the walls are high enough for him to get out of sight there.'

'OK. He might think we'll go flying straight past into Cromford. We'll probably find him sitting quietly with his headlights off, praying that we don't stop.'

'Let's hope so.'

The central storeys of the mill were lit up, picking out Arkwright's name on the brickwork. But the rest of the building and the roofs of the weaving sheds below the road were in complete darkness. At the entrance to the car park, a couple of attendants leaned against a wall, looking bored as they waited for owners to return for their vehicles.

Sensing that something was wrong, Cooper twisted his head round, and stamped on the brakes.

'Damn. The Citroën is on the forecourt in front of the main entrance. I almost didn't see it.'

Motorists in the queue of stalled traffic stared at him curiously as he reversed a few yards towards Mullen's car. It was parked at an awkward angle between two other vehicles that had been left there when the *Car park full* signs went up.

'He must have swung straight across the pavement as he went through the pedestrian crossing. And I bet none of these people noticed anything.'

'They don't look happy about the hold-up,' said Kotsev. 'Why should they report another driver for escaping it?'

Cooper parked the Toyota across the Citroën's tail end to block it in. As they approached the vehicle on either side, he spoke into his radio.

'Diane, we've got Mullen's car, in the main entrance to the shopping village. Right on the forecourt in front of the doors, you can't miss it.'

'You said that about Dinkie Donuts.'

'Georgi and I are right here.'

'Who's in the car?'

Cooper peered in through the windows, though he'd already guessed the answer.

'No one. They've legged it.'

'Where could they have gone? The shopping village is closed.'

'They can't have gone far.'

Then Cooper saw an iron stairway leading down from the forecourt. At the bottom was a door into the second level of the car park, just below the road. The door was painted red and lit up like a beacon. And it was open.

'That's the obvious way, Georgi, wouldn't you say? Especially if you were in a hurry.'

'Let's go, then.'

'Hold on a minute.' Cooper fetched his torch from the back seat of the Toyota. It was a four-cell Maglite, nearly fifteen inches long and weighing at least a couple of pounds. Not only would it give him a good light, but it was handy as a weapon, at a push. Then he found a spare torch from the car and handed it to Kotsev. 'You might need this.'

He turned at the sound of a horn, and saw Fry's Peugeot approaching, and her window winding down.

'We'll come in from the other direction,' she called.

'There's a roof level up the ramp, Diane. You might start there.'

'OK.'

She began to put her car into gear again, but Cooper put his hand on the door. 'How far are we going with this?' he said. 'I mean, Brian Mullen hasn't committed any crime that we know of.'

Fry gazed back coolly. 'He's running for a reason,' she said, as the Peugeot pulled away.

Cooper and Kotsev clattered down the iron stairs and through the red door. Inside, the parking levels were already half empty, the gaps between vehicles allowing a view right down to the ramps at the entrance. They shone their torches into the corners and along the sides of the ramps.

They hadn't been inside the car park long when Cooper heard a voice in his ear.

'We're coming in now,' said Fry. 'These attendants haven't seen anyone in the last few minutes, but I'll leave them to keep watch. How many parking levels are there, Ben?'

'Three, I think.'

Cooper found a door by the stairs, which led into the main building.

'Hey, there's a door open here,' he said.

'Be careful, Ben.'

'Aren't I always?'

'Actually, no.'

Cooper allowed himself a smile as he entered the darkened mill. The times Fry expressed concern for his welfare were so rare that they were worth collecting and treasuring for posterity.

He and Kotsev made their way slowly through the shopping floor. Although it was open-plan, there were far too many places to hide – counters and display units, racks of winter coats and free-standing shelves full of pottery. It would take dozens of people to search this place properly.

Without the presence of people, the dominant smell was the scent of polish rising from the wooden floors, as if they were walking through a low-lying mist. Cooper's torchlight reflected off mirrors everywhere, dazzling him with sudden bursts of glare. Time and again, he caught a movement across the other side of the floor and swung his Maglite towards it, only to see himself or Georgi staring back from a full-length mirror, pale and wide-eyed like ghosts.

When they came to the central stairs, Kotsev gestured upwards, and Cooper nodded. He watched until Georgi reached the top of the first flight, then he moved on.

And it was better on his own, without the distraction of someone else's footsteps behind him, another person's breathing in his ear, or that continual jump and flutter on the edge of his vision. Now, he could concentrate on the natural sounds of the building, he could listen for the subtle intrusions into the silence, the surreptitious movement in the darkness.

When he felt the floorboards shift and groan under his feet, Cooper knew he was near the wooden steps that led down to the museum at river level. Standing perfectly still, he held his breath and listened. The faint creak of boards came from below him, somewhere near the bottom of the stairs.

The stairs led down to two doors, one opening into the spinning room and the other into the weaving shed. A doubling machine and some of the looms had been running last time he was here.

The rattle of their bobbins and leather drive belts had seemed normal background noises then. Without them, the place was much too quiet, the long lines of wooden spindles dead and still, like rows of broken fingers.

His torchlight gleamed on white and pale blue walls, glared off red fire buckets, picked out the rainbow colours of the cotton on the bobbins. The weaving sheds had pitched roofs that were half glass to provide natural light for the weavers. Tonight, though, the glass only reflected his torch beam and the sporadic glint of machinery from the sheds beneath.

Cooper sniffed instinctively. The smell of lubricating oil and leather seemed stronger in the dark. Or perhaps in the silence. He wasn't sure which made the most difference. His jacket whispered against the wall, every footstep squeaked on the boards. At this level, he could hear a deep rumbling noise, and even feel a faint vibration through the floor. Common sense told him it must be the turbines running. If they ran at night, they were probably supplying surplus power to the National Grid. But their rumble sounded more like the heart of the massive building, thudding through the walls of the mill, beating much too fast.

Cooper felt his own heart begin to thump faster in rhythm with the turbines, and his chest tightened with anxiety. It was as if he was picking up a sense of fear from the building itself. *Be careful.* Aren't I always? *Actually, no.*

He froze to the spot, suddenly reluctant to go any further into the weaving shed. He didn't know what he was afraid of. But that was always the most frightening thing, the unknown. *You can only fear something that hasn't happened yet.* Damn right, Doctor. But lots of things had happened already. How many people had died? Too many to count.

For a moment, the rows of looms blurred and distorted. They seemed to change shape, mutating into crouching, angular beasts that lined a tunnel stretching away from him. They beckoned him further into the darkness, whispering with leathery tongues that had formed from their drive belts and pulleys.

Cooper shook his head, trying to drive away the illusion, to deny the lies that his senses were telling him. Then, at the far end of the weaving shed, he saw what his attention was being drawn to. His unsteady torchlight had picked out a shape on the floor. A bundle of rags, a pile of sacking? Well, it was possible in this place. Anything was possible. But Cooper knew it wasn't a bundle of rags, or a pile of sacking, or even a trick of the light. It was a body.

'Oh, shit.'

He recognized the smell of blood. This must have been the trigger for his anxiety, the message that his senses had been sending him. Blood meant danger. *Be careful.*

Suddenly, his surroundings came back into normal focus, and his feet began to move him forward again. Cautiously, Cooper edged around the looms and the other machines, checking the darkest corners of the shed, until he was bending over the body and feeling for a pulse. Despite the amount of blood matting the hair and spreading across the concrete floor, there were still signs of life.

There had been silence from his ear piece for several minutes now, and Cooper knew he'd lost contact. He pulled out his mobile, praying there'd be a signal. It wasn't guaranteed, especially since he was below road level. But he was in luck for once. First he called for an ambulance, then he rang Fry's number.

'Diane, I've found Brian Mullen.'

'Thank God. Is the child all right?'

'No, listen. I said I've found Mullen. He's unconscious – he looks as though he's taken a bad blow to the head, and there's quite a bit of blood. But he's breathing all right. I've got an ambulance on its way.'

'And Luanne?'

Cooper didn't answer for a moment. He was staring at the long rows of looms, the gleaming wooden bobbins. White walls and dusty shelves, the flash of his Maglite reflected and multiplied like stars in the glass roof of the weaving shed. And, almost too far away, a distant doorway that must lead out of the mill to the goyt, where the deep channels drew water from the river.

'Ben, are you there? What about the child?'

'There's no sign of her, Diane. She's gone.'

There was silence on the other end of the phone for a moment. Silence, apart from the distant sound of a car engine and faint, echoing voices. He pictured Fry still in the parking levels, struggling to cope with members of the public wanting to remove their cars.

'OK, Ben, hang on there. Stay with Mullen until assistance comes. Is Georgi with you?'

'I think he's still upstairs. But, Diane –'

'Just don't do anything stupid.'

And then she was gone. Cooper sighed as he ended the call, and checked Brian Mullen's pulse and breathing again. His skin felt very cold, so Cooper covered him with a bolt of cloth. There wasn't much he could do to stop the bleeding, but scalp wounds always looked worse than they really were.

He knew he ought to wait with Mullen, just as Diane said. But he was too conscious of time ticking away, too painfully aware that he might have been able to save John Lowther's life yesterday, if he'd acted more quickly. How could he sit here now and wait while a small girl was nearby, needing his help? Luanne Mullen might at this moment be at risk in the darkness. The thought was intolerable. He knew he'd never be able to live with himself if he did nothing.

Goading himself into action, Cooper ran back to the stairs to shout for Georgi Kotsev, at the expense of destroying the silence in the mill. He was saved the trouble when Kotsev appeared at the top of the wooden steps, looking huge framed in Cooper's torchlight.

'A problem, Ben?'

'Come down, Georgi, will you?'

Kotsev cursed quietly when he saw the body. 'And the child?'

'She's not here.'

'Dyavol da go vzeme.'

'Stay with him, will you, Georgi? Help is on the way.'

'Where are you going?'

'To find the child.'

They looked at each other for a moment. Kotsev seemed about to say something, but changed his mind. He nodded briefly.

'I understand.'

Then Cooper left him with Brian Mullen, and hurried down to the far end of the shed, tracking the sound of a closing door somewhere ahead. Noises echoed so much inside the mill that it was impossible to move around quietly. But it wasn't quite so easy to tell what direction the noise came from.

He had no idea of the layout at this end of the mill. Above Cooper's head, a bridge crossed over the looms to the mill entrance at road level. Ahead of him, a cavernous space gradually revealed itself to be the boiler house. Four black, riveted monsters glinted in his torch beam. Strangely, their upper surfaces were being used to store rabbit hutches.

He climbed back up the steps to a heavy steel door set into the outer wall. It looked like the entrance to a tunnel that would lead to the base of the mill chimney. He supposed someone must once have had to crawl in there to clean out the flue. Cooper paused for a moment, trying to decide between several doors and a series of smaller rooms, cramped spaces after the length of the weaving shed.

The door he chose turned out to be the bobbin room. The floorboards squealed and moved under the pressure of his feet as he entered. It occurred to him that he could be the ghost of Arkwright himself, prowling the mill at night, tracking down a fugitive child apprentice.

One flick of his torch showed Cooper a room like nothing he'd ever seen before. It contained dozens of musty-smelling hessian sacks spilling bobbins on to the floor. There were wooden tubs full of bobbins, bobbins in drawers and hanging on the walls. And above his head there were hundreds more of them strung in bunches – a thick layer of bobbins hanging as if they'd grown from the ceiling, like a strange fungal growth or a thousand stalactites filling every available inch. There were all kinds of shapes, sizes and colours, and they rattled slightly in a breeze blowing from an open door. Cooper could feel the chill striking through the doorway, and knew this must be the passage that led outside to the goyt, and to the river.

He slipped through the door on to a wooden walkway over the water channel. This area was open to the air, filled with the noise of the river and the sensation of empty space all around and above him in the darkness. The water that had once driven the mill's waterwheels still ran the turbines, and it flowed fast under the walkway here. He could hear its rush and feel the vibrations of the current.

But beyond the end rail was a stagnant basin. His torch picked out iron chains hanging from ancient pulleys, coated with dust and cobwebs. The chains disappeared into the murk, reaching down towards mysterious shapes that he barely glimpsed in the depths, metal structures with a forgotten purpose. Cooper shivered as he saw bits of dead vegetation floating on the surface. Even an adult might have difficulty in that water. Imagine getting tangled in the chains and dragged to the bottom.

His torchlight illuminated a warning sign. But was it the fast-flowing goyt it was warning of? Or the still, dark basin with its shadows below the surface?

Cooper turned sharply to the left, not sure what he was reacting to. His senses were confused by the adjustment from the silent interior of the mill to the noise outside. A series of explosions reminded him that the fireworks display was still going on over the village. The cascade of coloured light helped him to orientate himself. Beyond the goyt he could make out the bank of the river, and directly in front of him was an area of slippery concrete channels and sudden drops into black, lethal water.

It didn't feel any safer out here than it had inside. Of course, he ought to let Fry know where he was. So Cooper tried his phone again. But he was down by the river now, with the vast bulk of the mill behind him and the limestone crags towering on both sides. He raised his phone to head height and moved it in a different direction. No signal.

The roar of the weir sounded much louder at night. Now that he was close to it, it almost drowned the crack and scream of the fireworks launching from High Tor. Cooper strained to listen for sounds of movement above the rush of water from the weir and the hum of the turbines in the mill. The only other noise he could hear was a tap-tap-tap against the side of the channel as a polystyrene cup bobbed on the surface of the water. Tap-tap-tap on the concrete walls.

He thought he heard a shout somewhere, a woman's voice. But the words were incomprehensible. He was almost sure he saw a shadow flickering, and caught the rustle of a long skirt on concrete.

Then the tap-tap-tap became a clatter, the sudden sound of running footsteps. Cooper swung his torch, but he couldn't tell which direction the footsteps were coming from. The flashes and crashing of the fireworks were too disorientating, the reflection of his Maglite off the dark water too confusing.

So he spun round too late and didn't see the black shape that came at him out of the night, or the fists that smashed into him and knocked him off balance. He teetered for a moment on the concrete edge, drawing a breath to cry out. His torch dropped from his hand and plunged into the goyt with a loud splash. A second later, Cooper was following it. He plunged into the water, falling towards the light as it swirled and spun towards the muddy depths.

It seemed a long time before the light stopped falling, its beam swinging through the water to dazzle him. Cooper closed his eyes against the shock and the roar of water in his ears. He panicked when he realized he couldn't tell which way was up, and he began to thrash his arms and legs. He seemed to hit something, or something hit him, he couldn't tell which. The cold was already striking through to his soaking skin.

He opened his eyes again, and saw that the light was receding now, drawing away from him into the gloom. He seemed to be trapped by something, his clothes caught up on some heavy, rusty object under the water. He thought he must be sinking, and he thrashed harder. Just when he felt he couldn't hold his breath any longer, his head suddenly burst clear of the water and he gasped in a deep, ragged mouthful of air.

Dazed, Cooper realized that the collar of his jacket was being gripped by someone, and he was being dragged vigorously towards the side of the channel.

A deep voice laughed close to his ear.

'Bezopasno li e pluvaneto tuk? Are you sure it's safe to swim here?'

37

Sunday, 30 October

The following afternoon, Fry was sitting alone in the CID room at West Street. Everyone else who was on duty today had joined the search for Luanne Mullen. Most of them were expecting the divers of the underwater search team to have made a find by the time they'd finished dragging the channels of the mill goyt. Unless the child's body had been swept out into the river and was miles away from Matlock Bath by now.

Fry was thinking of her conversation with Brian Mullen early that morning. Same hospital, different ward. A Mullen who looked sicker and paler than ever.

'I always thought the adoption in Bulgaria was the wrong thing,' Mullen had said to her. 'I mean, I love Luanne to bits, and I wouldn't have parted with her, once we'd got her. I couldn't have taken her away from Lindsay. But I never thought it was right. It felt dodgy to me. I knew there'd be trouble. But Henry kept pushing and pushing, and Lindsay always went along with what he said.'

'I see.'

'It was all illegal, wasn't it? False documents, and everything?'

'Yes, I'm afraid so.'

Mullen had lain back, exhausted. 'I've never been involved in anything illegal before. Never. I knew they'd catch up with us.'

'Who?'

'I never knew who they'd be exactly, but I was sure someone would come one day, to take Luanne back. It was like we were living on borrowed time. And once that Rose Shepherd turned up again, that was the last straw. But no one else could see what I was afraid of. They told me I was being stupid.'

'Is that what you were having arguments with Lindsay about?'

'No, we never had arguments, I told you. We disagreed about some things. But I was right, wasn't I? They did come.'

'Possibly. But you have no idea who these people might be?'

'Somebody from Bulgaria, that's all I can guess at. They've got Luanne, haven't they? Have they taken her back there?'

'I really don't know, sir. I'm sorry. But we're doing our best to find her.'

It hadn't sounded convincing, even to Fry herself. Mullen had just looked even more sick.

'Can I ask you about something else, Mr Mullen?' she'd said.

'What?'

'Your next-door neighbour, Mr Wade.'

'Keith Wade? He's a good neighbour. He's always kept an eye on our house. I know he can seem a bit rough, and his wife walked out on him, poor bloke. But Lindsay saw a lot of him during the day when he was on late shifts, and he always took an interest in the kids.'

'Mr Mullen, when you say Mr Wade kept an eye on your house, what exactly do you mean?'

'We gave him a spare key. So if we were away for the weekend, he could get in to deal with any emergencies.'

'Wait a minute – he has a key to your house?'

'Yes, of course.'

Fry shook her head at the memory of her conversation with Mullen. As far as she was concerned, the question of who'd killed Lindsay Mullen and the two boys in the fire remained open. Despite his parents' protestations, it would be easy to blame John Lowther and leave it at that. But she was feeling guilty that she'd been so wrong about him. Her preconceptions had over-ruled her judgement. Bad mistake.

She considered Brian Mullen again. He was one of only two people she could definitely place at the scene around the time of the fire. Mullen had a key to the house, so he wouldn't have needed to break in through the side window. Of course, the damage to the window might simply have been a blind, to make everyone think there had been a break-in.

She wondered whether she ought to have seized Mullen's clothes for forensic examination at an early stage in the enquiry. But it would have been a pointless exercise, even immediately after the incident. Mullen had legitimate reasons for his clothes being impregnated with smoke, or even singed by the fire. He'd tried to get into the house to rescue his children, hadn't he? He had plenty of witnesses to that fact, including the two firefighters who'd physically dragged him back to the pavement. It took a bit of clever forward planning to contaminate forensic evidence like that. She couldn't believe Brian Mullen had it in him.

But no, she shouldn't rule out it out completely. No more false assumptions.

Gradually, Fry found her thoughts focusing on Keith Wade. The perfect neighbour, the assiduous member of Neighbourhood Watch. The keen amateur photographer. The only other person she knew to have been at the scene when the fire started.

Fry paused and checked her email. Wade had promised to send her some of his photos, but they hadn't arrived yet. She doubted if they ever would.

Then another thought struck her. Brian Mullen had an alibi for the time of the fire – he'd been at the Broken Wheel with Jed Skinner until the early hours of the morning. In Wade's case, it was that very same fact that had made it possible for him to get into the Mullens' house. If Brian hadn't been out late that night, the front door of number 32 would have been bolted on the inside. But Lindsay had left the bolts off for her husband to come home. Wade could have known that quite easily, couldn't he?

There was one person who wasn't out with the search teams. He wasn't on duty because he was at home, recovering from his unexpected dip in the trapped waters of the Derwent. Fry dialled his number.

'Ben,' she said, 'can I bounce something off you?'

'Yes, I'm fine. Thanks for asking, Diane.'

'Oh. Well, I can tell you're all right by the way you sound.'

Cooper sighed. 'What did you want to bounce off me?'

'Brian Mullen. You know that he denied the arguments with his wife?'

'Yes.'

'Whose word do we have that those arguments ever took place?'

Cooper considered the question for a moment. 'Well, the lady on one side of the Mullens heard the row about the carpet.'

'Which is the only one Brian admits to. And the rest?'

'We only have the other neighbour's word for those.'

'Keith Wade.'

'Yes, Wade. Why, Diane?'

'I'm thinking of getting Mr Wade in. Perhaps he wasn't such a good friend of the Mullens, after all.'

'But he seems to have been the perfect next-door neighbour.'

'Maybe.'

'Did the prints come back from the can of lighter fluid?'

'Yes, just today. I'm going to ask Mr Wade to give his prints for comparison.'

'He's lived next door to the Mullens for six years,' said Cooper. 'And they got on fine, by all accounts. Why would he decide to do them harm? What would have been his motive?'

'Motive?'

'Yes, motive. That's a bit of a problem all round, isn't it? Juries like a motive. They're never entirely happy if they don't get one, you know.'

'I'll be sure to let you know when I find out,' said Fry.

Cooper paused. 'Do you want me to come in?'

'No, you're recuperating.'

'I don't suppose there's any news . . .?'

'We're still working on the Rose Shepherd shooting.'

'That's not what I meant.'

'I know,' said Fry. 'No, there isn't any news of Luanne Mullen. Not yet.'

*   *   *

Cooper put the phone down thoughtfully. Neighbours had been a bit outside his experience until he moved to Welbeck Street. At Bridge End Farm, the nearest house had been several fields away. Even here in Edendale, there was only his landlady, Mrs Shelley, on one side, and a retired couple on the other, two former teachers who seemed to spend most of their time in Spain.

'Who was that, Ben?'

'It was Diane Fry.'

Liz was in his kitchen. Cooper wasn't sure what she was doing, and it felt wrong somehow for her to be there. A few months of living on his own, and he was already feeling territorial about his space. He just hoped she wasn't tidying up. He couldn't do with that.

Cooper put his head around the door and saw that Liz was talking to the cat, who'd taken to her straightaway. So that was all right.

'They still haven't found the child,' he said. 'You know – Luanne Mullen.'

Liz looked up, her eyes suddenly full of concern at something she'd detected in his voice. Her dark hair was loose today, curled round her ears in the way that he liked.

'It wasn't your fault if the child was snatched, Ben.'

'I didn't say it was.'

'No, but you were thinking it.'

Cooper raised his hands. 'It's a fair cop.'

Liz gave the cat another stroke, rubbing him behind the ears, creating a deep buzz of pleasure.

'Just so long as you weren't planning on going in to work,' she said. 'This is a rest day. We don't get much chance to spend a whole day together.'

'No, of course,' said Cooper. 'I wasn't thinking *that*.'

'Mmm.'

She stood up and came towards him. When she was close, he could feel her warmth. In another moment, he'd be distracted completely from what had really been on his mind.

'Diane says they're still working on the Rose Shepherd shooting,' he said. 'There's a suspect in custody, but it isn't going too well with him, from what I hear.'

Liz looked up at him, instinctively sharing the desire to see a satisfactory conclusion in a tragic case like the death of Miss Shepherd.

'Did I tell you about the gun, by the way?'

'The gun?' said Cooper.

'The gun you asked about, Ben. The Romanian PSL. I *did* tell you about the gun, didn't I?'

A defendant was always advised by his lawyers to smarten himself up when he appeared in court. It made a better impression on a jury, and even on magistrates, who ought to know better. Have a shave, comb your hair, and borrow a suit, even if it didn't fit.

But Keith Wade had gone a step further – he'd

smartened himself up for his interview at the police station. Not many people cared about looking good in an interview room. But at least he'd ditched the woolly Arbroath smoky, and Fry could risk breathing.

'Mr Wade, thank you for coming in earlier to give us your fingerprints.'

'For elimination purposes, you said. Is that right?'

'Well, that was the idea.'

'What do you mean?'

'First of all, I want to take you back to Sunday night again, when you first noticed the fire at your neighbour's house.'

He looked irritated. 'I think I've told you everything. Twice, probably.'

'How did you get into the house?'

'I don't remember.'

'Surely you must do. You saw the smoke, went to make the 999 call, then . . . ?'

'I opened their front door.'

'You opened the front door of number 32? Do you mean you broke the door down?'

'No.'

'Surely it wasn't unlocked?'

Wade decided not to answer that one. He began to look sulky. In a moment, she could be into 'no comment' territory.

'You've got a key, haven't you?' said Fry.

'Like I said, I knew Brian and Lindsay well. I keep an eye on their house when they're away.'

'They leave you a key. That's how you got in.'

'Yes.'

'You knew Brian was out that night, didn't you?'

'Well, yes. I always see him come and go.'

'Mr Wade, how did you get on with boys? Jack and Liam?'

'Oh, them –'

'They were nice lads, you said.'

'Little bastards, that's what they were.'

'One was seven years old, and the other four, Mr Wade.'

He stared at her sullenly. 'I know that.'

'You're a smoker, aren't you, sir? It was obvious as soon as I walked through your door.'

'There's no law against it, is there?'

'Actually, yes. But not in the privacy of your own home.'

'So?'

'Unfortunately, you took your matches and lighter fluid out of your house. You took them to your next-door neighbour's, in fact.'

'Brian's a good bloke,' said Wade, leaning forward urgently.

'He says the same about you, funnily enough. But he couldn't be more wrong, could he?'

'He's my mate. I look out for him.'

'So why did you go into his house that night, pour lighter fluid in the sitting room and set fire to it? Why did you murder his wife and children?'

'What?'

586

'There's no point in denying it. We have your fingerprints from the can of lighter fluid that you used and left in a bin down the street.'

Wade shook his head. 'Brian's better off without them. Look at me – I'm a lot better off without my wife. It was the best thing that ever happened to me when she went. I ought to have kicked her out a lot sooner. Once they start giving you trouble, the best thing is to get rid of them.'

'You mean you thought you were doing Brian Mullen a favour?'

'Well, you could put it like that. He was a brave bloke, but not that brave. I think that's why Brian went out so often, he couldn't face it. He needed a helping hand, like.'

'So you stepped in. Watching out for your neighbour, Mr Wade? That's just great. Thank God we don't all have neighbours like you.'

'I don't want to talk any more.'

'You've said enough.'

Fry began to get up, then stopped. 'When you said Brian went out so often, what did you mean?'

'He'd been staying out really late.'

'Like Sunday night, you mean?'

'Yes, Sunday. And Saturday.'

'Saturday? Brian Mullen was out on Saturday night as well?'

'Oh yes, all night. Past three o'clock, as I recall.'

'Why didn't you mention this before?'

'You never asked.'

She had a sudden memory of her conversation

587

with Jed Skinner, Brian Mullen's friend, his alibi. Had Skinner just slipped up when he mentioned Saturday instead of Sunday, the night of the fire? But then, why should he have thought that Saturday was the night Brian needed an alibi for? Did he think he was covering for an affair?

'That'll do for now, Mr Wade,' said Fry. 'You'll be charged with the murder of Lindsay Mullen and her two children.'

Wade looked at her with something like distaste. Surely it ought to be the other way round. But there was no accounting for what went on in people's minds, their rationalizations and self-justifications.

'You know, I thought Lindsay would welcome a bit of company, with Brian being out,' he said. 'A bit of male company, like. But she was a bitch, like all the others. Brian is a lot better off without her.'

Hitchens kept his chair still for once, instead of making it squeal on its swivel. Perhaps he was finally reading her thoughts, responding to the force of her unspoken will. Fry made a mental note to ask someone to come in and oil the thing when the DI was off duty.

'The SOCOs found Wade's digital camera,' he said. 'But all the photographs of the fire had been deleted from the memory card.'

'I'm not surprised,' said Fry. 'He was worried we might find something incriminating.'

'Like what?'

'I think he probably started taking photographs long before he made the 999 call. We'd have been able to see the time of each photograph on the memory card, wouldn't we?'

'Yes, that's right. Or even on a jpeg copy if he'd emailed them.'

'Well, then it might have occurred to us to compare them to the time of his call. And he'd have some difficult questions to answer. I don't think our Mr Wade is too technical. He wouldn't have known how to check the time stamp of each photo, so he deleted the whole lot.'

'You must have had him worried from the start, Diane.'

'He was an amateur. Look at how many mistakes he made.'

'Well, you always said the answer to the Mullen case would be close to home.'

'I didn't mean it like that,' said Fry. 'I was thinking about a member of the family. But I suppose your next-door neighbour is pretty close. The Mullens put their trust in him.'

Hitchens stood up from his chair. 'Let's go and see the DCI.'

In the DCI's office, they found that Kessen had just received the results of the latest actions from the incident room – a detailed assessment of Rose Shepherd's financial circumstances.

'Miss Shepherd had several savings accounts at

different banks,' he said, 'but they were practically empty. Unless there are some investments or deposits we haven't located, the victim's funds were getting dangerously low.'

'She doesn't seem to have had any income, either,' pointed out Fry.

'That's right. Apart from interest on her savings, nothing has been added to any of the accounts as far back as we can go. Since the house purchase, the flow of money has been in one direction – into her current account, where it's been used to pay bills. We had a quick calculation of her annual expenditure. At her present rate, she couldn't have survived more than another six months, I reckon.'

Fry took the print-out he offered her. 'Was she spending heavily?'

'Not really. Well, her big expenditure was on the house purchase and everything that went with it – solicitor's fees, and the work she had done, like the gates and the burglar alarms. That must have made a huge hole in her resources. But since then, it's just been normal living expenses. Council Tax, utilities, telephone bills. Not to mention food and general household expenses. They've all been increasing.'

'And interest rates have been falling.'

'She must have miscalculated badly, if she thought she could hide herself away in Bain House for the rest of her life.'

'In any case, she must have been able to see

what was going to happen not too far in the future. She was going to run out of money.'

'Bain House would have had to go, for a start. She could have survived a few years longer if she'd flogged it and bought a terraced property in the city somewhere.'

'She could have got a job,' said Fry.

'Look at the way she lived here,' said Kessen. 'Neither of those two options would have seemed possible to Rose Shepherd. She was too frightened of being tracked down.'

'Yes, of course.'

Kessen coughed. 'Are we nearly finished here? We need all the manpower we can get at Matlock Bath. Don't forget we're still looking for the child. And whoever assaulted DC Cooper, of course.'

'Thank goodness the Zhivko bombing is C Division's baby,' said Hitchens. 'We couldn't have coped with that as well. By all accounts, it's proving a big headache for them.'

'I'll send them our sympathy.'

'What about Brian Mullen?' asked Fry, turning back to the room. 'Should we interview him again? It does seem a bit tough on him, so soon after everything else that's happened.'

'Leave it for now,' said Hitchens. 'I'll have another try at Tony Donnelly first.'

'No, look,' said Donnelly a few minutes later. 'All I did was nick a car and torch it afterwards. That's nothing. You just get a ticking off for that.

Community service, that sort of thing. It's no big deal.'

'You've done it before, Mr Donnelly, haven't you?'

'Well, yeah. Everybody has. When we were kids, we did it all the time round our way.'

'But you're not a kid any more.'

'No. Well, I *had* given it up. This was just a one-off.'

'Found something more lucrative, did you?'

'I don't know what you're on about.'

'I think you do,' said Hitchens.

Donnelly shook his head.

'So why this one-off?'

'Look, it was a favour. Someone wanted a car for a bit, that's all. A decent car, a four-by-four. I found one for him, and I did it as a favour.'

'This would be the Shogun?'

'Yes.'

'Are you saying you didn't know what the vehicle was being used for?'

Donnelly chuckled. 'No, of course not. You don't ask questions like that.'

'*We* do.'

'Yeah, well . . .' He shrugged. 'I can't tell you, can I? No matter how long you keep me here, I can't tell you, because I don't know.'

'We don't need you to tell us that, Mr Donnelly. We already know. The car you stole was used to commit a murder.'

'Eh?'

'A shooting in Foxlow.'

'No. Well, I heard about that, but you can't—Well, you can't, that's all.'

'Mr Donnelly, unless you tell us who you did this favour for, you're our number one suspect right now.'

'For a murder? You've got to be joking.'

'Not at all, sir. I've never been more serious. I suggest you start being more co-operative, or you could be here for a lot longer yet.'

Donnelly stared at him for a long moment, his eyes flickering anxiously as he worked out the odds. Either way, they didn't look good.

'He was good to me,' he said. 'He gave me a job, and he helped me to set up on my own when things started to go pear-shaped. I owed him a favour, that's all. He's a good bloke. I did it as a favour, I don't know anything else.'

'Who are you talking about, Mr Donnelly?'

Donnelly took a deep breath before finally committing himself. 'OK, I'll tell you.'

Cooper caught up with Fry in the car park, between the security gate and the custody suite. A light drizzle was falling, and Fry seemed to want to get to her car quickly, but he stopped her.

'Ben? What the heck are you doing here? You're supposed to be at home recuperating.'

'I don't need to recuperate. I'm fine.'

He waited for the response he expected, wincing as he remembered what Liz had said to him when he put his jacket on to leave the flat. But, from Fry, it didn't come.

'So what do you think you're going to do here?' she said.

'I want to help. Are there any developments?'

Fry brought him up to date on Keith Wade, then told him about Rose Shepherd's dire financial circumstances.

'God, she must have been getting desperate,' said Cooper. 'There wasn't even anyone she could turn to for help or advice. She was dealing with that prospect alone.'

Fry leaned against the side of a police van. 'You know, in those circumstances, I think you'd probably get to a point where you didn't care any more. You'd be asking yourself what the point of it all was. I mean, how could her life have been worth living? Rose Shepherd was sixty-one – she was facing the prospect of another twenty or thirty years living like this, but with her deliberate isolation becoming more and more difficult to maintain day by day. Personally, I think Rose Shepherd might actually have welcomed her fate, when it came.'

Cooper stared at her, surprised by her sudden burst of empathy. Fry stood beside the van, a slight figure, hardly enough of her to catch the rain.

But Cooper wasn't at all sure about what she'd just said. He couldn't feel convinced that Rose Shepherd had welcomed death. In this case, there had been too much of a tendency for people to think they could let the dust settle and return to some kind of normal life, their offences forgiven or forgotten, their past put far behind them.

But dust had a habit of showing tracks if it was left undisturbed too long. And, like the dust gathering in the Mullens' smoke alarm, it could even mask the approach of danger, when it finally came burning out of the night.

'Diane, there *is* another possibility that Miss Shepherd might have considered,' said Cooper.

'What's that, Ben?'

'I wonder if she thought she'd found a lifeline. She might have made contact with someone she thought she could get money out of.'

'What?'

Cooper saw the sceptical look in her eyes, and started his train of thought all over again. 'I asked about the rifle. You remember, the Romanian semi-automatic?'

'Yes.'

'Well, apart from the military sniper rifle, there's a sporting version of the PSL made for export, the Romak-3. It's very similar, but has the bayonet lug ground off and some other modifications to comply with US import laws.'

'A sporting version. Do you mean a hunting rifle?'

'Yes. A hunting rifle.'

Fry tilted her head slightly to one side as she looked at him. 'What are you thinking, Ben?'

He smiled at the echo of Liz's words earlier. Liz

had known what he was thinking before he said it. She'd known, even though he denied it. But Fry was different – she wanted it spelled out. She wanted to hear him explain it. They connected on quite a different level.

'I listened to the tapes of John Lowther's interviews,' he said. 'You remember his sentence referring to hunting? He said some people go "hunting for whores. No, for babies . . ."'

'Yes, I remember.'

'I wonder if that was an example of what Dr Sinclair called "clang associations", a confusion of words with similar sounds or the same initial letters. I wonder if he meant some people go hunting *boars*.'

'Boars?'

'Wild pigs. They still hunt them in parts of the world. Bulgaria, for example.'

'So?'

'There's another thing. When Henry Lowther had that business trip to Bulgaria, it wasn't all vodka and red wine. His business contacts took him wild boar hunting.'

'How do you know that?'

'You asked him where he went and he mentioned the name of a place. Dounav. That was a mistake on his part, but I suppose he couldn't think of anywhere else in Bulgaria on the spur of the moment. There are some lies that you need to plan.'

'What's wrong with Dounav?'

'I looked it up,' said Cooper. 'Dounav is a state game preserve in northern Bulgaria. One of its hunting ranges is called the Bulgarian jungle because of its deep forests. Hunters go there to shoot deer, foxes and even the occasional wolf. But mostly wild boar.'

With the back of her hand, Fry wiped a bit of rain from her face and began to walk towards her car again. 'OK. So . . . ?'

'Well, how do you go about hunting boar?' said Cooper. 'Those are big animals. I doubt if you'd use a bow and arrow.'

Fry stopped in her tracks. 'You'd use a hunting rifle, right?'

'I think so, don't you?'

Her expression had changed. The rain was getting heavier, but she let a trickle run into her eyes and hardly noticed.

'OK, I'm with you, Ben. Let's see if we can check out Henry Lowther's financial status. He seems to have parted with money pretty readily when they were getting Zlatka Shishkov out of Bulgaria. But does he really have such deep pockets? I'm no expert on property prices, but I'd guess that bungalow at Darley Dale is probably worth less than Bain House.'

'If Rose Shepherd was making an attempt to blackmail Mr Lowther, she might have seriously misjudged his ability to pay.'

'Yes. But we've got to be discreet – I don't want him to know we're checking him out.'

'Right, Diane. And what then?'

'I'll talk to the DI. When we've got everything together, we'll go and see the Lowthers again.'

'They've lost both their children in the past week,' said Cooper.

'I know. No one said this was going to be easy.'

38

Rain spattered on the glass roof of the Lowthers' conservatory and ran down the windows in long, slow streaks. The stone angel had turned a darker shade of grey, puddles were forming on the backs of the flattened tortoises. Inside, the atmosphere was humid, condensation forming on the leaves of the tree ferns. It almost made up for the icy stares from Henry and Moira Lowther, sitting together on their settee.

Fry gritted her teeth, steeling herself to resist the waves of resentment surging through the foliage. For a few moments on the doorstep, she'd wondered whether they were even going to be allowed into the bungalow. Now, *that* would have been awkward.

'Luanne – she's still alive somewhere, surely?' said Mrs Lowther. 'The fact that you haven't found her yet . . . I mean, we *will* see her again, won't we?'

'I'm sorry, we can't say, Mrs Lowther. We're still looking.'

After that, the Lowthers just looked at her expectantly, offering nothing, asking no questions. And why should they? It wasn't their job to make it easier for her.

'I want to go back to what you told me about the adoption,' said Fry eventually. 'I understand the procedure for international adoptions can be rather complicated in Bulgaria.'

Henry Lowther grunted angrily. 'Complicated? You don't know the half of it. The whole business is like some nightmare from a Kafka novel.'

'A lot of hurdles in the way.'

'Absolutely. Right from the beginning, it was made as difficult as possible.'

She detected instant relief from the Lowthers at the direction of her questions. More obvious from Moira than her husband, perhaps. But Henry was prepared to talk now. Eager, in fact.

'Prospective parents have to obtain the consent of the Bulgarian Justice Minister in advance, before they can even think of starting court proceedings,' he said. 'And the application has to refer to a particular child, so you've got to find the child before you do anything else.'

'Hence the orphanage being the first port of call.'

'Exactly. Then we had to go to the ministry and demonstrate adoption would be in the child's best interests. Lindsay and Brian had to provide information about themselves: age, health, criminal records, that sort of thing. You need declarations of consent from the child's natural parents – or the chief physician of the orphanage, in our case. It was only when the minister gave his say-so that we could apply to the regional court in Sofia.'

'A lot of documents required, were there, sir?'

'Documents? A whole bloody library of documents. I could reel them off for you now, they're so imprinted on my brain. I used to go through the list every night before I went to sleep, I was so afraid we'd missed some detail that would bring the whole thing crashing down. Lindsay and Brian had to testify in writing to their motivations. They had to produce their birth certificates and marriage certificate. They had to give evidence about their home, their employment, their income, proof of their financial assets.'

Mrs Lowther was nodding in agreement. 'And their religion, their ability to raise children . . . They had to provide references, as if they were applying for a job.'

'Absolutely,' said Henry. 'And they had to produce doctors' reports – not just a physical examination, but their psychiatric condition, too. There had to be background checks, even for motoring offences. They had to make a declaration of intent, stating that they wouldn't use the child for medical experimentation. Medical experimentation! What sort of people do they think we are, for heaven's sake?'

'And all those documents had to be translated into Bulgarian, and certified by a notary public,' said Mrs Lowther, trumping him with what must have seemed like the final straw.

Her husband took a breath. 'Yes, the process was far too complicated. There were insurmountable obstacles put in our way at every stage, and we were defeated by the sheer bloody weight of bureaucracy. It was an emotional and financial drain on the whole family.'

'Financial, sir?'

'Oh yes, financial. Didn't I mention that? With lawyer's fees and notary's fees, and the cost of travelling backwards and forwards to Sofia all the time, the expense was crippling. And the worst thing was, we couldn't foresee any end to it. Not ever. Even Lindsay was so worn down by it all that she thought we'd have to give up.'

'But you didn't give up, did you?' said Fry. 'You found a way around the system, am I right?'

Lowther twisted in his chair to glance at his wife. They exchanged a look that carried too many meanings for Fry to interpret.

'Yes,' admitted Lowther finally. 'It was then – at the darkest moment in the whole process, when we were all at our lowest ebb – it was then that a miracle happened, as far as we were concerned. That was when we were contacted by Rose Shepherd.'

'So you weren't put in touch by a business contact, as you said earlier?'

'No, that wasn't quite true.'

'How did she first contact you?'

'She phoned the hotel we were staying at. Don't ask me how she knew where we were staying, or even how she knew about us. It was all a bit hush-hush – we had no way of getting in touch with her while we were there. We always had to wait for her to phone. But it was obvious from the start that Miss Shepherd had plenty of . . . well, contacts within the system. I'm certain she must have been working with some of the people at the orphanage, but it was never stated, and we didn't ask.'

'All right. What did she offer you?'

'She offered us a shortcut through the bureaucracy. She said she could arrange the necessary paperwork and deliver Zlatka directly to us. For a fee, of course. But frankly, the amount she asked was a good deal less than the cost we'd calculated for continuing the adoption process through the regional court. She told us she'd done it before for other foreign couples, and she even offered us testimonials.'

'And you believed her, Mr Lowther?'

'Certainly – especially after I met her for the first time. Rose Shepherd was very plausible, you know. She gave the impression of being completely nice and harmless, but a bit secretive, like a sort of maiden aunt. And it helped a lot that she seemed so . . . well, British. We were reassured by the fact that she was very like us – but she was Bulgarian, too. She was familiar with the ways of the country, so she knew how to deal with officials. She could play the system, if you like. Well, the upshot was that Miss Shepherd promised us an end to our frustration. She offered to provide exactly what we weren't achieving through the official channels.'

'And did she happen to mention that what she was offering was illegal?'

'No, certainly not. It was never hinted at. She led us to believe that it was entirely above board. She described herself as an international adoption agent.'

'Oh well, a bit of fancy language makes all the difference, doesn't it?' said Fry.

Lowther pulled a face and looked at her accusingly, as if disappointed rather than offended by her sarcasm.

'She seemed like a godsend at the time, you know. Particularly for Lindsay. Bear in mind that she'd already met Zlatka several times and they'd bonded like mother and daughter. Lindsay had already made a place in her heart for that child. The official process had demanded it, almost. It's very cruel to make a woman go through that experience and then tear the child away from her again. Don't you think so?'

'It's not my place to pass judgement on another country's legal system,' said Fry.

Mrs Lowther smiled sadly. 'You don't have any children yourself, I imagine.'

Fry stiffened. 'Are you really telling me that neither of you, nor any member of your family, ever suspected that what Miss Shepherd was proposing would be against the law?'

Lowther sighed. 'I think the only person who had any doubts was Brian. But he only wanted whatever would make Lindsay happy, you know. So he went along with it, despite his reservations.'

'And who paid the fees?'

'I did. And I was happy to do it. Miss Shepherd knew Bulgarian, and she was able to arrange things that we couldn't do for ourselves. She knew the system.'

'Was it difficult getting Zlatka out of Bulgaria?'

'Not so far as I know.'

'What do you mean?'

'It was Miss Shepherd who brought the child out of the country. The arrangement was that we would travel to Promahonas, just over the border in Greece, and she would deliver Zlatka to us there. So that's what we did. We stayed at the Hotel Olympic in Sidirokastro, about fifteen kilometres from the border.'

Lowther fiddled with the leaves of one of the pot plants, releasing a few drops of water that scattered on the oak floor. Fry waited for him to continue, recognizing it was best not to interrupt.

'From the balcony of the hotel, we could see a hill with a white church on top,' he said. 'Or it might have been a mosque, I'm not sure. But I remember it very well. The night we arrived, we spent some time on the balcony looking at it, because we didn't know what else to do with ourselves. I could see Lindsay didn't want to talk about the meeting – she was too anxious about it.'

'Was she worried that Miss Shepherd wouldn't keep her part of the arrangement?'

He shook his head. 'I think we both trusted her. Partly because she was British, like us. But also she seemed a very genuine person when we met her. No, it wasn't Rose Shepherd we had any doubts about. But we didn't know what problems might crop up, what could go wrong along the way. I'm sure Lindsay was imagining the worst – imagining that she would never see the child again.'

'So you were due to meet up the next day . . .' prompted Fry.

'Yes. In the afternoon, to give Miss Shepherd time to drive down from Pleven. That meant we had some time to kill. So the morning was even more difficult. But Miss Shepherd was as good as her word. She came down the E79 from Sofia to Promahonas, and the exchange took place in the back of our hire car. She handed over Zlatka, and the documents we needed. Everything seemed in order. Perfect, in fact. We were delighted.'

'And the money?'

'I paid for everything. I always wanted to help Lindsay as much as I could, financially. For example, I helped buy some of the things for their house.'

'A Smeg dual-fuel cooker, for example?'

'Yes, that was something Lindsay particularly wanted. Brian would never have been able to afford it himself. But for some reason, he seemed to resent accepting my help. It was very short-sighted of him. I only ever wanted to do the best for my little girl.'

'So how did the arrangement with Rose Shepherd work?'

'I paid half of her fee up front, and the remainder when she delivered the child. That was the agreement. It seemed very businesslike, and it was one more reason to trust her. I paid in pounds sterling, which was what Miss Shepherd had specified. I suppose they must have done it before.'

'In fact, they had quite a business going.'

Lowther looked dejected. 'They told us it would be all right. They said that no one really bothered about what happened to children like Zlatka. You know the sort of children I'm talking about –'

'Roma children,' said Fry.

'That's it. They said Bulgarian couples didn't want them. Well, it didn't matter to us that she was Roma. She's a beautiful baby. You've seen her, haven't you?'

'Yes, sir. Can you tell me who the person was you spoke to at the orphanage?'

'Her name was Piya. Piya Yotova. I hope she doesn't get into trouble over this. She was only trying to help.'

'Piya Yotova is dead.'

The Lowthers gaped at her in amazement.

'We didn't know that.'

'She was shot, along with a colleague, Dimitar Iliev.'

Fry took advantage of the shock clear on the Lowthers' faces at the news.

'Mr Lowther, now that we've got the truth about the so-called adoption, would you like to tell me again how you came to meet up with Rose Shepherd last Saturday.'

'I told you, Lindsay wanted to say thank you. She wanted Miss Shepherd to know Luanne was happy and doing well, that it had all been worthwhile. There was nothing wrong with that, was there? No matter how Miss Shepherd might have bent the rules in Bulgaria, she was a caring person. You could see that she genuinely wanted the best for the child.'

'And you got in touch with her by using the email address she'd given you in Bulgaria?'

'Yes, that's what I said,' agreed Lowther cautiously.

'Yet you've told me you had no way of getting in touch with her while you were there – that you always had to wait for her to phone you at the hotel.'

He hesitated, and Fry knew she was on the right track. There was more to be squeezed out of him yet.

'Actually, that's right,' he said. 'She gave me that email address when we saw her in Matlock Bath.'

'I see. And did she happen to give you her phone number at the same time?'

'Well, yes. So we could keep in touch in the future, you know.'

Fry could tell by the frozen expression in his eyes that Henry Lowther had no idea now whether he was saying the safe thing or not. If he denied having Rose Shepherd's phone number, would the police be able to prove he was lying? Poor Mr Lowther. He hadn't been as clever as he thought. He hadn't planned his story in enough detail.

'So the question remains, sir, how did you manage to get in contact with her before that meeting?'

'It was the other way round,' said Lowther. 'It was Miss Shepherd who got in touch with us. Perhaps you've worked that out.'

'Why on earth would she do that?'

Lowther had to think about that for a while. His dazed expression was starting to remind Fry of Wayne Abbott's lamping theory. This was the way she imagined the quarry would look, caught suddenly in a beam of light, not knowing which way it should run to escape.

'To be honest,' he said, 'I think Rose Shepherd was lonely.'

'Lonely, sir?'

'Yes. She knew no one in this country. I think she needed some kind of contact.'

'She risked a lot for a bit of conversation over a cup of tea, didn't she?' said Fry incredulously.

Lowther shook his head. 'What do you mean?'

'I mean, there wasn't much in it for Miss Shepherd, was there? She'd gone to a lot of trouble to give herself a new identity and made herself a recluse, all out of concern for her own safety. Why would she decide to risk all that for an hour with you in a tea room in Matlock Bath?'

'I really don't know. I just know that she asked us, and we agreed.'

Fry watched him, inviting him to say more, but he remained silent. She looked at his wife instead, and saw that a worried expression had come over her face, a grey wash of despair.

'It was our fault, wasn't it?' she said.

'I'm sorry, Mrs Lowther? Would you repeat that?'

'It was because of us that Rose died. We got her killed, didn't we?'

'Well, I wouldn't say that exactly.'

Mrs Lowther shook her head, dismissing her denial.

'The people she mixed with in Bulgaria, they must have come looking for her, to kill her. The same people who shot the couple in Bulgaria. And it was because of us that they found her.'

'Really? You think so?'

Lowther nodded at what his wife was saying, and sighed deeply. He thought he'd seen a way out, after all.

'It all makes sense now,' he said. 'That's exactly what happened, isn't it? It just goes to show what

610

awful consequences the most innocent of intentions can have. I'm only glad that Lindsay never knew anything about all this.'

Fry felt a physical surge of revulsion at his sanctimonious expression. She could see him relaxing now, smug in the belief that everything would be smoothed over and he'd get away with what he'd done. He thought he might escape the light, after all.

'Actually, Mr Lowther,' she said, 'that's not the way *we* see it at all. And it isn't what your former employee, Tony Donnelly, says either.'

Lowther just stared at her, shaking his head slowly from side to side.

Fry leaned forward and spoke to him quietly, fixing her gaze on his. Rain surged against the glass all around them, but she knew that he heard her perfectly well.

'Nor was it the reason your son killed himself. Was it, Mr Lowther?'

And that was the bullet he was waiting for. Right between the eyes.

39

Fry had bought a new packet of Paracetamol, but was keeping it in her pocket for safety. After the interview with Henry Lowther, she fished it out and found a few tablets left. She had just taken two with a cup of water when her phone rang.

'*Alo*. It's Georgi Kotsev.'

'Hi, Georgi. Will we see you today?'

'Diane, I'm sorry to tell you that my chief has recalled me. I would have liked to stay a little longer, but my duty is in Pleven now.'

'When do you leave?'

'There's a flight this morning, in three hours' time. Lufthansa, but what can you do?'

'Do you need a lift to the airport?'

'I have permission to obtain a taxi. My ministry is paying, so who can refuse? It will be here very soon.'

'I'm sorry we won't get a chance to say goodbye properly. It's been very interesting working with you.'

'Not like one of those bloody civilians, eh?'

'No, you're not like one of those bloody civilians, Georgi.'

'*Blagodariya*. Thank you.'

'Did you hear that we've arrested Henry Lowther for the murder of Rose Shepherd?'

'Yes, I heard.'

'We believe he killed Miss Shepherd because she was attempting to blackmail him over the child. Unfortunately, Mr Lowther no longer had enough money to pay her off. His export business was failing. I guess he hadn't kept up with the times.'

'A bad choice of blackmail victim,' said Kotsev. 'What a pity.'

'Well, Lowther wasn't going to throw away everything that he'd done for his daughter. There was no way he could let the child be taken away from her after all that. Not to mention all the money he'd invested in her happiness. When you've already been involved in one crime, it isn't a big step to the next one, is it?'

'No, that is true.'

'And Mr Lowther felt confident he'd get away with it, because he knew Miss Shepherd was a recluse and never talked to anyone.'

'It will be a tight case?'

'Yes. We found the gun when we searched the Lowthers' bungalow. And his son was driving the car. So we've cleared that up, Georgi. I'm sorry if it means you wasted your time here.'

'No, it was not a waste of time,' said Kotsev. 'Your theory is interesting. But it is a lot of *gluposti*. Bullshit.'

Fry was stunned into silence for a moment. 'You think we have it wrong?' Then she laughed. 'You have your own ideas. You want it to be connected to your Bulgarian Mafia. But, Georgi –'

'Where do you think the child is?' asked Kotsev.

'I don't know. Do you?'

'She was taken efficiently. She will be back home very soon.'

'Back home?'

'In Bulgaria. With her father.'

'Georgi, I hope not.'

'Could it not be for the best, Diane?' he asked tentatively.

'No, of course not. What do you mean?'

'No matter. And the Zhivko bombing? Entirely unrelated?'

'So far as we can tell.'

Fry wanted to ask Kotsev more. She wanted to ask him lots of things. But there was a hint of distance in his voice that made her hold back.

'I will be pursuing my own enquiries in Pleven. Meanwhile, if I'm not available, you may speak to my colleague, Inspector Hristo Botev.'

'Could you spell that for me?'

Kotsev spelled out the name. 'Hristo Botev. You pronounce the "H" in the throat, almost as if it was a "C".'

'It sounds a bit Welsh.'

'Yes, a bit Welsh. My friend Hristo is very celebrated in Bulgaria. A great hero.'

Fry smiled at his exaggeration. She didn't imagine that police officers were any more celebrated in Bulgaria than they were in Derbyshire. For most people, they were a necessary evil, at best.

Cooper came into the office, and saw at once that something was disturbing Fry.

'What's up?' he said.

'That was Georgi Kotsev. He's going back to Bulgaria this morning.'

'Well, his interest in the case is over, I suppose.'

'Not really. We still don't know where Luanne Mullen is. Or should I say Zlatka?'

'If she's not dead, she'll be back out of the country by now. Don't you think so?'

'Georgi does.'

'Well, then. Sergeant Kotsev will be more use back in Bulgaria, if she's ever going to be found. I think they did the right thing recalling him.'

'Yes, you're right.'

Cooper hesitated, wondering whether he should voice what was on his mind. The picture he had in his head seemed so unlikely that he was sure he must have imagined it. It was surely a false memory, an impression mixed up with something he'd seen in Derwent Gardens. Something, or someone.

'It's a pity, though,' he said tentatively. 'There was something I wanted to ask Georgi.'

'Anything important?'

'It was something I remembered from the incident at Masson Mill. Just before I ended up in the water.'

'Before you decided to take a swim, Ben?'

'Yes. Well, it was a very brief impression I had, but I thought someone else was there by the river that night.'

'Obviously there was – the person who pushed you in.'

'No, that wasn't what I meant. There was someone else, further away. I had the impression – well, I wanted to ask Georgi Kotsev whether he'd seen a woman.'

'A woman?'

Reluctantly, Cooper tried to describe his half-memory. It was no more than a shadow flickering in the darkness, perhaps the rustle of a long skirt on concrete. He might have been describing a dream. Or he might have confused it with the earlier glimpse of a woman who looked like a fortune teller, her blue scarf flashing briefly in the lights in Derwent Gardens.

Fry shook her head. 'There was no woman by the river, Ben. Georgi would have mentioned it if he'd seen her.'

'Yes, I suppose so.'

'I'm sure he would.'

Cooper looked at her closely. Her tone seemed to confirm what he'd been suspecting for a few days now.

'Did you like him, Diane?' he said.

But Fry looked away. 'He was a professional. It was a pleasure to work with him.'

'A refreshing change, then?'

'You said it.'

'Is he married, by the way?'

'I never asked him,' said Fry. 'Why are you interested in Georgi, all of a sudden?'

'I was reading some of this stuff that the intelligence unit sent us on Bulgaria. They went over the top with the information, for once. There are even some reports from the European Roma Rights Centre. Take a look at this one.'

Fry took the report he held out.

ROMA DIES IN POLICE SHOOTING

A police officer in Pleven shot and killed a 24-year-old Romani man. The officer apparently tried to apprehend the man, who had broken into a shop in a Mechka neighbourhood and stolen confectioneries to the value of seven thousand leva. When the suspect managed to escape, the officer shot him. He was taken to Pleven Hospital, but died of his injuries. A complaint was made by the dead man's family about the conduct of the officer, identified as a sergeant of the First Regional Police Department. The case was dismissed by the Regional Military Prosecutor on the grounds that the incident involved the legitimate use of a firearm.

'So?'

'There are dozens of these, Diane. The Roma seem to have a lot of problems with the police in Bulgaria.'

'Georgi Kotsev is different. That's not his attitude.'

'If you say so.'

Fry handed the report back. 'It's irrelevant anyway. We have incidents like that in this country, too.'

'Yes, I know. But they don't all involve gypsies.'

'Look, this is a report from the Roma Rights Centre. It's a single-issue campaign group. You're bound to get a distorted picture, because they're selective about the cases they publish. They're not interested in incidents that *don't* involve gypsies.'

'There are still quite a lot of them.'

'Ben, I must have missed your appointment as EU Commissioner for Human Rights.'

'What?'

'Well, that's what you're starting to sound like. Or are you still a Derbyshire police officer, by any chance? If so, just file those reports away. They're of no relevance to us. We're not here to solve the social problems of Eastern Europe.'

But before he put them away, Cooper read one last extract again:

PROTEST AFTER BURNING OF ROMANI GIRL

The Bulgarian newspaper Trud *reported that Roma from the Nadezhda settlement protested against recent cuts in electricity. Supplies had been cut to Romani settlements throughout Bulgaria for several hours at a time, every four or five hours. The measure had been taken by the National Electrical Company because of payment arrears by Romani inhabitants. The protest was sparked by an incident involving a ten-year-old Romani girl, who was burned when her clothes caught fire from a wood stove being used in the absence of electricity. The girl's injuries were made worse by the fact that, because there had been no running water in the settlement for eight months, there was no available water to put out the fire.*

Finally, Cooper found a website that gave currency exchange rates and looked up how much seven thousand leva were worth. He imagined it wouldn't be very much in sterling. But the conversion made it to be more than two thousand four hundred pounds. Surely that couldn't be right. No one could 'run off' with over two and a half thousand pounds worth of sweets and chocolate bars.

Then he saw a footnote to the conversion table. In 1999, the Bulgarian lev had been revalued at the rate of one thousand old lev to one new lev. Well, that was a different story. That meant the Romani man had got himself killed for stolen confectionery worth two pounds forty-five pence.

Oh, well. It was none of his business.

Cooper looked across to see what Fry was doing,

and peered curiously at some stapled sheets of paper on her desk.

'What's this?'

'An application form.'

'Oh, I see. For Europol.'

'That's right.'

'What happened to SOCA?'

'It's just another possibility to think about.'

Cooper picked up the form and flicked through it, wondering why she'd left it where he was certain to see it. He stopped at the qualifications section. Fry was a graduate, so that was OK. And she had the relevant law enforcement experience. But there was a problem here, wasn't there?

'How many languages do you speak, Diane?' he asked.

'Languages? Are you kidding?'

'It says here candidates must be fluent in at least two languages of the European Union, including English.'

'Oh, damnation.'

Cooper looked down, seeing that she was genuinely taken aback.

'Sergeant Kotsev will qualify when Bulgaria joins the EU. But I think you're going to have to do some studying if you want to get into Europol. Which language do you fancy, then?'

'I don't have time to learn languages.'

'Didn't you see that in the conditions of employment?'

'They didn't make it clear enough,' said Fry.

Cooper decided to leave the subject alone. 'You know, Henry Lowther said that one of the reasons they trusted Rose Shepherd was because she was British, like them.'

'But she wasn't British at all. She was half Bulgarian, and half Irish. According to the files from Sofia, her mother was a nurse from County Galway who met a Bulgarian soldier.'

'I know.'

He couldn't quite interpret the look that Fry gave him. Maybe she just wanted to change the subject, or maybe she really was concerned for his welfare.

'Are you all right now, Ben? You're not still bothered by John Lowther's death?'

Cooper was about to say no, he wasn't. But then he realized there were thoughts just below the surface that he hadn't had a chance to tell anybody about until now.

'He'd already stopped taking his medication, hadn't he?' he said.

'Yes, some weeks ago. Lindsay became completely absorbed with the baby. She forgot about her brother's needs, or maybe she thought he was well enough to cope on his own. But he wasn't – he began to slip.'

'I bet he knew there was something wrong. But once his thoughts became too disordered, he wouldn't know why, or what the problem was. Unless the voices gave him an explanation.'

'You're empathizing with a psychotic?' said Fry in amazement. 'Now I've heard everything.'

Cooper took no notice. 'John Lowther's problem was that he saw too clearly, wasn't it?'

'What? What did he see?'

'*The ghastly, naked spectre of insanity,*' said Cooper, hardly knowing whether he was speaking out loud.

'Where on earth does that come from, Ben?'

'I can't remember. It's just a phrase that stuck in my mind from somewhere.'

Fry sniffed. 'More likely he couldn't live with the knowledge that his father had involved him in a murder.'

'Yes, that as well. If he really understood what was happening.'

Cooper paused, considering his own comment. Because that wasn't what had been haunting John Lowther in those final moments, was it? His last words, as the air had snatched him from the tower on the Heights of Abraham, hadn't referred to Rose Shepherd, but to his sister and her children. *I heard them scream. I'll always hear them scream.* So those screams must have been inside John Lowther's head. Just one final illusion.

And Cooper knew there was something else he shouldn't mention to Fry. He couldn't help feeling sorry for both the Mullens *and* the Lowthers. The Mullens's desperation for a girl had brought terrible consequences for them. In a way, Brian and Lindsay had sacrificed two children for one, as if they'd been playing some ghastly game of chess. A game that they'd lost, in the end.

'The Mullens did it all for the sake of that third child,' he said, because that was a safe way to say it.

Fry nodded. 'And the child wasn't even theirs.'

'Not in a biological sense. But they'd gone to an awful lot of trouble to add her to the family, hadn't they? In a way, Luanne was the child they'd put the biggest investment into – time and effort, and expense, of course. But perhaps the biggest investment of love, too.'

'Do parents think like that?' asked Fry. 'I'd have thought their own children would be the most important to them. Their own flesh and blood.'

But she sounded uncertain, as if it was a subject she wasn't qualified to speak on. Cooper remembered the few details she'd once told him about her childhood in the Black Country, when she'd been taken away from her parents and fostered. He wasn't sure what had happened to Diane's real parents, or whether she ever had any contact with them. She'd never mentioned them at all, and it wasn't something Cooper felt entitled to ask her. Maybe one day – if he ever felt he knew her well enough.

'No, Diane, I'm not sure it always works like that,' he said, though he didn't really feel any better qualified. It was just something she needed to hear.

'There's still no sign of Luanne Mullen. She's disappeared completely.'

'Somebody has her somewhere.'

'She could be dead, couldn't she?'

'I have no idea. If you ask me, Georgi's right and she's back with her father.'

'If that's the case, it would all have been for nothing. We'd all have failed – me, you, Georgi Kotsev. What a waste of time.'

'Let's hope we hear something from Georgi, then,' said Cooper.

And, as he watched Fry's face, he thought that was one sentiment she probably agreed with.

'How is Henry Lowther doing?'

'We'll get the truth out of him. He's turned stubborn about talking, but at least he makes more sense than his son did.'

'You know, there was a question someone asked right at the beginning, when we were in Rose Shepherd's house after the shooting,' said Cooper. 'No one had any idea how to answer it then.'

'What question was that?'

'What Miss Shepherd's killer could possibly have said to her on the phone that would make her go to the window and walk into his sights.'

'There's no way we'll ever know that, unless Henry Lowther tells us.'

'Well . . .' said Cooper, 'if Miss Shepherd was in such desperate financial circumstances that she'd decided to blackmail Henry Lowther, there *is* one sentence that might have made her do exactly that.'

'What?'

'Rose, I've brought you your money.'

But as soon as he said it, Cooper knew he would

always feel sympathy for this person, too, though she might have been a blackmailer and a baby smuggler. And there was just one reason for that. No one had ever shed a tear for Rose Shepherd.

40

Three days later, Diane Fry received a letter in the morning mail at West Street. It carried a Bulgarian stamp depicting a yellow-winged butterfly, and the address on the envelope was written in tiny, precise black letters, with her name, rank and every word spelled out perfectly.

Inside the envelope, she found a postcard and a colour photograph. Was that all? It seemed very disappointing. Holding the postcard carefully by the edges, she looked at the front. The picture was a detail from the Pleven Panorama, depicting some epic battle that had liberated Bulgaria from five hundred years of Turkish rule.

But something about the picture unsettled her. Abandoned cannon and a landscape littered with bodies? It wasn't her idea of a tourist attraction, but perhaps it was considered art.

Then she flipped the card over and read the message. From the moment she'd seen the stamp, she had no doubt who it was from.

Honoured Sergeant Fry,
It was my privilege to work with you in this
recent investigation. I will remember it always,
because it will be my last. My chief has been
pleased to accept my resignation from the
service.

As you read this communication, I will no
longer be in Bulgaria. So where will I go now?
That is uncertain. Perhaps I will move to your
Derbyshire? As I told you, your beautiful hills
resemble those around my home in Miziya. I
hope you know you are very lucky!

Please give my regards to your colleagues.
And my apologies to your Constable Cooper. Tell
him, sometimes a man can see too much.

Ah, but you asked me a question once. You
asked me would a father really go so far to get
his child back? Would he go to any lengths
necessary? I did not answer you then. This
was because I knew what should be done,
but I felt certain you would say I was wrong.
You are a good professional. You have my
admiration.

So now I will tell you the answer. Would a
father go to any lengths necessary to get his
child back? The answer is 'yes'. The answer is
that I already did. May forgiveness be with God.

Довиждаие
Dovijdane,
Georgi Kotsev

Afraid to start figuring out what the message meant, Fry turned over the postcard again. This time she realized what she'd found disconcerting about the picture. The lower half of it was real, a photograph of an actual battlefield. Brown mud, abandoned weapons, a makeshift trench with a dropped water bottle, an empty ammunition box. But beyond the foreground, the scene was false. Those exhausted soldiers she could see weren't walking through a real landscape, but an imaginary one. The dead bodies were painted in, the drifting smoke was the product of an artist's brush. Reality and illusion had been cleverly merged, and the line where they joined was almost imperceptible.

Cooper put his head round the door, and Fry hastily slid the postcard under the papers on her desk.

'I'm sorry to tell you this, Diane,' he said, 'but I phoned the Interior Ministry in Pleven and asked for this colleague of Georgi Kotsev's. The name he gave you was Hristo Botev, right?'

'Yes. What did Botev say?'

'He wasn't there. He hasn't been there for quite a long time.'

'Oh.' Fry looked at him curiously. 'He's retired, perhaps?'

'You might say that. When I eventually got someone on the phone who spoke English, he made me repeat who I wanted several times, then burst out laughing. In fact, he seemed to be sharing the hilarity round the office.'

'Did Georgi play a joke on us?'

'A pretty pointless joke. When he could pull himself together, the officer explained that Hristo Botev was a Bulgarian revolutionary martyr, who died fighting the Turkish Empire in the nineteenth century. It seems Hristo was a cross between Robin Hood and Winston Churchill. They still commemorate his death every year on the second of June. There are several football stadiums named after him.'

'Football stadiums?'

'Well, Georgi did say he was very celebrated in Bulgaria. A great hero.'

Fry could hardly bring herself to speak. 'Yes. Thanks, Ben.'

'Don't worry. He was just pulling your leg. It must be the Bulgarian sense of humour. Pity, though – I still want to ask Georgi whether he saw a woman by the river that night.'

'There *was* no woman,' she said automatically.

When Cooper had gone, Fry put the postcard back and finally forced herself to look at the photograph.

The card had hardly been necessary, because the photo told her everything she needed to know. It showed two people standing in front of a wide, circular tower with a flight of steps and an entrance like a very tall letter 'H'. She wouldn't have recognized the building, but for the postcard. The Pleven Panorama.

Georgi Kotsev was in full uniform, with his

silver badge pinned to his breast pocket. And very smart he looked, too. The blue tunic and epaulettes suited him even better than a black leather jacket. Below the high crown of his service cap, Kotsev was smiling. It was a smile that had become familiar to Fry in the few days that she'd known him. It made her heart turn over until she felt queasy.

But here, the reason for Georgi's smile seemed to be the woman standing next to him. She was very striking, black-haired and dark-eyed, wearing a blue scarf and a red silk blouse, open at her throat. She was no taller than Georgi's shoulder, and he had his arm around her waist. She was like a dark rose in his hand.

But that wasn't all. Not by a long way.

There were actually three people in this photograph. And here was when reality and illusion seemed to merge again for Fry. Dr Sinclair had said that hallucinations could be just another way of constructing reality. Who was to say that anyone's perception of reality was the right one, or ever had been? It was an impossible question.

But one thing she was sure of. Sergeant Kotsev was a professional, all right. The woman beside him had the distinctive look of a Roma. And the child in her arms was the most beautiful baby that Fry had ever seen.

Black Dog

Stephen Booth

The long hot Peak District summer came to an end when they found Laura Vernon's body. But for local policeman Ben Cooper the work has just begun. His community is hiding a young girl's killer and a past as dark as the Derbyshire night. It seems Laura was the keeper of secrets beyond her years and, in a case where no-one is innocent, everyone is a suspect.

But Cooper's local knowledge and instincts are about to face an even greater challenge. The ambitious DC Diane Fry has been called in from another division, a woman as ruthless as she is attractive …

'An exceedingly good first novel'   *Evening Standard*

'Stephen Booth makes high summer in Derbyshire as dark and terrifying as midwinter'   VAL MCDERMID

ISBN-13 978 0 00 651432 9